A KINGDOM OF BROKEN OATHS

LAUREN LOWTHER

Visit my website at *www.laurenlowther.com*

Cover Designer: Books & Moods, *www.booksandmoods.com*

Editor: Jovana Shirley, Unforeseen Editing, *www.unforeseenediting.com*

ISBN-13: 978-1-7390333-2-3

A KINGDOM OF BROKEN OATHS

LAUREN LOWTHER
DARK TRUTHS TRILOGY

A Kingdom of Dark Truths
A Kingdom of Cursed Lies
A Kingdom of Broken Oaths

*For those who have realized that the world is not as they
told you it would be.*

PRONOUNCIATION GUIDE

Diana (Dye-an-uh)
Spense (Spence)
Aedan (Ay-den)
Maisie (May-zee)
Vera (Vare-uh)
Embris (Emb-ris)
Alwyn (All-win)
Sorin (Sore-in)
Badras (Bad-rass)
Olys (Ole-us)
Jweira (Way-ruh)
Jamey (Jay-me)
Eira (Air-uh)
Meske (Mess-kee)
Ryen (Rye-in)
Aislinn (Ash-lin)
Shela (She-lah)
Pik (Pick)
Hollaina (Hawl-ay-nah)
Demekol (Dehm-ee-coal)
Ilysia (Ill-ee-see-ah)
Lazansus (Laz-ahn-suss)

PROLOGUE

Alwyn knew with an impending certainty that she would not survive this.

But she was answering a call from deep within, a place she had not visited in years.

In her long life, nothing had ever been so certain.

It was her time to die.

As she stepped through the portal, the trap immediately took hold. Whatever *wrongness* that Diana had warned her about was evident, but she took it away. Crumpled it up and eviscerated it. So that her family wouldn't have to. So they could go home.

The magic was sticky and vile and warped—and it wasn't just one. It was many, stolen and taken. They stuck to the caster's magic like they were sewn together, with jagged edges and uneven lines.

Whoever had laid this trap had cut corners.

But it didn't seem to matter.

Her body felt weightless, empty, as it folded and hit a soft, mossy ground. The overwhelming smell of cedar surrounded her. Foresty and earthy and full of rich air.

Alwyn had not been born in Eira, but she would die here.

And she was okay with that.

Fourteen hundred years was too many for one soul. She had been on borrowed time anyway.

The warm, welcoming dark tugged her forward, and she did not resist.

She thought of her brothers, of Meske and Diana and the little fox, and she did not feel any pain. She was not scared.

She would watch over them, visit them often. They couldn't get rid of her that easily.

As Alwyn drifted away, a strong, determined essence clamped on to her.

Stay, it beckoned. *They need us a little longer.*

Alwyn had always wanted a sister.

PART ONE

ONE

SPENSE

COMPARTMENTALIZING

I had never understood anguish until now.

Pain, sure. Grief, yes.

But pure, unadulterated anguish? That was new. And it hurt like I'd never felt before.

Kneeling in front of my sister's lifeless body, cradling her head in my lap, physically caused me pain. There was no way to pinpoint exactly *what* hurt, only that my entire body felt like it was being sucked dry. Left an empty husk in the middle of the desert.

I was vaguely aware of someone calling my name. Nothing computed until a rough hand yanked my shoulder back.

Immediately, I was on my feet, my fist swinging wildly.

The emptiness that had threatened to consume me was replaced with fire, so strong and hot that it danced up my throat and tingled in my palms. This was not something quiet and menacing, like the soul magic that wrestled me daily. This was demanding, controlling.

It took nothing at all for me to give in to it, releasing the damper holding my magic inside.

Real flame expelled from me, blazing a hole in the dumping of snow that stretched on through the forest. The white ground became a grassy clearing, the wildflowers trampled in a mosaic of colour.

The fire raged, licking up tree trunks and melting more and more snow.

All this, and only a slight pressure was lifted from my chest.

"Stop." Badras's tree-trunk arms wrapped around me, holding my limbs down and crushing me to his chest. "Be calm, brother."

The flames disappeared, winking out as quick as they had come. They left no charred trees, and only the melted clearing proved they were real, not a hallucination from the depths of my battered soul.

"Don't you tell me to be calm!" I twisted around in his grip, but he held on like a vise. "Not when our sister is dead!"

"What happened?" Sorin's steady voice drove nails into my skull. He dropped to his knee to inspect Alwyn's delicate face, his brows puckering.

There was something unfamiliar inside me—inside my magic. It was me, but it wasn't. It wrapped around mine, but it wasn't coming from my own well. Finally stilling in my brother's arms, I followed the thread of magic all the way to its source.

Diana.

It wasn't just her magic. It was mine too. Only they were no longer distinguishable as separate. No more white mixed with purple; it was permanent lavender.

And from it, a deep, soulful horror was growing. Diana's horror. I could feel what she was feeling as if it were my own.

"Oh Gaia," she whispered, both hands coming up to cover her mouth. "I told her it didn't feel right."

Olys's face paled, his eyes widening as he joined us. "There are thousands of Folk freezing in this tundra. We need to direct them."

"How can you be so cavalier?" I spat.

His eyes grew cold as he stalked toward me. Badras's grip tightened, as if he could keep me from lashing out.

"I'm not cavalier. I'm compartmentalizing. Because if I don't, then I'll fall apart. And our people need us right now."

The ghost of a night I remembered all too well flashed on Olys's face, one where he'd held Kerisa's broken body, both of them red with her blood as his soulmate died in his arms.

If guilt was a splash inside me, then it was drowned in the tidal wave of anger pumping through my veins as steadily as blood.

"I'll go with you to direct them, brother," Sorin said, rising to his feet. "I trust you two can keep her safe until we can …" His voice trailed off, but the unspoken words hung in the air like a dense fog.

He joined Olys, and they started calling out orders to the bewildered Folk standing around the portal.

"Let go of me, Badras."

He hesitated for a moment, but loosened his grip, and I slid away, stretching my arms.

Diana was sitting cross-legged on the ground beside Alwyn. I recognized the way she stared unseeingly—she was conversing with Jweira.

A switch flipping, she snapped to attention and unclasped the emerald from around her neck. She placed it on Alwyn's still chest, carefully retying the strands. My heart clenched at the soft way she placed Alwyn's braid back onto her shoulder.

"Jweira was able to find her soul. She's staying with her, keeping her body alive until we can revive her. It's not a cure, but it'll buy us time." Diana stood and wiped the snow from her wet knees.

Badras's shoulders sagged. "Thank the gods."

"What did this to her?"

"I think something happened with the portal. Jweira said her body was in complete health, but she was still dying for no apparent reason." Diana joined me at my side. Her fingers entwined with mine, but it did not have its usual calming effect.

Badras looked between us. "Could this have happened from the portal being made wrong?" My throat tightened. He continued, "We wouldn't blame you. Alwyn always knew the risks of whatever crazy thing she did."

I shook my head. "The portal worked. It felt *right*. At least to me."

Diana bit on her lip. "What I felt must have come from the other side. She was attacked. And whoever did it might still be near."

TWO

DIANA
OPTIONS DWINDLE

There were a hundred things to think about right now, but the only coherent thought that I had was, *Why is there so much snow?*

It was the middle of summer. The North was known for its cold climate, but this looked like we had stepped into the dead of winter. Did the realms experience time differently? It could explain Urdan's incredibly long life span.

"We need to regroup." Badras cut through my spiralling thoughts. "We aren't prepared for this weather. Spense might have cleared some of this … stuff, but it's so damn cold. And correct me if I'm wrong, but doesn't water freeze when the temperature drops?"

I tried to hold back my shock. "You've never seen snow?"

He glowered. "Have you already forgotten what Ivywall looked like? Deserts aren't particularly known for their seasonal weather changes."

"It's going to get cold," I agreed. "Especially for those of you who have never felt such low temperatures. But this is uncharacteristic for this time of year. Something's wrong."

Spense squeezed my hand, and I realized how warm he still was. Hot even. The fire that had blazed through the clearing still raged within.

His overwhelming emotions had nearly sent me to my knees when we found Alwyn. They had been so potent and clear, rushing straight from his heart into mine. The magic of two soulmates were inevitably bound to merge together, but I had expected more of a warning. A gentle introduction.

This was agony.

Across the clearing, Sorin and Olys were directing the traffic flow emerging from the portal. Folk grouped together, huddling for warmth, their shock palpable.

My mind whirled. We needed to find somewhere sequestered from the elements. There were thousands of Folk counting on me, who had believed in our ability to keep them safe here. But, hell, if the North looked like this everywhere, what chance did we have to move a group this large? They wouldn't survive a trek south. Even going west would take weeks.

The palace was out of the question. My mother would see it as an attack. We needed to stay out of sight until I met with her. Our options dwindled.

"Here's what we'll do," I said, hoping my voice came out as steady as I aimed for. "The mountain range behind us should have caves and caverns for us to shelter in. Once we get there, we'll divide into groups for hunting and scouting. Ideally, we'll only have to be there a short time while I secure peaceful admittance for us."

Badras looked doubtful, but he nodded. "It will take a bit longer to get the last of everyone through. Pik and a few of our loyal council members will be the final group to join us."

"Will you be okay to carry Alwyn when we go?" I looked down at the quick-witted warrior we stood over.

She looked so young like this, her body small and vulnerable. I pushed down the emotion clouding my chest. It was too much. Grief, guilt, and worry were battling for dominance over my attention. It was hard enough, sifting through the waves that came off Spense without having to deal with my own.

Badras nodded, easily lifting his sister, who melded to his large chest. His jaw gritted as he looked down at her.

Spense's hand pulled suddenly from my grip. "I need a minute," he muttered.

We both watched as he stalked into the snowy wood.

"I hope he saved some of that fire for whoever did this," Badras growled.

He carried Alwyn into the crowd, where she would likely be warmed by the gathering of bodies.

Folk poured through the shimmering air. With every face of horror, every shiver or pulling of lightweight desert clothing to their chest, my heart broke more and more.

It was a horrible, hopeless feeling to admit to.

I had no idea how to fix this.

THREE

MAISIE
ENEMY OF EIRA

If I could pick one time in my entire life to have the kind of magic that Diana possessed, now would be it.

I would use it to keep everyone from raising weapons on each other.

I would use it to melt the tundra we were stuck in.

Maybe I'd even use it on Vera.

"My Queen."

The queen paced the library, red rug shifting under her heels. The grand room was not accustomed to Vera's meetings. It showed in the way the tables were pushed up against bookshelves, the eerie lack of familiar library sounds, like pages turning or pens scratching.

"What is it, Solis?"

The long-standing seneschal cleared his throat. "I have the list of names you were asking for—all the officials accounted for in the palace."

"And?" Vera snapped. Her voice had always been strong, icy, but ever since Diana's departure, she had turned downright cruel.

"The Southern representatives have all left, as we expected they would. Kashdan's entire party remains, and as for the East ..." Solis shifted on his feet. "They are all accounted for, except one."

Vera stopped pacing, her dress swishing around her ankles.

"Hollaina."

Solis did not need to confirm; his face said it all.

"If she left without her subjects, then it is clear she does not want to be found. Nor does she care that we know."

"That was my thought as well. Her party has not been able to offer up anything helpful. Unsurprisingly, the princess is notoriously untrusting."

Vera scowled. Delios, ever cognisant of his queen's mood, whined softly from under the table, where he'd made himself comfortable. The wolf had been seen less and less, which would intrigue me if I wasn't already laden with things to worry about. I would have thought, given the security measures being taken, he would be stuck to her side like glue. Especially since I had been under the impression that he was an added protection for her. Either way, a domesticated wolf's daily patterns were at the bottom of my list of problems.

The room sat charged for a moment before Vera finally spoke. "No matter. We move forward. The palace will be locked tonight, and anyone outside after the doors close will be considered an enemy of Eira."

If Solis had personal thoughts on this, he did not show it. With a small nod, he swept from the room.

Vera swung her icy gaze to me. "Oh, Maisie." She chuckled, sending shivers down my spine. "The pieces are moving on the chessboard. About time, hmm?"

She crossed the floor to cup my face. I tensed away from her, but her nails dug into the skin on my cheeks, holding me in place.

"Cheer up. I imagine my daughter will be paying us a visit soon."

When she released me, I staggered back, bringing a hand to my face to confirm it wasn't bleeding. Vera whistled to Delios and stalked from the room.

And I could only follow, wishing for the kind of magic that would release us from this tyrant.

FOUR

AEDAN
THAW

I t had been two days since I had felt my toes.

While ultimately concerning, I welcomed the numbness. It matched the state of my heart. I hoped it would spread through my body until I couldn't feel anything anymore.

The thin, patchy blanket thrown to me the night that my teeth had chattered loud enough to wake the guards did not do much to stave off the chill. The dungeons were always dank and cold, but with the temperatures below freezing outside, it was like living in a block of ice in my cell.

The slop food was getting harder to shove down my throat. As much as I rationalized that staying strong was important to get out of here, the light of hope in my chest dimmed smaller with every passing hour.

Escape, I scoffed. *Forget it. You're stuck down here for good.*

Despite my hatred for the meals I'd been given, my stomach growled. It was past dinnertime, and no one had shown up with my rations. The guard at the end of the hall remained still.

I sighed. Maybe today was the day they finally started to starve me. Movement in the halls echoed. A thud sounded, so loud that it reverberated off the bars in the cells. I leaped to my feet. That was the unmistakable thud of a body falling to the floor.

I peered through the bars as best as I could, pressing my face against them, getting coated in the slime that stuck to them. From the flickering of the flames down the hall—orbs did not work in this magic-resistant prison—shadows danced and swayed. Someone was punching and kicking their way through the half-dozen guards on duty down here. Grunts and fleshy hits drifted in the air toward me.

Finally, quiet blanketed the cells. Then … footsteps, even and steady.

Getting louder.

My heart raced in my chest. Anticipation coursed through my veins, shrugging off the cold that had held me tight for so long.

The last face I'd expected to see stopped in front of my bars. Eyes so light that they were almost white bored into mine, scars stretching around a wry smile.

"Bit of a predicament you've gotten yourself in."

"Hollaina."

"And you are Aedan Thesand, the deputy captain of the queen's army. I have heard quite a good deal about you."

"Why are you here?"

"I appreciate your forward nature. I'll be brief. I'm here to release you from this cell, contingent on your answer to my next question."

Awareness buzzed through my skin, making my muscles tighten up. "Ask away."

Hollaina chuckled once, almost to herself. "Why hasn't Vera killed you yet?"

I started. That was not the question I had expected. I would like to be able to say it was because she had known me since I had been a boy and cared enough about me to avoid my death at her hands. But that would just be a sad illusion.

"She needs me as a bargaining chip in case Diana comes after her."

"Diana values your life?"

Gaia, I'd like to think so.

"Yes. As much as I value hers. We grew up together. Planned to rule together."

Hollaina cocked her head to the side, studying me. "Rule together. Platonically, I assume. As queen and captain, not lovers, as you would prefer."

My jaw clamped, sending pain down the sides of my neck. "You said one question, and I gave you two. Either open the door or get out."

"Touchy. One more thing: I'm curious to know your favourite flavour of tea. Enlighten me, won't you?"

Tea? I had heard Hollaina was half mad, but this was full-blown nutcase. What could she possibly—

Oh.

"Lemongrass," I blurted. When Freya had told me the code word, I had been sure there was no way to bring that up naturally. But if it meant escape, then I was okay with being proven wrong. "That's definitely my favourite tea. Lemongrass."

"Took you long enough." Hollaina tsked, moving toward the cell.

Her fingers curled around an iron key, rested on the lock, and paused. I eagerly shifted from foot to foot as she eyed me.

"If I let you out, there's no going back. The Outcasts don't need anybody who is not fully committed. Either you're in or you're out. Choose now."

I could answer that in a heartbeat. "I'm in. All the way in. Vera is driving the land into a slow death. It's time to see real change."

Hollaina smiled, sending a ripple of chills down my spine that had nothing to do with the cold. The strange, ethereal air around her grew more prominent, the longer I was near her, even with the cell dampening any magic.

"Glad to hear it."

She swung the door open, and I charged out. Nodding at her, I took my first steps of freedom. She matched my stride, and we stepped over an impressive amount of bodies as we headed to the rebellion.

My toes were still numb—and likely would be for some time. But somewhere along the way, a thaw started around my heart.

FIVE

DIANA
FRIGID

There was an organization around here that could home or find homes for us all, but I was only half confident that the patrons would help. If I left right now, I could make it back here before dark, and that was reason enough for me to give it a try.

I found Spense near the edge of the group, pacing through the trees, fists clenched at his sides. Olys stood a few feet back, keeping an eye on him. He looked up when I quietly joined.

"Is he all right?"

Olys's brown eyes bored into mine, dull. "No, none of us are all right."

I bit my bottom lip, my own sorrow filling my chest.

"But he'll survive. That's what you do when you lose someone. Either you're strong enough to push through or you're not. Spense has always been strong."

My gaze flicked to his left arm, where I knew a faded, scarred soulmate tattoo was hidden by his sleeve. A constant reminder of his loss.

"We haven't lost her yet."

Olys's attention fixed on his brother, who hadn't yet noticed me. "Denial is a natural occurrence during grief. I won't begrudge you that today."

In his own strange way, that was probably the nicest thing he had ever said to me.

I felt Olys's eyes on my back as I trudged through the thick snow to Spense. The adrenaline coursing through me had evaded the cold so far, but it wouldn't be long until the nips of frost were impossible to ignore.

"Spense," I murmured, reaching out through my magic, which flowed into his force now.

His head snapped up, curls flopping, and the sadness in his face nearly broke me when our eyes met.

"I have an idea that might work better than caves. Will you come with me?"

He nodded, taking my hand. Despite the cold, he was feverish, squeezing my fingers with a strength that was near the point of pain.

"We're going to an abbey about an hour away," I told Olys as we passed. "We shouldn't be longer than two hours—three, tops. Can I trust you to handle things here?"

The second youngest of the Drakenis nodded. "Don't let go of him."

His words danced in my head. They were sincere enough, but some niggling part of me wondered if it was also a warning.

As we trudged through the knee-high snow in the direction of the Gaian Abbey, my heart panged for my horse. The drakes were useless right now, having been shocked from the sudden climate change, and some had even begun trying to hibernate. Their wings were firmly pressed into their hides, the frigid air hindering their cold-blooded need to draw heat from their environment. Finnvarra would have melted the snow in her path with her fiery disposition.

Soon, I promised. *We won't be apart much longer.*

Spense was quiet during our walk, but I didn't press him. The change in my magic—our magic—was still new to me, and it was hard to get used to the waves of feelings that pulsed from the lavender strands intertwined with mine. He was sad, but it was deeper than that. Anguish. Being stifled and pushed down by an overwhelming anger. It was terrifying to experience what he was grappling with.

And it made me feel selfish to wish that I couldn't.

Thankful for the closed-toed boots—which had kept my feet protected from the hot sand—that now kept out snow, I pulled my arms across my chest. The air was frigid, and though I was proud of my Northern blood, it could only do so much when my clothing was the lightest weight possible.

Wordlessly, Spense took the scarf from around his neck, which he had previously used to keep sun from his face, and settled it around my shoulders.

He did not look up when I murmured my thanks or change from the broody expression he wore. But it soothed a small part of me. He wasn't gone completely.

When the spires and red brick of the abbey came into view, I breathed a sigh of relief. The Gaians were absolute in their belief that the ancestors' word was law, and they recognized me as the formal heir. They would not send me away, but turning a blind eye to their religion to welcome the Unseelie they had been taught to repent? I wasn't so sure.

Ice lined the walkway to the main doors, and I was contemplating the best way around it when a melodious voice cut through the air.

"I wouldn't do that if I were you."

We whipped around.

Shock rippled through me. The Eastern princess, Hollaina, and my own friend Aedan Thesand were the last two fae I had expected to see together in the middle of the Northern forest.

"What's going on?" I could only sputter, caught between joy and confusion.

I raced over to Aedan, hoping to pull him into a hug, but his eyes locked on something behind me, his mouth setting in a hard line.

Before I could even blink, he punched Spense square in the jaw.

SIX

DIANA
SOLUTION

"Are you *kidding* me right now?"

Grunts sounded through the clearing as the males grappled, kicking up snow. Spense had Aedan in a headlock, which the latter was attempting to get out of by punching Spense's gut repeatedly.

I looked to Hollaina, still wildly confused about her involvement and hoping she would make a move to separate them.

But she stared at me with a brow raised, her colourless eyes reprimanding. "We don't have all day."

Snapping to attention, I pulled from my magic and sent flares toward them, causing each to stiffen. I marched in between the males and threw my hands out. The blast of magic had little effect on them with Spense's height and Aedan's muscle mass, but they backed away nonetheless.

"What the hell was that?" I demanded.

Spense glared. "He started it."

"You deserve that and more," Aedan spat.

His blond hair was entirely ruffled and *long*, nearly enough to tuck behind his ears. His usual healthy complexion had a pale pallor with dark circles under his eyes, and his scruff—I had never seen him sport anything other than a clean-shaven look. What had happened to him?

What didn't help his state of dishevelment was the shining bruise beginning to form on his cheekbone, along with the split lip.

"I know you are all young, but really? Petty squabbles over matters of the heart?" Hollaina scoffed. "We have real work to do. Lives are at stake."

Red flushed my cheeks. Everyone was aware of Aedan's feelings for me, it seemed. How could I have been so sheltered that I had never noticed? If I had known, maybe I could have drawn a line and allowed him to move on.

"What are you doing here?" I crossed my arms.

Hollaina had never left the East in all the time I had been alive. I had only met her once before, ten years ago. She looked the same, her white hair cascading down her back, scars still grooving deep and red into her skin.

"The deputy and I are making our way to the Outcasts to aid in the rebellion." She said it so matter-of-factly that it took me a moment to register.

"A rebellion? Against the queen?"

Aedan grimaced. "A lot has changed since you left. It's probably easier to go over it all once we get there."

"I'm not going anywhere until the fae I brought over are safe."

A ghost of a smile appeared on Hollaina's lips. "You've done it then."

Spense eyed her uneasily. "What does that mean?"

"The Unseelie are back? And the Folk?"

Aedan's head whipped back and forth wildly.

I held the princess's gaze for a beat before nodding. "They're all here."

Her eyes gleamed. "Wonderful. The Outcasts will protect them."

As much as I wanted to be wary of the offer, my heart sagged in relief. "Why would they do that?"

"Because they are eager to bring balance back to the realm. They wish to appease the gods."

Beside me, Spense stiffened. I could feel his excitement and trepidation pounding through our joined magic, matching mine.

"Can we trust them?" I looked to Aedan.

My oldest friend nodded slowly. "Yes. If not them, then me."

That was enough for me. "Where do we have to go?"

"The Unclaimed Land," Hollaina replied. "They have made a secure home base there."

I groaned inwardly. "That's a full day's ride from here. With such a large number of fae and no horses, it will take us days that we don't have. Especially in this weather. What is the deal with that, by the way?"

"The snow should start to melt soon now that you are back. As for the travel, I believe there is a solution. Is your portal still intact?" Hollaina started away, following the path Spense and I had made through the snow on our way here.

It was almost scary how much she knew. Either she was extremely lucky with her guesses or this group of Outcasts was entirely well informed.

She looked back. "Well?"

I nodded, joining her.

She smiled, the movement shifting the marred skin on her face. "Excellent."

SEVEN

MAISIE
DISOBEYING

The passing of time had never been something that affected me. Day in, day out, my life was the same. It lacked the grand lustre of someone like Diana's life, and while some might wish to trade places with her, I had always been fine with my position. Serving royals was a great source of pride for me.

Until now.

It was hard to wrap my head around how fast that had changed. Two months since Diana had disappeared, four since Spense had come tumbling into Eira and changed the course of her life—and mine.

Months had never felt like a long time to me. Everything significant in my life had been a culmination of years. Decades. Never such a short time as *months*.

It probably should have scared me how fast hatred had bloomed for the royalty I used to crave pleasing above my own happiness. From the depths of my soul came a full-bodied anger that twisted around inside me like flames, growing hotter every time I saw her face.

Her. The one who held Aedan's life in the palm of her hand, threatening to close her fist on it if I put a toe out of line.

The one who sat at a table of Northern royals, icy-blue eyes daring any to oppose her, while I placed steaming bowls of soup in front of them.

"Do we have confirmation of numbers?" she asked her seneschal as I placed her bowl down.

I had spat in it while taking it from the kitchen runner, but the temporary vindication that had elicited was gone.

She fixed me with a look that told me to stick around, as was usual these days. If I wasn't sleeping in my guarded room, I was within Vera's direct sight.

Solis picked up his spoon and stirred his meal. Steam wafted up and curled around his face. "It's in the thousands. But as for an actual army? It's hard to tell."

"How hard can it be to count the heads in armour?"

"Well"—Solis shifted in his seat, clearly uncomfortable—"there are quite a few different … races. Some are segregated from the rest while others seem to mingle. The armour is hard to decipher, as none have the same pieces or colours. The, Un—uh, *Dark* fae alone have close to five thousand, I would estimate."

Vera's lips twisted into a gruesome smirk. "So, what you're telling me is that it's a ragtag group, hastily pulled together. If they can't even coordinate armour, I don't see how defeating them will be an effort."

"I am not comfortable making estimates on how our numbers hold up to theirs. The captain would be the best for that job. Say, where is Embris?" Solis looked around the table, the others following suit, heads swivelling back and forth in confusion.

I had to agree that his absence was strange. The head of the queen's army had never missed a meeting.

Something flashed in Vera's face before she smoothed her expression away. "Do not concern yourself with things that are none of your business. Embris has his own duties to perform."

Solis hastily ducked his head. "My apologies, Queen. To

continue, to the best of my knowledge, our army was sitting at about fifteen thousand heads. That's not including the support from other regions—while they don't have full armies, their guards should be well-enough equipped to join the force. I would put each region at three to five thousand, no more. I, uh, should admit that the Eastern numbers have not been reliable for some time now. I am not confident where they stand."

His words hit a touchy subject with Hollaina's abrupt disappearance. The whispered word was that she was a part of a rebel group, looking to overthrow the queen. With all my heart, I hoped that was true.

"Even without the East, I don't anticipate having a problem. They will threaten a war on us, but it's a farce. They do not have the arms to back it up, and thus the power remains with me. And with the Nordians' imminent arrival, a clean sweep is easily done."

My stomach dropped. Hushed voices danced around the table.

"The Nordian warriors are coming down the mountain?" Nevelyn's head, Lord Rentin, asked, his voice low with concern.

"Mount Nord has been neutral for far too long. They are a part of the Northern Peninsula and answer to me. A reminder of that was overdue. With their approach from the mountainside and ours from the palace side, we should have the portal nearly surrounded. They can either run back to their own realm with their tails tucked or face our swords in battle."

My blood ran cold at her words. Her blossoming penchant for violence had been kept mostly to herself, and by the look on everyone's face, they had not seen this side of her. The one I had come to know and loathe.

"My queen, there are innocents—*children*—in that group. Surely, you don't mean to ..."

"As far as I'm concerned, Solis, there are no innocents. They marched on Eira and are now here against the wishes of our ancestors. If they stand in my way, they are in contempt."

Solis scratched the back of his head, soup abandoned. In fact, none of the officials had made a dent in their meal. Maybe Vera's twisted malevolence had finally disgusted them.

"I have reports that say Diana is among them."

My head snapped up. Relief coated my nerves, sending a gulp of air into my lungs. Whatever evil trap that had been placed around the portal did not ensnare her. She was okay—she had returned at last. If anyone could stop what was about to happen, it was her.

"That does not change our plan."

Every pair of eyes in the room was wide as they stared at their queen.

Good, I thought. *Let them feel the agony that I've been feeling. Let them finally see the tyrant who sits on the throne.*

"My daughter has been corrupted by the darkness. She cannot be trusted anymore. If she chooses to go against me, then she is to be treated as the enemy."

"The ancestors chose her," a brave official insisted. "She is our heir."

"Diana has abused the power given to her and spat on the name of her predecessors. Once I am able to communicate with our ancestors again, I am sure they will name a new heir. In fact, I have a strong feeling toward Jamey Pinois."

Surprise was as obvious on everyone's face as it was on mine. She couldn't be serious. There had never been an heir selected from another bloodline, let alone another region. The ancestors wouldn't replace Diana.

Right?

Solis's jaw was clenched, his knuckles white as he clutched his spoon. "There is also the worry that the group will move before the Nordians make it down the mountain."

Vera laughed, the sound cold as it pierced the uncomfortable silence. "A group of that size and lack of organization will move slower than molasses. If whoever is leading them is wise, they will attempt to make camp, especially in this cold. The Nordians are expected to reach the portal site by early morning. Once we have word they have arrived, we move. Any questions?"

To my great horror and non-surprise, the table was silent. Cowards, all of them. My gut twisted in the knowledge that I was no better.

Vera must have been feeling pretty confident because she dismissed me after the meeting to bring lunch to her chamber. Unchaperoned.

I wasn't sure what to do with my newfound freedom, and part of me itched to run. But the cold truth of reality set in—whatever I did, Aedan would pay for it.

So, I used my time alone to wander through the halls, finally unwatched. It would be my own quiet way of disobeying. Ensuring my feet were slow enough that she was served cold food.

Wow. How pathetic.

Quiet talking hit the air as I rounded a corner, making me pause. I pressed against the wall, trying to make out who was talking down the corridor.

"… Embris has been missing for the last two days," the voice of Ryen, Aedan's second, said. "The queen is keeping it quiet. She only told me so that I could lead in his stead."

"That's great news," the other voice said. "With you in charge, we can spring Aedan."

Hope clawed at my chest, looking for a way out. I tamped it down, long accustomed to keeping that emotion locked away. But this time, it refused to be put out, and I couldn't help but smile, thinking about it. I didn't even pass a thought about what had happened to Embris. He could become a monk and join the Gaian Abbey for all I cared. If Aedan was free, then I would be too.

"As soon as I'm confident we'll get away with it, I'm getting him out. I have to reschedule the guards in the dungeon with ones that I'm one hundred percent positive are with us. It should be by the day after tomorrow." Ryen's voice trembled with barely contained excitement. "I don't know what he's thinking, but we'll probably have to be ready to run."

With the army gone, Vera's plan would be halted. But her loyal region heads would send their guard, and the Nordians would arrive, and then she would be back on track. The only way to stop this war was to take her out.

I couldn't stop myself. It was terrifying and vulnerable and so unlike me, but my legs were walking with no regard toward my feelings on the matter, taking me to a future I had not foreseen.

"Instead of running …" I said, stepping into the corridor. Ryen and another soldier I didn't know by name wore matching wary expressions. "How about a damn mutiny?"

EIGHT

SPENSE
PATHWAY

The red hue tinting my vision had not dulled since arriving. Thankfully, the volatility that coated my bones had subsided a little after I was able to get some punches in on the dirtbag who had run at me.

Despite the way my soul sang, feeling Diana's magic entwined with mine, my world felt upside down. Being back in Eira brought up no lack of bad memories, and now, Alwyn …

I shoved the thought from my mind. She was going to be fine. She was too strong to give up on us so easily.

Diana was trusting of this haunting female, introduced to me as the princess of the Eastern Plateau region. Considering I had not seen her during any of the palace gatherings, it was questionable how trustworthy she could be.

Then again, perhaps her staying away from court politics made for someone who could think beyond the words of the Crown. I would never say it out loud because she was Diana's mother, but I hated the queen with a fiery passion. My soulmate was too kind, too gentle. She believed that she could reason with Vera. But I was preparing for war.

While we made our way back to the portal, Hollaina caught us up on the Outcasts. Aedan hung back, sulking as usual. He kept his distance from me, which was more than fine. It wasn't worth my time to go after him.

"Fae born without magic?" Diana's brows scrunched together. "That's impossible."

"How sad to hear such a naive statement come out of your mouth. Haven't you seen enough by now to know that nothing is impossible?" Hollaina held herself entirely in too high esteem for my liking, but there was something to be said for those who spoke their minds freely.

Diana's shoulders stiffened, but she said nothing.

"Once we get there, you should meet with the leader. She will help you adjust and make a plan," Hollaina continued.

"I'm surprised to hear that you aren't the leader."

The Eastern princess chuckled, the sound tinkling in the air. "Because I am in a position of power in the courts? While that does prove to be useful, I find my talents lie more in support rather than direction."

Diana hummed in thought as we approached the entirety of the Folk and Unseelie races. The number seemed smaller like this, hunched together in groups to stave off the cold. Sorin met us near the portal, all of us taking caution not to get too close to the shimmering lines.

Hollaina sucked in a breath as she took it in. "Beautiful."

Aedan's eyes were wild as his gaze darted around, absorbing all the Folk of vastly different races from Seelie. I had to stifle a laugh. It was only fitting that he'd become the confused minority.

"You're back," Sorin greeted. "I assume there's news?"

Diana nodded.

"There's a safe place we can bring everyone."

"Then, what are we waiting for?" Badras joined us, tree-trunk arms crossing over his chest.

"The problem is, it's in the Unclaimed Land, smack dab in the middle of all the regions. It'll take days to travel there with a group this size."

"The portal will work fine," Hollaina said. She had quietly wandered away from us and had a palm outstretched toward the shimmering magic. "That's what they were created for."

Badras eyed her. "Who's she?"

"Hollaina, princess of the Eastern Plateau region," Diana explained.

His gaze then landed on Aedan and flicked up and down once. "Picking up strays now?"

Aedan visibly bristled but wisely kept his mouth shut.

Diana fixed Badras with a stern look. "They're on our side. It's only because of them that we have somewhere safe to go. This is Aedan Thesand, one of my oldest friends. He's the deputy captain of the queen's army."

"*Was*," he muttered darkly.

Diana turned to him sharply. "What does that mean?"

"Things changed when you left. The queen caught me plotting with the Outcasts behind her back and slapped a treason charge on me. I'd still be under the castle if Hollaina hadn't gotten me out."

"Treason?" Badras growled.

Diana ignored him. "Why would you need to plot behind her back?"

Aedan's jaw clenched as he met Diana's stare with a pained look. "I didn't agree with the measures being taken to get you back. The Outcasts had a more accelerated timeline."

Clearly, Diana wasn't done interrogating her friend's half answers, but Hollaina cut in. "There will be time for that later. By now, Vera knows you're here. You have to move now if you want to avoid a battle."

Personally, I would love to put Bloodletter to use. My muscles were tense and tight, my anger only slightly dimmed. A fight would be a great way to refocus.

"There won't be a battle," Diana said, attempting to defuse the alarmed looks. "I just need time to speak with my mother."

Hollaina stared her down. "I have it on good authority that come dawn, you'll be surrounded on all sides. You're right; that's not a battle. That's a massacre."

"So, you plan on sending us all back through the portal?" Sorin demanded while Diana chewed over the princess's claim. "We would rather fight than go back to that human-ridden blithe."

Hollaina shook her head, white hair swishing. "While I admire your drive, your deductive reasoning needs work."

Sorin blinked in surprise, as did I. Not many spoke to the respected eldest Drakenis that way.

"Portals are not one-way. You came out here because Diana had lit a pathway with her intention of coming home. It is possible to do the same for another location."

Diana's mouth popped open, and I cut in before she could speak. "How do you know all this?"

Hollaina swung her white-hued gaze at me. "Do you want to argue about my education, or can I help you save your fae?"

My molars ground together, but Diana put an arm on my chest.

"There will be time to ask everything." She turned to the princess. "All right, do it then."

Hollaina shook her head. "It is better if you are the one. Let me show you."

Diana joined her closer to the portal, and I used this moment to zero in on Aedan.

"Diana believes her mother will listen to her. Is there any chance of that happening?"

For a moment, I didn't think he would answer me. But he sighed, steeling himself before meeting my eyes.

"No. The queen is not stable. She tried to set a trap on the portal—she didn't even care if it killed her own daughter. I think … I think she was *hoping* to. She's always been a hard-ass, but this?" He shook his head. "I'm relieved to see it didn't work."

Cold fury flooded down my spine. My fists curled in, nails digging into my skin to the point of pain. "It worked."

Aedan, despite his distaste for me, understood. "I'm sorry to hear that," he said quietly.

"She'll pay for what she's done."

"Diana won't fight her."

"I know." And I did.

I would go with Diana to appeal to her mother, play the part of the supportive soulmate, and keep my mouth shut. I would be there to comfort her when her mother's treachery came to light, and I would make the hard moves so that she did not have to.

I could wait for revenge. It would be worth it.

NINE

AEDAN
RELIEF

At some point, I gave up on the idea that I must be dreaming. Fae of every shape and size were scattered around the portal, watching me warily and keeping close to their groups. Sure, I'd seen depictions of goblins and the like in old texts during my studies, growing up. They were, however, hardly touched on and—I realized now—incorrect.

As shocking as this day had been so far, I praised myself on my ability to remain calm.

And, yes, punching Spense counted as calm in my books.

"It's ready."

Hollaina stood back, motioning for Diana to take the lead.

"Let's get everyone rounded up. It's going to take some time to move the group through again, and the more space we can put between us and the palace, the better. I'll go first—"

"No." My own voice shocked me as it rang through the air, cutting her off. "I'll go first. In case anything goes wrong."

Diana shook her head. "Aedan—"

"I agree," Spense growled, his arms crossed. "You're too important."

Diana swivelled her head between us, surprised to see us on the same side.

Don't get used to it, I wanted to warn her. *We'll only ever agree on your safety.*

"Fine, Aedan will go first with Hollaina. Spense and I will go last to make sure everyone gets through all right."

I looked to Hollaina, who nodded once and took my arm gently.

Together, we walked into the portal.

Whatever I had been expecting was far from the experience. My body felt like it was being twisted in a knot, like I was being wrung out. My mouth filled with the unmistakable taste of ash, and dizziness swam behind my eyes.

When we stepped out, it took a few minutes before my surroundings became clear. This was the camp I had been taken to in the Unclaimed Land, as lively and run-down as ever. And *warm*—not a snowflake to be found.

Hollaina was greeting some of the fae who had gathered around the portal. They were eager to know what was going on.

"Stand back from the portal," I called. "There's going to be a lot of traffic coming through."

The fae scattered, choosing spots off to the side to watch the rippling magic move as two goblins stepped through. The Outcasts gasped in delight, waving and calling greetings. It was commendable how accepting they were. If this had happened in the palace or even in Nevelyn, I wasn't sure the reaction would be this welcoming.

"I'll tell Freya what's going on," Hollaina said, her voice suddenly close behind me. "Unless you would prefer to."

I looked over my shoulder to see her pale eyes staring right through me, like she knew my relation to the Outcasts' leader.

"I would not."

She dipped her head and was gone.

Two by two, I watched Folk come pouring into the camp, welcomed into the arms of the fae who felt they belonged outside of society. Short goblins with glaring eyes and childish faces, tall and lanky beings with green skin and tails that I assumed were elves, tiny spirit-like shapes that sounded like tinkling bells when they spoke.

It was hallucinogenic.

Around midway, the fae that I had met at the portal came through, one of them holding a small, slumped form in his arms. They were directed to the healer's tent, and Spense's bitter words about Vera's trap working soured my stomach.

As much as I hated Spense's face and the way he looked at me like he was better than I was, it was a relief to hear that he wanted Vera gone. Diana would hate him for it at first, but there was no way for peace with the queen in the picture. And I would do whatever I could to help make sure Spense was successful.

Gaia, that feels weird to admit. But it was true. I wanted him to succeed in this. For Diana to truly be happy.

The twist in my gut that usually formed when I thought of Spense and Diana together never appeared. All that I felt was a flooding sense of lightness in my chest that she was all right.

I had been in love with my best friend for as long as I could remember. But in that moment, I realized that I no longer was.

And it was such a relief.

Finally, the chestnut hair of Diana appeared, and she walked through with Spense. Their faces were grim, and both were holding something in their cupped hands.

Voices shouted for help, and I took a few steps closer to hear what was going on.

Diana's face was pained as she allowed a group of tiny flying fae to take whatever was in her hands.

"The pixies were hit out of nowhere," Diana said. "They were attacked. By the shadows."

TEN

DIANA
THE WORLD TURNS OVER

My heart clenched as I watched the two stunned pixies being taken away by their family, Spense following them. It had been foolish of me to believe the shadows would disappear when we left Eira. It was another atrocity I needed to rectify.

Going through the portal, I'd known that the small, tiny lives I held in my hands might never wake up, and it sent waves of sadness through me. It wasn't fair for innocents to be caught in a war they had not chosen to be in.

And, Gaia, did I hate portaling.

The suction pulled at all my limbs, a horrible wind popped my ears, and there was an acrid, bitter taste that stayed in my mouth for way too long after. I would be completely fine if I never used one again.

I was home now. I shouldn't *have* to use one again. But that sense of familiarity, the comfort that should come with being home, was missing.

The Unclaimed Land was as strange and abnormal as usual. Its position—smack dab in the middle of the continent—made it nearly impossible to visit other regions without travelling through it, so I had experienced its unusual magic before. But I had never stayed long enough to tempt fate.

The Outcasts, as they called themselves, were seemingly happy and healthy, living here full-time, if not a bit on the lean side. As I took in their bustling camp, I was greeted with smiling faces and an eagerness to help settle the enormous group of Folk that had just poured into their home.

"Diana!"

I turned just in time to be wrapped in a crushing hug. The warm, crisp smell of pine enveloped me, and the twinge of nostalgia from it was incredibly welcome.

"Aedan. I'm so glad you're all right."

I would admonish him for picking a fight with Spense later. Right now, I was just relieved to see my old friend. I snaked my arms around his large torso and squeezed. We held on to each other like life rafts. I hadn't realized how much worry had been festering inside me for him.

Finally, he pulled back. "I knew you'd be back. You're too strong to be kept down."

"I want to hear everything that happened while I was away. But first, I need to speak with whoever's in charge here."

He nodded. "I can help you there." He started for the middle of the camp.

"How did you get involved with them?" I asked.

A grimace passed on Aedan's face. "I had a run-in with the Outcasts not long ago, when they ... *recruited* me for their plan to open a portal. Imagine my surprise when their leader turned out to be my mother."

I stopped dead in my tracks. "*What?*"

His mother had died before Embris was promoted to captain and he and Aedan had come to stay in the palace. From what I'd been told, he had been very young when she passed.

"That was my reaction too. Apparently, being married to a general in the queen's army and raising your son are nothing compared to living in the forest like a wild animal."

I touched his arm. "I'm sorry, Aedan. I can't imagine what it was like to see her again."

He raised one shoulder in a half shrug. "I'm over it. She's just a fae who happened to have birthed me. She's not my mother. Nor do I want to rehash the past."

His words sounded final, but his face did not match the indifference he claimed. Knowing my friend, I had a feeling this had shaken him to his core.

I spotted Spense near a small tent on the inner grouping, his impossibly tall frame making him hard to miss. He stood, head lowered, with his brothers as they looked over a small body placed on a table. An older male spoke to them, his hands moving as he seemed to explain something.

"That's the healers' tent," Aedan explained, following my gaze. "I don't know much about the head healer, only that he was trained in a different sort of medicine since no one here has magic."

My stomach knotted nervously. It was still so wild to me that this many fae had been born without any magic at all. "What do they use instead?"

"Herbs, I've been told, and roots. Plants. They make powders and salves for infection, which is interesting."

I sighed. "I don't think he'll be able to help Alwyn. There's nothing wrong with her physically."

At least Jweira would watch over her until we could figure out what to do.

Aedan said nothing, squeezing my hand gently, and stopped me in front of a tent that was half built into the side of the thick tree trunks surrounding this camp. "I'll be out here if you need me."

I gave him a grateful smile and pushed into the tent, not bothering to knock since there was no hard surface anyway. It was meagre on the inside, a privacy screen blocking what was likely a makeshift bedroom, a few chairs, and a desk overflowing with parchments.

A female waited for me like I was an expected guest, thin and small, with greying brunette hair and light eyes, closer to yellow than brown. It struck me that she didn't look anything like Aedan.

And then she smiled, and I saw it. It was his exact grin, down to the grooved dimples on her cheeks.

Freaky.

"You must be Diana. It is an honour to have you here in Shynin, our very own capital city." Aedan's mother extended a long arm to me, which I contemplated ignoring, but manners won out. "I am Freya, the leader of the Outcasts."

"Interesting. I don't remember the Unclaimed Land having an approved city within its borders."

Freya smiled. "Just because we live outside of the Crown, it does not mean we are uncivilized. I would hate to start on the wrong foot with you. Please, sit. Pawl has prepared us some tea."

With a start, I realized there had been a lanky, slightly balding male in the corner of the room this whole time, blending into the plainness of the tent. He brought over a tray with cups made from what looked frighteningly like bone while we settled in the wooden chairs. Pawl handed me a mug and poured steaming water into it. I tried to keep a neutral look on my face as the unpleasant smell wafted around my cheeks and nose.

"I should start by thanking you for your hospitality," I started, keeping the mug in my lap—where it would stay untouched if I could help it. "We brought no small amount of Folk back to Eira. It must be a strain on your resources."

"We are all equal here. The Unclaimed Land will provide, as it always does."

I didn't even know where to start with that. "How long have you been here?"

"The Outcasts have been calling Shynin their home for centuries. We were guided here by Queen Iave during her short rule."

"Iave? She is not a well-known queen." I myself had not even heard of her until meeting her during my ascension.

Pawl spoke up, his eyes alighted with passion. "Because of her attempts to bring back the Unseelie, any trace of her was erased when she abdicated the throne. Her daughter was too young to rule on her own, and her advisor was heavily biased. By the time Kvista took the throne, she had already been corrupted."

Embarrassment flamed my cheeks. It was a disgrace that I did not even know my true history. I hated being told what was real and what wasn't. Now that my eyes had been opened, I wasn't sure I could believe anything anymore. There would always be a question mark.

"We have continued working tirelessly toward her mission. As long as we serve the gods, the land provides for us." Freya stood and took a piece of rolled parchment from her desk. She unfurled it and handed it to me. "I'm sure you are aware of the prophecy by now?"

I didn't answer her as I read the page—or tried to anyway. It was written in another language—one of the old Folkish ones by the looks of the long, droopy lines.

"I can't read this." I shoved the paper back toward her.

"Neither can anyone here," she admitted. "I was hoping one of your Folk might be able to decipher it. The prophecy has been passed down from generation to generation, but the exact words have been lost over time. I think we are missing an important clue from it."

"I don't know anything about a prophecy."

Freya shook her head. "That is a shame, considering we believe you play an important role in it. But no matter. The prophecy was given by an anonymous fae around the time of the first Queen Diana's rise. It is our belief that it was removed from common knowledge to prevent any mistrust in the Crown."

She paused to take a drink from her tea, Pawl following suit. After a moment of them looking at me expectantly, I brought the drink close to my lips and pretended to take a sip, holding my breath to avoid the smell.

Satisfied, Freya continued. "It states, *Dark truths never prevail in a balanced world. And when two become one and the world turns over, the final battle will begin.*"

Even as I wondered about the seriousness of this "prophecy," a shiver worked its way down my spine. Those words were full of their own magic, and it pulled at something deep inside me.

"And you believe I am a part of this?" I looked between them, and both their gazes locked on to my left arm, where part of my tattoo was on display from my half sleeve.

"We have theorized that the *two become one* part could very likely be the joining of the Seelie and Unseelie, as represented by you and your soulmate. As for the world turning over, that becomes a bit more metaphorical. The snow that the North has been unseasonably experiencing, as well as some changes that all the regions have reported to have, could be argued to fit that line."

A prophecy was something that I did not have time for right now, especially when it was not urgently life-threatening. It called for a final battle, but I would do everything in my power to avoid that. I just needed to speak with my mother.

"I will see if one of the Folk can decipher this for you … but I need a favour in return."

It occurred to me that Freya did not owe me anything—in fact, it had been a huge ask for her to open her home to everyone who had come over from Rathe. There was nothing stopping her from speaking to an elf or a goblin outside of my knowledge. She said herself that they lived outside of the Crown here.

But perhaps Aedan had inherited his good nature from her, for she replied with, "Anything."

"I need to get into the palace."

ELEVEN

DIANA
DEAL

Two hours and three undrunk cups of tea later, we had a somewhat-sturdy plan. Joined by Spense, Sorin, Badras, Olys, Pik, Aedan, and a few of Freya's counsel—Hollaina among them, which was still a huge shock to me—we sat in a giant circle on whatever chair or surface could be dragged in. The tent felt incredibly full and a little too hot, but I welcomed it. This was *real*.

"Vera's guards are on a tight rotation schedule, but the army's soldiers take over for the night shifts. I think she believes an attack is more likely to come in the darkness. That's why our best bet is to sneak you in during the shift change first thing in the morning." Freya had procured a map of the palace—unnerving—and probably knew more than Aedan and me combined about the staff and weak areas.

I could tell it threw him off, sitting here and having to work with his mother and listen to her break down the weakest parts of his responsibility—the safety of the palace. But he took it like the stoic soldier he was, only giving away his discomfort in the way his jaw flexed every time Freya directed a question to him.

Sorin rubbed at his chin, a bit of stubble growing there. "Aedan, you are the deputy captain, correct? Would your soldiers not recognize you and stand down?"

"I was labelled as a traitor and imprisoned before Hollaina let me out. I'm sure, by now, the captain has spun whatever story he needed to get the army to turn on me."

Aedan's face was pained, and my heart broke for him. His whole life had been the queen's army. His second had been his best friend.

Spense looked to me. "Are you sure you don't want to just walk up the front door? You are the heir. Surely, they would look past their *shoot first, ask questions later* policy for you."

Pawl slammed the parchment down in front of him. "Absolutely not! You would risk the High Princess's life in the hands of some mindless monkey trying to prove himself with a bow and arrow? Preposterous!"

Spense growled, his magic swirling while Aedan snapped, "My soldiers wouldn't shoot Diana."

Freya raised her hands in a calming motion. "Pawl, my love, that was perhaps not the best way to communicate your severity. But I have to agree. Your soldiers are impeccably trained, loyal to their last breath, as I understand it. At least, that was the case when my husband was involved."

Aedan's teeth clamped together so hard that I could hear the snap. "They obey orders. There is no wavering or hesitation."

"Then, would seeing their princess be enough to bypass that loyalty to their orders? I am not willing to take the chance, if there is no hesitation, as you say."

Aedan had started to stand, but a hand on his shoulder calmed him. "Fine, we'll go in undetected. Okay?" Everyone nodded. "The best place to try to sneak in would be through the servant's entrance, but it's tight. It'll make our window of being unseen even smaller. But my maidservant would help us; perhaps I can get a message to her somehow."

"My spy could potentially get something through, if you knew the exact place she would be." Freya looked to Maltin, introduced as her spymaster.

He nodded, the hood never slipping to reveal his face.

"That won't work," Aedan cut in. "Maisie was … compromised. The queen found out she was working against her. She's being kept on a tight leash on the threat of my death—oh Gaia, what if she's been harmed now that I'm out?" The words came out in a rush as the thought took over him.

Seeing fear in Aedan's eyes was rare. It made my throat thick as nerves danced in my stomach.

"My mother wouldn't hurt Maisie," I pushed, even as the words fell flat in the air. It was horrifying to realize that I didn't trust my own mother not to harm someone I cared about. Seeing her in front of the portal that day had broken the glass of illusion, and now, the shards of it had lodged into my heart.

Thankfully, no one contradicted me even though the silence said enough.

"If things go south in the palace, you need to get her out," Aedan said to me, his brows drawn and mouth tight. "She's not safe there."

I placed a hand on his arm. I hadn't realized he and Maisie knew each other past a professional level. "I wouldn't leave without her. But it won't come to that—a civil conversation is very achievable, and even if it takes a while to sway the queen to our side, she wouldn't chase me out of my own palace."

Aedan didn't look like he believed me, but he nodded. For the first time, I noticed how his usually slick, tidy blond hair was falling around his ears and the back of his neck, longer than I'd ever seen it and with a slight wave to it. A fine stubble had cropped up around his chin. How long had he been kept in the dungeons?

"A word, if you would allow it, Princess." Hollaina's melodious voice floated through the air, as if propelled by its own wind.

I nodded even though I was positive that she would have offered her opinion even if I had said no.

"Having been in the palace the last month and witnessing everything that happened, you should prepare for a hostile environment. I know it is not what you want to hear, of course. I am one of very few who can sympathize with you princess to princess. Vera is not in a good state. She is volatile, dangerous. It is my opinion that you do not approach her unless you are ready to go to war."

My teeth clenched, heat trickling up my spine. "It will not come to a war. You underestimate my position, *Princess*. The heir has the right to object against the queen's decisions. If you had deigned to attend the meetings in the North instead of sending your lackey, perhaps you would be up-to-date on court policies. You would know that I could force a vote between the region heads."

Hollaina chuckled, making my attempt at power sound childish. "I am well aware of court proceedings. It cannot come to a vote because you will not win."

I crossed my arms. "I know Kashdan is a lost cause, but I believe Leo would vote with me. And I would hope, so would you."

"You stand a good chance of winning the majority—it's true. And Vera knows this. She is no fool. Do you think she would let it get as far as a vote, knowing the inevitable outcome? She would delay it until she could force one of us out and replace the position with a pathetic official looking to move up the ladder by pleasing her. It is commendable that you wish to play fair, but it is stupid to try when your opponent will not." Hollaina was so calm, eerily quiet, even as her words carried so much weight. She was outspoken and powerful, making me wonder why Nimshar had always attended meetings in her stead.

"I know my mother. She might be cunning when it comes to political moves, but she wouldn't turn her back on the laws our ancestors made. Thank you for your concern, but I can handle it."

Hollaina tilted her head slightly—a submission. Only it hardly felt like one as she studied me, her scars glinting in the dim light of the tent.

Freya cleared her throat. "Even without inside help, I still think it's possible to make our window. Obviously, the fewer in your party, the less chances of being seen. You should limit yourself to no more than five. That way, you still have a chance to stave off attackers in a retreat, if need be."

It frayed at my nerves to hear everyone preparing for the worst-case scenario. Logically, I knew it was practical. But it felt like a punch to the gut that there was seemingly no trust in my ability to see this through.

"I'll go, of course, and Spense. I'd like Badras as well, if you're comfortable with it." I looked to the large, hulking male, who grinned wickedly as he rubbed the hilt of the blade at his hip.

"Count me in."

"I'm coming too." The conviction in Aedan's voice made it hard for me to tell him no.

"I need you here, Aedan. I need to be able to count on someone to make decisions for me. I trust you with my life."

"Which is why I should be going with you—to protect you," he insisted.

"She can handle herself," Spense growled from my other side. "And if for whatever reason she can't, then her mate will be there. I'll *always* be there."

The sentiment was almost sweet enough to distract me from the obvious territorial battle, but Aedan's responding glare reminded me of the feelings I had found out that he harboured for me. It was a problem for another time, as long as they could tolerate each other for now.

"Please, Aedan," I murmured softly. "I'm asking you as a friend. Please don't make me order you as your princess."

I didn't want to tell him that the real reason for keeping him away was that I didn't know how he would react in the palace. I hadn't been caught up enough to know exactly what had gone down and why he had been imprisoned. Not to mention why his father hadn't fought to free him. I didn't need any surprises. They would only hinder my mission. He stared at Spense, jaw clenched, until finally, he sighed and met my gaze, his eyes softening.

"Fine. And for the record, you're not my princess." My breath hitched in my chest for a split second before he continued, "You're my queen."

All I could do was nod. "Thank you."

Sorin spoke, his confidence in a strange environment enviable. Though, I supposed, when you had lived for as long as he had, confidence must have become second nature. "I can recommend two of our own soldiers to accompany you," he offered. "I think it wise not to have too many cooks in the kitchen, as they say."

"Good idea," I agreed. "Are you able to manage overseeing the Folk while Badras is away? It won't be a walk in the park to get everyone settled."

"Olys and I will handle it." He looked to his younger brother, who nodded once, his usual downturned mouth present.

Hope fluttered in my chest, like a nervous bird testing out their wings after a crash. I was proud of this plan.

"Now that we've settled that"—Freya steepled her fingers

together—"I believe a part of our deal is still unfinished."

I nodded. "Pik?"

The blue-skinned goblin looked up, his childish features eager. "Yes, my lady?"

"I have a task for you. Can you find out what language this is in and translate it?" I pulled the rolled parchment from the pile in the middle of the table and passed it to him. "It is of utmost importance that it gets done swiftly and correctly. I trust you to do this for us."

Pik unrolled the paper and surveyed the words. "It is not a language I recognize, but it does look similar to an old Elvish tongue that was used before the Great War. I will ask around, of course, but it might take me longer than usual without my texts and normal resources."

"You are welcome to all the research we have," Freya said. "I will set you up in our library."

I wasn't sure how accurate the term *library* was, considering it was likely a tent filled with scribblings and dusty tomes, but it would have to suffice. Pik's work was certainly cut out for him.

"Perfect." I glanced around the circle, gaze landing on each member briefly. When I reached Spense, I held it, his small smile filling me with warmth and confidence. "We need to be prepared to leave tonight if we want to reach the palace by the sunup changeover."

Everyone stood, ready to get moving.

I couldn't help but smile, even as the nerves in my chest fluttered wildly.

"We have a castle to storm."

TWELVE

MAISIE
NO MERCY FOR SINNERS

"It's time."

Fear choked me, rooting me to the marble that I stood on, closing my throat until it was hard to swallow. Vera's presence never failed to illicit that response in me lately, and today was no different.

After being woken by the light orb that summoned me to the queen, I had raced there to find she was already dressed, her hair coiled in braids at the nape of her neck. Usually, she expected me to get her presentable for the day, and the fact that she had chosen to get ready without me sent rocks tumbling to the pit of my stomach. It was past dawn, but still early for her. Her habit of staying up late into the night meant she normally didn't wake until mid-morning—something that had never been the case before Diana's disappearance.

"Would you like me to get breakfast for you, My Queen?"

"No. Our morning plans just became much more exciting than breakfast, Maisie." She grinned. Her usual poise had been slipping more and more since Diana's return, showing cracks of mania and bloodlust below the queenly surface. "The prodigal daughter has come back to her mother."

My hands wrung together, unable to be pulled apart even if I tried. No, Diana couldn't have been that dumb. Surely, she had an army waiting to reclaim her throne from the terror reigning over it. She wouldn't have walked into the lion's den without armour.

Vera laughed at the look on my face. "Come along. Let's see what she has to say, shall we?"

She no longer had to drag me with her anywhere, considering my obedience was tethered to Aedan's life. I followed her willingly, a conforming servant, just as she wanted.

I was surprised to see the throne room empty when we entered. Vera positioned herself in her large ivory chair, instructing me to stand on the dais a few feet behind her. Delios was noticeably absent—he was usually stuck to the queen's side during times when she wanted to put on a show of power. Times like this.

The sunrise flooded through the floor-to-ceiling windows, painting the room pink and orange. Another new day without an end in sight.

The usual guards who stood at the door were absent, replaced by soldiers from the queen's army, fully decked in battle wear, down to the multitude of weapons. A breath of relief filled my lungs when I recognized them as Ryen and Trent.

Footsteps echoed through the room, and Solis entered. "They are almost inside the palace. Should we apprehend them?"

"No." Vera crossed a leg daintily. "Let them believe they made it here unnoticed."

Solis nodded. He closed the heavy oak doors and stepped away. Within a minute, the same doors slammed open. Diana strutted into the room, palms outstretched from blasting her magic. My heart clenched. Hers was the face I had wanted to see for months, but now, all I wanted was for her to turn around and run the other way. If I wasn't a coward, I would've yelled. Told her to get out while she still could.

But I was a coward.

The change in Vera was palpable. Magic poured from her, and an energetic fizzing haloed around the throne. She was excited, but it didn't feel like the happiness that came from a mother seeing her daughter after a harrowing time apart.

It felt like a wolf zeroing in before the kill.

"Mother." Diana's familiar voice rang through the room, strong and clear. She wore her hair up in a way I'd never done for her before, braided and wrapped around her head like a crown. Wisps had broken free, bracketing her face, which looked wiser. Older.

Spense and three fae I did not recognize fanned out behind her, creating a triangular effect. It was a power move, and it filled me with pride for her.

"My sweet child. I am relieved beyond words to see you safely returned," Vera crooned, voice dripping in honey. "Although I have to say, it breaks my heart that you felt the need to sneak in to your own home like a common thief. Were you concerned your own mother would reject you?"

Diana moved closer, her companions following. She stopped at the edge of the dais, and her hazel eyes narrowed as she looked up. Her gaze landed on me for a half second, softening slightly, before returning to the queen.

"Last time we spoke, you tried to have my soulmate killed. I'm sure you can understand why I felt cautious about coming back here."

Vera's back was to me, stopping me from being able to read her face, but from the way her nails dug into the arms of her throne, I could tell she was not pleased.

"It is troubling that you still do not see the hold this Dark fae has on you, my dear. I was trying to protect you, our land. Seeing him at your side after what he did tells me that you are not here in peace."

Diana bristled visibly. Beside her, Spense tensed, his eyes flicking between her and the queen. His steely gaze gave nothing away, only that he looked ready to jump in front of Diana at a moment's notice.

"Let's get one thing straight, Mother. Spense is Unseelie, not Dark. There's no such thing as Dark and Light fae—that was something made up to create a fearful narrative. And how can you say that he's controlling me? We are *soulmates*." She shoved up her sleeve, revealing swirling black ink, the lines starting at her wrist and disappearing up her arm.

I felt my mouth pop open. Aedan had told me about the tattoos, but deep down, it hadn't registered with me. I couldn't believe that Diana was tied to *him* so permanently.

"You had a soulmate once. Or have you forgotten my father already?" she continued icily. "How can you have felt this bond, the pure love and power of it, and refuse it for me? Are you really so stuck in your ways that you cannot look past his heritage—something he has no control over—and wish me happiness? It is *my* heart that is broken, Mother, not yours. You have no right to be heartbroken."

Vera was quiet for a few moments before standing slowly, her dress gliding down her body to the floor like water. "Diana Lightbringer. You disgrace your namesake. How dare you speak to me this way? Jago was my husband for nine years before he was your father for two months. The soulmate bond leaves a *scar* when it is severed, one that pains me every day."

She took a step forward, and below, Diana took a reacting step back. I wanted to hang my head. If she was already retreating, it didn't bode well.

"Your precious soulmate came here to bring war to our peaceful lands. He conspired with the biggest blight the realm had ever seen to poison your head with thoughts of doubt. Your ancestors would be ashamed."

Diana's jaw clamped, and she sucked a breath through her nose. "That's where you're wrong. These are no peaceful lands. The same ancestors you believe admonish me are the ones who guided me to heal the portal, to bring back balance to the realm. Everything we know about the history of our ancestors, our court, is wrong. The story of the Seelie queen and the first Diana has been misconstrued and twisted. The Unseelie were driven out all those years ago. They belong here, as do the Folk. We are supposed to live in unity."

"Unity," Vera sneered. "I thought I'd raised you better. Are you that naive that you truly believe I will not be attacked if I were to lower my defences? The Darks are looking for a crack, and right now, that crack is you. But I will not be weakened. It is my duty to ensure the work our ancestors did was not done in vain."

"Please, Mother, just listen to me. King Urdan is no longer a threat. The Unseelie and the Folk want peace. They suffered in the realm they were banished to. Why should they be punished for something that happened eight thousand years ago? This is their home. They belong here."

Diana's voice bordered on desperation, and it wrapped a fist around my heart. She had always been like this, believing the best in everyone. It was a blessing and a curse. She had not seen the disintegration of the once-reasonable Queen Vera. It was a lost cause, but I feared she would not see that until it was too late.

"Urdan will be a threat as long as he lives and breathes. He is Eira's enemy. And now, so are you." The queen's words hit the air like knives, sharp and cutting.

"How can you say that?" Diana breathed.

"I know how to make hard choices for the better of the realm.

Unlike you, I can separate feelings from my decisions. It brings me no joy to do this, but if you will not see reason, if you will not forsake the evil that plagues you, then you will be treated as one of them. And I will not hesitate to send you back through that portal, kicking and screaming if I have to."

Instinctively, my hand flew to my chest. This was truly the end. The days as I knew them would forever be changed. No matter what happened next, their relationship could never recover from this.

This was war.

"I don't want to fight you." Diana's voice shook, even as she held it as steady as she could, her eyes swimming with tears. "I want peace, just like you. Give me a chance to show you how it's possible. You raised me to be strong and smart. Mercy over justice, remember?"

Without looking back, her arm flew to the side, referencing the words that were carved into the wall above the door.

"There is no mercy for sinners."

Vera's mind was made, and I knew as well as Diana that it would take an act of Gaia herself to change it now.

Come on, just get out of here, I pleaded in my head, hoping that by some force of nature, Diana would hear my words. *Regroup and come back with a better plan.*

"Think about your next words wisely, Diana," her mother warned. "I am not bluffing."

One tear slid down Diana's cheek. She looked broken, the way her arms hung limply at her sides, the way she stared forward without any more fight behind her eyes. She took a shuddering breath and looked directly at Vera. "I am the rightful heir to this realm. I have the right to a say in the choices regarding this land. *My* land. If you will not listen to me, then I invoke a vote. Let our peers voice their opinions on this matter like the civilized court we used to be."

The queen sighed heavily, and for a brief, fluttering moment, I thought she might concede. But I should have known better. "You might be the heir, but I am still the queen, chosen by our ancestors. It is my right to eliminate threats to our court how I see fit."

She raised a hand in the air, and the soldiers at the door stood to attention.

"What a waste," she said, her voice almost soft as she shook her head disdainfully at her daughter. "We were so close."

Diana looked to the guards warily as her companions shifted to a defensive position, weapons slowly being drawn. Her throat worked on a swallow.

"Soldiers, eliminate the threat."

There was no time to react before all hell broke loose.

THIRTEEN

MAISIE
FRAY

As much as I wished I could say I jumped into motion, that would be a lie. My feet remained planted on the dais as I watched in disbelief while Ryen and Trent ran from their positions at the door.

Swords drawn, they raced toward the throne. Spense arced his weapon over his head, ready to push them back, but they did not stop to fight. In a truly shocking move, they ran right past the group and at the queen.

Although I supposed I shouldn't have been that surprised. I was the one who had suggested the mutiny after all.

It was so gratifying, seeing Vera's face when she realized what was happening. The five on the floor stared in shock while the queen backed up, jolting when she bumped into the throne.

"Your tyrannical rule has come to an end," Ryen snarled, his sword dauntingly close to her throat. "Surrender your crown, or we will do it for you."

As if on cue, a sea of soldiers flooded into the room, surrounding the dais.

Vera's slack jaw turned into a nefarious smile, growing bigger and wider until fear clawed in my belly at the sight of her wicked grin.

She began to chuckle, which quickly turned into howling, stomach-clutching booms of laughter. Terror shot down my back, leaving ice in its wake.

Still shouting with guttural laughter, Vera drew her arm back and blasted power outward, so strong that it sent the nearest six soldiers flying backward. "You think you can stop me? You will all burn for your treason."

She began hurtling power across the room, so wild and uncalculated that she looked completely unhinged. Soldiers darted to and fro, trying to dodge the streaks of magic while inching closer to take her down.

Hands suddenly gripped my arm, yanking me backward off the dais. I screamed, the sound lost in the noise of the room.

"It's me! Maisie, it's me."

I looked into wide hazel eyes and felt air return to my lungs.

"Come on," Diana urged, pulling me with her. "We have to get out of here."

Like hell I was going to turn that down. I kept stride with her as we caught up to her party and aimed for the door.

"Wait!" I tugged on her arm. "We can't leave without Aedan. He's being held in the dungeon. She'll kill him."

Diana shook her head. "Aedan is in the Unclaimed Land, waiting for us. He escaped with Hollaina."

Holy hell. Relief flooded through me, loosening my legs enough to keep up with the breakneck speed with which we tore through the palace. Soldiers ran around us, dodging and ducking out of the way. Officials fled, eyes wide with terror and unsure where to go. At one point, we passed a fire that was creeping up the walls, swallowing paintings and wooden furniture like a hungry drake.

It wasn't until we fled down the front steps and took off down the cobblestone road to Nevelyn that the thought occurred to me: Aedan had escaped and left me there alone, thinking he was one wrong move from death. I was ready to run into the fray for him, risk getting trapped again to get him out. So he could be free to help Diana. That was how much I had come to care about him.

But apparently, he hadn't shared that sentiment, if he felt comfortable letting destiny take its chances with me.

So much for him and me against the world.

FOURTEEN

SPENSE
RHETORIC

Nevelyn was a ghost town.

Every home, shop, and building was boarded up. No lights, no sign of any life. It was as if the entire city were gone.

Diana's face was pained as she took in the once-vibrant and marvellous city, still panting from our mad run here. My heart ached for her to see what had happened in her absence.

Maisie bent over, resting her hands on her knees as she fought for breath. "The queen ordered a shutdown in every city once we saw the portal. They have orders not to open up until it's been lifted."

"They can't go that long without supplies."

Her maidservant nodded. "We probably have a week or two before the code will be broken by those in search of food. Until then though, they're going to keep everything locked up tight. They were warned of a war."

Diana shook her head, gazing around at the unwelcoming city as if she might be able to find a hole somewhere, a way in.

"We need to take cover somewhere safe until we can regroup," I said, stepping forward. "We can't stay out in the open like this."

"If all the cities are like this, then we might have to go to the

Abbey and hope they let us in." Diana moved closer to the buildings and into a shadow, and we followed suit. "Shela would hide us, but the City of Scholars is too far away."

Badras grabbed at a large chunk of wood that had been haphazardly stapled over the front window. He pulled the edge, but it didn't budge.

"I might have an idea," Maisie said nervously. She eyed the big, armed males and gave me a disdainful look. Speaking only to Diana, she continued, "I know of someone with the resources we need. He deals in bargains."

Slowly, Diana nodded. "Can he be trusted?"

"Can anyone?"

"Fair enough. Lead the way."

Her words couldn't be true enough. Diana was putting on a brave face for the sake of us—or maybe it was the only way she could function right now. Either way, I knew there would be a huge crash once she allowed herself to deal with what had happened in the throne room.

We followed Maisie along the shadowed sides of the streets all the way to the Marketplace. Had it not been for the giant sign above and the tipped-over cart at the entrance, I would not have recognized it. Without the vendors and busy patrons, it looked like any other street.

We ventured farther into the Marketplace than I had ever been, where the shops were older, more established, and less boarded up. Just as I was thinking we must be getting near the end, Maisie halted us in front of a black shop with no windows. The sign above the unguarded door read *The Curator.*

Whatever you're looking for, The Curator has it.

This place was as ominous as ever, and respect blossomed for the maidservant. I had been aware of her less-than-innocent reputation in the palace, but having contacts like this was a surprise.

Maisie looked to Diana, expecting her to take the lead, but the princess motioned for her to go first. Hesitantly, she raised a fist and knocked on the door.

Before she even pulled her hand away, it swung open. Immediately, I made to move in front of Diana, but she stopped me with a gentle arm and followed Maisie inside.

"Stay by me," I murmured in her ear, trapping the hand she'd outstretched in mine.

She only gave me a little pat on the arm.

Inside, the shop was smoky and smelled so strongly of incense that my eyes began to water. There was a small sitting area with a long, curved couch that wrapped around a large armchair. There were six cushions on the couch, which seemed like an oddly large number for such a small seating area.

A door I hadn't noticed behind the armchair opened, and a tall male stepped into the room. Badras and the soldiers Nome and Pyter tensed, fanning out instinctively.

"Welcome." The proprietor smiled.

He was young and handsomely dressed with an earthy power that bled from him. It was not something you felt every day, and I knew from one look that Badras noticed it too.

"Maisie, my dear. How good to see you again. Although this is unexpected; I had thought those stones would keep you busy for a while."

Diana's head snapped to her friend.

"Kol, this is the high princess, Diana Lightbringer. I'm sure you've heard of her." Maisie's tone was dry, a departure from the meek, quiet voice I knew. She motioned to her left. "She's seeking refuge."

The stranger—Kol—tilted his head, his gaze raking over all of us before snagging on Diana. "Does the princess not speak for herself?"

Diana squared her shoulders. "Maisie told me that you deal in bargains. I would like to make a deal for our safety."

"And you assume that you have something worth my time."

"The deal is a courtesy," Diana said, her voice steel. "Need I remind you that refusing aid to the high princess is treason? I could have your head."

Kol grinned, the air charged, and my hand went to rest at Bloodletter on my hip. He did not move from where he stood, but the room seemed to shrink.

"Somehow, *Princess*, I doubt you are in a position to be making those kinds of threats right now." He waved his arm out in front of us. "Sit, everyone. Let's be civil about this, shall we?"

There was a moment where no one moved, but finally, Diana broke her stare from him and moved to the couch, where she perched on a middle cushion.

Maisie, who had dropped into the spot on her right, looked around. "Done some redecorating?"

The Curator settled into the armchair, hands folding in his lap. "I like to be prepared for my guests."

I took the spot on Diana's left, and the others filled in the couch.

"I must say, I was glad to hear of your return," Kol said, sounding earnest. "The realm needs their high princess now more than ever."

Diana narrowed her eyes. "That's an interesting change of tune."

He shrugged. "I am nothing if not interesting."

Maisie leaned forward. "Are you aware of what's happening in the North right now?"

"I heard some scuttlebutt about a lock-in order. I assumed you were the reason for that."

Diana frowned. "Scuttlebutt? Guards would have gone door to door, telling everyone about that kind of order."

Kol smirked. "The Crown has not been brave enough to darken

my doorstep for quite some time."

I could sense Diana's wheels turning, her brain firing in about a hundred different directions. "Let's get to the point. We need somewhere safe to stay the night. What will that cost us?"

The Curator looked over each of us, his lips moving as he counted the bodies. Something clearly done for show. It seemed less and less of a coincidence that he'd had the exact seating we needed when we came in.

"Six, hmm. That's a lot of safety I'm promising. But I can do it—for a favour."

"What kind of favour?" Diana asked, her eyebrows scrunching together.

"Well, if I knew what I wanted, I would have just said that, wouldn't I?"

I crossed my arms.

Diana shook her head vehemently. "No. Absolutely not. I don't deal in unknowns."

"I think you will find that in life, everything is unknown."

Gods, this fae was strange. I was beginning to feel unsettled, but I fought the urge to shift around in my seat.

"I don't know you or trust you enough to give you an open-ended favour. Especially not with my position."

Maisie looked down at her hands, which were wringing themselves. Kol noticed this, too, but did not waver.

"That is my price. If you'd prefer, I would happily make the deal with your new soulmate here instead."

We locked eyes. It was unusually hard for me to get a read on him, but for as strange and frighteningly confident as he was, with the connections he clearly had, he didn't give off malintent.

Or he was just very good at hiding it.

Diana pursed her lips. "How did you know we're soulmates?"

She was right. Our sleeves covered our arms.

Kol sat back in his armchair, that infuriating wry grin never slipping.

"He's involved with the Outcasts," Maisie said in a low tone. "Spies, among other things."

"We're done here. I'm not bargaining on behalf of Spense," Diana argued.

"I'll do it."

"Excellent." The Curator stood.

"What are you doing?" Diana hissed to me.

I pulled a strand of her chestnut hair away from her face gently. "We need somewhere safe to spend the night. I can handle him, promise."

She didn't look convinced, but I gave her a small smile as I stood, extending a hand toward Kol.

He took it, long fingers wrapping around mine firmly. "I look forward to working with you, Prince."

A shudder worked its way down my spine at the way he used the title. He could easily be using it as an extension of Diana, but somehow, I was sure he knew who I really was.

"If you'll follow me through this door, I can show you to your accommodations."

The heady smell of incense thankfully faded as we left his meeting room, entering into a hallway of sorts. Steep stairs twisted up to our right, but we went past them and out another door, which deposited us on the street.

Diana looked around, confused. "Where are we?"

Kol didn't look back as he led us down the cobblestone. "So many questions." He tsked.

Even Maisie didn't seem to recognize this street. "Has this been behind the Marketplace all these years?"

"That sounds like rhetoric, my dear friend. Seems an obvious answer to me."

We stopped in front of a pub. *Lodging available*, it read on the sign, below the large letters donning it as *Lara's*.

It was surprisingly normal inside, well lit, and clean. There were a few patrons at the bar and less at the spattering of tables, and they all stared when we came in.

A gruff-looking female behind the bar with close-cut black hair lifted her chin at us. "Kol. Who are you bringing in here now?"

"Relax, Lara, love. It's unlike you to turn down good business."

Lara curled her upper lip. "I have a right to refuse customers, you know. Even if you bring them in. With everything going on, I'm not taking any irregulars."

Kol dropped his forearms on the bar, his long legs crossing. "I'm hardly irregular." He raised a brow, seemingly referencing something between them. A deal, no doubt.

She shook her head in exasperation. "Fine. But you're responsible for them. And keep your damn elbows off my bar."

She swept a towel across the shiny surface to shoo him away, and he smiled.

Turning to us, he opened his arms. "Let's eat."

FIFTEEN

DIANA
LITTLE REBELS

The Curator made for an interesting dinner companion.

I couldn't shake the feeling that Maisie knew him from making a deal. He was an eccentric character, but he kept calling her variations of his "dear friend," and she spoke to him with less hesitancy than usual.

But then again, she had changed enormously since I'd left. My friend had always been sweet and kind and inquisitive, but now, she paired that with a can-do attitude and grit, which she'd never shown before.

It made me uneasy to think of what Maisie could have gone through to cause such a change in her. Guilt was already squirming in my gut before adding on that she might have made a sketchy deal with this powerful male because of me.

The seven of us sat at a round table, thankful to eat hot food, even if the bartender looked like she had spat in it first. There were soft conversations between us, nothing too serious due to the wandering eyes. Kol sat in silence, watching us all keenly. He had not been brought a plate, but it seemed to suit him fine.

"Do you think we should be worried about why he's not eating this?" Spense hissed in my ear.

"Maybe he's been struck by food poisoning too many times before."

"I was thinking more along the lines of *real* poisoning, but you're probably right." He lifted a piece of stringy meat with his fork, examining it. "What do you think this is?"

Badras's tankard—specifically requested—of ale hit the table with a thunk. "Since when do you care, little brother?" He wiped beer from his beard with his sleeve. "You've grown so soft since coming here. Where's the Spense who scarfed down kelpie droppings on a dare?"

I coughed to cover up my snicker while Spense emptied the remainders of his dinner onto his brother's plate, who shrugged and forked it into his mouth.

"What's a kelpie?" Maisie asked.

"Nasty creatures," Badras said, his words barely understandable through a mouthful of food. "They live in the water and pull you down to the depths, where they feed on your soul."

Maisie's eyes widened, looking to me for confirmation.

"I wish he were joking." I grimaced.

"And you brought them *here*?"

"They're as a part of the Folk as we are. It wouldn't have been fair to leave them behind because we're scared of them."

My eyes skittered across the table to Kol, who stared with open interest.

"Balance and all that crap, right?"

The corner of his mouth lifted slightly.

"You seem like you've been around a fair bit," I hedged.

He cocked his head. "An astute assumption—I'll give you that."

"Considering how much you love to talk, you're not very chatty when it comes to yourself." It was infuriating, trying to get an answer from him. All evasion and half answers.

"I am of the opinion that mystery is a most attractive quality in someone. Why give it all away for free when you can work for it? Much more of a reward that way."

I rolled my eyes. "You're definitely in the right line of work then."

He grinned, shockingly beautiful and intimidating. "I'm glad you agree."

Beside me, Spense coughed. From the way he'd been subtly keeping me within arm's reach all night, I could tell he didn't trust The Curator. I sent a small tendril of magic his way and took a deep breath with the comfort that surged when it touched his. It was always like coming home or finding a piece of me that had been missing too long.

He placed a warm hand on my knee under the table, his thumb stroking over my leg comfortingly.

"How did you get into this work anyway?" Maisie asked, her half-eaten dinner long abandoned.

Kol looked at her for a moment, as if wondering whether or not to answer, and finally said, "It was not something I chose. But necessity demanded it, and I have come to enjoy it. I know how to make good of the hands the gods have dealt me."

The Unseelie members of the table each whipped their gaze up.

"You know of gods besides Gaia?" I breathed.

"I have never understood Eira's obsession with just worshipping Mother Earth." Kol smiled. "How blasphemous of me."

Maisie shook her head. "I still can't believe this. How many gods are there supposed to be?" She looked to me, worry etched into her face.

"Two," I said gently. "Gaia and Ouranos. And then there are their children—the deities."

"Four," Kol cut in. "Unless you count *their* children, of course."

My head spun.

Badras harrumphed from across the table. "The deities were never documented to have children. And if they did, the knowledge was never passed along to their subjects."

Kol lifted a shoulder. "They lived among us, in mortal bodies. How can you blame them for reproducing, really?"

I thought to the history lesson Alwyn had given me—it seemed like months ago, not mere weeks. My heart panged.

"So, you mean to say that there could be fae still alive that are distantly related to actual *gods*?" Maisie's mouth parted.

"Don't quote me on it," Kol replied, his smirk returning.

Spense shook his head. "There are no records that say the deities ever took mortal form."

"Seems like you haven't been reading the right records then."

I sucked in a breath. This *Curator* was dangerous. He had way too much knowledge and enough personality to make us believe him, whether he told lies or truth.

Badras fixed him with a dry look. "Teases stop being fun when they never lead to anything."

Kol laughed, the sound jarring in the tense air. "That is delightful indeed. You're right, of course. But unfortunately, there is not much I can give you if you don't ask the right questions."

"Sounds like cowardice to me," Spense growled.

I expected Kol to shrug or brush off the statement with a sly one-liner. But it was a shock when his eyes darkened, his mouth setting into a firm line.

"Do not speak to me of cowardice, boy. You do not know nearly enough about me or this world."

There was a charge in the air, and even without a magic presence, it was powerful. I placed a hand on top of Spense's, still resting on my knee.

"We don't mean to offend you, Kol," Maisie said gently. "There's a lot of pressure on all of us right now."

Kol straightened his jacket lapels, sighing. "It troubles me that this is the group that's supposed to lead the rebellion. And you don't even know your own history."

Spense exchanged a look with me. He knew that was something that weighed heavy on me since finding out my ancestors' true past. Lies that were so catastrophic that I was now part of a mutiny against my own mother. Not only part of it, but leading it as well.

"That history was kept from us. How can we know when those holding such volatile information, like you, do not speak up?"

"You are still young, Diana. You have a good heart and integrity. But you will learn that while speaking up might be the right thing to do, it is not always the smart move. This world is not yet ready to hear the truth. You must be able to see that in the way they blindly follow their queen's lies, even when it goes against their beloved princess. It is more difficult to convince someone that they've been deceived than it is to deceive them. A sad truth of this world." Kol's eyes softened, showing years of maturity beyond his youthful face.

"That will change under my rule."

"In that, I have full confidence."

"Can you share more about the deities? Are they involved in how to stop the Seelie queen?"

Kol looked straight into my eyes and held the contact. They were nearly black, pairing neatly with his well-kept dark hair. After a moment, he said, "I think the best way I can help you now is to tell you a story."

"A story?" Badras raised his eyebrows.

"Yes, and this one's free of charge, so I would keep your thoughts to yourself," The Curator snapped.

Badras raised his hands mockingly, leaning back against his chair, which groaned under his massive size.

"A long time ago, after Gaia and Ouranos were satisfied with the creation of their worlds, they decided that they would keep one realm to themselves. Here, they would send their exciting new beings—the Folk. But because they could not enter the realm themselves, only watch over it, they needed a way to be able to reach their creations.

"So, the deities were created, each made from different aspects of the Folk—to better blend with and understand them. Two sons and two daughters would rule their own magical distinctions. The deities were not mortal, not by any sense, but they needed to be able to walk among those on the plane of physical existence. And so Gaia called to the Folk, one from each faction, and with their help, she was able to tie her offspring to the land, using four magical artefacts from the earth that she and her other half had created. So long as they remained intact, the deities could walk as mortals.

"They were, however, given one strict rule—do not interfere. Gaia and Ouranos were ageless beings, and as such, they did not want to sway their creations. Free will would be given. With some guidance, they wanted to see how they would govern themselves. The deities agreed to this, knowing that if they were to do something that altered the natural progression of Eira, the artefacts would be destroyed, and they would be banished from the mortal realm forever."

Kol spoke like a gifted storyteller, his voice rich and smooth. His words made sense, and considering all I had learned in the last few months, it was hardly the most difficult story to believe. But one thing stood out.

"If Gaia and Ouranos couldn't come to Eira, then how would they destroy the artefacts? I can't imagine their siblings would do it, if it was a punishment to them all."

The Curator held up a slender finger. "First, the deities were *not* siblings. They were created, not born. Gaia and Ouranos were gods, not mortals. They did not procreate. Secondly, that was supposedly a simple fix. The Folk that Gaia chose to help her would have the power to do it, and when they grew too old, the duty would pass to whomever they chose as their heir. When the gods called to them, they listened. In times of great need, they could commune with them by accelerating a willing soul's journey to the ancestral plane."

Whoa. "Meaning ... they would die?"

Kol nodded. "Once they spoke with Gaia and Ouranos, they would be able to relay the message with the rest of the council of Folk through divine spaces, like the Endless Cave in the East or the Sacred Pool in the North. They were revered, honoured, to have given their lives serving the gods."

That felt so wrong. That the gods had to resort to the death of one of their precious creations in order to right a wrong in the world they'd built.

Kol leaned back in his chair, one leg gracefully folding over his knee. "I hope you use this story wisely. It is one that has been lost in time. I was trusted with it, and now, I am entrusting it to you."

As grateful as I was to learn more true history, it only added more pieces to the puzzle. How were we supposed to use this information to defeat the Seelie Queen? And without my mother's cooperation, it would be even harder on our band of misfits.

Lara, the pub owner, stopped at our table to collect the mostly empty plates. She fixed Kol with a look, balancing the tower against her hip. "Rooms four through six. If you stay past breakfast, it's extra."

"Thank you, my dear." Kol gave her that wicked grin, which did more to intimidate than charm, in my opinion, but she ate it up.

My chair slid along the floor as I stood. "I think we should all retire so we can get an early start. Wouldn't want to overstay our welcome past breakfast. Thank you for your help."

Kol smirked at me and remained sitting as we all collected our things—like Badras's sword, which he had placed on the table like a centrepiece. "Rest up, little rebels. I expect we shall meet again soon."

His gaze landed on Spense, who did not shy away from the reminder of their bargain.

We made our way through the pub upstairs to the lodgings, which was just ten rooms down a long hallway.

"Okay, Maisie and I will take room four, Spense and Badras in room five, and Nome and Pyter in room six. Make sure you get up early enough to eat something. We leave for Shynin by sunup."

The others nodded and dispersed.

Spense pulled me aside. "I don't want to be away from you." He pulled me close by the waist. "Not in this weird place. Don't you want to be roomies?"

I placed my hands on his chest. "I'll be fine. As appealing as it is to room with you, I'm not leaving Maisie to spend the night with one of those soldiers she doesn't know. It's not fair to her."

He nodded. "You're right." Kissing the top of my nose, he sighed. "Why are you always right?"

Chuckling, I stepped away to look for Maisie. "Wait, where is she?"

We both looked back and forth down the hall, and then her honey-yellow curls caught my attention, bouncing up the stairs.

"Everything okay?"

Her face looked ashen, eyes darting between us.

"Just feeling a little off from whatever was in that dinner," she said, a hand on her stomach. She stared straight ahead. "This our room?"

I nodded. "Yeah, go ahead."

She pushed the door open and didn't look back as she disappeared inside.

Spense looked as concerned as I felt. "That doesn't bode well for the rest of us who ate that food."

"I'm sure the stress of the day is catching up to her. My mother, she —" I shook my head, unsure of what I had even been trying to put into words. "I'll be glad to put this day behind us."

Spense wrapped me in his arms, resting his chin on my head. His scent and warmth enveloped me, filling me with the first comfort I had felt all day.

"I needed this," I mumbled into his chest.

A low laugh rumbled through him.

"We're going to get through this, I promise. Whatever you need from me, it's yours."

I looked up into those grey eyes I'd come to memorize. "I love you."

He placed a soft kiss on my lips. "I love you most."

It was hard to leave his arms, but I was looking forward to reconnecting with Maisie. I had missed her friendship terribly.

The room was dark, but enough light slipped under the crack in the door from the hall that I could make out her form on one of the two cots. She was breathing deeply, already passed out.

It was just as well—we needed the sleep. I pulled the blanket up over her shoulders and tucked into my own bed. Tomorrow would be better.

SIXTEEN

AEDAN
HOLD IT DOWN

It had been too long. Two days—that was what Diana had told me as her party left.

"If you haven't heard anything by the third day, then you can worry."

It had not been two days—in fact, it had only been about ten hours. But it was well into the night now. Surely, if they had been successful, they would have sent word that everything was okay.

And that was why, despite Hollaina's tsking and Freya's blatant disapproval, I was saddling up one of the resident Shynin horses. She was small and lacked the muscle tone boasted by the palace-bred mounts, but she would have to do.

I had never been one to ignore my instincts, and this was no different.

We set out into the woods, both shivering once we passed the border into the North. The poor mare had probably never seen snow, but I would make sure she was well cared for once we reached the palace.

I led us to the back entrance, where we would reach the stables first. After we had travelled for a few hours, the building was finally in sight. I slowed the mare, allowing her to catch her breath. Her skin had a sheen of sweat layering it, as did mine. Best we cool down and approach without drawing any attention.

I hopped off once we reached the cobbled path, which had been shovelled recently. We made it into the barn entirely unnoticed, which was incredibly strange. On a regular day, the soldiers would never have let a stranger get that close.

But as I took in the barn, I realized there seemed to be no soldiers here. Only a young stablehand sleeping against a pile of hay.

I nudged him awake with my foot. "Are you the only one here right now?"

He blinked groggily, sitting up straighter once he recognized me. "I'm on the night shift alone on account of us being low on staff right now."

"What are you talking about?"

"Er"—he swallowed—"a lot of the workers left to be with their families after the region lockdown. The ones of us who stayed are on our own."

I took a deep inhale through my nose, holding it for a few beats before letting it go. This had gone on too long. The effects of this power struggle were spreading farther than they needed to.

"I need you to put this horse away. Blankets, a mash, the works—she's had a long night."

The stablehand nodded eagerly, taking the reins from me. I gave her one last pat on the nose and headed down to the barn.

I stopped briefly at Kali's stall to see that she was in good shape and stroke her neck. Finnvarra pinned her ears angrily as I passed her, which confirmed she was her usual, healthy self.

A pit grew larger in my stomach, the longer I walked toward the palace. By the time I reached the back entrance, it was like a stone was rolling around my belly. The place was a disaster. Furniture was tipped over, curtains ripped, burn marks up the walls. The smell of ash burned my nostrils, the eerie silence ringing through the air.

What had happened here?

I broke out in a run, heading for the throne room.

"Hey! Stop there!"

I spun at the booming voice. A soldier ran toward me, sword drawn, freezing when he saw my face.

"Ryen!"

My second continued charging, thudding against me as he pulled me into a hug.

"Aedan, thank Gaia. We heard you'd gotten out. What happened?"

"Hollaina rescued me—I know it's crazy," I added at Ryen's raised brows. "But more importantly, why does the palace look like it's seen a war? Where's Diana?"

"She was here with Spense and a few others. They were trying to make peace with the queen. They ran when she ordered us to attack them, but we turned on her. The army has been loyal to you for a while now. Vera's powerful, but she couldn't take on all of us at once. She fled to Gaia knows where. I'm sure we haven't seen the last of her though."

Upon closer inspection, I noticed Ryen had cuts and scrapes along his armour. His jaw was bruised, and dried blood was caked under his nose.

"She did that to you?"

"I think she broke one of my ribs, but the face was courtesy of Lord Devlin. Some of the officials fought back and were surprisingly well trained. Anyone left in the palace has turned against the queen though. We're calling it the Rebellion."

I shook my head in amazement. To think, I had blamed Ryen at first for turning me in when he was my greatest ally.

"That's impressive," I told him, squeezing his shoulder. "Your loyalty is a gift I don't deserve."

He shoved me once. "Never say that. Besides"—he smiled—"we're really loyal to Diana. You're just lumped in there."

"Well, I'm glad to have you in charge—that's for sure."

"I'm relieved I don't have to be in charge anymore now that you're back. I thought I knew how much responsibility was on your shoulders, but experiencing that pressure myself—wow." Ryen shook his head.

"While I appreciate the sentiment, I'm going to need you to helm the ship a bit longer. I have to meet up with Diana, figure out the plan. Now that the palace is ours, she'll want to come back. Where did they go anyway?"

Ryen rubbed the back of his neck. "I'm assuming into Nevelyn since they wouldn't have wanted to go far on foot. I'm not sure where they would be able to get into though, considering the lockdown."

"I'll head there then. Did Maisie get out with them?"

"Last I saw, she was with Diana."

Good. That simplified my plans.

Ryen sighed. "I'm guessing I can't convince you to spend the night."

"You know me too well."

"I get it. Your girl is important."

I fixed Ryen with a look. "Diana's not my girl. Surly, tattooed Unseelie—any of that ring a bell?"

"Duh. I'm talking about Maisie, you dolt."

I blinked in surprise. *Crap.* He was right, wasn't he?

"Also, you should know," Ryen started, and his tone concerned me, "Embris is missing."

I scoffed. "It doesn't surprise me that he fled with the queen."

"No, he went missing a few days ago. That's why I could make the moves I did after Vera appointed me in charge. She said he was on some sort of mission, but I don't know. He didn't talk to any of us, and there weren't any horses missing. He left without a trace. Just seems strange, is all."

For a twisted moment, I wondered if he had decided I was worth saving and Vera had punished him for it. How would I feel if my father had died, trying to save me? Was I supposed to feel guilty?

It didn't matter anyway. Embris would never have gone against the queen, even for me. Wherever he was, it couldn't take up space in my mind.

Ryen shook his head. "Get out of here. Just make sure you check back in once you get things sorted. I can hold it down until then."

I clapped my second on the shoulder. "You're the best."

Ruined furniture, paintings, and windows blurred as I passed at a clipped pace down the hall.

"I want a raise!" Ryen called after me.

Without looking back, I replied, "Clean all this up, and we'll talk!"

SEVENTEEN

MAISIE
FEIGNED

"Maisie, a moment." The voice was calm, quiet, but filled me with dread.

Slowly, I turned to face The Curator.

"What can I do for you, *friend*?"

Kol chuckled, his chair sliding across the floor as he stood up. "I like your attitude. It will serve you well as I call in my debt."

My throat suddenly felt dry. "All right then."

"No pushback? No begging for me to reconsider because you were finally reunited with your friends?"

I shook my head, feeling my hair bounce. "I know the deal I made. Let's get it over with so I can move on with my life."

Kol's smile was far from comforting. "I'm impressed, Maisie. I can see I was right about my decision to work with you."

I only crossed my arms, waiting. Hoped he didn't see that I kept them crossed so that my hands didn't shake.

"What I need from you is really quite simple. You have connections with the high princess and thus *her* connections. The Eastern princess, Hollaina. Do you know of her?"

I nodded, unsure whether or not to divulge how well I *did* know the princess. In fact, a part of me wondered if he already knew that, as impossible as it might seem.

"Excellent. I need her to pay me a visit."

"That's it? That's the favour?"

He cocked his head to the side. "Were you expecting something else? Nefarious or violent perhaps?"

"Well, kind of, yeah."

"I make deals with those I believe can help me. While some might be more useful to me for their muscle, that was never the case with you."

I was … oddly touched?

"So, you just want me to bring a summons to Hollaina? And we'll be clear?"

"The moment she steps foot into my shop, our deal is done."

I chewed on my bottom lip. It seemed too easy to be true. "Is there some reason you can't go to her?"

Kol's dark eyes hardened. "That is hardly your business, is it?"

Gaia, he could go from jovial to terrifying in the blink of an eye. This was not someone I wanted as an enemy. The sooner this deal was over, the better.

"You're right; I'm sorry. I'll see it done."

"I look forward to it. May our paths cross again one day."

I hope not.

"Good night."

Kol gave me a nod, holding my gaze, and I didn't wait any longer to turn tail. I could feel his eyes on me as I hurried through the pub and up the stairs. Diana would be wondering where I was by now.

She seemed to buy my feigned illness, which was pretty realistic, considering how nervous I was. And that the food was sketchy as hell.

Guilt threatened to choke me as I waited for Diana to fall asleep in the tiny cot across from me. She was the last person I wanted to lie to. I had been hoping to stay up with her, catching up on every part of our crazy lives since we'd seen each other last.

Soon, I promised myself.

When Diana's breaths grew even and deep, I slipped from my cot, stopping to leave a note on the table between us.

With one last glance at her sleeping form, I tucked her cloak under my arm and crept from the room.

EIGHTEEN

AEDAN
IN THIS TOGETHER

Kali's ears were ramrod straight as she stood frozen, staring down something that I could not see. Her locked limbs sent a trickle of awareness down my spine, alerting me.

We were only at the bottom of the cobblestone path, the palace still within eyesight. But the woods bordering the road were deathly quiet, and my horse's reaction was enough to confirm my suspicions.

"I know you're there!" I called out. "Show yourself!"

For a moment, nothing happened. Then, birds shot into the air from the trees, and a hulking form came into focus. Many hulking forms actually.

Kali danced on the spot. I ran a hand down her light-grey neck, trying to soothe her. From the looks of it, we were gravely outnumbered. But there were no horses in sight, so a quick getaway was still an option.

Even if my sword arm twitched in anticipation.

The forms wore no armour, but were covered in red and black paint. It decorated any bare skin, almost distracting from the giant weapons they carried. A few bared their teeth menacingly as they lined up on the outskirts of the trees.

A giant hulk came from the middle and pushed through the

line. He grinned wickedly, white teeth shining against the red paint. "Deputy. How fortuitous to meet you here."

"General Maverick." I nearly breathed a sigh of relief, but the way the Nordians stared me down made me think twice about loosening my guard. "Long way from home, I see."

"On your orders," Maverick growled. "From the impersonal summons to the lack of direction leading us here, I must say, we're not off to a great start."

"I did not summon you. I've been … *indisposed* up until very recently."

The Nordian general pulled a balled-up parchment from his pocket, unfurled it, and read it aloud, "*The great region of the North and the almighty Queen Vera of the Lightbringer line request your immediate assistance at the capital. Signed, Deputy Captain Aedan Thesand.* Sure sounds a lot like your name."

I cursed under my breath. If Vera had had her hand in this, what else had she been cooking up? Being exiled from the palace would do nothing to deter her.

"That was not sent by me, I can assure you. The queen has turned on her heir, and in my attempt to stop her assassination plan, I was captured. I only got out yesterday."

Gaia, had that really only been mere hours ago? It felt like a lifetime had passed.

"You mean to say that Vera had a plot to kill her own daughter?"

I nodded once, hoping my grim face showed enough sincerity.

Maverick growled, crumpling the parchment and chucking it at the nearest tree. "Where is she now? Don't tell me you're still her errand boy."

It was my turn to bristle. "First of all, I was *never* her errand boy. Secondly, we don't know where she is. The army mutinied, and she fled. I assume she's off licking her wounds, but I don't think we have long until she retaliates."

The general studied me for a moment and finally nodded once. "My agreement still stands. We will fight with you. Any chance to rip into that tyrannical bitch."

The Nordians grunted their own approvals, some jeering and others raising weapons in the air.

"Diana has always been the right choice to lead us. I knew it from the moment I met her. We will fight for her."

I wanted to bring up the fact that Maverick had broken her heart into pieces before, but I bit my tongue. Once all this was over, I'd let him meet my fist for that.

"The Rebellion welcomes you." I couldn't help a small grin at the sound of those words.

This cause was important, and my role in it was far from small. Responsibility had never scared me. In fact, it fuelled me. From deep within, my soul sang at the chance to lead others—and lead them *well*.

The fire inside had erupted from an ember to a blaze since Diana's return.

And I was only getting started.

Someone was trying to slink unnoticed through the streets, and they were doing a horrible job.

Nevelyn was near pitch-black without the usual streetlights, and I *still* tracked the would-be spy's every move. They crept along the sides of the buildings, not even aware of the brightness of the moon and how it sent shadows rippling down the alleys.

I waited, ducked down behind empty mead barrels, keeping one eye on Kali the entire time. She stood patiently, one leg resting, at the hitching post in the middle of the square.

The nighttime creeper was steadily getting closer to her. They darted from one building up the road to the closed-up bakery front. The way they were going, it would only take one more "stealthy" move before making a play for my horse. And that was when I would—

Oh crap. They were just flat-out running for her now.

I leaped to my feet and caught up quickly before they could get too close to Kali. The hooded figure was small, easy for me to wrap one arm around their waist and one around their mouth.

"Not so fast."

The figure went still in my arms, stiff as a board. A familiar scent greeted me, one of honey and apples.

Immediately, I dropped her. *"Maisie?"*

She turned, her hood falling back in the movement. She looked as shocked as I felt, her blue eyes wide.

"Were you about to steal my horse?"

She crossed her arms, a stubborn expression appearing on her face. "Well, I didn't know it was Kali until right before you grabbed me. Thanks for the heart attack, by the way."

Her glare was so unintimidating that I let out a small laugh, which she did not appreciate.

"What are you doing out here? I thought you were with Diana."

"Oh, sure, now, you're worried for my well-being."

I reared back. "What are you talking about? I came out here to make sure you were okay. In case you have forgotten, I was being held in a dungeon."

"When did you get out? Because I can assure you that it was before I did. While I waited on the queen hand and foot, terrified of what would happen to you if I breathed wrong, you were free. Did you even think about bringing me with you?" Her voice lost its edge, hurt dancing in her eyes.

My heart clenched.

"I was always going to come back for you, Maisie," I said gently. I reached a hand out to touch her arm, but she moved away from me. "It all happened so fast. Hollaina got me out; we fought a bunch of guards and didn't even get far because we ran into Diana, who was trying to find somewhere safe to bring an entire realm's worth of Folk. I never had a chance to think."

Maisie's hard exterior gave way at the trembling of her lips. "I was scared. I was terrified, Aedan. And you never even came back for me."

"Diana didn't want me to come. I swear, I tried to. After a few hours, I couldn't take it any longer, not knowing. That's why I'm here now."

"She told you not to come, and you're here anyway?"

I nodded.

"She's going to kill you." Maisie shook her head, a small smile working her mouth.

I breathed in relief. "It's worth it to know you're all right. I meant it when I said we were in this together."

She finally softened, any remaining hardness on her features gone. Before I could even think, she crossed the space between us and wrapped herself in my arms. Stunned, I gently wrapped them around her small back, savouring the feel of her against my chest, her steady breaths.

Too soon, she pulled back, and my hands fell to my sides. She looked up at me with those big eyes, gaze darting once to my lips. I swallowed once and felt the need to lower my head, the pull of her intoxicating and inescapable.

Maisie blinked, and awareness washed over her. She stepped out of my arms, leaving cold air in her wake.

"Diana and the rest of them are staying the night in a pub called Lara's. It's in a hidden alley, but it's reachable through the back of a few places. It took me a few tries to find somewhere that wasn't boarded up, but thankfully, the theatre was unlocked. You can get in through there." She pointed in the direction of the street.

"Where are you going?"

She pursed her lips. "There's something I need to do."

I crossed my arms. "Alone, in the middle of the night? Diana doesn't know about this, does she?"

Maisie shrugged. "I left a note."

"Well, at least I don't have to worry about being first on her hit list because she will definitely kill *you* for that."

"It's not like I have a choice! The sooner it's done, the better."

I studied her, still clad in her palace-approved plain dress, the overcoat not doing much, considering it only reached to her knees. "Does this have to do with your deal with The Curator?"

She didn't say anything, but her silence was answer enough.

"I'm coming with you."

"No." Her tone was vehement. "I'm going alone. And don't you dare follow me!"

"What part of 'in this together' did you not understand?" I untied Kali and threw the reins over her head. In one motion, I placed my foot in the stirrup and swung into the saddle. I reached out my hand. "Now, get on."

NINETEEN

MAISIE
IMMINENTLY

By the time we made it back to Shynin, I was thoroughly exhausted. The sun had broken and was well on its way into the sky, and the birds were annoyingly chipper.

"Where's Hollaina?" I asked a passing fae as I slid from Plum's back.

She pointed to Freya's tent.

I met eyes with Aedan, who had just dismounted from Diana's fiery mare. He had led Kali back to conserve her energy. Plus, he'd added, Finnvarra needed to let off steam.

"You don't have to come with me."

Diana had mentioned the Outcasts' leader was Aedan's estranged mother and their rocky relationship.

"Of course I'm coming."

After securing the horses with the fae tending the fenced lean-to—calling it a barn would be too generous—Aedan slipped his hand in mine.

My heart thundered in my chest as we walked to Freya's tent. As we opened the tent flap, I let go of his hand, but he squeezed my palm in his, keeping me tethered to him.

"Aedan, what a surprise." A tall, lithe female with dark brown hair rose from her chair. Her gaze flickered over our joined hands once. "And I don't believe we've met. I'm Freya."

"Maisie."

Out of complete habit, I felt myself dropping into a curtsy, as I always did when around my superiors. Aedan yanked my arm, keeping me level. I appreciated that he wanted to keep me from creating a line between us, but the unfortunate side effect was that it looked like my knees had randomly buckled.

Freya's tracking eyes looked amused. "To what do I owe the pleasure?"

"Actually—"

"We're not here for you," Aedan said in a vicious tone I'd never heard from him before.

If his mother was offended, she hid it well.

"We were hoping to speak with Princess Hollaina, if we could," I explained in a much gentler voice.

Freya gestured to her guest, who had not risen when we arrived. She sat with her hands folded over her lap, that ethereal poise engulfing her.

"By all means. We are finished with our conversation anyway."

Hollaina tilted her head, studying us, but eventually stood and followed us outside. "What can I do for you?"

Aedan looked at me. I loved that he didn't ever trample over me or try to speak for me. No one else had given me that luxury before.

"Well, uh, this might not be the best timing, considering the rebellion and all, but I'm hoping you'll help me out with something. You see, a while back, I made a deal with someone called The Curator."

Hollaina's lips pressed into a thin line, her gaze going stony. "You must be extremely brave or extremely stupid."

"So, you know of him then?"

"Kol is an old acquaintance of mine. I hope whatever you got from him was worth it."

My hands wrung. "It was of great value actually. The problem is that I promised him a favour in return, and now, he's collecting."

Hollaina arched a brow.

I cleared my thick throat and continued, "He wants to see you. Or more specifically, he wants you to go to him. To his store."

The Eastern princess huffed a laugh. "That is just like him, using you to get to me. It might not come as a shock to you that trucking through the snow to have a conversation is the last thing I want to do right now."

"Yes, of course, I get that. It's just that I'm not sure how else I can fulfil the deal. He made it clear it would not be wise to break it."

"He would take something he deemed of equal payment. He's right; you don't want to break a deal with him."

Aedan growled, "So, there are two options: either you complete the deal or you help us kill him."

I gaped. "I'm sure that's not necessary!"

"It *would* be the safest way out of the deal. But I believe we can avoid that by coming to our own agreement."

They spoke of murder as casually as if discussing the dinner menu.

"No. Enough deals." Aedan shook his head.

"I will go pay our old friend a visit and free you from your bargain with him if you procure something for me that I need."

I narrowed my eyes. "How come you can't get it? Aren't princesses supposed to have power?"

"Do you want me to go to the North or not?"

Aedan opened his mouth, probably to object, but I spoke before he could. "Fine, yes. I'll do it. What are you looking for?"

Hollaina smiled, and Aedan shot daggers at me.

"It is an old gemstone, nestled away in a temple in the middle of the Unclaimed Land. Bring it to me, and I will go."

"That's all you're giving me to go on?"

"That's all there is. Are you incapable?"

I squared my shoulders. "Get packed. Your trip North leaves imminently."

Hollaina's answering grin was the last thing I saw before spinning on my heel. Aedan quietly followed as I marched back to the horses.

"Don't say it," he warned as I turned to face him. "I'm not letting you do this by yourself."

"Fine. Not much use trying to stop you anyway."

Deep down, a large piece of me sighed in relief. It felt innately comforting to have someone fight for my safety.

I reached for one of the Shynin horses, choosing to leave Plum and Finnvarra for their respective partners. Hopefully, Diana wouldn't be too mad at me once she saw that I'd brought her favourite horse back for her.

Aedan deftly got Kali ready. "Are you sure you want to ride alone? I know you don't have a lot of experience. It might be tiring for you, considering we don't know how much riding is ahead of us."

"I'll be fine," I answered quickly.

The thought of riding in front of Aedan again, in such close proximity, set my nerves on fire. The way his entire front had plastered against my back, his strong arms holding me to him, our hips way too close together, was too much. It'd filled me with a warm, tight feeling, beginning in my belly, giving my cheeks a flush that didn't fade until I dismounted Kali at the palace stables.

Even if my legs fell off from soreness, I would take my own mount, thank you very much.

Once we were situated, Aedan let me take the lead after showing me which way to start. Gratefully, I rode ahead, happy not to have to look at him the entire trip. Even if the feeling of his body ghosted against my skin.

Gaia, let me get to this temple in one piece.

TWENTY

DIANA
UNCHARTED TERRITORY

"I'm still mad at her. I don't care what her reasoning was."

Spense looked over at me from his spot atop Plum, the little bay mare he had come to love during his first visit to Eira. He raised a brow. "I thought you accepted her peace offering."

I looked down at said gift—my own fire-coloured mare, Finnvarra. An Outcast member had given her to me upon our arrival back in Shynin, looking quite relieved to no longer have to deal with the uncontrollable horse. He'd claimed that Maisie and Aedan rode through the camp on their way to an undisclosed location and dropped off the two mounts.

"She scared the crap out of me. As thankful as I am to have my girl back, Maisie has to take more care for her life. What if something happens to her and we don't know where she is?"

When I had woken that morning at Lara's, the tiny scrap of parchment that read, *Don't look for me. I'll see you soon*, had filled me with a dread beyond belief. Where could she have possibly gone? I had a horrible feeling that, somehow, The Curator was involved, but he was nowhere to be found the next day to press about the matter.

"She's not alone. Aedan's with her." Spense deftly steered Plum away from Finnvarra's flattening ears after they got too close.

"Don't even get me started on him! He rode into Shynin *with* Maisie—meaning he left the camp after I specifically told him to stay put."

The whole thing was entirely confusing. In the middle of the night, Maisie had stolen away, somehow met Aedan, gotten in and out of the palace stables, and passed back through the Unclaimed Land.

All while we had been none the wiser. And completely unaware of this alliance between the two of them.

I hated being kept in the dark.

"I know you're used to everyone listening to you, but these are unprecedented times," Spense started. "They are grown adults. We have to trust that whatever they're doing, why they're not sharing it with you, there's a good reason."

I grumbled under my breath.

"Besides, we have more important things at hand right now."

I looked ahead through Finnvarra's orange ears at the moors ahead. They seemed to stretch on forever, the sun sinking low on the horizon in front of us. At this rate, we weren't going to make it to the West court in the daylight.

"You're right," I sighed.

Behind us, the rest of our party dutifully followed on borrowed horses and mules from Shynin. Freya had not been thrilled to hear of our leaving the palace or how my new plan was to demand an audience with Prince Kashdan and earn his allegiance.

We had swapped Badras with Sorin, taking into account his easy way with words and the ability he had to make everyone trust him. Badras, sensing he wasn't going to get the chance to put his sword to use, had agreed to stay behind and watch over Alwyn. She was being kept in a cot away from the prying eyes of the inner camp, along with the casket that Urdan was … *sleeping* in.

"How much longer?" The eldest Drakenis trotted a few steps on his mount to catch up with us. "It might be wise to consider making camp for the night to approach fully rested tomorrow."

"The Western palace is close to our border. I've never come to it from the Unclaimed Land, but I recognize the moors. It shouldn't be too much farther, less than an hour."

Sorin nodded. "We can push through then. The only worry is being tired should we meet a less-than-hospitable welcome."

It was exhausting and foreign to me, all this planning for fights. The peace I had been living in might have been false, but at least I hadn't spent my life worrying about deaths on my hands.

"There." Spense pointed at the now-dark moors. Through my squinted eyes, a tall palace spire came into view. "Are there no gates around the court? It seems very trusting to have this epicenter in the middle of the moors, unprotected."

"They don't need a gate or a wall," I explained. "Look around; it's only flat land for miles. They've seen us coming for a long time now."

The wind across the flat land was not as muggy as expected. Though they didn't have the snow the North was plagued with, the usual summer warmth was missing. The Western Shores was basically open area until it met the ocean, which was where most of the residents chose to live. They endured seasons of cold, where the South did not, but otherwise, the two regions were similar in the sandy landscapes and warm sea breeze.

A strangled cry from the back of the group sent the horses spinning around.

"What the—"

There was only inky blackness. It surrounded us, closing in tighter. The air was sticky and bitter, the magic around it like sludge.

"Don't touch the shadows!" I warned. "Is there any way to get out?"

"We're locked in," Sorin said grimly.

Fear flashed on everyone's faces. I fought to keep my own terror under control.

I reached down deep into my well of magic, feeling Spense's wrapped up with it. I summoned as much light as I could and sent it outward, hoping the brightness would send the shadows receding.

Spense pulled it all back, blinking out the light.

I whipped around to face him, trying to keep Finnvarra steady as the horses danced around, bumping into one another. "What are you doing?"

"The light only fuels them! Look, can't you see how it's grown from that?" He pointed up to where the shadows swirled higher, looking to close us in from the top as well.

"I want to try something!" Spense called to me.

Without waiting for my answer, I felt him dive into our shared magic. He sifted through it, seemingly untangling his from mine. It was vastly uncomfortable, my body reacting to the displeasure of his magic separating from me like my heart was splitting apart.

When Spense opened his palms, a dark, wavy magic poured out of him. It swirled through the air, touching the shadows, which then merged into it. Slowly, they fused together until the shadowy being surrounding us was hued by Spense's indigo-tipped colour.

"He's controlling them," Sorin breathed.

As if through a veil, I could feel it. The way he had the shadows bending to him, to his will. They receded, dissipating into the air. Finally, the night sky was empty, save for the light of the twinkling stars.

"How did you do that?" I stared at my soulmate, taking a

shuddering breath when he released his magic and it came slamming back to mine.

His grey eyes were wide, his face flush. "I don't know. I just felt like I knew the magic. And that if I answered it, I might be able to send it away."

"Answered it?" Sorin asked sharply. "Don't tell me the shadows that have been tormenting this realm have just been trying to relay a message."

Spense shook his head, causing the messy black curls on his head to flop around. "No, it felt more like it was looking for something. But I just tried to match it, and when it accepted me as part of the shadows, it was easy to send them away."

Disconcertment danced in my belly. The shadows were so dark and inherently evil, considering what they'd been doing to their victims. And yet they recognized Spense as one of their own.

Sorin looked pensive, gathering his thoughts on his own.

"Back before Spense had his memory, I had a theory that Urdan was sending them," I told Sorin. "Do you think even in his state, he could be in control of them?"

"I suppose anything's possible. We are in uncharted territory, as it were. He's being kept in an unconscious state, but given that this was the realm he was born in, it's entirely possible his subconscious could be tapping into the land."

"It would explain why the shadows listened to me," Spense offered.

We both nodded. Gaia, I hoped that was the reason.

"Even so, I don't think we should wake Urdan until we are absolutely sure we have a plan for him. I would hate to see him let loose out here. It would be yet another problem we don't need."

If the siblings wanted to keep Urdan like that forever, I would have no qualms. He was not someone I wanted to interact with. "I agree."

Spense steered Plum toward the looming palace. "Then, let's get some Western allies and get out of here."

I clucked my tongue, and Finnvarra charged forward. We were nearing the path to the front door when a booming voice stopped us in our tracks.

"ARCHERS, READY!"

TWENTY-ONE

DIANA
EMPTY-HANDED

"Stand down! I am Diana Lightbringer, and I come in peace to speak with Prince Kashdan!" I screamed so loud that my throat hurt.

The arrows, nocked in their bows from the highest turrets of the palace, stared us straight in the eyes.

Vaguely, I was aware of Spense drawing deep into our magic, preparing himself.

Whoever had called out was quiet now, but the rustling sounds of feet shuffling and armour clanging meant that some sort of discussion was happening up there.

Finally, a head poked over the side of the high window above the dead-bolted front doors. "The prince is not accepting visitors at this time." The soldier had a nasally voice, giving us a haughty look from under his visor.

"Unacceptable. As his high princess, I demand an audience. You will tell him I said so."

The soldier pursed his lips, but dipped his head and disappeared.

The horses shuffled their feet as we waited.

A few moments later, Kashdan himself popped into the window. "I'm afraid to say that I cannot see you, Diana," he said gruffly. "Your mother has advised us of your unfortunate recent change of loyalty, and it should come as no shock to you that I remain fully committed to Queen Vera."

I steered my horse closer to the Western wall. "There is much you do not know. We go back a long time, Kashdan. Do you renounce me so much that you would not hear me out? I come with a small, unarmed party—I am of no threat to you or your court. I only wish to tell you my side of the story."

"Do not insult my intelligence." Kashdan's eyes flashed angrily. "You will not use Dark tricks on me!"

The Western prince's greatest flaw had and would always be his immovable stubbornness. Once his mind was made up, you would have better luck moving a mountain than swaying him. Still, I had to persist.

"You're on the wrong side!" I yelled. "You can change your mistake before it's too late. Please, let us in. Let me explain."

"There is nothing I wish to hear from you—unless you repent the Dark forces you are dallying with. You are not welcome in the Western Shores. Leave—*now*." Kashdan flicked his hand in the air, and the archers pulled their bows taut with a whoosh.

"We need to get out of here," Spense urged. "You're not going to get through to him."

"I am the heir! The West is not yours to lock up. Everywhere in Eira bows to *me*." In some faraway part of my brain, I hated how I sounded. But I was getting sick and tired of nobody taking me seriously.

Kashdan shook his head. "You might be the heir, but Vera is still the queen. Her word carries more than yours. And while the crown rests on her head, you mean nothing to me."

My heart crumpled, bitter and icy. Hearing those words come out of the mouth of someone I had known and trusted since I was a young girl sent acid through my veins.

A loud whizzing sounded close to my left ear, and I flinched away.

There, embedded in the grass not two feet away, was an arrow.

I snapped my gaze up, locking eyes with the prince. "You're going to regret this." My voice was soft, almost a whisper, but from the hardening of his face, I knew he'd heard it.

"Diana!" Sorin called. "Let's go!"

With one last glare at the West, I nudged Finnvarra's sides. The others followed me as I galloped back the way we had come. Tears pricked at my eyes, the wind pushing them across my face and into the air. I only slowed down when I could take a deep breath again.

This was absurd. I was still in shock. Not only had my request to talk been refused, but I had been chased from my *own damn constituent.* I had truly overestimated my ability to broker peace. There was no easy path here, only rocky, uphill terrain. And I was just beginning the climb.

With hopes that the wind had pushed the redness from my face—or at least replaced it with a flush from the cold—I turned to face the others.

"What's the plan?" Spense asked softly. His handsome features were turned down; he was no doubt feeling my rampant emotions through our shared magic.

There was no plan.

Gaining the allegiance of the West was what I had been counting on to show my mother that she was the anomaly. But I had been playing a fool's game. It was naive to think I could appeal to the masses with simple words when they had been under false histories for millennia.

No, they would need something bigger. Unmistakable.

"We go South, to see Leo. Only this time, we won't be leaving empty-handed."

TWENTY-TWO

SPENSE
FORBIDDEN FLAME

We made camp as soon as we were outside of the Western border. The fire Diana had started pulled at my magic, leaving a faint taste of smoke in my mouth. I was still getting used to feeling her so strongly. Her emotions, her magic, her essence. It was like I was meeting a new part of myself.

I had felt her gut-wrenching sadness after our encounter with Kashdan. Then, I felt her spiky fury igniting my own fuel. It was delicious, how it drew from deep within, strong and sure. Intoxicating.

I'd wanted to feed it, to grow her power and support it.

She was so close to becoming the strong leader she had been born to be. Which was why, when it was my turn to keep watch over the camp, I slipped a bit farther away and called to the shadows.

I had stuffed it as deep as I could, but after the initial shock wore off, I was filled with a thrilling elation when the shadows merged with me.

Maybe I should have been concerned that I felt the need to hide this from Diana. But she had enough on her plate, and worrying about me was the last thing she needed.

In fact, I would love it if she gave some of her worries to me to handle.

Starting with forcing that dolt of a prince to submit to his true heir.

I took a steadying breath and dived into our magic, being careful not to disturb the parts that were joined. Diana needed her sleep.

It wasn't hard to recall that twisty, shapeless shadow. It longed for partnership, and I willingly offered it. I called on the darkness of the night, pulling from the trees and clouds and anything that had hidden the sun before.

It was heavy, this magic. And if I wasn't careful, it was plenty grabby.

But I could handle that just fine. Let it cling to the outer ridges of my magic, where it would be easy to release when I was done.

The shadows were an extension of someone—or something. It acted on its own, but was not sentient. Remarkable really. I'd never experienced anything quite like it.

How they were sending victims into an unconscious slumber was another question. Although from my touching and interacting with the shadows, the maliciousness of that kind of magic never showed up.

Meaning the shadows saw me as one of their own. Which almost guaranteed that Urdan was involved.

I called out to the darkness and immediately felt the responding tug. Shadows began to form around me, weaving and swirling. It almost seemed to stare me right in the eyes, questioning.

How far can I send you? I mused.

I pushed it away, focusing on the boulder a few feet away. After a moment, the shadows disappeared and rematerialized where my gaze was.

Excitement built, creating a flurry in my belly. Heat rushed down my arms and into my palms, which bunched with energy.

I took a deep breath through my nose and closed my eyes. I pictured the Western Shores palace and their arrogant lack of defence. Sure, they could see a normal enemy approach, but these shadows had a way to render that useless.

Go here, I urged. *This is where you want to be.*

The shadows winked out of sight, and from the thrill I felt deep in my core, I knew that it had worked. Kashdan would pay for his insubordination until the sun came up and banished the shadows. That was a fitting punishment.

Before returning to the camp, I let some of the magic calm down and smooth out. When I joined the party at our makeshift camp again, pride warmed in my chest like a forbidden flame.

Diana was beautiful and innocent when she slept, her face younger. I was happy to take this onto my plate so that she did not have to. Her soft, open heart would say that she could never endanger bystanders in the crossfire.

But she had yet to learn that in war, there was no other way to deliver a message.

TWENTY-THREE

AEDAN
THRUM

"**D**o you think this is the place?" Maisie ran her hand down the temple's giant grooved columns, tracing lines. Ivy and other plants grew up the sides, but for as lifeless as it looked, it was still in good shape.

"Considering this is the only sign of *anything* we've seen since leaving the camp, I'd say this is a good bet."

I studied the temple, stretching high into the sky on its massive pillars with a gabled roof. There were walls, but no door, and it was too dark inside to see what lurked in there. Above the threshold, a symbol was etched into the temple, depicting a sun and moon overlapping.

Maisie straightened and braced her hands on her hips, staring the entrance down. "Well, let's go in then."

I grabbed her elbow before she could take another step, ignoring the spark of energy that travelled up my arm from touching her. "I'll go first."

She looked like she wanted to roll her eyes but allowed me to take the lead. I took the three steps gently and looked for anything that might seem out of place on the tiling or outer walls. Part of me felt silly for taking such precautions on an old, abandoned temple, but the Unclaimed Land had its own magic, and I didn't trust it.

With no alarm bells blaring, I entered the temple and stopped a few steps in. It was large and open, mostly empty. There were no windows, but at the top of the ceiling, a skylight allowed light to flood in, landing directly on an altar in the middle of the room. There, atop a small pedestal, sat a sapphire, as large as a head, reflecting the light in every direction.

"Holy mother of Gaia," breathed Maisie from behind me. "What is this place?"

While still trying to stay aware of potential threats, I had to share her sentiment. As simple and empty as this temple was, hidden by a decrepit exterior, there was a thrum to it, an ancient life that whispered of a time long ago.

"We should be careful in here." I took a few more steps forward, noticing for the first time etchings in the tiles below my feet—the same symbol as the outside of the temple.

"The sun has long been associated with Gaia," Maisie murmured. "I wonder then if the Unseelie stories are right and the moon is for Ouranos. It would make sense with the two of them merged like that."

"It would definitely explain why this place feels so old. If it's truly an altar to both gods, then this has been standing for more than eight thousand years." I looked over my shoulder and almost stuttered a step.

Maisie's eyes were bright as she took it all in. The light dancing off the gemstone washed her in sparkling tones, making her look like she deserved her own temple to be worshipped. When she caught my eye, she smiled, and my heart leaped.

I cleared my throat, which had gone weirdly thick, and continued until I stopped in front of the sapphire. I could feel Maisie's presence beside me as we both stared into the deep blue. The gem was not perfect, with jagged lines and uneven edges, but it was smooth. And it was beautiful.

"This must be what Hollaina is looking for."

"I don't see why she couldn't just come get it herself," I scoffed. "Unless we're going to be blasted down by Gaia for temple-robbing."

Maisie's head tilted as she looked at the sapphire. "I don't think this was originally on display here," she noted. "See how the pedestal seems to be weighed down by it? It's practically touching the altar."

It did look like too heavy a gem for its holder.

"Still, it feels … wrong somehow. To take something meant as a gift for the gods. What if it's like the emerald that Diana has? What if this is less of a shrine and more of a prison?"

Before I could react, Maisie reached out and stuck her palm flat on the sapphire. She took a deep breath through her nose and closed her eyes. Her arm shook as she clung to the gem, her eyelids fluttering. I watched with bated breath, scared to disrupt in case it could harm her.

Her eyes flew open, her face still. "Nope, nothing."

"That wasn't funny."

She fought a smile, her eyes crinkling. I fought one of my own as I shook my head.

"Well, if you're so sure that it's not going to get us killed, let's grab it and get back. The sooner you're out of that deal with The Curator, the better."

Still smiling, Maisie reached out her other arm and wrapped it around the sapphire, grunting with effort as she pulled it from its spot.

There was an audible *click*, filling the air with an uncertain silence, and my stomach dropped as I realized where it had come from. The pedestal that had been weighed down from the gem had snapped back up and was slowly getting taller.

Deep, untethered fear wormed in my belly. There was something innately wrong happening. The alarm bells that had been silent before were blaring in my head, filling me with the undeniable need to run.

Like waking up from a trance, I jumped into action, grabbing Maisie's arm and turning us away from the altar. "We need to get out of here."

There was a deep rumbling from below, and the temple started to shake. Dust snowed from the ceiling, and a horrifying crack sounded.

"Run!"

The doorway was becoming smaller and smaller as a slab from the top started sliding down. I cursed under my breath and yanked Maisie faster, pulling us both across the tiles.

Only half of the doorway was still visible.

"You're going to have to duck!" I yelled, letting go of her hand as I dropped into a roll and slid under the door.

It was getting more and more obstructed with every second.

Maisie followed, her roll clunkier, less smooth, and if it wasn't for me grabbing her shoulders and yanking her through, she would have lost her legs.

The heavy clunk of the doorway sealing itself off rattled through us. I was on my back, having pulled Maisie on top of me, and we stared at each other with wide eyes, our breaths coming in pants. I could feel her everywhere, her warmth a relief that she was okay. We were both okay.

One moment, there was space between us, and the next, there wasn't. Suddenly, I was kissing her with a fervour that I had never experienced before, one driven from adrenaline and passion and desire.

And she is kissing me back.

I'd never been one for music, but her mouth on mine was a symphony that sang through my veins. She was pure and sweet and confident, matching me move for move. One hand wrapped around the small of her back, pulling her to me. The other cupped her neck, getting tangled in her hair. I twisted my finger through one of her curls and delighted in the small gasp she made against my mouth.

This—*this*—was Maisie, my friend, my confidante. When we'd both decided we were more to each other didn't matter because we were here now. And I never wanted to go back. *Could* never.

Because kissing her was finally something that felt right. In this world of stormy days, she was my clear sky. Even the sun didn't compare.

Maisie's hands were on my chest, and I was certain she could feel the thrum of my heart beneath. Just as I could feel hers reverberating through her body and into mine. They made a melody of staccato beats that thundered proudly.

Hands moving to my shoulders, she pressed me into the stone tiles, the cold a jagged contrast to the warmth between us. My head clanged against it, breaking our contact.

No, damn it. No. I didn't want to wake up from this.

Her blue eyes were wide as she took me in. Her lips were swollen, and there was red in her cheeks. It occurred to me that I wanted to be responsible for this look *always*.

I let her compose herself as she pushed off of me and sat a few feet away, running a hand through her yellow curls, as if that would fix what I'd tangled. The loss of her weight was sad and lonely as I sat up and let my legs hang down the steps.

"Okay." Maisie blew out a puff of breath. "I, um, think we should get back to the camp."

She stood, aiming for the sapphire that sat near the front of the temple, where it had gotten tossed on the way out. Nimbly, I leaped to my feet and reached it first, holding the massive gemstone out as she placed her hands on the other side of it.

I didn't let go yet though. "I'm sorry, Maisie. I never want to scare you or push you into anything you don't want. Say the word, and we can pretend like it never happened." I swallowed. "But you should know … I don't want to forget this. The way you make me feel—I always want to feel that. I want to be with you and not just casually. You don't have to say anything right now, but I need you to know I'm not messing around here. This is real for me."

Maisie's flushed face was mostly unreadable as she nodded. She was still taking those deep inhales, which I took as a good sign. Slowly, I let go of the sapphire and stepped back.

Speaking my mind had never been much of a problem for me. Being in charge of an army meant making hard calls, no matter who might not agree. But for some reason, saying that admission out loud to Maisie had made my heart clatter in my chest, my stomach knotted up like yarn. It'd made me feel vulnerable in a way I wasn't used to.

Unrequited love—now, that was something I was sadly well versed in. This was different—or at least, it *felt* different—but it still sent nerves running wild. It made me want to close up my heart and lock it away where it could stay safe and unattached.

"Come on. Let's get your deal finished."

As we walked side by side back through the bendy trees to rejoin the horses, what had started as a weighted silence became an easy one. Every time she brushed against me and didn't flinch away, I could breathe clearer.

If she needed time, she could have all my days and all my nights. Because at the end of the day, locking up my heart wouldn't matter anymore.

It was already hers.

TWENTY-FOUR

MAISIE
THE CAUSE

I'm standing in a pool of water, and my hands are blue.

Actually, they're red.

Red with blood. And I think it's my own.

Oh—yes, that's where it's coming from. My abdomen is steadily flowing my life force into the pool. And it doesn't even hurt. I'm not afraid.

I turn to see the figures at the water's edge as black rims my vision. There are ten of them, watching as I slowly die. One of them—the tiny one with brown skin—holds the sapphire.

They give me their gazes as a symbol of respect, of honour.

I will see them again soon.

The ridges of the gemstone are the last thing I see before I slip away from my mortal body.

When I am free from the plane of existence, everything feels lighter. I have never known such weightlessness. I am joy incarnate.

But I cannot rest yet. The others are depending on me.

Then, I will be able to find my peace.

A warm, soothing voice wraps around me. "There you are, my child." It cradles me, holds me close, and I know I am safe.

"We need your help, my goddess."

"I know you do. Now, listen close, and I will tell you exactly how to fix this."

The dream stayed with me throughout the entire day. I'd woken in a damp sweat, my hair sticking to my forehead. The humidity of the tropical forest we were discovering the Unclaimed Land to be did not help matters when I went for a walk this morning.

When I returned, our bedrolls had been neatly packed away, and Aedan was stirring something over a fire.

"A lot of work to go through when we're mere hours away from an easier breakfast in Shynin."

He shrugged, the movement of his shoulder causing his hair to loosen up from behind his ears. It was so long now, the white-blond getting a slight wave to it now that it wasn't slicked back neatly. I remembered what it had been like to wrap my fingers in it and stifled a shiver.

"Are you all right?" Aedan asked. "I heard you leave. If I had known you were going so far, I wouldn't have let you venture off alone."

I took a seat across the fire from him, crossing my legs. "I appreciate that, but I needed to be alone. I didn't go too far, promise."

He paused, hand still hovering over a pan of what looked like scrambled eggs. "I hope I'm not making you uncomfortable."

"It's not you," I replied. "I just had a weird dream and felt like I needed some air."

My mother had always taught me, growing up, that a good night's sleep, followed by a walk in the fresh air, was the remedy to all conundrums. And that had proven itself to be true over and over, except today. My brain still felt foggy, the haze of the dream sitting heavy. It had been so real. I knew it was impossible, but it felt like a memory.

Aedan passed me a wooden bowl of breakfast. It was clearly his first time making eggs by the looks of it, but the gurgling in my stomach was impossible to ignore.

"I don't even remember you packing bowls," I mentioned as I took a bite.

Mmm. Runny.

"I found them in my bag this morning—I must have left them in there from a previous trip. How are the eggs?" His face was so hopeful that I shovelled another bite into my mouth to avoid answering.

"Do I want to know where you found these?" *Please don't be baby birds.*

Aedan rubbed the back of his neck. "This is going to sound crazy, but I think the Unclaimed Land sent them."

I just stared.

"They were with the packed food, and I know for a fact that they weren't in there last night. So, unless an animal got into a closed satchel, laid a few eggs, and left without a trace, someone put them in there."

"That doesn't make sense. Maybe you just didn't see the eggs before."

"I didn't pack them. Did you?"

My silence was enough for him to continue. "The Outcasts keep saying how 'the land provides' for them. I thought it was a load of crap, but maybe it's true. I mean, there doesn't seem to be a shortage of food since tripling the number of mouths in Shynin. How can that be possible?"

Maybe that made the Outcasts feel protected, but it set me on edge. I didn't like the idea of the *land* watching over me. Creepy.

"I don't want to know. As far as I'm concerned, the eggs were always there."

Aedan smiled softly. "Yeah, it's definitely weird. Best not to dwell on it when we have more important matters at hand." He stood, taking our bowls and packing them. He extended a hand to me. "Like getting you in the clear with The Curator."

I allowed him to help me up, trying to ignore the firm, warm grip of his hand and how the muscles in his corded arms flexed.

I checked on the sapphire again, now safely stored in Plum's saddlebag, and we set off.

Back in Shynin, we handed the horses over to the stablehands and found Hollaina right where we'd left her.

"Do you think there's something going on between them?" I murmured under my breath as we made our way to Freya's tent.

Aedan wrinkled his nose. "Romantically? Probably not with Pawl in the picture. Although maybe—"

I smacked his arm playfully before he could finish his inappropriate thought.

"You know what I meant."

He smiled, and damn if those dimples didn't draw my gaze right to them. "I wouldn't put it past them to have their own agendas beyond what they've been telling Diana."

Gaia, I hoped that wasn't the case. There was way too much going on to keep track of as it was.

"Back so soon?" Hollaina set down a glass as we entered the tent. It was empty, save for her, Freya, and Pawl, who were bent over a large map.

I pulled my satchel off my shoulder and cradled the heavy sapphire in my arm as I took it out of the bag. Even under the dim lighting from the candles burning, the gem shone. It held everyone's attention as they took it in, seeming to glow from their gaze.

"It's real," Pawl breathed.

Hollaina stood, floating over to take a closer look. She reached out, and I surprised myself with the speed in which I yanked it away.

Aedan gave me a confused look. Now that it had happened, I couldn't figure out why I'd done it. I just really didn't want her to have it in that moment.

I didn't want anyone to have it.

"You do want me to visit our little friend, don't you?" Hollaina asked, her voice amused.

"Why did you need us to get this?" I demanded. "You easily could have gotten it yourself. It was in an unprotected temple in the middle of nowhere."

"Mostly unprotected," Aedan muttered.

Freya's eyes bounced between us and the sapphire. "It is of great importance to the cause."

"You say an awful lot about 'the cause,' but there never seems to be a clear answer. What exactly do you need it for?"

Gaia, these Outcasts were starting to piss me off.

Hollaina's pale eyes bored into mine. "You are right to wonder, Maisie. Those who never question will not get very far in life. The Outcasts' cause is the same as yours—peace in Eira and Diana leading it. The sapphire you hold is ancient, as I'm sure you have felt by now. It holds great purpose for defeating our enemy. That is all I can say. You will have to trust me if you wish for your deal with The Curator to be over."

My arms were leaden as the sapphire's hard edges dug into my skin. My body felt tight everywhere. It felt wrong—innately wrong— to let go of it. To see it in another's arms.

"Maisie," Aedan said softly, "you can let go of it."

I turned to meet his gaze and suddenly felt like I could take a deep breath again. Without looking away, I pushed my arms out from my body. It was gingerly taken from my grasp, and the second it left my touch, all the anger and possessiveness faded away.

Hollaina took a deep inhale as she held the sapphire, running a hand along the edges. "I will leave tonight for the North. I gave my word, and I will keep it."

I closed my eyes in relief. "Thank you."

The sooner I was out from under Kol's thumb, the better. For Diana's sake, I hoped Spense had known what he was doing, making his own bargain with him.

The tent flaps abruptly swung open, hitting both Aedan and me in the process. A large, hulking mountain of a male strode in, long hair flowing behind him. I recognized him as one of the fae who had come to the palace. He had been with Diana when I left the group. I couldn't remember his name—had we even been properly introduced? It was all a blur.

Whomever it was seemed incredibly angry. He narrowed in on Hollaina and pointed a finger at her. "You."

"What's going on?" Freya moved to stand in between them.

"Urdan is missing. And *she* was involved."

PART TWO

TWENTY-FIVE

MAISIE
BRAVER THAN ME

"I can assure you, I had no part in that," Hollaina said calmly.

"Whoa, whoa. Urdan's gone? As in the Unseelie king, who was being kept unconscious for everyone's safety?" Aedan's brows leaped up, his face incredulous.

Fear coursed icy cold through my veins. This was the first I was learning of such a dangerous fae being kept in the camp I'd thought was safe.

The intruder gritted his teeth as he slowly turned to glare at Aedan. "I just said that."

"Calm down, Badras," Freya urged. "Explain what happened."

I remembered him now—he was Spense's brother.

"Urdan had been kept under constant supervision since arriving here. When I went to administer his tincture, I found the casket empty. The guards stationed had not seen anyone go in or out."

"How is that possible?" Aedan crossed his arms.

"Perhaps your guards have been compromised," Hollaina said.

Badras stalked forward, easily pushing out of Freya's grasp when she attempted to grab his arm. He didn't stop until he was practically nose to nose with the Eastern princess, who did not shy away. She stared evenly up at him, as calm as ever.

"I know you had something to do with this. Your scent was all over. Not to mention how useful air magic would have been to mask the sound of you slipping in."

Hollaina was not shaken. "I didn't realize we knew each other well enough for you to recognize my scent. Certainly, I could not pick yours out."

"Don't patronize me. I met you the first day we arrived. I have been around for a long time. Such trivial things as smells become ingrained in my brain whether I want them to or not. If you still don't believe me, why don't we have someone who knows you confirm that the smell in our private tent is yours?"

Aedan and I shared a confused look. Badras didn't look very old, a few years older than us. He definitely seemed younger than the princess he was threatening.

"That would be my fault," Freya interjected. "I asked if Hollaina could check on your sister, Alwyn. To see if anything might be done to help her. I was there, supervising, the entire time. Sorin agreed to it."

Badras clenched his jaw. "Aren't you lucky that Sorin isn't here to back up your claims?"

Freya put her hands out in an attempt at a soothing motion. "When he returns, we will sort this out."

"Why is no one taking this seriously?" Aedan exclaimed. "Urdan is missing! Who gives a damn *how* he got out?!"

"My brother Olys has already left to search for him. When Diana's party returns, I will join him, along with Sorin and Spense." Badras glared down at Hollaina. "And if I find out you had anything to do with this, you'll be answering to me."

She smiled. "I'm not worried."

She sent a blast of air at his chest, forcing him to take a few steps back from her. Badras growled, the air becoming electric—literally. It seemed to pop and fizz in my ears, and my hair started to grow static. Whatever power Badras had, I didn't want to be on the other side of it.

"I can pass along the message to your brothers if you want to join Olys," Aedan offered.

Badras finally looked away from Hollaina. "And leave my sisters and niece here, unprotected? Out of the question. And no offense, blondie, but I don't trust you."

"Fine. Do you have any clue where he might go? I need to warn my soldiers in Nevelyn."

"My father is not exactly the sharing type. The gods only know where he slinked away to. A lot has changed since he lived here. He likely wouldn't recognize it on a good day."

Father? A rock dropped in my stomach. I hadn't known that Spense was related to Urdan. It made me fearful for Diana.

Aedan gently steered me from the tent. "I need to go to Nevelyn for a few days, maybe longer. I hadn't planned on leaving the soldiers with the Nordians for so long, but now that I know you're safe, I should make sure they haven't killed each other. Are you going to be okay here?"

"Of course. I understand. You should go."

Even though I had told him over and over that he didn't need to come with me on my various trips, deep down, I was glad he'd insisted on it. But I couldn't hold him back from his duties anymore.

He pressed a kiss to my forehead, and the smell of pine enveloped me. It would be all too easy to fall into his embrace, consequences be damned. Which was why I just gave him a smile as he stepped away.

"Diana should be back soon, I would think—hey, Badras, wait."

The surly male, who had been stalking toward the healer's tent, spun slowly. Aedan was brave. Much braver than me and probably most in this camp. Badras scared the living daylights out of me.

"Weren't you with Diana's travelling group? What happened?"

"They headed West two days ago," Spense's brother answered gruffly. "Traded me for my more diplomatic brother. They planned to be gone about a week."

Aedan nodded. "And you plan to hold off that long to look for Urdan?"

"I don't have a choice," he growled. "My sister in her vulnerable state is far more important in my eyes than that poor excuse of a king."

Strangely, as scary as it was to have Urdan in the wild, I understood Badras. Diana was more kin to me than my own family. My mother, who I didn't trust with my rebellious thoughts, was closer to her job than she was to me, and my father and I had stopped being close when he moved to the East to be with his new wife. Maybe I would regret it later, but I was prioritizing Diana and the Outcasts over my mother right now. She would be safe in the palace now that Vera had been removed from it, and truthfully, I didn't want to have to worry about her in Shynin, as competent as she might be.

Badras disappeared into the healer's tent, and Aedan nodded in that direction. "Maybe the healers could use your help."

I scoffed. "The only skills that would transfer over from my training would be making beds."

"You have magic; they don't. I doubt they'd turn you away."

Aedan was just trying to be nice, giving me some sense of importance. The healers in Shynin had long been without magic, and if I had learned anything since coming here, it was that they were quite happy without it.

But I appreciated the gesture, so I agreed. "I'll see what I can offer."

"Be safe, Maisie. Don't go making any more deals or wandering off to find hidden temples, okay?"

I pushed his arm, smiling. "Just get out of here already."

His blue eyes shone, and for a moment, he looked like he might say something else, but he shook his head gently and sent a hand running over his hair, attempting to tamp it down. "I mean it—don't do anything dangerous."

"Hypocritical of you, but fine. It might be hard to believe, but I actually don't like getting into life-threatening situations."

Aedan grinned, setting off for the horse pen. "Could've fooled me."

I watched as his blond head retreated farther and farther away, until I couldn't see him anymore. My smile didn't fade until I reached the healer's tent.

Taking a deep breath, I pushed inside.

TWENTY-SIX

DIANA
THE SOUTHERN ISLES

"I'm glad you finally came to your senses," Leo's arrogant voice drawled, echoing through the huge room.

With four tree-sized pillars and an entire open wall to look out into the southern ocean, this room was as showy and extravagant as its ruler.

Although, I had to admit, the warm sea breeze coasting off the calm blue waves and the golden sunset painting the sky brilliant hues of yellow and orange and pink were stunning. I would never say it out loud, but the view was something I could get used to.

"How did you know all that about the realm being unbalanced and the portal anyway?" I crossed my arms, remembering the conversation we'd had while dancing in the grand ballroom at the palace.

Leo raised a brow. "I'm no snitch, Princess. But I believe you have already met my informant from the East."

"Hollaina sure gets around, doesn't she?" Spense muttered under his breath. "She's got a hand in everything."

I had noticed that as well, but with her advocating for my side, I had put it in the *not as concerning right now* part of my brain and left it there to simmer.

"So, I assume I can count on your numbers to join the cause?"

With Sorin on one side and Spense on the other, I felt powerful. Strong.

"I have wanted Vera removed from power for quite some time," Leo said, a wry smile on his face. "It would be a great pleasure to assist you."

Well, this had been much more successful than the West.

"There's one problem."

I shouldn't have spoken so soon.

"During my long absence from the South, some of my officials did not react well to the gossip mill. Without me here to control the damage, there has been unease in my court. I returned to find it divided."

I bit down on my lip. Leo was a strong figurehead—that was for certain—but he had been in his role for only two years. He was still gaining the trust and loyalty of his court, and it didn't surprise me that his absence had been missed.

"So, what does this mean?" Sorin asked.

"It means that I cannot guarantee my full guard at this current time. I am working to fix that, of course, but this is war we're talking about. I cannot force my officials to give the lives of their citizens."

"I must say, I'm surprised, Leo."

He had always come across as someone who ruled with an iron fist.

The prince raised a brow. "I have always valued free will above all others," he replied. "I expect a lot from my court, but willingly."

I still didn't trust the male, who would never *not* look like an adder in my eyes, but my opinion of his character certainly had grown.

"What kind of numbers are we talking then?" Spense asked.

Leo grimaced. "A few thousand. Twenty-five hundred at most."

I sucked in a breath. Less than half of what we had hoped for.

"We'll take whoever you have that is willing to fight for Eira. Would it help if I spoke with your officials who aren't sure?"

His gaze landed on my tattooed arm and then on Spense. "They would all know you from the—uh, what was the queen calling it? Mid-spring mania?" A smirk crossed his face. "I think it best they see your actions instead of the same words they have heard from me."

"Fair enough. We will head out in the morning then. No time to waste. Will your guard be ready at a moment's notice? I don't know when we might need them." I stood, the two Drakenis brothers standing with me.

Leo nodded, signalling to the servant waiting by the door, who bustled over. "I will make sure of it. I'll send a few hundred with you now and a runner that can call for the rest when needed. Are you back in Nevelyn now?"

"I would like to get back there before this all goes south—no pun intended. But until we have an idea of where Vera's hiding out, I think the safest place is with the Outcasts."

Leo's lips twitched. "Ah, the Rebellion."

I shook my head. "It's not something I ever thought I would see in my lifetime—let alone be leading."

"You're doing right by Eira. I am not one to swear fealty, but my loyalty is to this realm and its rightful heir. I will go to battle for its peace."

"I was trying to avoid war," I said softly, almost an admission.

Leo's eyes gentled slightly—something I had never seen in him. "Starting a war and fighting in one are not the same thing. This is not your doing, Diana."

I appreciated his words. They could not touch the storm of guilt and worry brewing inside, but they were a buoy for me to cling to.

"Come. I'll walk you to the guesthouse. It has a lovely view of the ocean."

Leo led us through his open-air castle, the pillars creating shadows from the setting sun. Even though the day was waning, it was still warm, the wind soft.

We climbed a set of ancient-looking stone stairs that led outside the palace into the open courtyard. From this high, the ocean stretched on forever, not a lick of land in sight. It was magnificent. The shoreline was sandy and quiet, a few bodies mingling to watch the sunset. The tide crashing was loud enough that it could just be picked up from here.

"What's that?" I pointed to the right, where a piece of the shore had been blocked off with wooden barricades. The water was darker with rocks jutting out between the waves.

Leo followed my aim and frowned. "Shark Cove. As the name suggests, we've been having some issues with the local sea predators. It used to be a great diving spot when the tide was low. Lots of minerals and gems. But lately, the sharks have been a terror, and because of the rocks, we can't use boats. Free divers won't risk it."

"I wonder why the sharks are so bad."

"They have no other predators, and we certainly don't hunt them. The numbers have been steadily increasing over the years—our fishers are fighting them for the fish. At this rate, we might have to consider a culling." Leo shook his head. "Damn shame. Nature used to be able to sustain itself."

An idea sprang to mind. "I might have a solution for you."

All three heads swivelled to me.

"Do tell," Leo drawled.

"The kelpies," I suggested, to which Sorin and Spense instantly agreed. "They're extremely violent Folk that we brought from the other realm. They live underwater and pull things to the bottom to feed. We weren't sure what we were going to do with them, honestly. Maybe they could help with your shark problem."

"I've heard of them," Leo mused, drawing a hand to his chin. "But aren't they lovers of fae meals as well?"

"There are ways to … deter them," Spense said, a dark shadow crossing his face. "And they are not social beings. They'll spread out. With such a big shoreline, I don't see it being much of a problem as long as you keep an area separate for swimming and leisure."

Leo considered this. "There hasn't been much leisure with the sharks so close anyway. Okay, let's try it."

I tried to control my grin. "I'll get it organized."

"I must say, it's thrilling that the Folk have returned at last. Please know they are all welcome in the South." Leo stopped us in front of a one-level home with white boards panelling the sides and lots of windows facing the view.

Nome and Pyter were already inside, judging by the scuffed-up boots that had been abandoned at the door.

I remembered what Leo had said at the mid-spring mania ball, conveying his opinion that the Folks' absence was causing the land to die. While I wasn't sure yet how the land would change with them here, it felt good to know that the Southern Isles was a safe place to send those seeking refuge.

"Thank you, Leo. Not just for this, but also for always wanting the best for Eira. Even when it made you unliked."

The prince laughed once, the sound foreign, but not unwelcome. "I look forward to working with you, Diana."

When he left, we rested in the modest lodgings, happy to watch the last colours fade from the sky from the cosy sitting room. We faded to bed with the darkness, and a quiet calm settled over us that hadn't been there before.

Sleep came easier than it had since Spense had first appeared in my life.

My spirits were finally at a normal level again, thanks to the success of finding a home for the kelpies as well as securing Leo's allegiance. I was getting the hang of this thing.

I ran a hand down Finnvarra's mane, delighted to be reunited. Maybe I had been too harsh on Maisie. We would sit down when I was back and hash it all out. I didn't want her to hide anything from me.

Secrets were as good as weapons in war.

Sorin rode beside me today, helping me strategize how we would prepare for an attack. I agreed that we should take back the palace and reopen the cities. It was time to let the citizens know what was going on.

And more importantly, Spense had chimed in, I was the one they could trust.

It filled me with a bitter taste to think of turning my cities against their queen. My own mother. But I needed their support, and showing them the truth was the only way I felt comfortable doing that. Having the wool removed from where it had covered my eyes hurt like a physical wound, but now that it was gone, I would choose that pain over and over again before going back to ignorance.

Eira deserved the same.

"When we get back to Shynin, I want to prepare a large group to go to the palace. The army will have taken control of it, so Aedan will need to come. As for the—"

Finnvarra halted in her steps, and I froze in my saddle.

"Not again," I muttered.

The others noticed the change, too, the air growing heavy and quiet.

"Shadows?" Sorin murmured.

"No." Spense pulled up next to me. "They don't feel like this."

Damn it. We were so close to the Unclaimed Land. I debated our chances if we made a break for the cover of the trees within the border.

Without a definitive idea of what *this* was, it would be stupid to run.

A bird caw resounded, reverberating through my body, and three ravens flew overhead, violently close to clipping us.

"Gods above," Pyter cursed. His white horse shimmied, bumping into Plum.

For a few drawn-out moments, nobody moved. Silence rang in my ears, louder than the bird call had been. And then a horrible feeling pummelled into my stomach at the sound of my mother's voice.

"You shouldn't be out here."

TWENTY-SEVEN

SPENSE
SO BE IT

The second Vera's voice pierced the air, a red haze clouded my vision.

She wasn't getting away this time.

Diana's eyes were wild as she whipped her head around, trying to find the source.

"A leader shouldn't be so unguarded." Her mother's voice tsked. "Especially the leader of a mutinous rebellion."

"Is that why you won't show your face, coward?" I couldn't help myself from calling back. My proverbial hackles were raised, my blood boiling.

An unearthly chuckle filled the air. My spine tingled from the heightened magic around us. One of the ravens cawed from a nearby shrub, and suddenly, Vera's voice was coming from its beak.

It was horrifying.

I wanted to know exactly how she had done it.

"I am just following my own advice," the raven said. "If I may offer a piece of wisdom to you, my daughter, do not underestimate me."

Diana's stricken face visibly smoothed as she stared down at the black bird. "And you should not underestimate *me*. How did it feel to be turned on by your own army? That should be proof enough that what you're doing is wrong."

The raven's feathers rustled, the small creature struggling to control its rage. "Right and wrong is such a naive way to look at things. It's subjective, darling. For example, one could find it morally wrong for you to attack the West out of anger."

Sorin sidled up close to me, speaking in a low tone. "She's stalling. She has to be close by to use this much magic—we should prepare for an attack."

Diana scoffed. "Kashdan is feeding you lies. We were turned away before we could even enter the castle."

Vera laughed through the raven, the sight completely unhinged. "You are making it too easy for me, dear. You have no control over this rebellion you claim to be heading. The Western Shores guard spent the night evacuating and attempting to fight a rather large group of shadows. I have not heard from Kashdan yet the number of casualties, but I have to guess it won't be low, considering they did not let up for hours."

Diana faltered, and my heart leaped. I heeded Sorin's words, taking Plum to the edge of our group, searching for telltale signs of magic sources. The raven sat on its perch, staring us all down with its beady eyes. If I couldn't find Vera's hiding spot, taking out the bird would be a good way to stun her.

"We were attacked by the shadows as well. We have no bearing over them."

I pulled the small dagger I kept strapped to my hip, settling it in my palm. I aimed for the bird's chest, pulled my arm back, and—

"You might not possess the ability to control them, but your dear soulmate does."

Before I could release the blade, Diana's eyes met mine, and I felt her fury through our shared magic. It rippled through me, shocking me enough that I felt my grip on the dagger loosen.

She took in my raised arm and the weapon that I had been about to launch. Her voice was as hard as her face when she spoke next. "Spense, tell me that's not true."

My mind whirled for what I could say in that moment to calm her down, to let her see my side. I didn't regret it, not for a moment, but the way her jaw clenched at my silence sent a cold fear rippling down my spine.

The others kept their gazes trained on the bird or the ground while Sorin continued his scan.

It was only Diana and me as she said three words that broke something deep inside me. "How could you?"

The horrible voice of Vera cut through our stares. "Good luck to you. I will be back for my crown. Seems it doesn't fit your head anyway."

This time, I did fire the dagger, and it made a high-pitched whizzing sound as it flew through the air and was lost in the bush. The raven flapped overhead, unharmed.

Sorin galloped his horse back to us, not stopping as he shouted, "Go! Get to cover!"

Instantly, we all took off, following him toward the Unclaimed Land's border and the safety of its low-hanging trees. And it was soon made clear why—the darkening sky, the deafening sound of flapping wings, ravens flying everywhere.

They dived at us, grabbing at our hair and clothes, their sharp beaks cutting into skin. The horses bucked and bolted, as driven as we were to get into the trees.

I cursed loudly when a bird tore at my side with its talons, forgoing the beak. Immediate pain burst, and I knew without having to check that it was bleeding.

Diana's screams were piercing at my nerves, and my gut clenched at the sight of her raising one arm above her head, attempting to keep the birds from pulling more of her hair.

The roots of the heavy trees hit us before the protection of their branches did, and the horses had to slow down once they started tripping over them. Nome nearly came tumbling off the side when his horse fell to its knees before righting itself.

"Thank the gods," Sorin panted as the last few birds got caught in branches and abandoned us.

We all slowed to a walk, checking for injuries. Thankfully, the horses seemed okay besides some cuts and scrapes. We fared mostly the same, save for the gash over my ribs and Diana's arm. It was dripping blood onto Finnvarra's neck, the jagged lines crossing and meeting, deep in more spots than I liked.

It was the wrong time to think about this, but I wondered what would have happened to the soulmate tattoo if she had raised that arm. It was infused with enough magic that I would hope it wouldn't have marred the design. Maybe it would have even kept her from harm had she raised that arm instead.

"Are you okay?" I asked her.

She nodded, inspecting her arm.

"Hey," I started. "We should talk about—"

"About what, Spense?" When Diana finally met my eyes, she was angry, her mouth set in a flat line. "About the fact that you went behind my back to attack one of my regions? That you put innocent lives on the line because you couldn't control yourself? Is that what we should talk about?"

"Maybe it's not the right time," I mumbled, sensing her intensity rising. "We should get that arm looked at."

"My arm is fine," she spat.

My own rage sparked at her anger toward me. I had helped her. Doing what needed to be done. If she didn't like it, then that was too bad. I was accustomed to war; she wasn't.

"You would have had to make a move on Kashdan eventually," I growled. "I saved you from having it on your hands. I saved you from having to make a decision I know you didn't want to make. So, forgive me for being strong when you couldn't."

Diana whirled around in her saddle, Finnvarra following the weight change. "Being strong? That's what you think that was? That was *cowardly*, Spense. Sending a malevolent entity we know incredibly little about to do the dirty work for you is shameful. I knew I'd have to make a move eventually, but I deserved the right to do it *my* way."

"This is war, Diana. You don't get the luxury of time to think things over."

She shook her head, an emotion in her eyes that I had never seen directed at me. "I used to think you weren't capable of this. Where is the male who saved an innocent girl from drowning by jumping into a rushing river? *That's* the male I fell in love with. And you're not acting like him. You betrayed my trust."

My whole body stiffened, ice forming over my limbs. "You knew what I was capable of back in Ivywall. I will not apologize for doing what had to be done."

Diana's nostrils flared, her eyes glistening as she struggled to keep tears from slipping down her cheeks. "Go away, Spense. Before one of us says something we can't take back. I don't want to see you for a while."

She trotted Finnvarra away, her hair swishing as she forged ahead. Nome and Pyter followed close behind, giving her enough room to avoid her wrath.

Sorin sighed. "Spense—"

"Don't," I snapped.

He fixed me with a look I knew all too well. One that said he was disappointed and that this wasn't the last of this conversation. My whole life, my siblings had been perfecting that look, eager to correct insolent young Spense for whatever cruelty he had committed this time.

If only they could see that everything I did was in consideration of *them*. Of my family, my Folk, and a better future.

If I had to be the bad one, the shoulder to place the blame, so be it.

TWENTY-EIGHT

AEDAN
FOREBODING

The overwhelming scent of Nordian pipe barrelled into me the second I walked into the palace.

Guards stationed at the door nodded to me as I passed, and it was easy to follow the smell and sounds of jovial laughter to the large ballroom. The doors were propped open, and I could see why.

"Put the fire out." I strode into the room, heads lifting from the makeshift firepit, where a mix of Nordian and queen's army soldiers sat cross-legged, passing around the herb responsible for the strong smell.

Trent, one of my own, gave me a sheepish look as he smothered the flame.

"Where's Ryen?"

Several hands lifted to point toward the balcony leading from the room.

The laughter started up again when I slipped through the glass doors into the cool air of the night. A sniff of annoyance surfaced. Surely, they had better uses of their time with what we were preparing for.

Ryen was leaning against the rail, looking out into the frozen landscape, where the River Nord slithered down through the trees like an icy serpent. Maverick stood beside him and turned at the sound of the door closing.

"Thesand. Find it smoky in there?"

I snorted. "Marginally."

Ryen twisted around, propping his elbows on the rail. "How are things on your end?"

"Urdan, the Unseelie king, escaped his hold. We need to be on guard in case he tries to come here. He's dangerous."

My second was instantly alert. "We'll send a scouting party in the nearby woods to make sure."

"Considering his current search party is a party of one, it might be prudent to have that group try and find him as well. If we can spare the swords."

"I'll see it done."

Before I could thank him, Maverick patted him on the back. "What a good little helper you are."

Ryen shoved him off, flashing a particular finger at him. "You're just jealous I'm not *your* little helper."

Maverick laughed, the sound deep and gravelly. "Guilty."

"You two are certainly getting along better than I hoped."

The Nordian general crossed his tree-trunk arms, grinning. "Raises morale to see the leaders get along."

I looked back over my shoulder to the group now almost impossible to see through the thick layer of smoke—both from pipe and the dying fire. "Might be a little too high."

Ryen snorted. "Good one."

"I meant the morale. But, yes, that too."

"It's a de-stress for them. We've already been promised their lives in battle. I don't think we can ask much more of them." Ryen was right, as usual.

Maverick nodded. "Let them have their fun. I sense something coming."

I furrowed my brow. "Like what?"

"I'm not sure yet, but I can feel it in the air. It's foreboding. And it's coming to us."

"A *feeling* isn't enough to keep the entire region under lockdown."

"They are already safe as they are. You would risk the lives of your citizens because you don't believe me? What's the harm in keeping the order another week or so?"

Ryen met my gaze, and I could tell he shared my thought. "It's not that simple," he said. "There will come a point where they won't listen to the order anymore. If we keep extending the lockdown, eventually, our word will lose importance."

"If they disobey a strict order from the palace and get killed because of it, that's their fault, not yours," Maverick growled.

"Maybe so," I agreed. "But I want to protect them regardless."

"So, you're saying you want to open the cities back up?"

I nodded. "Slowly. There will be a curfew in place, and no one goes anywhere alone. With a few soldiers stationed at each city, we should be able to create a good line of communication across the North as well. It will be harder for Vera to catch us unawares."

Maverick tilted his head. "If you are positive, then I will not fight you on this. But I want to make sure you're taking my hunch seriously. I'm rarely wrong about this."

"Nothing is being taken lightly, least of all your gut feeling. We're a team, General."

"I suppose time will tell."

Ryen and I shared a glance. As well as his Nordians were getting along with our soldiers, it was evident that the general kept his trust close to his chest. And frankly, that made me less trusting of him as well. Our agreement had its work cut out for it to hold together our tentative peace.

"So, let's move forward with a slow opening. Knowing Diana, I think she would want to start gaining their trust again. We're not at liberty to make any statements regarding the queen or the state of the palace, but at the same time, I want to make sure the civilians are talking among themselves. Whispering. Wondering about why the queen turned her back on the high princess. So, the soldiers need to know that while we cannot start any rumours, they might … *encourage* them."

Maverick smiled, the upturn of his mouth giving away a wicked interior that had undoubtedly helped earn his role.

Ryen clapped his hands once. "Done. We'll send runners to the bordering cities and go door to door in Nevelyn. Should we be worried that integrating the Nordians with the soldiers might be frightening for the citizens?"

"Aw, you think I'm scary?" Maverick smirked.

"Get a grip, General. The scariest thing about you is your breath."

Maverick laughed deeply while I shook my head. I was starting to wonder how much pipe these two had indulged in too.

"I think it will show a united front. No one here has ever seen a Nordian with their own eyes, so their presence will make the danger we've warned them about that much more realistic."

My second nodded. "Are you sticking around for a while?"

"For a few days. Diana's party is expected back in Shynin by the end of the week, and I want to meet with her as soon as she's in. I must say, it's a weight off my back to see how well you've handled things here."

Pipe not withstanding.

"And Maisie?" Ryen asked.

I narrowed my eyes. "What about her?"

He shrugged nonchalantly. "Last time we spoke, you seemed to be concerned for her. I'm just wondering how she fared getting to safety. She was the one who came to me with the idea of a mutiny."

I smiled. That did not surprise me. Nothing about Maisie surprised me anymore.

"She's handling herself well."

I didn't miss the wry look Ryen sent my way, eyebrow raised.

Maverick pushed through us, grunting. "If you two are quite done with your gossiping, I'm getting in on that pipe before it's gone. I've used my brain enough for one day."

Without waiting for an answer, he swung open the door and joined the group still shrouded in smoke from the doused fire.

"He's sure something."

Ryen laughed. "It could be worse."

I had to agree.

"You coming?" He motioned with his head toward the palace.

"You go ahead. I'll catch up later."

Turning to rest my arms on the railing, I took a deep inhale of the forest air I loved so much. The door clicked shut behind me, and then it was silent.

The snow-capped trees were bright against the moonlight, giving much more visibility than I was used to. The River Nord glistened, shiny and still.

If I hadn't been looking at it already, I would have missed the splitting of ice in the far distance, accompanied by a resounding crack that pierced the night air. The unmistakable sound of rushing water picked up, and my face broke out into a grin.

The North was melting.

TWENTY-NINE

SPENSE
SUBDUE

Badras marched out of the healer's tent the moment we dismounted in Shynin. "Sorin. Spense. I need to speak with you now."

"Can it wait, brother?" Sorin's gaze landed on his wife, Meske, who was seated at the firepit, helping their daughter, Aislinn, roast something in a pan over the fire. "We've had a day, and we could use some food."

"Your day's about to get worse." He pointed to Diana, who was taking off Finnvarra's saddle. "Her too. Tent. Now."

Sorin let out a heavy sigh. "Go. I'll get her."

The irritation that had been slowly building after today's events was turning into a simmer. I was starving, the tiny fruit bowl breakfast in the South not nearly enough to sustain me. I was tempted to make my brother wait. But Badras, being the ever-hungry beast he was, would not have summoned us before dinner without due cause. And as I followed him into the healer's tent, my heart clenched in fear.

Alwyn's all right, I told myself. *She's stronger than any of us.*

My sister's tiny body lay out on the makeshift bed by the back of the room, her chest rising slowly. So slowly. I bit at my bottom lip, wondering if she knew what was going on right now or if she was unaware, just sleeping.

I hoped it was the latter.

Sorin and Diana joined us not a minute later, and Badras did not waste any time.

"Urdan is missing."

We were silent as the words digested.

"Excuse me, what?" Sorin's low voice had a sharp ring to it.

"You heard me. I came in to check on Alwyn, and his guards were gone. So, I opened up the coffin to find it empty. Olys is out now, trying to find a trail."

My heart thundered in my chest. "Why is he out alone? Urdan could be anywhere by now."

"I wasn't about to leave Alwyn and Meske here, unprotected, was I?" Badras growled. "Whoever did this had intimate knowledge of his condition and how to wake him. I haven't left this tent since then."

Looking over by Alwyn's bed, I could see where Badras had made up his own cot on the floor. He was staying at her side, protecting her, and it made my chest feel warm.

"We need to get search parties going immediately," Diana said, walking over to the empty coffin. She peered inside, her brows wrinkling. "This scent is familiar."

"Hollaina."

She snapped her gaze up. "Yes, that's it."

Badras turned to Sorin. "The leader of this camp said she spoke with you about Hollaina looking over Alwyn to see if she could help. Is that true?"

Slowly, Sorin nodded. "Freya asked if it would be okay to have a friend look at her who knew a lot about healing, which I agreed to. She never said who it was."

"And you didn't think to ask?" growled Badras.

Sorin's mouth set. "Considering Meske has been with the healer this entire time, I was confident in her ability to watch over Alwyn. I assume you've kicked them all out of here?"

Badras crossed his arms. "They were treating patients in here. It was too much to keep track of."

"You broody asshole! How are they supposed to heal their fae? They have no magic."

"They can make their little potions just fine outside—"

"Okay, all right," I cut in. "I'll head out with you to look for him. Maybe I can reach out to his magic, if it's still working right with all the sedation. Sorin, if you want to stay with Meske and Ash, I understand."

"There's no way I can stay here, knowing he's out, causing inordinate amounts of trouble. I can head up another party, and we'll assign some of our trusted soldiers to look for him as well." Sorin looked to Diana. "As long as they're not needed. I trust you'll be able to protect my family—*your* family."

"Of course," Diana said emphatically. "I'll have someone trustworthy stationed with Alwyn at all times as well."

Sorin nodded. "Then, we should get going. We're wasting time."

"Olys headed east to cover more of the Unclaimed Land. I think we should head north. I just have a gut feeling that Urdan will try and find the Seelie queen, and the palace there is the last place he saw her before they left this land." Badras heaved two saddlebags into his brother's arms. "Let's go."

"I should get you a map," Diana started.

"Already got one." Badras pulled a rolled parchment from his bag and tapped it in the air. "This handy thing even shows entrances into the palace."

Diana moved to snatch it, but he was quicker, yanking his arm above his head, where she had no chance of reaching it. "Where did you get that?"

"Relax. I'll bring it back in one piece." He stared at us. "Well? Are we going?"

"I'd like to see Meske and Aislinn for a few moments before we head out. You two get fresh horses saddled, and we'll go." Sorin left the tent, Badras following him.

A strange tension sat in the air between Diana and me. I hated it. But I also hated that she was mad at me for something I had done out of love.

"Don't waste any bodies on Urdan. You need them more in case of an attack. They won't be able to help us against him anyway."

"What will you do when you find him?" Diana finally turned to me, her arms folded over her chest.

"Subdue him, I suppose. Bring him back here while we figure out what to do with him."

"You should bring him to the palace in Nevelyn. The holding cells underground are protected against magic."

"Oh, I remember."

Diana sighed. "Be safe, Spense."

A bit of my anger faded because it was impossible to stay mad at her when she was incapable of holding a grudge herself.

"I will. It'll be easier to focus, knowing you'll be safe here."

Diana averted her eyes for a moment. "I might not be here when you get back."

I stepped closer to her, forcing her chin to tilt to look me in the eye. "What is that supposed to mean?"

"I want to go back to Nevelyn, Spense. To my home. The palace is full of soldiers awaiting direction. My mother might try to reclaim it at any time. I plan on finding Aedan, wherever he's disappeared to, and set up a new reign while I have the chance."

The parts of me that were trying to let go of being angry were trampled by the mention of Aedan's name. The tattoo on Diana's arm might be proof that he would never have her, but I still hated him. The thought of him at Diana's side, ruling her army, made it difficult to quell the urge to throw something.

I had an army, too, and it would never be led by a Thesand.

"Well, hopefully, you can find him, and he's not been captured by the enemy again."

"Don't be like that," she snapped. "We all have roles to play in this. I'm trying to find peace for my fae. For yours too."

Badras's head poking through the tent flap saved me from growling out something I would likely regret. "I gave you more than enough time to kiss goodbye. Get a move on." He disappeared.

"You'd better go."

I pulled at strands of my hair. I didn't want to leave it like this between us.

"Look, I—let's talk when I'm back. I'll find you, wherever you are." I leaned down to brush a kiss to her lips, but she moved her head to the side, and my kiss ended up on her cheek. My chest clenched uncomfortably.

"I'll see you soon."

Diana nodded, her face unreadable.

Outside, Badras handed me the reins to a small sorrel horse. He raised an eyebrow at my scowl.

"Don't bother," Sorin said, mounting his black mare. "Lovers' quarrel."

"Another reason I'm fine without a soulmate." Badras swung into his saddle, and I followed suit. "Seems like an awful lot of work."

"It's not easy to get used to someone seeing the worst parts of you and holding you accountable for them." Sorin let Badras lead the way as we headed out of Shynin. He turned to level me with a look. "But it's worth it. Even the tiniest slivers of happiness outshine the biggest storms."

Badras made a gagging noise. "That was corny, even for you, brother."

The two continued joking, but Sorin's message was clear. And he was right. We just had to get through the storm.

THIRTY

AEDAN
LAST DAY

The peace I had felt last night disappeared by dawn.

I was looking out my window into the wooded area behind the stables when I saw it. Her.

Standing at the palace gates like some sort of bad omen.

By the time I shoved a jacket on and stalked to the grand foyer entrance, there was a small crowd. Soldiers and Nordians watching her through the glass and waiting for instruction.

I didn't hesitate as I pushed through and blasted open the doors. I wasn't one for blatant shows of magic, but it needed a release.

Ryen was at my side in an instant. "No sign of backup. She came alone."

"Either she's extremely stupid or she has something up her sleeve. Keep looking," I growled.

"Aedan," Jamey Pinois purred. "How lovely to see you again. Glad to see you aren't too malnourished from your time under the castle."

I reached for the sword at my side, swinging it through the air. She backed up a step, but kept that arrogant smirk.

"Now, now." She tsked. "No need for violence. I'm only here to deliver a message."

"I don't care." I plunged forward, sword directed at her neck, but

Jamey held a hand up, and a burst of magic wrapped around her like a bubble. The force of it pushed my weight backward.

"Really? So childish."

"Where did you get magic like that?" I demanded.

In all the time I had known her, even before becoming romantically entangled, she had never shown power that strong. Not even her family line could wield anything much more than water.

Jamey smiled, her perfect teeth not as attractive as they once had been. "It's a gift, to keep the new heir safe."

"You can pretend all you want, but you'll never be the heir," I spat.

Her smile hardened, and it thrilled me to finally break through her facade.

"I don't see anyone else doing the job here."

"Who says Diana isn't here?"

Jamey crossed her arms. "You might think me an idiot, but surely, you don't expect me to believe that Diana would stay inside and let you do all the work for her. I know my friend better than that."

I bristled at the term *friend*. Jamey wouldn't know the meaning of that word if it struck her across the face. Which I was aching to do.

I shrugged. "Maybe you're just not important enough for her to waste her time on."

She sneered, "When Diana returns, please inform her that the queen wishes an audience."

"She won't agree to one."

"It wasn't a question. She'll be waiting." Jamey stepped into my space, staring up at me, close enough that our noses could almost touch. "Do take care now. I expect your days are limited."

Behind me, I was aware of the sounds of weapons being drawn. The sharp graze of metal swords and the stringy whisper of bows being stretched taut.

I smiled. "Your last day will come before mine—that I promise you."

Jamey raked her gaze from mine to the band of soldiers behind me and flipped her hair over her shoulder as she walked away. She didn't say another word, her figure getting smaller as she followed the cobble path toward Nevelyn.

"Take the shot."

The air was filled with arrows whizzing by me. They all deflected off of whatever borrowed magic she was using, like I had thought.

But it felt good anyway.

THIRTY-ONE

DIANA
AN ADMISSION

"I've heard from Hollaina's officials in the East—their guard is ready to march. They're on their way to the Unclaimed Land as we speak." Freya flipped through a stack of parchment on her lap, updating me with the various correspondence I'd asked her to oversee.

"That's good news." I was sitting in the chair across from her, where my butt would have to get used to the rigid discomfort of it.

In a few moments, Pik would be updating us with his findings on the prophecy.

"Will you be able to house them here for a few days? Once I reclaim the palace, we'll have more than enough room for the guard."

"The Unclaimed Land provides, as I have said. And get used to calling these soldiers what they are—an army. *Your* army. You will have a hard time stepping up fully into the role of queen if you believe in your mind that you are only pretending."

Freya spoke out of turn—and often. Miraculously, I was starting to get used to her unveiled truths. Her words now pestered me like a fly would. I just had to swat them away.

"Army, guard, no matter. We're a rebellion. I don't think such formalities are necessary."

Freya frowned. She opened her mouth, but whatever she was going to say was cut off by Pik entering the tent.

He bowed low, the tips of his long blue ears nearly touching the ground. "My lady. Freya." He held the tattered scroll we had entrusted him with.

"Pik." I sat straighter. "I hope you come bearing good news."

"We are making progress on this," he said. "I believe I have figured out the language it was written in. It had the markings similar to goblin dialects, but not one I had ever seen. Upon consultation with some of the Burrowing Goblin elders, we all agree. I had not thought there were any Burrowings left—it seems word of the departure from Rathe made it to them in the far reaches of the West Dunes, where they had been hiding out, and they were able to get to the portal in time."

"That's great news, Pik." I smiled. "So, the prophecy is decidedly of goblin descent then?"

He nodded, his childish features passionate. "It is an old dialect, but we are still looking. The books Freya has so kindly provided are full of information; however"—he looked at her warily—"they're not the sort we are looking for."

"I wonder what's happening in the City of Scholars," I mused aloud. "I would love to send you to the Academy for your research. I just worry about how they will react to—well, to the Folk."

Freya leafed through the parchment in her lap before pulling out a piece. "This is the last report I have on the Northern cities."

I leaned forward, trying to get a look at it. "You have spies reporting on my cities?"

"It is only the basic things—hardly spying." Freya waved me off. "They obliged the palace's shelter-in-place command, and it seems they are slow to open up, even after the order was lifted. It might be hard to sneak him in. Perhaps if you had someone on the inside?"

It seemed Aedan was busy in his new role in Nevelyn. A splash of worry pooled in my stomach about opening the cities while my mother was still a threat, but I had to trust that Aedan knew what he was doing. He always had my best interests at heart.

Much like Spense.

"I have a friend who can get him into the Academy—or at the very least help retrieve the needed tomes. Do you think we could spare a runner to send a note, as well as a few guards to escort Pik and his research team?"

"Are you asking me or telling me?" Freya asked. "A queen takes charge without saying words like *do you think*."

I bristled. "I'm telling you," I ground out. "To send a runner with my note and send a guard with Pik to the City of Scholars."

"Better." Freya nodded.

My teeth snapped together so hard that I was surprised they couldn't hear it.

"Consider it done."

Hastily, I scribbled a note to my old friend Shela, who would jump into action to help, although she would undoubtedly send me a scolding reply for not visiting her the moment I'd stepped foot back in Eira.

With a runner sent, Pik returned to his team to pack for their trip.

Maisie found me standing on the edge of the forest while I was hand-grazing Finnvarra in the lush, tall grass. The mare snorted as she yanked at the blades, happy to be away from the overcrowded barn.

"So, you got my apology gift."

I turned. Maisie was wearing the homespun look of the Outcasts with a plain, long tunic and loose pants underneath. Her honey-yellow curls were tied back, her bright blue eyes nervous as she waited for me to respond.

I dropped Finnvarra's lead to wrap my old friend in a hug, savouring the familiar homey scent of her. I pulled back to attempt a stern look. "I'm mad at you."

She looked down sheepishly. "I'm sorry. I had to do something—but it's done now. Promise."

"I'm just glad you're all right." I leaned down to retrieve the rope attached to my horse. "I don't suppose you'll tell me what you were up to?"

Maisie drew her bottom lip in. "Hopefully, you can forgive me for not sharing. I think it will do no good, except to worry you."

"You've changed a great deal since I left." At her worried expression, I added, "In a good way. You're more confident, sure of your decisions. I just can't tell you how sorry I am to have left you in a situation that forced you to change."

She came over to stand next to me, running a hand across Finnvarra's orange shoulder. "You couldn't have known what would happen to you or how your mother would react here. But you're back now, and you'll make everything right again."

I swallowed, my throat tight. Rocks gathered in the pit of my stomach. "Was my mother truly so horrid to you?"

Maisie levelled her gaze with me. "She's gone, Diana. She's not your mother anymore. She's hardened and cruel. I'm sorry to have to tell you this."

I worried about the things she wasn't saying. What had truly gone down in the palace after I left?

"I just don't think … that I can kill her." My voice came out soft, a whisper. An admission from deep in my soul.

Maisie nodded, her eyes full of sorrow. "Maybe it won't come to that."

I looked into the forest, at the odd, spindly trees that seemed to bend in all sorts of directions. My mother was redeemable—that was what I had to keep telling myself. Otherwise, I would spiral.

"Come," Maisie said softly, taking her hand in mine. "They have the best bonfires here at night."

THIRTY-TWO

ÆDAN
PROXIMITY

Early mornings were my favourite in the palace because of the quiet that accompanied it. Only a handful of the slowly returning staff were awake, and the morning birds had just begun to sing. It was the calm before the storm of a busy day.

Now, standing in what used to be a garden of peonies before the snow covered them, not far from the path down to the stables, it was too quiet.

There was a difference between the quiet hum of a normal morning and the charged silence that had become regular since Vera's departure. Perhaps it was just the lack of officials and servants staying in the palace or the fact that everyone here was trained to walk with soft steps—whatever the reason, it unnerved me.

I continued my stretches as I waited for General Maverick to arrive. The only sound was the swish of wind through the trees. It rustled the hair around my ears, reminding me how direly it needed a trim. But it was growing on me, the length. I would be able to tie it back soon, and I looked forward to that. Even though I had gone my whole soldier career with it cropped close, the longer it was, the more I felt like a warrior.

"Thesand." Maverick's form came into view, emerging from

behind a shrub that had been shaped to resemble a wolf's head. "What on Gaia's green earth are you doing?"

"Stretching." I pulled my arm across my chest, feeling the tug of a sore muscle. "So I won't be as brittle as you when I'm your age."

Maverick's booming laugh was a stark change to the quiet air. "My body is always prepared. Stretching is for weaklings."

We started jogging at a gentle pace, weaving a path through the gardens.

"Are you going to tell me what's really going on?" The delicious burn of running began in my calves, striking a match of familiarity and comfort.

"I suppose it wasn't really believable that I wanted to use your workout program." The general picked up the pace, forcing me to match him. "I thought you would like to know that one of my patrols tracked her. The one who came yesterday to threaten you."

"I didn't realize you'd sent out a tracking party."

Maverick looked sideways at me. "I assumed you had already sent one and thought to double our odds. Surely, you didn't mean to let her slither back to the hole she'd crawled out of without a tail?"

Truthfully, I had assumed she wouldn't be traceable with Vera's protective magic. An oversight I would not make again.

"Where is she hiding out?"

"A sanctuary not far from here. We can go now."

"A sanctuary?" I repeated. "Do you mean the Gaian Abbey?"

Maverick shrugged, running faster. My arms pumped as I kept up with him. He led the way, the grass making squelching noises as we ran. The temperature had picked up significantly, and the snow was rapidly melting away into the ground.

It was obvious very quickly that we were indeed heading toward the Gaian Abbey. And when we arrived at the front door, the red brick gleaming against the sunlight, two cloaked Gaians were already waiting for us.

Their hoods were pushed back, arms clasped in front of them underneath billowing sleeves.

"Deputy Captain," the female on the right said, her tone a warning. "We ask you do not enter the Abbey on grounds of violence."

I was tempted to shoulder right through them, but Diana would not condone the mistreatment of the clergy. "You know why I'm here then."

The Gaians did not say anything, their faces stoic.

I stepped closer, feeling a sickening sort of pleasure when the male on the left flinched slightly. "Bring me Jamey Pinois, and I won't have to commit violence on this sacred ground."

The female cleared her throat. "She is seeking sanctuary, Deputy. We cannot withhold this from her. It was decreed by Mother Gaia at the beginning of this world that we not turn away anyone in need."

Maverick, quiet until now, reached out and grabbed the Gaian by her cloak. He pulled her in close. "Then, you are disobeying your goddess by not allowing us entry. We wish to shelter here from the incoming storm," he growled.

Both Gaians glanced upward, where the sky was blue and sunny for the first time in weeks.

But she swallowed, nodding slowly. "Let me speak with the High Mother."

Maverick released her sharply, and she fell back a few steps.

"Do that."

She hurried into the Abbey, the other Gaian following quickly behind. The heavy black door slammed shut.

I looked to the Nordian general, who shrugged.

"I didn't commit violence."

I couldn't argue there.

Within a few moments, a dark-haired female wearing the robes of the High Mother swung the door open. She waved us through. "Guests of the Abbey, please join me inside the sanctuary."

The high-beamed wooden walls had not changed since I had last been in here as a boy. I was pretty sure the chairs and table were the exact same, too, old and cracking. I could recall sitting with Diana in front of the window across the room, staring into the forest while we were supposed to be meditating.

"Close your eyes, Aedan," she urged, sending a tiny—albeit sharp—elbow into my side.

"How do you know they were open?" I asked, squeezing them shut.

I opened one eye to peek at her, finding her smiling through closed lids.

"I just know," she said.

I shook my head to clear the memory. It made my heart clench to remember how young and innocent we had once been, unencumbered by the war that plagued us now.

"Where is High Mother Cretis?" I said, choosing to stand as the imposter took a seat in front of us.

"There has been a change in leadership. I am Bandra, the new High Mother."

"The palace was not informed."

Bandra tilted her head to the side. "Queen Vera gave her full blessing when I was anointed. Perhaps it was just *you* that was not informed."

I gave my head a shake. There was no time to worry about Cretis or the fact that Vera had gotten to the Abbey before us. "You know why we're here."

"Aedan"—she shook her head—"I cannot give her up to you."

"Bandra," I replied, forgoing her title if she was not going to use mine, "Jamey Pinois is an enemy of the realm, a direct threat to the heir. Holding her here, no matter what rules you might have about sheltering, is bringing harm to Diana."

"It's treason," Maverick growled.

The new High Mother folded her hands in her lap, gaze raking over the Nordian. "I do not appreciate being told how to run my Abbey. I have been interpreting Gaia's word longer than you have both been alive."

"If you don't bring her out, we will go in and find her ourselves."

Bandra narrowed her eyes. "We do not condone violence within these sacred walls. Violate the sanctuary I have given, and you will regret it."

Cretis had been firm, but possessed a gentle way about her that radiated kindness. This Gaian was hardened and impenetrable.

I took a step closer. "Is that a threat?"

In that moment, a blurring shape streaked across the room, running for the exit.

"It's her! Let's move!" Maverick took off after Jamey, leaping over the couch.

"We're not done here." I pointed a finger at the High Mother as I backed away.

She only watched, her brows drawn. I held her gaze for another moment and tore after Maverick.

I followed him deep into the woods, where he was keeping up with Jamey. She was surprisingly fast and agile. Maverick's giant step alone should have caught her by now.

We came up on the River Nord, and though I had nearly caught up, a horrible feeling started in my chest. Jamey was about to do something stupid.

She ran full force at the river, which was wide enough that no one in their right mind would attempt to jump it. But clearly, that was her intent as she barrelled toward the edge.

It happened in slow motion. Jamey's feet left the ground, and suddenly, she was flying through the air. Maverick, three steps behind, leaped after her, but he did not reach the air. Instead, he slammed into it with as much force as if he were ramming into a brick wall. He crumpled, his body dropping to the water's edge.

Jamey landed on the other side with a thump, falling to her knees and rolling. She got to her feet slowly, although much quicker than Maverick, who was groaning as he pulled himself to his hands and knees.

I slowed when I reached him, testing the air with my hands. They hit a barrier and bounced back toward me.

"Your boundary magic won't last long, Jamey!" I called across the water.

They required proximity to hold, and she was about to take off again.

Dress torn, hair wild, she laughed open-mouthed. "You might want to reconsider pursuing me. Your palace is about to be visited by a few of my friends. It needs all the help it can get." And then she took off at a run, disappearing into the trees.

Maverick swore colourfully as he got to his feet. "Foul, wretched thing."

"Can you run?"

He nodded, shaking his head to clear the wobbles. One of his bones cracked. We started off at a run along the side of the River Nord.

"Like I said, my body's always ready."

THIRTY-THREE

MAISIE
MOULDED

The alcohol in my cup did nothing to soothe the storm inside. Unlike the rest of the abnormally large group of patrons in the Unclaimed Land, letting go did not come naturally to me.

Blame it on the years of servitude with no days off.

Even on the horizon of the biggest war this realm had ever seen, no one seemed as nervous as I felt. A bonfire had been constructed in the middle of the camp with flames dancing high above even the tallest heads. Groupings had formed all around with Folk of all different types mingling, but I chose a log farther away, where the heat of the fire dimmed before it tickled my shins.

The wood groaned as weight shifted it beside me. Diana sat down, perched like only a princess could. I doubted she was even aware of it—that unnatural, straight, poised back and uptilted chin. She sat with her hands in her lap, folded around a twin cup to mine. The only difference was, while mine had a few sips left, hers was untouched.

Staring into the flames, she sighed deeply. "How are you faring with all this?"

I answered with a sigh of my own. "How are *you*?" I countered.

Diana laughed humourlessly. "I feel like this isn't real. It has to be a dream."

"You never thought you would be leading an army made of up Folk we'd only ever heard stories of in a war against your mother?" I clucked my tongue drily. "Come on. Even I saw that one coming."

She smiled, and I was happy to see it was a real one. "You're right. How could I have been so blind?"

We sat for a few moments in easy peace—until shouting at the other end of the bonfire caught our attention. A group of males—easily recognizable as Unclaimed patrons in their ratty tunics—were getting rowdy as they passed a large slab of meat around.

"How can they be so cavalier?" It was not meant as an admission, but my voice gave away the irritation biting at me.

Diana watched them. "It's okay to be scared. I am. I think they are too. I don't blame them for taking a normal, happy moment when it comes. They are so rare these days."

Tears pricked at the back of my eyes, but I blinked them away. Her words lifted a strange weight that had been pulling on my heart. I didn't have to feel guilty for finding a bright spot in these dark times. Not when those moments were the only thing that kept me trudging through the night.

Diana scooted closer and took my hand in hers. "We'll make it through this. I have to believe that. I *do* believe that." Her arm stood out against mine, almost wholly covered in swirling lines of ink that seemed to move as she did.

She caught me staring and flexed her arm, twisting it so I could see more angles without letting go of my hand. "Weird, right?"

A laugh escaped me, so unexpected that it came out more as a cough. "You could say that."

She smiled. "Strangely, it's one of the only things keeping me sane right now. It's always there, you know? And no matter what, no matter how far we are or how much danger we're in, I always know that Spense is all right."

I took a breath. "It's still weird for me to hear you talk about him like that. I hated him for taking you away. I think … I think I still do."

Diana squeezed my hand. "I know you went through a lot when I left. Believe me, I didn't want to go. I never wanted to leave Eira. But I'm glad I did. Even though we're in this huge mess because of me, I really do think there is a reason for it all." She twisted her shoulders to look me straight in the eye. "Maisie, I'm terribly angry with Spense right now, but I really do love him. I know it'll take time, but I would like for us all to be friends. You're both so important to me."

Slowly, I nodded. Diana was one of the biggest parts of my life, and thanks to that tattoo, Spense would always be a part of hers. I couldn't have one without the other. And she was important enough that I could at least pretend to tolerate him for the time being.

"I've seen how he dotes on you. I'll give him a chance—only because he treats you how you deserve to be treated. Actually, I'm surprised he separated from you willingly."

For the first time, Diana took a long swig from her cup. "If you knew Urdan, you would understand why it's so important that we find him," she said darkly. "He's trouble. Something we already have enough of right now."

The storied Unseelie king, known for his ferocious and insatiable nature, was not someone I ever wanted to come face-to-face with. I was in full support of keeping him locked up.

"Besides"—Diana's voice lightened as she bumped my arm—"we can handle being on our own, can't we? Even though I have a feeling you're feeling the same way I am about being separated from your guy." She gave me a knowing look.

My heart rate spiked. "He's not mine," I muttered, heat blooming in my cheeks.

Someone like Aedan could never be with someone like me even if he thought he wanted it right now. That truth was a sharp thorn in my heart.

Diana laughed gently. "So, it's true! Maisie, I love the idea of you and Aedan together. I don't know why I didn't see it earlier!"

I drained my cup. "I know why—because I'm a servant and he'll be the captain of the army. How could anyone believe that a decorated, respected member of the royal court would be interested in a lowly maidservant?" The words came out bitter and harsh, and although I meant them, I immediately regretted speaking them aloud. It somehow made them real, true, as if I was daring the universe to prove me otherwise.

She stared into the fire, eyebrows pinched together. She took a deep breath and chugged the rest of her full drink, cringing when she swallowed.

"Listen." She turned to me again. "I'm not going to say that I haven't enabled my own share of prejudice. I was raised a certain way, whether it was intended or not. And I have to credit my time away from Eira for making me see how wrong I was. If I become queen—*when* I become queen—things will be different. There is change coming, starting with equality for all. I don't want there to be a hierarchy, a ladder that doesn't allow for movement between rungs. And the best part of that is, my most important circle of fae already thinks the same way I do. That includes Aedan. I've known him almost his whole life. When he sets his mind to something, he will see it through. If he's told you how he feels about you, it's not a lick of a lie. He's honest and loyal and committed. It doesn't matter his status or yours. He won't let what others think stand in the way of what he wants."

"I don't even know that he wants me." Somehow, that didn't feel like a lie.

"You say you've seen how Spense reacts around me. It's impossible to ignore, right? I've seen it in Aedan. It's like every move he makes, he's calculating for you too. He might not be as obvious, but when you've known him as long as I have, it's clear how he cares for you. Before we went to the palace, you should have seen him. He was not letting any of us forget about you. Not that I would let that happen either," Diana added.

I looked down, my borrowed boots scuffed and dusty. "I'm scared."

"Has he done something—"

"No, no, it's not that. Actually, it's the opposite. He—he's so good to me. I haven't had a lot of positive male experiences in my life. I'm scared that I'll finally believe it's real, and then I'll lose it." The words shuddered out of me, loosening my chest as they flew away, dissipating into the air.

"I understand that. You know I do."

The difference was, she had gotten through her heartbreak and found her soulmate. That meant something. It was real. It wasn't just for fun or to pass time. They were in it for life, and they were one of the few lucky ones who could trust in that.

My arm was bare, as was Aedan's. It terrified me to think that, one day, his tattoo might show up for someone else. It terrified me even more that I wanted it to be me.

"I don't know if there's anything I can truly say that will make you feel better. But just know that love is worth it. It's worth the pain, the heartbreak, the days of darkness. *It's worth it.* And you will find it. If I have to track down Gaia myself and demand to know who your soulmate is, I'll do it." Diana straightened, her posture looser since she'd finished her drink. "Now, with all that heavy stuff out of the way, I want to know *everything.* Starting with how it began between you two."

Despite myself, I smiled. It had been too long since I had indulged in these talks with her—and so rarely were they about me. "Well, I think you'll be happy to know it started while we were scheming to rescue you."

She put a hand over her heart. "I'm going to take credit for this forever."

I laughed. "I don't know. It just was so easy. Unexpected. But, oh, did he tell you about his tryst with Jamey? That definitely slowed things down."

"Jamey Pinois." Diana shook her head. "I can't believe what she did. Or that he would fall for that. She's a better liar than we all thought."

"She's dangerous. The queen has been using her as her personal right hand. She means to replace you with her."

Diana looked down at her feet, hunching inward. "If that was what the ancestors wanted, then I would oblige. But I know it is not. It only makes my job more difficult."

I squeezed her hand. "Anything to lift that weight off your shoulders, you know I will do."

She shook her head, as if to clear the shadows again, a somewhat-forced smile returning. "Okay, I'm curious. Aedan—good kisser?"

My cheeks warmed, and I had to look away for a moment. "*Good* might be too small of a word."

Diana laughed, her hands coming together joyfully. "I knew it! How long has this been going on?"

My hands moved on the cup, and I wished there were still drink left inside. "I mean, we've only kissed the one time. It's kind of nice actually that we became sort of friends first while we were conspiring. Although I think … I think I had feelings for him since the beginning."

Diana smiled, and it was so radiant and happy that it almost made me forget why I was being cautious with my heart in the first place. She made me want to believe in love and happy endings.

"But enough about me." I pointed my cup at her. "Why are you 'terribly angry' with Spense?"

She pursed her lips. "He's complicated. Since his memories returned, he's been struggling with who he is. I think … he wasn't very good before coming here. And he's trying to let go of that—I truly believe he is. But sometimes, moments come up where I feel like I don't even know him."

I didn't like the male, but I would still try to help Diana through this. "It seems unfair to ask him to let go entirely of who he was before Eira."

"I've never asked him to be anyone or any way. I just wasn't expecting the real him to be so impulsive and easily aggravated."

"There's a lot of pressure on you both right now. I mean no offense, but not everyone is as pure and squeaky clean as you. We're not all heirs to our own realms. Just because you haven't outright asked him to change doesn't mean he doesn't feel the expectation to."

Diana raised her eyebrows. "Have you always been so wise? Or perhaps I have not been as observant as I thought."

You've been moulded by the palace to look like a caring ruler without committing to the role fully, I thought. *But you're breaking that mould every day.* I did not voice those potentially emotionally damaging words. She didn't need that.

Instead, I said, "I have only recently found my voice."

"I'm sorry if I ever made you feel like you had to live up to a standard, Maisie. Actually, not *if.* I know I must have. But I want us to be equals, moving forward."

"Don't forget that I was a willing servant, Diana. I was happy to serve you, and I still am proud of it. But I'm happy to be your friend too."

"You've always been my friend."

I rested my head on Diana's shoulder, and we watched the Shynin residents, old and new, enjoy their night around the fire. At one point, music started, and we were pulled into a trot step with some rather dashing elves.

We all knew that there might be war tomorrow. So, we enjoyed tonight.

THIRTY-FOUR

SPENSE
WHAT PEACE MEANS

"Another dead end."

Pissed off, Badras kicked the nearest thing he could find—a loose stone. It flew through the air, landing in the River Nord with a splash. Now that the snow was melting, the ice on top had broken apart and softened. Soon, the rushing waves would be too strong to be held back by a layer of ice.

"We're getting closer," Sorin consoled. "Look, this was used as a firepit." He gestured to a pile of rocks that had been fashioned into a circle with black ash in the centre.

I stepped forward to inspect it. "Feels like his magic. But a fire right on the riverbank? It's so visible. I know he's not all there anymore, but he's not stupid."

"He's leading us on a wild goose chase," cursed Badras.

"Or," Sorin mused, "he wants us to find him."

"It would explain why no one else is able to pick up any trace of him." I crossed my arms. "But I don't like the idea of him having the advantage over us."

Sorin sat on the edge of the river, the grass now visible as it melted into the water. "I don't trust anything to do with Urdan. If he's not alone, then we need to be prepared to come back with more forces."

Badras and I both joined our brother. The grass was a bit damp, but the sight of it after entering Eira in a tundra was like a breath of fresh air. Warmer air too.

"I don't know if I can live in the cold all the time," Sorin admitted. "I've been in a desert my whole life. I think my bones might be at risk of splintering from all the shivering I've been doing."

Badras grunted, smiling slightly. "I won't miss the sand—that's for sure. There's only so much of it you can take before it's as annoying as the Night Pixies."

"And no humans." I pulled my knees up to my chest, letting a Northern breeze lift my hair. Sure, it was cold. But it felt like home now.

"No humans," repeated Sorin.

"Just a senile old male, a corrupt queen, and a divided kingdom," Badras growled.

For the first time that I could remember, I laughed. Somewhere in my magic, Diana was lightening too. Knowing that she was finding a reason to smile made it easier for me to take steps further and further away from her every day.

"Do you think our Folk will be happy here? That they will follow Diana as their queen?"

Sorin paused before answering, "There will be an adjustment period, no doubt. But look at this land. It's beautiful and accommodating. And most importantly, it will be *safe*. When they see that Diana led them here, fought for their peace, they will happily follow her. She's worthy of the title, and she's kind."

My throat burned with pride at Sorin's words.

"Plus," added Badras, "they'll have you as their king."

I jolted in surprise. It was perfectly reasonable, just not something I had put together on my own. Eira felt like it belonged in Diana's hands, not mine. I hadn't thought about ruling since before I lost my memories.

"Do you think we'll know peace when it comes? Or have we been fighting so long that the concept will be lost to us?"

If my brothers were surprised by my wonderings, they did not show it.

"That is something I have often pondered," Sorin admitted. "I suppose we have to decide what peace means to us, and then it will be easier to recognize it."

Badras lifted a shoulder. "I don't think there will ever be peace entirely. Isn't that the point of this whole balance thing? Without the bad, there's no good—all that crap."

"So, there's no rest for us—is that what you're saying? There will always be some war to fight because without battles, there's no triumph?"

"I didn't say that."

"To me, peace means no longer waking up every morning with fear in my heart," Sorin said, wistful as he stared over the water. "That even if there are struggles and times of strife, it will all be manageable because I know my daughter can go outside and play without an armed guard."

His words settled me, as they often did. Peace was relative—I knew that—but I could find mine. Whatever it might be.

"That's why we call you the wise brother," Badras said, clapping Sorin on the back heartily.

"Thank the gods," I agreed. "We'd be lost without you."

"Spense," Sorin started with a tone that I knew meant he was about to get sentimental.

But we were interrupted by a flashing light in front of our eyes.

I squinted at the brightness as a pixie came into focus. Her little wings flapped as fast as a hummingbird's, and she had pointed features and an undeniable glimmer.

"Oh!" she squeaked. "I am so delighted that it worked!"

Sorin smiled, holding out his palm so that she might land in it. "I'm so glad to hear that, Josette. It was very impressive."

The Floral Pixie preened, delicate wings slowing as she stood in Sorin's hand. Her skin and hair were the same rose pink as her dress, which flared out at her hips. "Pixies have been without our jumping abilities for far too long. We were meant for this land indeed."

Even Badras, the perpetual grump, couldn't fight his smile.

"Do you have news for me?" Sorin asked.

Josette nodded, looking around the empty riverbank, as if she did not want to be overheard. "Olys is tracking a trail not too far from here. He seemed encouraged by it, although it was hard to get anything out of him. Nasty attitude." She sniffed.

"Don't take it personally, Josie," Sorin reassured her. "He's like that with everyone. Would you be able to point us in the right direction? We've hit a dead end here, so we might as well join him if he's close."

Josette nodded eagerly. "I'll take you there myself!"

Without warning, she disappeared with a *poof*, only for that bright light to pop up along the tree line. A jingling noise carried through the air, as if she was beckoning us to follow.

"Hopefully, Olys has something good." Sorin stood up and brushed the dirt from his pants, and we did the same, following the pixie deeper into the forest.

THIRTY-FIVE

AEDAN
WILD FERVOUR

Blood spattered across my chest as I ran through the thick of the fight. I had no armour, so the warmth of it seeped through my thin running shirt. It went against every instinct to run through the fray instead of fighting alongside my soldiers, but I needed to get to Ryen. And a weapon wouldn't hurt either.

Nordians and soldiers blended together as they worked to defend the front of the palace. The enemy did not have any identifiable colours or insignia; in fact, the fae used old-fashioned weapons, their clothing battered and torn. Most had heavy chain mail, the clinking sound mixing with metal scraping, shouts, and the horrifying thud of bodies hitting the ground.

They seemed evenly matched, quick and nimble. Whomever this was, they fought in relative organization. They came in a steady stream from the forest surrounding the palace, the uninhabited wild that led to the mountains.

It didn't make any sense. This army shouldn't exist.

But they were very real—and more importantly, a very real threat.

And I knew in my bones that Vera was responsible.

I charged through, dodging fights and helping as much as I dared to without engaging in my own battles. I tripped a hulking fae who had been holding his own against two Nordians as I slipped past, and the stumble was enough to give our side the opening needed to incapacitate him.

Without warning, an assailant jumped into my path, waving a sword. She rushed forward, swinging in a large arc. I ducked, feeling the air from her blade *whoosh* across the top of my hair. With her arm stretched out, I popped back up and aimed a kick straight at her chest. She fell backward, and I kicked her weapon across the cobblestone before continuing on my way.

The sun was warm today, hot enough that I could feel it for the first time in what felt like years. I did not have the luxury of enjoying the welcome change; all I could do was hope not to slip as I narrowly avoided the increasing puddles.

Along my way up the path, Mikale caught my arm. "Ryen went to the roof for a perimeter scan!" he yelled before jumping back into the fray.

When I reached the doors to the palace, I slipped between two of my soldiers and into the foyer. Outside of the melee, the noise was muted, making my ears ring from the sudden lack of it. I charged up the steps, my footfalls echoing, and slipped into the servant corridor to access the stairs to the roof.

There were six sets of stairs that led up, and I made it onto the fifth landing when the door to the roof slammed open. Ryen burst from it, his longsword in hand.

"What happened with Maverick?" he asked, barely pausing to wait for me as he tore back down the stairs.

I kept stride, my quads burning. "He joined the fight, but he likely won't get past the outer edges. He took a hard hit when we were chasing Jamey."

Ryen blew out a breath. "I wondered what happened on your run.

Did you get her?"

"No."

He cursed. "They've got us nearly surrounded. The stables give us a wall of protection, but every other angle is being attacked. The archers took out a few at the beginning, but once we started close combat, I called them off to join on the ground."

"Who are they? How can we have not known of an army of this skill and size?"

My second shook his head as we ran through the halls of the palace toward the weapons room behind the queen's office. "They came nearly as soon as you left. We were already surrounded. They knew how to get past the wards in the forest."

"It has to be Vera."

Ryen nodded. "I think that's most likely. As to where she acquired this on such short notice, I'm at a loss. Kashdan would have given her whatever arms he had, but even then, there wouldn't be this many. Maybe she's been building this in secret for a while."

We were missing something huge here. I racked my brain while we rummaged through the weapons room, adding various blades to our bodies. I found my weapon of choice—trenching knives—and slid them into the belt I'd donned with sheaths on both sides for exactly this.

"What's the plan, Captain?"

I hesitated for a split second, the title making me think of Embris. What would he do in this situation?

My father's voice echoed in my mind. *"Weakness comes from the unwillingness to do whatever it takes to win."*

The words made my stomach sour, and I pushed all thoughts of him aside. I could do this without him.

"Bring the iron walls down around the palace entries and drive the forces toward the forest. If you see anyone on the other side who looks like they're giving orders, I want to know about it."

Ryen nodded, recognition flashing in his eyes. "You want to send them into the forest and then come from behind with the cavalry."

The sandwich. It was harder than just driving them away, and it was an act of finality. There would be no escape routes open.

Thankfully, for them, I wanted surrender, not a massacre. I wanted to speak to someone who could give me definitive answers.

"If we can spare the arms, that's the end goal."

Strapped up, we started back for the battle.

"Send a runner to Shynin, requesting Diana's immediate aid."

Ryen nodded. "Done. Although, given the travel time, the best we can hope for is their arrival tomorrow."

"It will have to do. We can hold that long, and if it starts to go south, she'll bring the fresh troops we need."

"And if she doesn't come?"

"She will."

I leaped from the front steps of the palace, flinging myself back into the battle. The sounds were as familiar to me as a lullaby, the smell of dirt and blood and sweat the very scent I had grown up with.

Nordians were easy to spot, their giant forms and warrior paint sticking out against the bland grey armour. They fought with pickaxes and other various long weapons that kept the enemy far from them, and those that got past the staffs were welcomed with skilled hand-to-hand combat. They were deadly.

Maverick himself stood out to me, as steady on his feet as he had claimed he would be. He showed no signs of fatigue as his menacing scythe swept through the crowd like a silent wind. When the body before him crumpled to the ground, he looked up at me, grinning wickedly.

I used his wild fervour to fuel my own as I lunged forward with my knife.

THIRTY-SIX

DIANA
UNASSUMING

I was dreaming of waltzes and rum and elfish tails when the screaming woke me.

Jumping to my feet and grabbing Soulweaver from its place under my cot, I was out of the tent before rational thought could settle.

Bodies ran about, Freya in the thick of it. She ordered fae left and right, and when she locked eyes with me, she beckoned urgently.

"What's going on?"

"The palace sent a runner—they're under attack. I'm gathering the guard. They await your orders." Freya held up a parchment with Aedan's signature on the bottom.

Dread washed over me. "Attacked by whom? My mother can't have mustered up a force so soon."

"It doesn't say, only that they're requesting immediate backup."

Nodding, I tried to enter the place in my mind where I could put my fears aside to focus. *Breathe*, I told myself. *You might not have Spense, or Sorin, or Badras to help you, but you have Aedan. And you will not give up the palace.*

"Leave behind enough guards to keep a safe perimeter around Shynin. The rest come with me. Are the horses being saddled?"

Freya nodded. "But I'm afraid there aren't enough for all the soldiers we've amassed. And we'll need a few in case of emergency. Half will have to go on foot."

Not ideal. "The drakes won't be able to fly through the snow either. So, those on foot will have to be the most fit. I want a party of healers sent out tonight, to wait in the city of Nevelyn for assistance into the palace."

"Understood," Freya confirmed. "What of the party of researchers? They left last night. We could retrieve them in less than a day."

I paused. I wasn't sure how much of the whole prophecy business I believed, but if it had even the smallest chance of being something useful, then we had to pursue it.

"No, let them continue on." I prayed to Gaia that I wasn't making a mistake.

It took longer to prepare than it would have with Aedan's practiced army, but we were en route to the North as quickly as we could go. With half the army on foot, it slowed us significantly, but I was unwilling to ride ahead into an unknown battle and leave the rest to fare for themselves upon arrival. Aedan would have to hold the line.

I rode in front, Finnvarra's chestnut mane flapping as we crossed the Northern border. The snow was slushier than the last time we had been in it, easier to push through, which was a relief. I spared a glance behind me, at the group fanned out, following in my tracks. Seelie, Unseelie, goblins, elves, gnomes, dryads, those without any magic, all carrying their weapon of choice, all in mismatched armour. It wasn't shiny or synchronized, but our unassuming look would be our biggest advantage.

By the time the sun came up, boasting a blue sky with streaks of red and pink, we were close enough to hear the yells of battle.

THIRTY-SEVEN

SPENSE
BEACON

Watching Olys interact with Josette was the most hilarious thing I had seen in a while.

She turned from rosy pink to tomato red when she got worked up, which had been constant since reuniting with Olys.

Josette had *popped* up right in front of his face, causing him to swear and fling his arms through the air wildly, one of them sending her flying into a nearby tree trunk. She screamed words at a decibel so high-pitched that it was unintelligible while hovering in the air, brushing herself off.

"Oh, it's you," Olys had mumbled when we came into view. "Did you send her? She's been pestering me all day."

"I have *not!*" Josette proclaimed.

"She's been very helpful," Sorin said to Olys. "She was kind enough to use her new jumping ability to lead us to you."

Josette crossed her arms, sniffing.

"I hadn't realized that you no longer possessed the ability to track your own brother," Olys snarked, "and that you had to rely on glorified woodland nymphs."

Josette had sputtered, "Well! I have never been so insulted in my *life!*" And then started to pelt acorns at Olys's face, at which point we had stepped in between the two.

The pixie now sat on Sorin's shoulder, sulking as Olys led us through the brush, tracking the trace of magic he'd picked up.

"It's getting stronger," Badras remarked. "I can feel it now too."

As the words left his mouth, I felt it. The trail that Urdan had left behind from using his magic as he went could only be described as oily.

Immediately, it sent a shiver of recognition through me, causing anger to flare up. "That's definitely him."

Olys glared over his shoulder. "Obviously. I know what I'm doing."

"You don't have to be rude." Josette sniffed daintily. "You must have been sick the day your brothers were taught proper manners."

"Not sick," he drawled. "Just didn't care."

"Now, that I believe," Josette muttered.

Badras rolled his eyes. "Children, please. Let's all get along."

I snorted. "Such eloquent words from the head of fae-folk relations."

He rounded on me, but we were interrupted by Olys halting abruptly. "Do you see that cave?"

Following his line of sight across the clearing, I nodded. It could have been easy to miss with trees positioned to hide it more and more as they grew, but the unmistakable slate-grey rock was there, tucked away behind some particularly thorny blackberry bushes.

I reached into my magic, sending a feeler out toward the cave. It only got halfway before I sucked it back, Urdan's magic strong and on alert. "He's in there."

"Let's go." Badras started to march forward, but Sorin caught his arm.

"Can we at least agree on a plan before we dive in headfirst?"

"Simple. We go in there, subdue him, drag him to this magic-blocking prison. It's four-to-one; he's not going to stand a chance."

"Five-to-one, thank you very much," Josette piped up.

We all ignored her.

"He *will* stand a chance, and you know it," Sorin warned. "We have no idea who or what he could have with him. Let's send Josette to scout."

The pixie stood up, cracking her neck.

Olys shook his head. "No way—"

The hair on the back of my neck stood up, and I whirled around. "What's that?"

Everyone stopped, the strange feeling buzzing through the air. If I really concentrated, it sounded almost like it had a pulse.

Josette waved her tiny hand. "Oh, those are my sisters." She smiled. "They're trying to send me a message."

She squinted her eyes in concentration, and the buzzing thankfully stopped as she listened intently.

"Did you know the pixies had these abilities?" I whispered to Badras.

"There were legends of what they used to possess the power to do," he answered. "I suspect a lot of legends will come to life now that the Folk are back where they belong."

"Which means our relationships with all Folk factions are incredibly important, moving forward," Sorin said quietly, sternly. His eyes were fixed on Olys, who nodded once.

"Oh dear," Josette said, her hands coming up to cover her mouth. "The message was from Shynin. The palace in—what was it, Neverlin? It's under attack. Diana is leading a group from the camp to help."

An attack on the palace? Impossible. How could Vera possibly retaliate that fast?

Diana wasn't ready.

"I have to go." I looked to the cave where my father was hiding out, my resolve faltering. Our plan was to head to the palace anyway, with Urdan in tow. "How long do you think it would take—"

"You go," Sorin cut in. "Take Bad. We can make a plan and get Urdan to the palace without you. If we rush into it now, we risk losing him."

I hesitated, but my brothers voiced their own agreement—Josette's as well, as unhelpful as it was—so Badras and I took off the way we had come.

Sparing another glance over my shoulder, I wished on all the gods to send them luck.

"They'll be fine," my brother said, leading us out of the tightly grown bush to where we had tied our horses. "We've been dealing with Urdan for longer than you've been alive."

Sometimes, I forgot that I was such a tiny blip of time compared to my brothers. They had seen the fall of our father and our kingdom as we receded from the humans. While they didn't have the magic that I did—the kind strong enough to match Urdan—they didn't need it.

Diana, on the other hand, did need me, no matter how much she tried to convince herself she could do it her way. She would realize that soon, and I would be there.

We mounted our horses and headed toward the river.

"Do you know where this palace is?" Badras asked, bumping up into a trot.

"I have a vague idea."

Truthfully, I had no clue where we were in relation to Nevelyn or how to get there. But when I reached down deep and tugged on the magic that entwined with Diana's, I was confident. She was my guiding light, a beacon leading me straight to her.

I let that take us all the way there.

THIRTY-EIGHT

DIANA
FAUX CIVILITY

There was nothing comforting about being back in the palace. What had once been a serene, lavish place was now contaminated with fear, blood, and death. If I could ever feel at home again here, it would be a miracle.

When we had arrived, the Shynin warriors eager to join the fray, the battle was waning. In fact, *waning* might be too small of a word. It had all but disappeared.

I found Aedan exactly where I'd expected him—pacing the front line on the forested side of the palace, watching the enemy retreat. His hand came up to scratch the back of his head absently.

"Seems like you didn't need me after all," I greeted.

Aedan turned, and he wore such a hardened expression that I almost didn't recognize him. His armour was blood-spattered, his hair spiked with sweat and dirt. "I don't get it. They were winning."

A live current of trepidation tunnelled through my veins. "What do you mean?"

He threw one of his short knives into the soft, muddy ground, where it sank in, handle just above the surface. "What I mean is that we were outnumbered and surrounded, being backed into the palace. Then, all at once, they retreated. It's as if they were told only to fight until dawn broke." His jaw worked as he stared into the trees.

"That's … troubling."

Aedan ran a hand through his hair. "You made good time at least. You must have left as soon as you got the message."

I nodded. "The volunteer warriors from Shynin are made up of many different styles, but they were all eager to help. They actually look disappointed now." I glanced over my shoulder, where the makeshift army I had marched with now mingled with the queen's army—and Nordians, which was a sight beyond startling.

"Well, I appreciate it anyway; we would have needed you."

"What's going on, Aedan? Where did this army come from that's not only strong, but also organized enough to outnumber both your soldiers *and* the Nordians? I thought losing the queen's army would cripple my mother—at least enough to buy us time."

He blew out a breath. "That's what I've been thinking about too. Unless you've somehow made another enemy this large, I don't see who else could be behind this."

And then, as if conjuring her from our words, Vera stepped out from the tree line.

My heart fell to my stomach.

My mother's eyes bored into mine, icy and dangerous. She was barefoot, gliding toward us with the grace of falling snow. The air she possessed was crackling with electricity. A stark difference to the strong but kindhearted mother I had grown up with.

She stopped at the edge of the forest, almost directly on the line that separated it from palace property. The dawn's pink and orange rays coloured the sky, the sunlight landing on her in a hazy glow.

"Diana," she said, smiling widely. Too widely. "I was hoping we might have another chat."

My throat was so tight, my mouth dry. I had never been unable to formulate words to my mother, but my brain was spinning like a pinwheel, offering no options, except, "Um," and, "Uh," and, "Er."

I could feel my heartbeat in my throat, fast and erratic.

A hand grasped my arm, and I spun around to see Spense, dishevelled and panting, staring right back at me. His magic enveloped mine, and my brain was clear. He ran his hand down my arm to link his fingers through my own, and I took a deep breath.

He nodded once, an encouragement and a comfort.

I looked back to my mother, whose head had tilted as she watched us like a bird stared from the safety of its branch.

"Are you to blame for this?" I swept my arm wide, but her gaze didn't follow over the mess of a battlefield between us.

She kept her eyes locked on mine.

"I raised no weapon today. This is the first I've seen of my palace since being untimely chased from it. You've certainly failed with the upkeep." Her voice was as familiar as ever, and the hardened edge brought me back to being an adolescent, flinching as she'd reprimanded me when all I ever aimed to do was please her.

"That does not mean she isn't responsible," Spense growled from my side.

"This isn't your palace anymore," I said, heart racing as I willed my voice not to shake. "That became evident the minute your army turned against you."

Vera bared her teeth in a sneer. "Those disloyal brutes have not been mine since your friend Aedan got it in his head that he wanted to play rebel." She waved a hand. "No matter. Their deflection to you no longer bothers me. Rather, it makes the sides a little more even." She grinned. "Emphasis on little."

"Since when are we on opposite sides, Mother? All I want is peace. I'll let you be queen still. We don't have to fight."

From within my magic, I felt Spense's churn angrily. His entire side was stiff, his jaw clenched. I tried to send calming waves his way. The last thing I needed was for him to blow up right now.

My mother raised her eyebrows mockingly. "*Let me be queen?* Your arrogant insolence has gone too far. I was chosen by the ancestors. There is no question. I was the queen, I am the queen, I will forever be the queen."

"You were never going to be queen forever, Mother. I would have been crowned after you. The ancestors chose me too, remember?" As soon as the words were out of my mouth, I knew they were a mistake.

Whatever leash Vera had on her rage snapped. The power that flowed from her was palpable, strong and angry and incredibly cold. She stepped forward, her hair whipping through whatever wind her magic was creating. Not wind, but flame. White fire that licked out, tasting the air. She was unrecognizable.

Only, I realized, she *was* recognizable.

But not as my mother.

Her auburn hair cascaded down her back and front, long enough to reach her lap. A crown of emeralds sat upon her head, commanding power from the room. Her face was concealed by a white wolf mask, leaving only her eyes in view, which were strikingly blue.

No. It couldn't be.

Jweira glared at the Seelie Queen, her stature never failing. "And if I don't?"

"Then, you, too, will become a casualty in my war on the Unseelie." The queen turned, her hair swishing as she stalked back to her throne and sat down.

It wasn't possible.

The Seelie Queen grew enraged. Red flame burst out of her, giving her the appearance of being on fire.

But it *was* possible. In a horrible, sickly, gut-wrenching way, I knew it was.

The last thing I saw before the world melted around me was the Seelie Queen's head turning directly toward me and staring me down with her eyes of ice.

"It's you," I breathed. I felt as if I were tumbling through time, unable to hold on to anything or slow my descent. Wildly, I fumbled at my neck, only to grasp air, not the chunky emerald I had expected.

Vaguely, I was aware of Spense trying to get my attention, through magic and by repeating my name over and over.

Blinking, I lifted my gaze to him.

"Where did you just go?" His concern radiated off him. "I could barely feel you."

I sucked in a shuddering breath, looking back to Vera, who grinned wickedly, and in that moment, my heart shattered. She knew that I knew who she was. And she was enjoying my miserable revelation.

"I am the true queen of this realm. I always have been, and I always will be. For millennia, I have conquered this land, bending it to my will. There is nothing you can do to release my hold. Eira is mine." She seethed.

Spense squeezed my fingers. Fear had started to pool in my stomach, but he held me strong.

My mother, the abhorrent evil that had split this land so long ago, stared me down. "You won't win this war, Diana. You didn't the first time either." The magic around her started to pulse, her eyes flickering with the fire that engulfed her. "I will not tolerate insolence on my land, even from my own blood. But I am not without mercy." She smirked, faux civility dripping from her words. "So, I offer you a choice: secede to me, or I end you all. It will be no great problem for me, I assure you. The army you saw today was only half of what I've amassed."

End you all. The words bounced and echoed in my head, digging deeper into the cracks of my broken heart. This was not my mother.

It was some shell of a being, twisted and wicked.

She started to slink backward into the forest. "You have until the next sunup to decide."

THIRTY-NINE

SPENSE
LOW MARGIN FOR ERROR

In the orb-lit library, there was a certain peace, even considering the impending doom.

Diana had held herself together as long as she could, shouldering bravely in front of both armies as well as the officials who had stayed behind and now sought her leadership. I had steered her away from the battle—the second one I'd now witnessed her emerge from distraught—and didn't stop moving until her legs gave out.

There, in the hallway between the ballroom and the formal dining room, we both sat on the floor, and I held her as she worked through the bomb that had been dropped on her. She didn't cry, as I'd thought she might, instead staring blankly and tunnelling deep within her magic to clear her mind.

When she finally rose, it was on steady legs, and she led me wordlessly to where the others had gathered. I mentally thanked whoever had decided on the library instead of the council room. Diana needed a place that was untainted by her mother.

My brothers had returned from the Unclaimed Land in good time; it was a surprise to see them seated along with Meske, Aedan, his second, and a hulking male dressed in unfamiliar battle leathers and colours. The plush, overstuffed chairs had never seen so much use, and even then, some seats from the dining room had been brought in to accommodate the large number of bodies. On the level above the seating, in and around the towering bookshelves, stood the officials of Eira; some I recognized from my time in the palace, and others were new.

One thing was certain: all the fae in the room were here to fight.

The quiet chatter silenced when we entered the room.

Diana's gaze swept over everyone, and she took a deep breath. "So, here we are."

The sentiment was echoed back a few times, bringing whispers of smiles to some faces.

Aedan, sitting on an ottoman with his ankles locked together, cleared his throat. "What's the plan?"

"I could ask you the same thing," she replied on a shaky laugh.

Aedan gestured to the group assembled, his arms outstretched. "Everyone is here because we all follow *you*. You were chosen by our ancestors to lead. If you say you trust these Folk, that they are necessary for the success of Eira, then we will uphold that peace however you need."

Diana's appreciation showed on her face, clear as day. "Okay then."

Wordlessly, the room listened raptly as Diana shared everything we now knew. Everything about Vera's true identity, the ultimatum she'd dropped, and all the things in between.

When she was finished, she sat with a definitive *plop* on the chair Meske had quietly brought over for her. I stood behind her, as I always would.

"Vera is the Seelie Queen?" Aedan finally said, his shock surprisingly well maintained.

"Seems tyrannical parents aren't that rare after all," Badras murmured.

There was a split second where he tensed, waiting for a tiny but mighty elbow in the gut, and his face when he realized it wouldn't come was soul-crushing.

"Nice of her to give us time to stew in the decision," Aedan said drily. "If she had the forces ready, why risk us having the time to plan?"

Badras said, "Dramatics."

At the same time, I said, "She's stalling."

Diana ran a hand through her hair, the regularly shining strands limp and dirty. "Unfortunately, Badras is right. She told me herself she wants to give us a sense of 'even sides.' She's over eight thousand years old, and she has an army twice the size of ours—more skilled too."

"I beg to differ," scoffed the giant male in battle leathers.

"Nordians, vicious as they are, make up less than a quarter of our forces."

I eyed the male. I had never met a Nordian, but despite that, he fit the description of the warrior tribe perfectly.

"Surrendering is out of the question for us," Sorin said, heads swivelling in his direction. "The Unseelie and the Folk did not endure millennia of hatred and war to roll over to a new threat. We have nothing left to lose."

"I assure you, surrender is the farthest thing from my mind," Diana said firmly. "My mother will only use glamours and tricks to make Eira believe her narrative. Clearly, she's been doing it for years already. We fight for everyone to know the truth."

"How did she do it?" Olys mused. "She had the power of Jweira, sure, but I recall you saying that the emerald disappeared after the fae were separated. Where did she get all that power from? Glamours of the size she created are no easy feat, even with allies."

Diana paused. "Honestly, I'm not sure. I remember my grandmother, Maeve, so vividly as the queen during her time and how she would openly disagree with my mother. If Vera's truly been the one behind this for generations, then she must have had some kind of control over them. But as far as I'm aware, she never tried to control me—at least not in a magical sense." She chewed on the inside of her cheek. "And why did the ancestors not warn me during my ascension?"

"We might never know. What's important right now is our plan of action," Badras put in with a tone that suggested we move along.

"Knowing Vera's capabilities and patterns is a valuable weapon toward defeating her," Aedan argued.

"If you have months." Badras crossed his arms, giant bicep muscles bulging across his chest. "I hate to burst your *captain of the army* bubble, but I've been doing this a lot longer than you. If we waste our precious few hours trying to spy on someone who's infallible, we'll lose."

Aedan readied himself for an angry retort, but Sorin jumped in before he could. "Diana has the most intel on Vera's abilities, and even then, the information is compromised now that we know she's a highly skilled liar. While it would be ideal to spend time learning her weaknesses, it's true that we must plan with what we've been given. What are your thoughts on this?"

To my surprise, he directed the last question at me.

I cleared my throat. "I agree. Alwyn's drake unit should be able to fly again soon now that the weather's warming. I can find a suitable rider to lead them." My throat burned as I thought of the only drake rider I really wanted and how I wished for her input. "The only issue with the drakes is that if the battle is brought within close range of the palace, they'll be useless unless we're considering friendly fire."

Diana shook her head. "We'll have to draw the battle somewhere open."

"Open?" Badras snorted. "Good luck. This place is absolutely *covered* in trees. I wouldn't be comfortable with a cavalry, let alone an air force."

Internally, I chuckled. Badras had lived in a desert for two thousand years. It was no wonder he felt stifled here.

"Our cavalry is well accustomed to forests," Aedan's second said, a touch of pride in his voice. "But an open space is optimal. Perhaps we can lead them to Silver Lake."

"That might actually be perfect, Ryen," Diana said slowly. The wheels in her head were practically visible as they turned and turned. "I forgot about it entirely. There are trees, of course—it's a forest after all—but the lake is fed from River Nord. There's a huge clearing around it, made from when it overflows after heavy rain. If we can bring the battle there, that'll be the most open spot we have without travelling south for days."

Slowly, the room began nodding collectively.

One of the officials I didn't recognize piped up, "How will we lead her there? If we wait for her to find us, we'll leave Nevelyn unguarded."

"I know we can't spare many arms, but I would never leave the citizens without protection," Diana vowed. "We'll have to stage it. She'll come to the palace first to see if I've considered her offer and attack from there. She'll likely have it surrounded, and it will be hard for us to break through the lines." Her voice rose, getting faster as an idea hit her. "If we set up the armies farther into Nevelyn, we could march from behind her forces. It'll be risky at first, but they'll have to turn around, and then we can lead them to the lake."

"How far is the Silver Lake from here?" Sorin asked.

"About an hour on foot," supplied Ryen.

Sorin considered this. "It's possible. Leaves us a low margin for error though."

Badras grinned. "That's how we live our life, brother."

"So, we have the drakes wait there until there's a clear shot," Diana continued, almost oblivious to everyone as she worked through her thoughts. "Can we count on the pegasi joining us in the sky?"

The Nordian smiled wickedly. "They have missed the taste of blood."

"What if we placed kelpies *in* Silver Lake?" Olys suggested curiously.

"Drop our enemies into the water, and those bastards will do the work for us." Badras grinned. "Nice idea, Ollie."

Our brother shot him a glare at the unwanted nickname.

Diana shook her head. "What if our own forces end up falling in? Or dropping in the lake from the sky? I won't risk the loss of our own, especially not once the enemy sees that the kelpies won't discriminate their meals."

Badras looked mildly disappointed.

"Besides, I've already arranged for their delivery in the South. They should be arriving within the next day or two, which means it will take far too long to reroute them."

"Speaking of the South," said the official from Leo's court, "there has been quite a flood of new support, and another group of soldiers arrived last night."

My eyebrows rose. Leo had been so adamant on his court conducting their own alliances. "What spurred that on?"

"From what I've heard, Vera attempted to … gain some of their support by force. It wasn't received well."

Vera would be her own ruin. I relished in watching her crumble.

"Do we have any leads on where Embris might be?" Diana

asked, directing it toward Aedan and Ryen. "His expertise would be extremely helpful, seeing as he's been at my mother's side for nearly twenty years. Him being missing is extremely unusual. If Vera's not holding him, where is he? It's not like him to stay behind during this kind of fight."

Aedan drew in a great breath. "I've wondered that too. If he's not with Vera, he's likely dead. Pursuing him would be a waste of resources."

The room tensed slightly. Strangely, I understood him.

Diana studied him for a beat before nodding. "So be it."

Whatever was going to be said next was lost to the wind as the door to the library slammed open with a surprising force.

All those armed—nearly everyone in the room—jumped to their feet immediately, only to pause in confusion. The intruder was tiny, hosting a head full of flaming red hair, and had her hands on her hips, staring down the room as if she were an angry mother.

FORTY

DIANA
TRANSLATOR

"**S**hela!" I jumped to my feet in time to be nearly barrelled over by my old friend.

When she pulled away, she gave everyone in the room a once-over, pausing to wink at Aedan. The sheer unabashed way she swept her gaze over the most important fae in Eira was so completely *Shela*.

"I see my invite was lost in the mail." She tsked.

"It's a long way to the City of Scholars. Easy to get lost," I teased back. "What are you doing here?"

"You honestly didn't think you could send an honest-to-Gaia *goblin* to the Academy in search of me, give me a prophecy in a long-dead language that might save the realm, and I wouldn't show up to debrief you in person, did you?" She raised an eyebrow. "Do you even know me at all?"

"That door slam was certainly on brand," Spense said. "And you do have a habit of showing up unannounced."

Shela nodded exasperatedly. "See? He gets me."

I opened my mouth to assure her that I'd indeed planned on visiting her once my life was no longer held hostage by war, but she cut me off.

"No time for apologies. I'm here on important business after all." She pulled the aged, rolled-up parchment from within her cloak and brandished it in the air.

At that moment, Pik entered the room, out of breath and disgruntled. "My Princess." He bowed, his nose close to touching the floor. "You have my sincerest apologies for the interruption. My colleague here is rather hard to keep tabs on."

Shela rolled her eyes. "I wasn't going to wait for permission in the foyer like a commoner with all the time in the world. Diana might think she's important these days, but I am also important—and busy."

Pik's cheeks flamed as he sputtered, clearly offended.

"It's all right, Pik," I assured him. "Please tell us what you've found."

Shela didn't wait for the goblin to fill the air. "This prophecy—are you confident it's real?"

Freya was an ally I was still trying to figure out. But if I could trust her on anything, it would be the fervour with which she followed these words. "I believe there's a claim to its authenticity—though I can't confirm that it pertains to me." I wouldn't tell Shela, but the prophecy had all but slipped my mind through the haze of the last days.

"Oh, it definitely pertains to you." Shela unrolled the parchment and cleared her throat. She rattled off the words, the language guttural and jagged. Totally unrecognizable.

The room stared at her, mouths dropping open.

"What on Gaia's green earth was that?" Aedan asked, incredulous.

"That was the lovely, if not difficult, language of the Green Impish Gnomes. According to our research, it has been out of use for around two thousand years." Pik clasped his hands in front of him, and it brought me back to the days in Ivywall, watching as he debriefed whatever news of the day to the Drakenis siblings.

"It took us a while, but we found the key to the translation. Turns out, it's a very metaphorical tongue," Shela continued. "What you thought was right. The words translate to, *Dark truths never prevail in a balanced world. And when two become one and the world turns over, the final battle will begin.*"

I nodded, remembering the chills that had crept down my spine when I first heard them. "So, you think you understand what it means?"

"I don't think." Shela grinned. "I *know.*"

"Do tell," Badras drawled, his voice laced with an edge. "We don't have all day."

Shela fixed him with a look I would never dare to and continued, "The beginning and ending are as literal as you're going to get. But the middle, that's where it gets interesting. The idiom used for *two become one* can also be translated to opposites *furhallen.*"

"What's *furhallen?*" I asked, completely butchering the pronunciation.

"We don't have a word for it, but it means to join together against a common enemy." Shela shook her head, smiling. "Isn't that wild?"

It certainly hit close to home.

"The most interesting part is when it says, *the world turns over.* Now, that sounds like a metaphor, but when translated, it means to turn over. As in the world turns on its axis. Becomes something completely new." She was grinning wildly, her hair flying as she bounced on her toes. "Don't you get it? The world turns over—it means *death.*"

Her words floated in the air, no one reaching to grasp them.

"I don't understand." Spense ran a hand through his hair. "The world has to die? As in Eira?"

She shook her head. "The world is only as alive as its people—and who represents the people?"

"You're talking about my mother." I sat in my chair. "Vera has to die."

Shela nodded. "Sorry, kid. But last I heard, she kind of has it coming."

I sighed, fighting the urge to hide my face in my hands. I wasn't ready to face head-on what was steadily marching for me.

"That doesn't make sense," Aedan said, his brow furrowed. "Once Vera dies, the final battle begins? If she's not the final battle, who is?"

Shela held up her hands. "Don't look at me. I'm just the translator."

"Again, this is fine and all, but a prophecy doesn't help us that much." Badras's words earned him a sharp glare from Shela.

"*Fine?* Do you even know the hours of time we put in to translate this? The amount of cross-referencing and volumes we had to hunt down? You insult me." She seethed.

Pik backed away from the glowering female.

"Vera was going to die anyway—we need to focus our time on ensuring that happens. The scroll is redundant."

I whirled on Badras. "I'll thank you not to speak of killing my mother so flippantly."

He had the good grace to look somewhat remorseful even if he didn't break my stare. Everyone else in the room had conveniently found somewhere else to look with the exception of Spense, who placed a hand on my back.

I took a breath through my nose, pushing everything from my mind. "Shela and Pik, thank you for your hard work and haste. Please stay in the palace as long as you'd like, but I suggest getting somewhere safe, considering we'll be under siege by morning."

Shela nodded once, offering a sad smile that inexplicably filled me with anger.

"We go ahead with our plan. Officials will refer to Captain Thesand for placements. Now, where were we?"

FORTY-ONE

SPENSE
ANTICLIMACTIC

After a few hours, Diana released everyone to get prepared.

"My mind feels like mush," she admitted quietly to me, placing her hands on her forehead. She looked to the door, where Shera and Pik spoke with one of the officials from the East. "I should speak with them, apologize for earlier," she murmured.

Now alone, I crossed the room to join my brothers, who were watching Meske as she left the library, likely to rejoin Aislinn and the healers.

"You seem relaxed, brother," Sorin noted.

"This land has been under a false peace for millennia. For as long as the Unseelie have been fighting a real war, these soldiers have only been practicing. Training will only get you so far when it comes to preparing for battle. I can't help but feel our forces will have an upper hand."

Badras shook his head, the bun housing his long sandy-brown hair flopping. "Arrogance will get you nowhere in battle. Surely, you've learned that by now."

I shrugged. "I like to think of it as confidence."

"We're grossly underprepared, in my opinion," Olys said, his discerning gaze flicking over everyone in the room. "This is the same

Seelie Queen that managed to banish us thousands of years ago. I can't imagine she spent all that time twiddling her thumbs. She has to have more up her sleeve."

"We're as prepared as we can be," Sorin said. "We're using every resource available to us, and our plan might be ambitious, but it's solid. And we have the rather bittersweet advantage of having nothing to lose."

We were silent as we soaked in those words. In truth, we had each other to lose. As well as Diana, and Meske, and little Ash, and our sister's comatose body. But we all understood what Sorin meant. With no home, no future, we risked it all. There was no going back to Rathe, to the dying desert of Ivywall.

We won, or we died trying.

"Those Nordians are tough business," Badras remarked. "I was speaking with their general earlier—he's good blood. I could see myself learning a thing or two from their tribe."

From Badras, such an esteemed remark was practically unheard of. I stared across the room at the hulking male in battle-decorated leathers, his muscular form not all that unlike Bad.

Sorin nodded. "Maverick, I believe. He's definitely an asset in this war."

The name was familiar, dancing around in my head until it landed in a memory. One where I had sat on the floor of Diana's room, and she poured her soul out to me, remembering a male who had broken her heart and left her in pieces.

"Maverick, did you say?" I said, abruptly cutting off whatever Olys was talking about.

He gave me a look of annoyance.

"That's what I said." Sorin eyed me, and it was probably a good thing he was paying such close attention because his arm shot out as I moved to stalk across the room.

"Why don't you tell us what's going on before you act on whatever feeling has that look on your face?"

Badras leaned in and snickered. "Yep, that's the one. Spense's *get out of my way or you're next* look."

I shrugged off Sorin's arm, but tension still rolled through me. "I just want to chat with him, is all."

My brothers exchanged a look, and Sorin sighed, always volunteering as the voice of reason. "I'm not even going to ask. Can you not wait until this is over, Spense? The last thing we need right now is civil war on top of the war we're already fighting."

I rolled my shoulders. As usual, my eldest brother was right, and although that hadn't always stopped me in the past, this time, his words struck true. Based on the ferocity of the Nordians and the sheer size of him, one punch wouldn't go unanswered, and I needed my strength for tomorrow.

"Fine."

I kept one eye on Maverick as my brothers continued speaking. If he approached Diana, I was gone, Sorin be damned.

"As much as I hate to admit it, a small piece of me really did think that being back here might heal him," Olys was saying. "But I should have known his insanity ran deeper than that."

"How did you manage to get back here so fast?" I asked. "I expected Urdan would be more of a challenge to subdue."

"We left him there," Olys said simply. "And before you start yelling, of course we thought it through. You didn't see him, Spense. He's gone beyond reason. Even on his worst day in Ivywall, he was ten times more lucid than he was in that cave."

Sorin nodded. "He'll likely die of thirst or starvation within a few days if we don't go back for him. He just sat on the ground the entire time we were there, muttering to himself. He's in no shape to fight or even walk farther than a few steps, in my opinion."

"The only time he reacted was when we tried to take the staff from him," Olys added. "Once we let go, he went back to his chanting."

"Staff? He didn't have one on him when we arrived."

Olys shrugged. "Guess he found it in that cave. Some long stick with a big, dark gemstone on the end."

Despite the strange nature of Urdan clinging to a jewel like it was his life force, it seemed that we were finally done with our father. He was lost, succumbed to his mind, like we had known he one day would.

"So, I suppose we just go check on him again after this is over? Put him out of his misery?"

Olys looked me in the eye, his face dark. "If what he says about his life being tied to Vera's is true, he likely won't be alive when we go back to check."

The finality of that didn't register like I'd always thought it would. No joy, or relief, or even sadness. Just … apathy. And a sighing sense of an anticlimactic ending.

FORTY-TWO

"**C**an you fit any more in there?"

I looked up from the satchel that I was currently cramming yet another roll of gauze into. The bag was near bursting, but I kept pushing the rolls in, praying that it would close when the time came. We were going to need as much as we could carry. Meske held another dozen in her hands, clearly hoping to pass them off to me.

"I could maybe stuff those into my pockets?"

Meske shook her head, the raven-black hair she kept tied at the nape of her neck shimmering under the harsh lamplight. "I suppose we already have enough packs to carry as it is."

Healers shuttled back and forth from the tent, bringing supplies to the two horses we were left. They would be loaded up, and all of us on foot would likely have to carry at least two packs each as well.

"What's the yarrow plant for?" I asked, looking into one of the stores the healer kept. "Oh Gaia, that smells awful."

Meske chuckled. "It's a great way to stop bleeding, made into a paste or a drink. And it tastes worse than it smells, unfortunately."

The Outcasts' head healer, Grogio, shouldered his way back inside, trailed by Meske's daughter, Aislinn. The little girl was vibrant with life, her mother's nearly identical twin.

"What are you doing now, Gorgo?" she asked, stuttering over his name.

"Still packing."

"I can help!"

"You can help by counting to three hundred."

She wrinkled her nose. "That doesn't sound helpful."

I hid a smile. Aislinn was whip-smart and eager to be involved, and she would fight for that opportunity every chance she got. In the short time I had been helping the healers, she was already becoming my favourite part.

Meske steered her daughter away from Grogio's thinning patience. "Why don't you braid Wyn's hair? She'll love it."

Aislinn took up a spot at her aunt's head, playing with the strands of sandy-brown hair. "When will Wynnie wake up?"

The tent grew quiet, healers slipping out as they continued packing silently.

Meske sighed gently, placing a hand on her daughter's shoulder. "We don't know yet. She's still healing. See this?" She pointed to the glowing emerald on Alwyn's chest. "That's your other aunt. She's keeping Wyn safe until her body is strong again."

Aislinn reached out tentatively to stroke the emerald, which pulsed under her touch. "I miss Wynnie."

Her mother dropped a kiss on the top of her head. "She knows."

I fumbled with the strap on the satchel of gauze, tying it as tightly as I could. I looked around, and the tent was nearly bare. All the packs had been loaded, and there was no more time to waste.

Meske joined me outside, where she surprised me by donning a pack.

"You're coming with us?"

She nodded. "This is my calling. I can't imagine my family at a battle where I'm not there to help."

"And Aislinn?"

Grogio finished his head count, and the group of healers started the walk to Nevelyn.

Meske readjusted the straps across her shoulders. "She'll be safe here with her tutor and a few others from Ivywall I trust. As much as I want to stay with her, I can't sit and wait, knowing what's going on out there. I've been healing for a long time. It's selfish of me not to share my gift regardless of my personal worries."

"You're a warrior, Meske."

We fell into step together, following the line through the forest.

She smiled, shaking her head. "You're kind, Maisie. I hope the war doesn't take that away from you."

"It hasn't taken away your kindness yet."

From what I had been told, all of Spense's siblings were absurdly old, a side effect of having a death-defying tyrant as a father. If she hadn't soured by now, I didn't see what could change that.

"It has taken plenty other things from me." Meske's face was withdrawn, near haunted. It aged her.

I placed a hand on her arm. "You have love and a daughter. That is a blessing."

She was lucky. Love, a family, a life away from servitude—it had always been something I was too afraid to allow myself to wish for.

"They are blessings, Maisie. You're right."

"Aislinn is amazing." I smiled. "She has so much care for others."

Meske nodded. "I hate that she has to see Alwyn this way. She loved her so much. Called Aislinn her little fox."

"Alwyn will be okay though, won't she?"

There were a few moments where silence stretched between us.

"I think she's already gone."

I jolted. "But … the emerald. Isn't that—"

"The emerald is a crude holding cell for the soul of a sister long lost to the Drakenis family. None of the siblings have even met her. She's doing us a great service by preserving the body, but I fear Alwyn's soul might have moved on. She was never one to sit still," she added, a bit wry.

How sad for their family.

"I'm sorry," I murmured. A thought niggled at the back of my mind, of how the magic holding the soul inside the emerald worked. "Could you not put Alwyn's soul into a gemstone as well so that she could be reunited with her body eventually?"

Meske looked sideways at me. "That kind of magic is sacrificial. Jweira, the one in the emerald, lost her body when her soul was preserved. It was done by the Seelie Queen so that she might use Jweira's power unchecked. It's a prison, Maisie. I would not wish that on anyone."

We continued our trek, following the steps of the healers in front of us, sometimes having to climb fallen trees or avoid puddles from the rapidly melting snow. Through it, light conversations stirred, but I couldn't concentrate. Something about the emerald sat in the front of my mind, heavy and persistent.

My thoughts whirled for hours before landing on the vibrant blue sapphire Aedan and I had found. That Hollaina now held. I remembered what it had been like to hold it, to sleep with it near my body. I was almost certain it was the reason for the strange dream I had that night.

Was it possible that Hollaina had trapped a soul inside of the sapphire, the same as Jweira? The magic was old, vile, and widely unknown.

What if it wasn't a soul trapped inside, but a power source?

I picked up my pace. A thought had placed itself in my mind, and there was only one fae I could think of who would be able to confirm it

FORTY-THREE

ÆDAN
COAX

There—a figure on the tree line, sitting sidesaddle on horseback with a deep blue cloak covering their face.

It might be hard for another to distinguish their identity.

But I knew.

I knew from the way she sat ramrod straight, near rigid, hands stiff in front of her. I didn't even need the strand of blonde hair peeking from the hood to confirm what I already knew deep in my gut.

My hand curled tight around the hilt of the throwing knife at my side. My jaw clamped, molars grinding as I stood at the library window, looking out into the grounds. If I could make it to her without her taking off, I'd be there in an instant.

But Jamey Pinois was a coward, and she would run.

A coward and a liar, and there was a reckoning coming her way. And I would enjoy every second of giving her the punishment she deserved.

Long after Jamey had retreated back into the forest, I stood in the library, letting my thoughts wash over me. The group of fae that had rallied for Diana, for Eira, was remarkable. Hope fluttered quietly in my chest, like the sun trying to emerge after a storm. But I held that hope tight in my fist, nervous to let it run free.

Earlier, I had walked halfway to the farthest east part of the palace, only to halt in my steps when I realized where my feet had been taking me. To see my father.

His absence had been like a noose loosening at first, but now, it set me on edge. As much as I hated to admit it, I wanted his counsel.

Soft steps sounded behind me, and I spun around. None of the fae I knew would tread so lightly without announcing themselves.

"What are you doing here?" I grabbed Maisie's shoulders, my relief at seeing her almost outweighing the drive to send her somewhere safe and far away from here.

She wore the plain clothes of Shynin, a bag slung over her shoulder.

"I came with the healers, but I've been looking for you. I have a hunch, and I'm going into Nevelyn to see if it's right." Her blue eyes shone, her face alight, and it killed me to have to take that from her.

"The palace just got attacked. I have to stay with my army, Maisie. I'm sure you understand why I can't just drop everything and go to Nevelyn with you."

Immediately, her light dimmed, and she closed up. "I wasn't asking you to. I can go alone."

Maisie moved to push past me, but I caught her elbow.

"Like hell you can."

We locked eyes. There was something in the set of her jaw that dared me to try and hold her back. And it sent a thrill down my spine. There she was, the warrior inside that she had spent so long trying to coax out, and I was trying to shove her back in. Unacceptable.

"Fine. Let's go."

"I can handle myself, Aedan." The way she said my name should be a crime. "You've got a duty to stay here, and I won't stand in the way."

I shook my head. "Ryen and Maverick can handle it. And with Diana here, there's no better time to go. As long as we're back by the morning."

After ducking inside the palace to pull my second aside—who was adamantly trying to sew up his own cut without the help of a healer—I rejoined Maisie in the stables, where we mounted up and set out.

As we clipped along the cobblestone, I noticed Maisie staring at me. "What?"

She shrugged. "That was easier than I'd thought it would be."

I sighed. "You should know by now that I have no ability or desire to say no to you."

FORTY-FOUR

DIANA
THE QUEEN'S BLESSING

"Again, I'm so sorry," I said, clasping the hands of the elderly male who had answered the door. The fourth door I had knocked on in Nevelyn. The one I knew belonged to the baker who operated the charming eatery down the street, where the banana bread was unparalleled.

"My dear," he said, his wrinkled hands shaking as they gripped mine. "Whatever are you sorry about? You could not have predicted this."

"I wish I didn't have to turn you against your queen. That you didn't have to see such unrest in your home."

He smiled softly, a sad sort of smile. "I was alive to see Vera take the throne at a young age, and even then, I knew she was not a queen of her subjects. She would never have done what you are doing now. If her reign is indeed over, then I am happy to see you succeed her."

Fissures in my heart warmed at his words, even as the last door's visit replayed in my head. *Why should we trust you? You brought the enemy here. We're as good as dead without Queen Vera's protection.*

"You are too kind." My hands felt cold as the elder's fingers slid from my grip.

He stepped back a few paces and gestured to his interior. "Would you like to come in? We have lots left over from dinner. Potato leek soup. Eating from the stores until the snow melts." He chuckled.

"I'm afraid my night is only beginning, but thank you for the offer." I turned to leave, catching sight of Spense and the Nevelyn official at the bottom of the steps. "And as for the snow," I called over my shoulder, "it should be gone soon, if I have anything to say about it."

Spense took my hand when I reached them. "Three good, one bad. Seventy-five percent is not too shabby," he said, placing a kiss on my temple.

"I don't think you can count the word *okay* and a door in my face in the good category," I answered drily, remembering the scared face peeking from a crack in the door that barely waited for the words to be out of my mouth before retreating.

"I have to agree with the high princess," Rentin stated.

Spense threw him a look that I assumed was disapproval, but I shook them both off. "Where to next?"

Rentin pulled his parchment from his cloak and surveyed the list. "Well, Rory from the amphitheatre Nordside holds a lot of sway in the community. He employs nearly a thousand performers, as well as providing entertainment to the whole of Nevelyn. He is a staple here."

"Perfect. Lead the way."

Rentin cleared his throat. "There is one thing you should know. Rory was—last I knew—an avid follower of the Gaian law. He has loudly voiced his support of not only Vera, but of the entire anti-Dark cause as well in past years." His eyes caught on Spense for a moment before flicking back to me. "You might want to visit him alone."

Spense's magic turned ashen, a dark cloud forming. He tried to keep it from travelling down to me, but we were still working on boundaries. It was awkward and clumsy, not even taking into consideration the fact that we hadn't yet reconciled about the shadows he had sent to the West.

I shook my head. "Spense is a part of the cause and a part of *me*. I won't pretend to be something I'm not in order to sway Rory to my side."

Rentin inclined his head. "As you wish."

When we arrived in the art district, Rentin led us in the opposite direction of the amphitheatre and instead toward the apartments on the outskirts that lined the River Nord. There, we waited at the door of one of the nicer-looking buildings while the porter retrieved this *staple of Nevelyn*.

Rory appeared at the door a few moments later, his eyebrows raised as he took me in. He was middle-aged, if I were to guess, but his stark white hair opposed that.

"When the porter told me the high princess was calling for me, I didn't believe him. Thought it might be a prank," he said by way of greeting.

"Yet you came anyway." I surveyed this short fae, wondering just how much attitude was kept in such a small form.

He shrugged. "Curiosity got the best of me."

Rentin reached out a hand. "Good to see you again, good sir. I must say, the last opera at Nordside was absolutely mesmerizing. *Swans at Dusk*, if I recall correctly?"

"You do, Sir Rentin. One of my finer pieces, if I say so myself. Many were theorizing it would be the box office's best of the past hundred years. Unfortunately, we'll never know, thanks to the city-wide shutdown." His eyes shot daggers my way, and that did not sit well at all.

Before I could take my deep breath and form a civilized response, Spense made his feelings clear.

"That shutdown was for your benefit," he growled. "Would you have rather your precious play be interrupted by the sounds of war? That would certainly mess with the acoustics, I would imagine."

Rory scowled. "Play," he scoffed. "I have never been so insulted. And even if the shutdown was of real merit, I highly doubt this falsified attacker would choose to hit the opera first."

"That's enough."

The second my magic hit the air, Rory's face whitened, and he sobered. He would most certainly feel it around him, like a gentle pressure from all sides. Not painful, but not gentle either. A reminder of whom he was speaking with.

"Sir Rentin tells me that you are highly regarded in Nevelyn. I have sought you out so that you might understand on a more personal level what has been going on in Eira and pass it along to those in the community since I am unable to visit each and every citizen personally."

The opera writer eyed me, his own rough magic coming to the surface as it tried to get in between mine, but to no avail. "Rumour around here is that you and the queen are in some sort of standoff. Why should I trust you when she's been the one leading us for years? I don't even know what you stand for."

I released the magic from him, and his shoulders slumped before he regained his stick-up-the-ass posture.

"Let me tell you what I stand for. I stand for peace between the Folk, not just the Unseelie, but all who were forced out. I stand for the right for all to choose who they follow even if I don't agree. But most of all, I stand for the truth. Transparency. And the truth is that my mother, Vera, is not the merciful queen she pretends to be. She is in fact the Seelie Queen from the first stories of Eira, taking the place of every ruler for the past eight thousand years. She has twisted the minds of her subjects and kept an iron fist on the throne after driving the Unseelie and Folk from this land so long ago. She is a plague that needs to be eradicated."

Rory stared, disbelief written plainly on his face. "What a tale." He finally laughed. "Even if that were true, she's hardly a villain to us. Living prosperous and free doesn't seem to be the work of a tyrant." He shrugged again, his flippancy setting my teeth on edge. "I don't pretend to know what all goes on in a queen's day. She makes hard decisions so we don't have to. If this is how she's protecting her subjects from what she perceives as a threat, then I stand with her."

"The land is dying from the lack of balance. The snow is only part of that," I said, trying to keep a calm exterior. "Vera attempted to kill me when I tried to negotiate peace for the Folk. You might not see filicide as a problem, but I was chosen by the ancestors to be high princess. The heir. It goes against every Gaian law to harm me. Isn't that proof enough that she isn't who she seems?"

Rory's defiance was crumbling. "The Folk aren't real," he whispered, almost to himself. "They're just a story."

"They are real, and they're here," I urged. "Spense is one of them."

At my words, Spense lifted the hood on his cloak, revealing his horns. Rory stumbled back, horror etched into his face.

"N-no, it can't be—" he spluttered. "Demon!"

I pulled my sleeve back, as did Spense, to show our tattoos.

"Soulmates are chosen by Gaia," I said gently. "If the Unseelie were truly this great evil, why would the great Mother Earth tie my soul to his eternally?"

Rory seemed at a loss for words as his mouth opened and closed, resembling a fish. "What are you asking of me?" he asked, voice barely above a whisper. "My support as you drive Vera from the throne? I'm no one of importance."

"You are important, Rory. This city knows you, respects you. All I'm asking is for you to spread the word about the truth you heard today. So that the war that's about to break won't be a total shock." I stopped myself from reaching out to him, aware of the fear in his eyes.

Finally, slowly, he nodded. "My faith is everything I have. I was at your ascension, at the Sacred Pool that day. I remember that the ancestors picked you."

I swallowed my guilt. Anyone present that day, save for a chosen few, would have no recollection of the chaos that had ensued. I promised myself that when this was over, I would find a way to reverse the glamours my mother had put on this city. Hell, maybe even the entire region. *Realm.*

"If they have chosen you and this … Unseelie, for whatever purpose … then I must have faith in them. In Mother Gaia. I will spread the word," he promised.

Weight like a boulder lifted from my chest, and I took a shuddering breath. "Thank you."

We made a dozen more stops, each with varying answers, and by the end of the night, I felt more prepared, knowing I had appealed to my subjects honestly and openly. My stomach still churned with the anxiety and stress of tomorrow, but at least I knew that no matter the outcome, the truth was out there.

"There is one last place I'd like to take you, if you're not too tired," Rentin said, sparing a glance at the sky, where the sun had begun its descent.

My feet throbbed, and my stomach growled, but I nodded. "Absolutely."

As we entered the Nevelyn Orphanage, my fatigue faded away.

High Mother Cretis met us at the door and swept me into a hug. "You have been so brave, my dear."

"High Mother, it's good to see you. I'll admit, I wasn't sure how you would react to all this."

I pulled back to look her in the face. She had aged since my ascension, bearing the lines and spots of a long life. It was shocking how her appearance made it seem like years had passed since that day.

Cretis folded her hands in front of her. "I have always been an advocate of what is *right*. That is the Gaian way. And you were prophesied to do great things."

"You know of the prophecy?" I exchanged a surprised look with Spense.

"As High Mother, certain knowledges were passed to me. I regret not being more aware of Vera's extracurriculars. I fear I could have helped you."

I took one of her hands. "No matter. You're here now. And what's better is that the support of the Abbey will go a long way toward helping Eira see the truth."

Cretis looked down. "Unfortunately, I no longer hold sway with the Abbey. There were some recent differences of opinion that led to my relief of the position. Bandra is the High Mother now."

I frowned, anger building. "They can't do that."

"They can, my dear. The Gaians have always respected a democracy in the Abbey. Many thought my 'outdated' way of thinking was holding them back. I fear Vera might have gotten to most of them."

It was shameful that I hadn't thought to go there first. That my mother had wrapped her tendrils around the purest souls, the voices of Gaia. It was blasphemous.

"I don't wish to add more to your plate, my child," Cretis said, leading me into the orphanage. "It's a relief that so many Gaians were able to get out with me before the infectious ideas reached them. Besides, more importantly, there are some fae here who were very excited that you were coming to visit them personally."

The Gaians she mentioned stood in the common room, smiling genially at me. Many still wore the Gaian habit, but others donned simple day clothes. A male with a braid that reminded me of Alwyn opened a door.

And six children came spilling out into the room, jumping all around as they surrounded me. I knelt in the middle, accepting hugs and returning hellos.

The joy of children was unmatched in purity and unconditionality. It practically poured from them as they played with my hair, asked me questions, told me stories. It was a sobering reminder of who I was fighting to bring peace to. These children would grow up in a new era with Folk all around them, and they would lead the future of Eira.

There were two I recalled from previous work with the orphanage, and they remembered me as well. They asked for stories of Finnvarra the Mighty, and my heart clenched. My life used to be so easy. It seemed silly to think of how overwhelmed I used to be. Before this. Before the war.

When Spense knelt beside me, I introduced him as Unseelie, a race wronged long ago, and they stared in awe and shock, not fear and horror. His smile lit up his face as he listened to their rambling, and it was impossible not to match it with one of my own.

"What have you been learning in your studies?" I asked.

The eldest of the children, an outgoing male named Tareq, piped up immediately, "We learned about how the queen is chosen by our an—an—what's the word?"

"Ancestors," Cretis supplied.

"Ancestors!" Tareq exclaimed. "And that she is the most powerful fae in all the realm. And her job is to keep us all safe."

"That's right," I agreed, my throat tight. "She has a very big duty indeed."

A small girl looked up at me with wide blue eyes. "Will you be the queen one day? That's what the governess told us."

Spense's eyes flicked to mine, and in them, I saw all the pride and love that I could feel from his magic. So much faith in me. It was a weight as well as a blessing.

"Yes," I told them, pulling the emerald family ring from my finger to hold it up. "I come from a very long line of queens. See the sigil of the wolf on this? That's the Lightbringer crest."

They all took turns passing it around until it came back to me, warm and slightly sticky. That was children, I supposed.

"We also learned this." Tareq stood, waving at his peers to stand as well, and directed them to line up behind him.

I watched curiously as he constructed his masterpiece.

When he was satisfied with the lineup, he left the line, walked three steps to stand directly in front of me, and knelt down on one knee. He hung his little head and waited. When I did nothing, he reached up blindly, fumbling for my hand, and placed it on his shoulder.

"Oh," I gasped softly.

He peeked up at me. "Do you know what to say?" he whispered.

Tears welling in my eyes, I nodded, and he hung his head again.

I squeezed his shoulder gently and cleared my throat.

"Go with my blessing."

Tareq grinned as he stood and tore off to the back of the line. One by one, the children came to kneel beside me and receive the Queen's Blessing. An act of high honour and respect for a queen from an army about to do great battle.

When they had all had a turn, they ran to me, grinning, while I wiped stray tears from my cheeks. They enveloped me in a hug, and over their little heads, I caught Cretis's suppressed smile.

Thank you, I mouthed.

She only shrugged, as if to say, *It wasn't me*.

FORTY-FIVE

DIANA
I KNOW

After we parted ways with Rentin, the official stating that we would see him on the battlefield, Spense and I took a walk through Nevelyn's inner city. I had been walking all afternoon, and soreness crept into my bones, but the thought of sitting still made me wring my hands.

It was aimless at first, until I realized we were retracing the steps from the first time I'd toured him through these streets.

Many of the businesses were still boarded up, the roads quiet. In the North's busiest, most bustling city, we were alone.

I hadn't realized Spense was leading until we stopped at a bridge over the River Nord. *No, not just any bridge.*

He leaned over the railing, looking out into the rushing water. It was higher than usual with the melting snow and was nearing the riverbank edge.

"I can't believe I jumped from here," he remarked.

That was a day I'd never forget. Watching him leap over the rail to save a small child who had fallen into the water, without memories or magic, was the first time I'd thought differently about the Unseelie. About my education.

I joined him on the ledge and blew out a breath. From here, it looked like a death wish; the drop was bigger than I remembered, the water sloshed angrily, and rocks jutted out.

"You always were the kind to act first, think later." The words came out more jaded than I'd anticipated, and I felt a pinprick of guilt.

"Yeah, I deserved that one." Spense grimaced, hair flopping into his face.

I sighed. "I'm just exhausted, Spense. And so overwhelmed that I can barely think straight. I thought I could trust you to help me, not add more stress to my plate."

"The last thing I want is to cause you more stress, Diana."

"Yeah, well, sending shadows to my own fae is sure not the way to go about that."

Spense flipped to his side, his eyes flashing. "You seem to forget that you're not the only one under massive duress right now. My entire race, all the races of Folk I'm responsible for, have been evacuated from their homes and brought to this strange land, where the inhabitants don't even want them. My sister is possibly dead, my father is completely insane, and I can't remember the last time I felt normal."

I swallowed. "I understand that. But it doesn't excuse how you endangered—"

"Diana, this is war. It sucks that you have to come to terms with it this way, but it's all I've ever known. Those fae in the West? They *aren't* yours. They were ready to fire arrows into your heart. Fighting for them is only going to drag you down."

"I—"

He waved a hand. "I know that I could have reacted better. And I'm sorry for not involving you. We don't know a lot about the shadows, but I can control them, which makes me think I have some connection to getting the victims to wake up. And even if they don't, then I'll gladly shoulder that responsibility. Because I don't regret it. Not when they stood between you and taking back the peace *we all* deserve."

Tears pricked at the back of my eyes, and I slammed my tongue to the roof of my mouth to try and stop them, but to no avail. They were hot, angry, dripping off my face and nose with surprising force.

At once, Spense softened, and he wrapped his arms around me. "Don't cry. Not over me, Diana, please."

I fisted my hands in his tunic. "I'm … mad. Angry. Frustrated. And not really at you. I understand that you're different from me and you're going to do things I don't agree with. We grew up in opposite situations. I'm … I'm *pissed* that I have to do this. It's too much. But I have to because it's my responsibility. My prophecy."

He ran a soothing hand down my back.

"I think I've been using my anger with you to channel all of my troubles. I just—I need you to know that I'm never going to be okay with you putting innocents in harm's way, no matter how they feel about me."

Spense pulled away, his grey eyes searching mine. One gentle finger caught a stray tear. "Innocents, I can agree with. But anyone who goes against you is unforgivable to me. I won't apologize for protecting you."

I would never be able to change Spense completely, mould him into my exact replica. That wasn't why we worked. His ability to make hard decisions challenged me, and when I really looked inside, I was grateful for that. I just hated how it felt to admit to myself when I needed to relent. Let go. Pride was something that was hard enough to navigate, but throw in the near-impossible job of proving to an entire kingdom that I was worthy of being followed was a line I was still learning to straddle.

The question was, was I was strong enough to look for my own flaws and accept them when I needed help? I could try. For Eira. For Spense. For myself.

"I'm lucky to have you looking out for me. Can we agree though to run major decisions like that past each other from now on? We might not always agree, but we deserve to know what the other is thinking."

He nodded, those black curls flopping softly on his head. "That sounds good to me."

I stepped back into his arms, and for a few moments, he held me close, his heartbeat the only thing I could hear over the sound of rushing water.

"Diana?" he murmured against my hair.

"Yeah?"

"If it comes to it and you're in danger, I won't care who it is; I'll kill them."

A shudder worked its way down my spine. "I know."

He paused. "Even if it's your mother."

I closed my eyes against his chest. "I know."

FORTY-SIX

MAISIE
REVELATION

"So, Vera is the Seelie Queen." My mind was blown.

Aedan nodded as he tied Kali to the hitching post in the middle of Nevelyn's square. Now that the city was opened up again, a tentative busyness had returned. Fae still lined the streets, going to and fro, but the difference was that no one seemed to linger long. The safety of being inside was still fresh in the city's mind.

"We were all shocked," he added, helping me finish my tie for Plum. "I can't imagine what Diana must be feeling."

Aedan had given me a full update on our way into Nevelyn, and while I appreciated the honesty, the truth made me nauseous. Eira was a realm shrouded in darkness, slowly suffocating through thousands of years, with an unkillable monster at its helm. We were but a small blip of time on that scale.

Still, if anyone could defeat her, it would be Diana. And if I was correct, my information would help her win this. If it wasn't enough … well, at least we would die trying.

Horses secured, Aedan took my hand in his as we started to walk.

Ignoring my spiked heart rate, I tried to wiggle out of his grip. "Aedan, we should talk about this."

His blue eyes bored into mine, a sadness between his brows.

"Maisie, we could all be dead by this time tomorrow. Can we table the *what are we* discussion until after the war?"

Swallowing, I nodded. A smile threatened at his mouth, and I fought the urge to brush his full lower lip with my thumb.

"Will you tell me where we're going now?"

I bit the inside of my cheek, shifting my weight. "You're not going to like it."

We turned onto the street where the abandoned theatre stood, and Aedan halted suddenly. "No," he said, his face darkening.

I tugged on his hand. "I have a hunch, and he's the only one with the knowledge."

"You just got out of a deal with him," Aedan argued, his feet firmly planted. "I'm not letting you get sucked back in."

"You said yourself that we might die tomorrow. If I could find this information without him, I would. But we don't exactly have the time for it, do we?"

He sighed, using his free hand to rub at his eyes. "Fine," he said finally. "But if it comes to a deal, let me make it this time."

If I told Aedan what my hunch was, he would likely agree that Kol was the unfortunate best option. But I was afraid that if I spoke the words aloud, they would sound insane, and I would try to back myself out of it.

Pushing forward without thinking about it was the only way to make myself do something I feared.

When we made it to the back door of Kol's shop, it was already open.

Aedan stepped in front of me and peeked his head into the doorway.

"Hello?" he called out.

There was a scuffling sound, and footsteps echoed as they got louder. A body emerged from the shadows, one with tanned skin and piercing eyes that I knew all too well.

One that I'd never expected to find at The Curator's shop.

"Leo," Aedan growled. "What are you doing here?"

The Southern prince flicked his gaze over us once and sighed. "Might as well come up then."

Aedan and I shared a glance as we followed Leo inside, and I was glad to see he was as confused as I was.

Instead of Leo bringing us to the shopfront, we turned and headed up the stairs to the left, which opened into a large room. There was a table and desk, as well as a curtain that cut across a corner.

Kol sat at the small table, as poised as ever, holding a handful of cards. Hollaina sat across from him with her own hand. They both turned as we entered.

Leo flopped into another chair at the table, leaving us standing. I fought the urge to look down as Kol's gaze met mine.

"Maisie," he said in that knowing voice. "I wondered which of you would be the one. I must say, I rather thought it would be your fearless leader. But I suppose she was too caught up in all her juggling to allow the pieces to come together."

Hollaina smiled softly, her scars grooving into her cheeks. "I knew it would be you."

I tried not to be alarmed. "So, you know why I'm here then."

Kol lifted an eyebrow, not looking up as he placed a card down between them. "I suspect you've come to ask me about the tale I told you at our last meal. Please, sit. I mustn't forgo my manners, even at the edge of the end."

I took the last open chair while Aedan stood behind me, shaking his head.

"This is so much weirder than I thought it'd be."

Leo smirked.

"The end? That's not very optimistic." I watched as Hollaina placed her card down, grinning when it trumped Kol's.

The Curator made a disgruntled face and took the entire deck to shuffle. "The world makes its own magic, you know, Maisie. It spins stories and weaves the lines of fate through the grass, the sky, the sea. If you know how to listen, you can hear the whispers of what's to come."

Aedan muttered under his breath, a few words floating to me that sounded like *raving lunatic.*

I waved off Kol's doom ramblings. "In your story, you said that the deities used to walk among the fae. In Eira. If those deities were still alive … how might one know for sure how to spot one?"

All the eyes at the table swivelled to me.

"You wouldn't," Kol said passively while starting to deal out a new hand.

He was always infuriating, but this time, I couldn't take it anymore. I reached across the table and slapped the deck out of his hand, sending cards flying. They scattered across the table and onto the floor.

"You listen to me, and you *answer* me—and none of your nonanswer bull. You're a deity, aren't you? And instead of helping us fight the Seelie Queen, you're sitting here, playing cards, when we could use you! Don't you care about Eira? You *had* to have been alive when Vera took over eight thousand years ago. How do we defeat her, Kol?" I held his unflinching gaze as anger clouded his face. "Or should I say Demekol?"

He rolled his shoulders back, stretching as he worked his jaw. "Was there a specific question you wished to ask me, or shall I give nonanswer bull to cover your rapid-fire accusations?"

"Are. You. A deity?"

Kol's unflappable demeanour crumbled into a terrifying look, and I worried for a moment that I might have put myself into grave danger, provoking him like this.

We should get out of here, I thought.

Then, "Yes."

With the admission, tension released from the air, and it was like taking a deep breath for the first time. I almost didn't believe that he'd said that or what it implied—that I was right. That a child of the *actual gods* sat before me, and I had just slapped a card deck from his hands.

"Was that all?" Kol asked drily.

"No—I mean, how …" I shook my head, trying to form one cohesive thought. "Why haven't you stopped Vera? She's been ruining your realm for millennia!"

"We are forbidden to directly interfere with the mortals."

He shared a look with Hollaina, and suddenly, the words came tumbling, unbidden, from my mouth.

"You're one too."

Hollaina's pale eyes flicked to me, and she nodded once.

My limbs felt weak. If I hadn't been sitting, I would surely have collapsed by now. It was remarkable that Aedan was still standing.

"You're telling me you can't do *anything*? Not even one small thing to help indirectly? Your power must be enormous compared to Vera."

Kol slammed a hand on the table. "How many times do I have to tell you that I have no power?"

"A deity with no power doesn't make any sense. Hollaina has power; I've seen it. And I've felt yours too."

Kol glared, opening his mouth to snap back, but was cut off.

"Ilysia has been alive as long as we," Hollaina said. "In her years, she has learned dark practices, and her power has grown substantially. She uses tricks and cheats in order to bolster her abilities."

"Like the sapphire you asked me to get for you."

Hollaina smiled. "See, Kol? I told you she was smart."

He only shrugged.

"So, if we can destroy the items that are feeding her magic, she would be weakened?" It was a long shot, but at least it was something.

Kol shook his head. "Even if you somehow found a way to destroy her conduits, she's still much more powerful than you. Or even our darling rebel leader, Diana. Only an act of the gods will save us now."

"What happened to you?" I said, disgust crawling up my throat. "You used to be so full of wit and zest. Now, you've given up."

"He's right, Maisie," Hollaina resigned. "Ilysia has played this game since the creation of this realm, and she's finally won. Now, we wait for the gods to step in."

For the first time in several minutes, Aedan spoke. "Vera—Ilysia—we thought she was just the Seelie Queen. But she's a deity too, isn't she?"

"She's worn many faces and titles through the years," Kol bit out. "I would wager she doesn't know which one she is anymore. But, yes, her first name was Ilysia. The deity of the west."

With that revelation, I turned to Leo. "Are you the fourth then? Hiding out here with the rest of them?"

His adder-like grin was not as full of life as it used to be. "I'm not Lazansus, no. Although I suppose I *am* a deity in the same way Diana is. And her soulmate, I've been told."

My head spun. There was so much there to digest. "You're Hollaina's *son*?" I breathed, mostly to myself.

"But unlike Diana, you're hiding while she's amassing an army, facing Ilysia head-on." Aedan's voice was pure, deep authority, threatening to turn my limbs molten.

"I have given Diana my army," Leo said. "And I plan to join them in the fight. Forgive me for spending a few hours with my mother while I still can."

"And Lazansus?" I prodded. "The other deity? Where is he hiding?"

Leo raised a brow. "I would imagine your friends could tell you that. Most of your rebel group is related to him after all."

The last of Leo's first statement finally clicked. Lazansus was Urdan.

"He's become just as twisted as Ilysia," Kol warned. "When she tied her life to his, it ruined them. Sure, she could draw from his power source, but it stripped away her divinity, as well as his. She became a mortal in an immortal's body, one with mortal thoughts and desires and fears. Lazansus will have fared much worse. He won't be of any help to you, if that's what your little brain is thinking."

It was what I had thought, but I wasn't going to admit it.

"What about the fail-safe?" I asked. "Didn't your story say something about the gods giving you a way to stop the others?"

Kol nodded. "Ilysia has the items and has hidden them across the realm. All except one. Even if you could find the other three gems, there would be no way to use them. Gaia's Council has long since died out, thanks to Ilysia."

Hollaina pulled the sapphire from her lap and set it on the table with a thud. "This is my representation," she said. "Ilysia thought she took mine when she killed the Eastern court rulers twenty years ago. By the time she realized she had a fake, I had assumed the role of princess, ensuring she could not act against me without cause. I hid this one in the Unclaimed Land, as you know. The magic there has always protected what needs safety."

"So, the real Hollaina died with her parents?" Aedan asked.

"Yes. My gods-given name is Ilex."

Aedan's hands rested on top of my shoulders, sending flitters of electricity down my arms. Whether it was his magic or just my body's reaction to his, I had no idea.

"You just happened to be in the East when it was attacked?"

Hollaina grimaced. "The attack was no accident. Ilysia had discovered where I had been hiding and tried to use the fire to flush me out. She murdered an ancestral-chosen ruling line in the process."

Hiding? What a contradiction of the word *deity*. They had been made by the gods, immortal and powerful. How could they possess the ability to shape peace and forgo it out of fear? It wasn't right.

Disgust must have shown on my face, for Leo said, "You would have hidden, too, if you had known what Ilysia was capable of. My mother watched how Kol's power was stripped from him. Ilysia saw their attempt to call the gods back when she first split the fae, thanks to a spy, and got to them before they could. She had already been meddling in dark, evil magics, which was how she was able to seal the realm in the first place. She took Kol's magic from his mortal body—in his own region, no less—and placed it into a familiar. A conduit for her own power. What you feel from him is a branding of who he used to be. Do you see now how futile it is to go up against her?"

Aedan growled from behind my chair, leaving me to stand in front of Leo, a menacing figure. "Futility is only a word used by those who have no ambition."

Leo's throat worked, but he said nothing.

"Our hands are tied," Hollaina said gently.

"That's pathetic," I spat. "And cowardly."

Kol sighed, and it was a heavy sigh, filled with the weight of thousands of years. "All I can offer you is information, Maisie. Now that Vera has revealed herself to you, I am unbound from speaking of our past. The gods will take us regardless of what I say now."

I considered just walking right out of the room and marching back to the palace to pursue Urdan instead, who seemed much more likely to offer aid in taking down Ilysia. But another idea formed just as I was leaning back, ready to scrape the chair across the floor.

"Fine then. Tell me of Gaia's Council."

FORTY-SEVEN

ÆDAN
GAIA'S COUNCIL

Leo followed us from Kol's home, stating that he would rejoin the rebel movement in Nevelyn.

"Does Vera—Ilysia—know of your true lineage?" I asked, helping Maisie mount Plum.

"She has never liked me, but I don't believe she knows the truth. I suspect I would be long dead by now if that were the case."

"Good." I swung into Kali's saddle. "Let's keep it that way."

By the time we reached the Unclaimed Land, it was well into the night. Inky blackness bled from the sky into the forest, making it near impossible for us to see farther than a few feet ahead.

"How much farther to Shynin?" Maisie asked from her mount in front of me.

"Don't tell me you want to stop now." As it was, there was a rapidly shrinking chance that I would be making it into Nevelyn before the dawn. Meaning I wouldn't be there to lead my army. It was unacceptable, treasonous even, which was why I was putting all my faith into this plan.

If it didn't work … I didn't know what I would do.

Maisie spun around in her saddle to fix me with a glare. "I'm not tired. I'm *impatient*. Do you think we can make it the rest of the way at a gallop without stopping?"

I spurred Kali's sides, and she leaped forward. "Let's find out."

"Do you want me to go in without you?"

Still slightly panting, my hair sticking to the back of my neck with sweat, I tied Kali and Plum to the post in the middle of the Shynin camp. Despite the late hour, lights had come on in several tents, indicating they were aware of our arrival.

"No," I told Maisie. "I'm coming with you."

She stared at me for a moment before nodding, and I followed her in the direction of the leader's tent.

Freya was waiting at the flap, wearing regular clothes, as awake as if she never went to sleep that night. Concern splashed across her face as she took us in. "I must say, you are not who I expected."

Maisie lifted her chin. "We have a plan to end this once and for all."

Slowly, Freya nodded. "And what do you require of me?"

"We need several volunteers. Ten in fact. One of each Folk race. And as soon as possible."

If the Outcasts' leader was surprised, she did not show it. "Come with me."

When Diana and I had been young and in schooling, we had learned very briefly of the types of Folk that used to live in Eira. There were the Unseelie, of course—rebranded as Dark—and goblins, elves, gnomes. But no one had prepared me for the pixies.

Josette flitted around my head, the whirring of her wings only slightly less annoying than the chattering of words that had not stopped since meeting her.

"Where are we going?"

"Is that a gnome? Oh, how wonderful! The Folk were always meant to be reunited!"

"Watch your step; that's a three-petaled daisy. They're rare!"

"Is tonight a full moon? If so, we should really be walking backward to ward off evil spirits."

"You could use a haircut, you know. Females like a tidy look."

Gaia must be mad at me.

When we reached the clearing Freya had steered us in the direction of, the line of fae halted in their tracks. A pond larger than the Sacred Pool spread out before us, the mirrored surface of the water blinking in the sunlight. A waterfall bigger than I had ever seen fed into it, the roaring sound filling my ears now that there were no trees to block it. It was giant and strong, seemingly fed from the mountain range beyond it.

"I didn't realize there were mountains in the Unclaimed Land," Maisie breathed, her eyes open in awe.

"They range from the North," I replied, seeing a map of Eira in my mind's eye. "This must be where they stop before the East turns into a plateau."

"It's stunning."

Josette, having been quiet all of one minute, spoke from my ear, startling me. "Is this where we'll do the ceremony?"

It matched Kol's description, and as I took a few steps closer to the water, I recognized the haze that floated within, similar to the Sacred Pool. "I think this is it," I said to Maisie.

And there was no time to waste. Dawn had passed, and the sun had begun its rise. By now, my absence had no doubt been noticed. My stomach clenched as I thought of Diana realizing I was gone. We'd had no time to leave a note, and I was counting on our years of friendship that she would know I would not have left if not for good reason.

Maisie nodded, her jaw setting. She turned so her back was to the water, and she faced the rest of us—the group of eleven she had set out to gather.

Me, a Seelie.

A sharp-looking young Unseelie female.

A taller-than-life green elf.

A flittering chatterbox pixie.

A waist-high, farm-worn brownie.

A strange, well-dressed leprechaun with a long, wispy beard.

A tall, transparent, unformed spirit, known as a nymph.

A small, orb-like spirit that dropped leaves, called a dryad.

A child-like, blue-skinned goblin.

A heavyset, kind-natured gnome.

And lastly, a dark, opaque box with a sinister hissing coming from inside, containing a kelpie—one held back from the trip South by Freya (without permission) in hopes of studying it.

Maisie's own version of Gaia's Council.

We made an interesting group, and sometimes, it was hard to know where to look, but I could not fault them for being different. They had all listened to Maisie's plea, her untested theory, and one by one, they had agreed to join our mission.

That was more than could be said for a lot of the Seelie we were working to protect.

Maisie took a deep breath, locking eyes with me. I could tell she was debating on asking me to stand with her, take over for her. She was starting to doubt her power to motivate.

I just gave her a smile and a nod, hoping it communicated all the faith I had in her. She had done so much already—more than I could do. I was floored by her. The quiet, ignored servant was long gone. A warrior stood in her place.

Maisie's throat worked, and she nodded back.

"Okay," she said, her gaze flickering over each of her assembled council. "Here is what's going to happen."

FORTY-EIGHT

DIANA
IMPERFECT AND FRACTURED

It was a relief when I finally sat down on the stool in the kitchen, shoving whatever leftovers we could find into my mouth.

Badras chuckled at the ferocity of which I forked down barely cooked rice, plopping himself onto a counter with a burlap bag of vegetables in his lap.

"Those aren't washed, you know," Olys pointed out.

The giant male only shrugged, taking a monstrous bite out of a bell pepper. Seeds coated his beard.

The lights in here were dim, and with hardly anyone left to take care of the palace, it was dusty, and dishes were stacked haphazardly. I knew Ada would never run her place like this, and even so, I was glad she wasn't here. I hoped she was somewhere safe.

"Sorin with Meske?" Spense asked, his long legs dangling off his own countertop.

Badras nodded. "They spent some time in the gardens with Aislinn, and last I saw, they were taking her to bed."

"That's nice," I managed, even as my heart clenched in fear of that family shrinking.

Before the dawn, the healers would be setting themselves up on the outskirts of Silver Lake, taking any young children and those unable to fight with them.

Shrugging, Badras threw the core of the pepper over his shoulder and dug in the bag for another snack. "You'd think they'd be used to it by now. War."

To my surprise, it was Olys who spoke first. "Sorin has had plenty of time to familiarize himself with battle. But having his family—his *soulmate* and *daughter*—on the front line, in imminent danger, is new. And I can tell you, it's terrifying."

Badras didn't speak, his eyes only flicking once to the faded tattoo on Olys's left arm. My lungs tight, I looked to Spense, and I understood. I didn't want to imagine a scenario in which something happened to him—*couldn't.*

"I'm sorry, Olys. I know you don't like to speak of it, but I am truly sorry."

He looked to me, and for a second, I prepared myself for one of his harsh barbs.

But he looked to his hands, sighing deeply. "I'm sorry too. She wouldn't want me to live like this—to be too lost in my own grief to even speak of her. She was smart and witty and brave. It's been twenty years. But that kind of thing—I just … I'm not ready."

My heart broke for him. There was nothing I felt I could say to ease his sorrow.

"This would be a great time for one of Alwyn's one-liners," Badras said, and we all smiled. The thought of her was warm even if it was another reason we were all grieving. He jumped off the counter. "I'm off. See you all at dawn. Brothers. Sister," he added, giving me a nod.

I smiled.

Olys left soon after.

Spense stood, taking my plate gently, and tidied up as best as he could. "Are you ready to sleep?"

I shook my head.

"A walk?"

I laughed. "Gaia, no."

He smiled. "What do you want to do?"

I suddenly couldn't stand to be in this palace any longer, not with its memories and reminders. "How about we visit the garden?"

***

"These flowers got annihilated by the snow." Tsking, I dropped the head of the yellow daffodil I'd been inspecting. It drooped sadly.

"I'm just glad it's melting," Spense admitted. He ran a hand over a patch of pink peonies, and water splashed from the petals. "Did you ever find out why it snowed in the first place?"

I stopped in front of my favourite alcove, where the purple lobelia I loved so much was dried up and brown. I sighed. "I think it was something to do with me leaving. The balance upset, all that."

Spense followed me to the bench, where we sat and looked at my sad flower bush. "The flowers will come back," he said, planting a kiss on my shoulder. "As will you. This is just a patch of winter."

I smiled. "I love you."

Grinning, he flicked the top of my nose. "Love you too."

His eyes were so pure, so filled with emotion that I could barely stand the overwhelming love I felt. It gathered in my magic, in his, and bubbled to the surface. His gaze dipped to my mouth, and my stomach flopped. He was so handsome, so alluring, and sometimes, I had to pinch myself that he looked at me this way. With desire.

I crossed the distance of the bench easily, kissing him with all the emotion that had welled up inside me. By the way he kissed me back, I knew he was also caught up in it.

And it was lovely.

The way his hands roamed only drove my own, and when one hand moved from the curls at the back of his head to his horn, dragging a finger up one, the other smoothed over the muscles in his abdomen. I delighted when he sucked in a breath.

"Diana—" he choked out. "I—my horns—they're sensitive."

I didn't let up.

He placed his hands on my waist and tugged me away. "I'm serious. You need to stop if you don't want—"

"I do want." I looked into Spense's face, his cheeks flushed and his lower lip slightly swollen. To accentuate my point, I took his hands and travelled them up my body to my chest. "I want you. All of you."

"Are you sure?" His grey eyes were steely, shining as he looked at me. At our joined hands.

The black ink of our tattoos blinked in the starlight, an encouragement and a comfort.

"I've spent the last few months—hell, my whole life really—second-guessing every decision I've ever made. This, you and me, this is the first thing I've been completely sure of. There's not a whisper of doubt in my mind."

Spense's smile was radiant, and I was certain in that moment that the moon was jealous of how he glowed in this garden.

"You are the best thing that's ever happened to me," he told me as my arms wrapped around his neck. "You saved me. I would have become something ... horrible without you."

I pressed a kiss on his mouth. Firm, blazing, to say what words couldn't. *I see you. Your soul is imperfect and fractured, but so is mine. We'll heal each other.*

I guided his hands down my body, and he shuddered, his eyelids flickering.

"Diana," he murmured between kisses. "I know that you have ...

experience. And that's okay. But you should know that this … I've never …"

I pulled back to look at him, at the open way he waited for me to respond to his vulnerability. "Really?"

He smiled crookedly. "Is that so hard to believe?"

"I just thought there would have been hordes of females eager for your attention. I mean, look at you. You're gorgeous." I touched his cheek softly.

He pressed a kiss into my palm. "I never gave myself time to pursue that sort of thing; any distraction from training was unacceptable in my mind. But I see now that my soul knew. That it didn't matter. You were coming for me."

My heart flopped over on itself, and I could no longer think of words as I kissed him, my hands tangling in his curly midnight hair. No coherent thoughts, just feelings. My soulmate. He was mine forever. And I was his.

He laid me down in the grass, the blades still damp from the melting snow. Slowly, gently, our clothes vanished, until there was nothing between us, save for our magic, pulsing as wildly as our hearts.

He kissed me with all the love he could muster, and I felt that love in the pull between us, in the air, in our touch. He was kind and yielding, strong and sure, playful and teasing. Every move he made I matched with my own, easily and wholly.

Spense was my equal in all ways. He didn't let me slip back or let my flame dim. He pushed me to be front and centre, to take back what my birthright demanded from me. It was the same way that I led him from the darkness, allowing his just, protective nature to shine through.

With him by my side, I was not afraid. I could face tomorrow. I could make the hard choices, not just after the sun rose, but every dawn after that too. Because he saw every flawed part of me and loved all of it. With his body pressed against mine, our magic swirling happily, like smoke curling from a fire, I was certain that we would be all right.

PART THREE

FORTY-NINE

SPENSE
THE QUEEN IS HERE

"You look beautiful in this armour." I snapped the last strap across her breastplate and stepped back.

Diana was elegance personified. Her hair was braided in the fashion that Alwyn had preferred, and her sword hung from her hip, where she rested a hand on its pommel.

But the look in her eyes—that was the real difference in her. She had been presented with an unthinkable destiny, one where she would have to defeat her own mother. Others would crumble under this weight, but my soulmate held her shoulders high.

I had never loved her more.

We had woken in the grass to find that flowers had fallen from the bushes surrounding us and decorated our hair. Diana giggled as she stopped me from pulling the lilac-coloured petals out, kissing me gently and telling me that they would be good luck. It was fitting, I agreed, that the flowers were nearly the exact hue of our bonded magic.

It was agony to let go of Diana, knowing what we would face today. I held her in my arms for as long as I could get away with, until the sky turned from black to navy to pink.

Then, we joined our group of rebels and sat with them quietly as we enjoyed possibly our last peaceful morning together. When the sun had touched the sky, we had risen and readied for war.

"I wish I didn't have to wear it," Diana admitted.

She reached out to cup my head in her hand gently, and I leaned into it.

"I know."

With my own armour in place, I unsheathed Bloodletter, watching the light of the dawn dance off its red blade. Badras whistled from across the room.

"I've always loved that blade," he remarked, tying his long hair into a knot on the top of his head. "It's unmatched. Can't say the same about its wielder though," he added, smirking.

I let the easiness, the light laughter, fill me up, holding it close to my heart. It was a reminder of everything we were fighting for. Happiness. It would fuel me on the battlefield.

Through the laughter, Diana started looking around. "Has anyone seen Aedan?"

There was a collective shaking of heads. It was strange for him not to be here. Maybe he was with his army, making sure everyone was prepared.

"I haven't seen Maisie either," Meske spoke out. "She was supposed to help me with inventory this morning."

Diana's eyes flicked to me, worry filling them.

"They're probably together," I reassured her. "Didn't you say they had something going on between them?"

She nodded, pulling her bottom lip into her mouth to chew on it. "They should be here."

Truthfully, it didn't feel right that both of them were missing on a morning of this calibre. But this was war, and they were capable of taking care of themselves. Diana would only worry for them the longer she sat on it.

"Well," I drawled, hooking my finger into her weapons belt and pulling her closer. Our armour made a distinct, almost-comical clinking noise when it touched. "I know that I would have done anything to make our morning last a little longer."

She flushed, a smile creeping up onto her lips.

"Relax. They're probably on their way here right now."

Diana nodded, and inwardly, I breathed a sigh of relief. I kissed her gently until Olys grumpily and very loudly informed the room how much he hated public displays of affection.

The doors to the throne room we occupied swung open, a red-faced runner from Aedan's army nearly collapsing into the room. We all knew by the look on his face whose presence he was about to announce.

"She's here." Diana took a deep breath, and it caught in her throat.

The runner nodded, and she dismissed him.

I took her hands, gazing at her hazel eyes, more stunning than the sunset, before kneeling in front of her. Her eyes widened slightly, and then she understood. She placed a hand on my shoulder, and even through the cold metal, I could feel her warmth.

"Go with my blessing."

I stood and then smiled as she repeated the Queen's Blessing to each of my siblings when they took their turn, kneeling at her feet. My heart could have burst with the pride I felt for her. For earning the respect she deserved.

When we were all standing, I led her to the ivory throne on the dais, where I had seen her mother sit with cold eyes. She swallowed once, her vulnerability only for me to see, before settling into the large chair.

She placed her hands on the arms, crossing a knee over her leg. A deathly still calm washed over her, and she was almost unrecognizable, except for the magic that waved out, daring anyone to come near.

I stood behind her, and my siblings each lined up below the dais. Motion stirred behind the doors, and a guard slipped in.

"The queen is here."

I looked to my Diana, her small frame commanding the throne as if she had sat in it her whole life.

Yes, I thought, *the queen is right here.*

I drew my weapon, and the others followed suit.

Diana set her shoulders, lifting her chin. "Send her in."

FIFTY

DIANA
FRIENDLY FIRE

The guard who had alerted us was barely out of the way before the doors blasted open, a finery-draped figure gliding into the room.

"My daughter returns. I rejoice." Vera opened her arms out, the fabric of her gown falling from her outstretched limbs like flames, the red hue abrasively bright.

This was my mother … but it was not.

Her face was gaunt and sunken, her eyes dark around the rims. She seemed to bare fangs instead of teeth as she grinned maniacally at me. The frenetic energy that poured off her was sticky and ill, reminding me of something that I couldn't place.

Whatever I had been expecting when I finally came face-to-face with my mother again, it wasn't this. I swallowed, my throat thick.

"Well? Have you nothing to say? Here you sit, upon my throne, and not a word about it? Come on now. I was expecting a speech at least. I'm *bored*."

I was launched into the memory Jweira had shown me on a day that seemed like decades ago now. The Seelie Queen, wolf mask adorning her face, poked and prodded at the Unseelie princess until she got what she wanted from her. A fight.

"This might have been your throne," I said, willing my voice not to waver, "but you lost your right to it the moment you condemned the realm to teeter, unbalanced, for millennia, its fae separated and suffering. In fact, I don't believe the ancestors ever truly blessed you to rule, Ilysia."

My mother tilted her head to the side, her smirk never leaving. "Let's hear your theory then. I would love to learn how discerning you turned out to be."

I hated the condescending tone, the way she stared into my soul as if she knew how to reach into my deepest weaknesses and exploit them.

She is my mother, I reminded myself. *She knows me better than anyone.*

Spense's hand landed on my shoulder, and I felt a surge of warmth. No, not anyone. Vera never knew the real me. She never tried to look past the dutiful daughter she could keep on a leash at what was truly in my heart.

Just like her first daughter.

The one I had been named for.

The sudden realization that I was a *replacement* turned my stomach to ash. She hadn't even given me my own name. I could have thrown up in that moment, the heaviness sitting on my chest in a pressure I had never known. I was Diana, but really, I was the second try at Diana. A pawn.

"You pulled the strings from the moment the Unseelie were driven from Eira. Every ruler was under your complete manipulation. You used dark magics to do unspeakable things, and now, you're twisted and ugly."

Badras spat on the ground, driving my point home.

Vera rolled her eyes. "Yes, yes, the obvious facts. That's all you have? Surely, you aren't that daft. Naive and gullible, maybe, but you were always smart."

I ground my teeth together. "What more is there? You've sat on a false throne for eight thousand years, and you are going to be punished for it."

She laughed then, the sound merciless and cold. "Punished? By you? How terrifying."

"By Gaia, by Ouranos, by the other deities, and whoever else on that plane that has a bone to pick with how you treated this realm."

"Gaia has no power here. Certainly not over me. If you're going for a fear tactic, I would try again, my child."

"I am not your child." I seethed.

"Oh, but you are." Vera grinned. "Born from this very body, the result of an incredibly bold male who declared himself my soulmate. It was fun while it lasted," she added, a twisting smirk pulling at her lips. "And his appearance meant I could finally take back my rightful place, front and centre. But once I had what I needed—*you*—he became a nuisance."

I felt bile creep up my throat. "You murdered your soulmate?"

"When you've been alive as long as I have, you'll realize that there is no such thing as love. It's all a farce, driven by an innate base desire to procreate. I will say, the time it took to repair my magic after Jago's death was cumbersome. Nearly worth keeping him alive actually."

I could barely draw a breath. I was related to this malicious creature. "You make me sick."

"Again, I'm *bored*. Your insults are so very drab."

"Well, when I've had millennia to come up with creative ways to spew hate, maybe I'll be more entertaining."

Vera moved closer to the throne, stopping when my guard raised their weapons. "Now, now." She tsked. "We don't play with swords here. If you want to play, we use magic."

Her eyes glinted, and she raised a hand. Before I could yell out a warning, Sorin was blasted through the air, landing against the window in a sickening crunch and sliding to the floor.

Spense immediately stepped forward, a dark, choking fog coming from his palms and heading right for Vera. While she eyed it, the first time I'd seen caution cross her face, she kept her hands out, the fog parting around her like a river slipping over a rock.

"You're outnumbered," Olys said, his voice steely. Of everyone in the room, him speaking up was a shock. "Don't try anything stupid."

Vera flicked her gaze over him, trailing up and down like a hawk circling its prey. "My, you have the gall, don't you? Although I suppose I should expect nothing less from a son of Urdan." She bared her teeth. "Surprised I know of your lineage? You shouldn't be. The longer your life unnaturally extends, the more you stink of the bastard."

Badras flung his sword with no warning, the movement so slick that I barely registered it. Vera staggered back, her hands catching the hilt as the blade slid into her abdomen.

I stared, open-mouthed, as the lilac smell of her magic filled the room, and the sword dissolved into smoke. The hilt clattered to the marble floor, not a drop of blood spilled.

"Like I said," Vera growled, stretching her jaw, "we don't play with swords here."

Magic gathered around her, creating a thick tension in the air and sending flowery perfume into my nose, and then the room shook with a massive thunder.

Yelling ensued from the halls, and as I ran to the window, I could see why.

The entire left parapet of the palace was crumbling, fire climbing and rocks falling, skittering down the roof and breaking holes. The palace continued to shake as the parapet collapsed, until there was nothing left of it and the walls were bare and open.

Thank the goddess we moved the army.

Then, everything stilled, the quiet deafening.

It didn't give me a moment to catch my breath before the throne room began showing effects of the blast. Cracks ran up the walls, and from them … fire. It poured through, seeking more air to take over as it searched for anything flammable.

Flames licked up the curtains, thankfully not climbing the stone walls. The smoke steadily gathering and the tremor running through the floor did not fill me with much confidence in the throne room's integrity.

"Friendly fire?" Vera asked, surprised. "I didn't think you had it in you."

"Don't pretend that wasn't your doing," I spat.

She picked at a piece of ash that had landed on her shoulder. "Please. If that had been my intention, there would be no doubt it was me."

I spun toward Spense. "Tell me that wasn't one of ours," I growled.

He shook his head, jaw set. His gaze landed on something behind me, and murder danced in his eyes.

I turned.

And could only stare in disbelief.

Because stalking toward us, clad head to toe in polished iron armour I would never be able to forget, was a human.

FIFTY-ONE

MAISIE
SPIRAL

"**I** don't like this."

"Oh, really? I thought you were joking the other eight times you said so." At the edge of the pond, I pulled my shoes off. The water glinted at me, and I was struck with an uncanny feeling that resembled the Sacred Pool's magic. I felt … watched. But unlike my experiences at the Pool, this water did not send fear rippling up my spine. I was not afraid.

"Let me do it at least." Aedan hung back on the grassy part before it turned into pebbling rocks.

I didn't look back at him, knowing what would happen if I let myself fall into those blue eyes. "And steal my credit? I don't think so, Captain."

He made a sound that could only be described as a harrumph.

My cloak fell next, and although the air was usually stifling and hot in the Unclaimed Land, a lovely breeze danced off the water. It ruffled my hair and filled my nose with the scent of flowers.

"You are my Seelie representative," I said, watching the regality of the waterfall melt into the pond almost seamlessly. "And your magic is much stronger than mine. I need you here, on the outside, to make sure everything goes all right."

His hand at my elbow was warm and electric. "Maisie," he said gently, and I sighed before giving in to his gaze, nearly the same colour as the gorgeous blue water. "I can't lose you."

I forced myself to keep my eyes open, to drink in every detail in Aedan's soft face. His jaw was defined, his brows drawn, and yet he still exuded tenderness. The way he looked at me was how I had always dreamed of being looked at, and I wanted to live in this moment forever. To take his hand and wade into the water, splash and play under the waterfall as if we were two souls with endless time to spend together, enjoying nothing but each other's company.

But there was a war on our doorstep. In fact, it had likely already begun, by the looks of the sun's high position in the sky. So, I took the fantasy of who we might have been and tucked it away to keep it safe.

I was certain he suspected it. What I was prepared to do. But we didn't speak of that fact—the one that pointed to me not waking up from this.

Gaia's Council had always needed a sacrifice. We were working around the original system because we did not have the time or resources to find the anchors of each deity. In my vision, I could only see Hollaina's sapphire—a memory the stone had transferred to me, I had learned—but Kol had assured me that all four were needed. When I had suggested this plan to him of using just the one, he could not guarantee it would work. But he also could not say that it would fail, which was what I held on to.

I touched Aedan's cheek gently. "I don't want to be lost."

He leaned into my palm, and the scruff on his face tickled me. "But there's no backing down now." His sigh was resigned, final.

I nodded, and my hand slipped away. "We'll do this, Aedan. We'll stop Ilysia, and then Diana can take control. There's no other way." At least, none that we had been able to find.

"I still don't like it," he muttered.

I managed a smile and stood on my tiptoes to give him a swift kiss. He was having none of that though and hoisted me to his chest when I went to pull away. Aedan kissed with all his emotion, his mouth firm and pressing on mine. A promise, not a goodbye.

With one last look into those quickly hardening ocean eyes, I stepped away and dipped my toe into the water.

Immediately, I could feel the magic imbued in the waves, and I took a shuddering breath as I allowed it to flow into mine. I waded farther into the pond, and from the sounds of light splashing behind me, everyone else was coming in too.

I could only go so far, as some of our patrons were not very tall, and when I got waist deep, they circled around me.

"Float on your back," suggested the brownie, Hala.

Glancing at the kelpie circling around us with unflinching black pits for eyes, I slid down in the water and pushed onto my back, letting the water hold me up.

I cradled the borrowed sapphire to my chest, its weight anchoring me. Energy buzzed all around—from the stone to the water and everyone in between.

"The kelpie won't harm us," Josette said, her voice entirely too confident.

"How can you be sure?" The Unseelie female nearly shook as she watched the spiny creature lazily swish its tail to propel itself through the water, keeping us in its beady gaze.

Josette smiled. "Because I spoke with him!" When no one looked convinced, she sighed. "It's sad no one learns languages anymore. Pixies are fluent in every form of communication there is. It's one of Gaia's gifts to us," she preened.

The nymph spoke in its dialect then, its voice like the wind and the words like chimes dancing in it.

Josette flushed, turning up her chin in a pout. "Next time you want to test my abilities, I would appreciate more *polite* words."

"Focus." Aedan's army voice moved across the water, sending goose bumps up and down my arms. "Let's get started."

Without fuss, everyone obliged. One by one, each of Gaia's creations placed one hand on my body and the other on the Folk to their left. If I could look at us from a bird's-eye view, I would imagine us in a spiral similar to a snail's shell.

There was a tug on my magic as everyone began tapping into their own. Aedan's wrapped soothingly around me, staying close. The combined feeling of all these different magics was addictive, exhilarating, satisfying. It was strong, and it danced in colourful waves as it reached me.

My eyelids started to droop. For the first time, fear kicked in, warning me to stand up, get out of here before it was too late.

But I couldn't move if I wanted to. My limbs felt like stone, the water a restful bed. All the fatigue, the muscle soreness, the terror of the last few weeks settled into my bones and made my mind numb.

I wanted to yawn, but I couldn't make my jaw open. Not with the smothering magic keeping me immobile.

With one last look up at Aedan, I fell into darkness.

FIFTY-TWO

AEDAN
LIMBO

My molars ground together as magic started to fatigue me. Maisie's limp body floated in the water between us. Us—a group of mismatched beings who didn't have training or anything other than basic knowledge of this ancient ritual.

It hurt to look at her face, staring blankly up toward the temperamental sky. I wanted to close her eyes, but somehow, even if I could free up a hand to reach for her, it felt wrong. Like it was final.

So, I stared at her, even as my heart fell to the pit of my gut and my stomach churned uncomfortably. How long should this take? Surely, calling out into the netherworld for the goddess of all fae couldn't take that long? She was there to deliver a message and get out. Maisie had been adamant on this.

Time felt entirely too fast and slow. Sometime after she fell unconscious, after we swayed against the gentle lapping of the water and channelled magic into one another and Maisie, the Folk began to show their worry. What started as swift glances around the circle quickly turned into chittering whispers of doubt.

"We should think about a plan," Hala said, eyes locked on me. "How much longer are we prepared to hold her for?"

"As long as it takes," I ground out.

The Unseelie female, Indra, shifted her weight. It was barely a movement, but the already-moving water was the catalyst of a chain reaction. It threw everyone off-balance, and soon, we were gripping each other with white knuckles to keep from disjoining.

"Does the water seem choppier to anyone?" Josette asked, her pink light flickering with her shivers as she sat on top of the waves like a leaf.

She was right. The sky was dramatically stormier, any blue in the sky replaced with grey. The air seemed colder, more bitter, as the water churned unpredictably.

"It's the kelpie." The goblin shot a daggered look at the swimming beast, who still kept close, its tail thrashing against the tide.

"It is *not*!" Josette huffed. "He's trying to keep the water steady for us."

A spattering of arguments broke out, but I cut right through them, my well-practiced captain's voice booming across the water. "Enough! Something's happening in the atmosphere—a storm of some sort. It could be caused by the battle in the North, but it's more likely that we're the only ones experiencing it."

I looked down at Maisie's body. Her limbs had started to twitch gently.

"She's losing her grip on the magic," the gnome said. "If we don't pull her out, she could be lost for good."

The elf, tallest of the group and wispy, fought for balance against the white-capped water, clinging to the gnome next to her to keep from breaking the chain.

The druid spoke, its voice tinkling, and Josette translated. "How do we bring Maisie back without harming her mind?"

My mind spun, anxiety weaving a pit in my stomach. I never should have agreed to this plan.

Everyone stared at me, as if I were the one to come up with this absurd idea of twisting an ancient ritual and cheating the way Gaia had demanded it to be done. I was valuable with a weapon and with a map of army movements. Not this. Never this. Diana had always been more in tune with magic. Hers had bloomed like an entire garden exposed to the sun while I struggled to care enough to use mine on a daily basis.

"I don't know!" I nearly yelled. "Surely, *one* of you can think of something? An idea? Anything!"

Then, without warning, Josette yelped, "Her ear!"

Maisie's shockingly open eyes blinked rapidly, her lips parted. A fine trickle of red blood snaked from her inner ear down her jaw, dripping into the water. It hissed and sizzled as it made contact.

"Oh dear." Josette stood, her little pink shoes not heavy enough to break the surface of the pond. "The kelpie finds himself struggling to resist his baser desires."

Indeed, the kelpie seemed to be warring with itself as Maisie's blood entered the water, thrashing closer and then back away. Any success it was having at keeping our area steady was lost, the waves threatening to pull us apart once more.

"What happens if we separate?" the goblin asked. "I don't want to be unconscious in the water with that thing!"

Wild eyes and frenzied magic were all around, and if I wasn't in the middle of it, I wouldn't have believed the intense power that thrummed. All these Folk were something different, blessed in unique ways by Gaia. And with all of them together, fear causing their magic to act on its own, a foreboding sense of urgency bled into my mind.

They were going to cause an explosion.

"Stop! Everyone, calm down!"

The feeling grew stronger, and I was sure we were about to be torn apart when it stopped.

Everything stopped.

The water smoothed, the magic stemmed, and even the clouds began to part in the sky. I took a deep breath, finally able to think properly.

And only then did I realize what had caused it.

"She let go of it." Josette stared down at Maisie, walking on the water's surface to place a tiny hand on her cheek. "She's in there alone now."

Without the magic to hold them, everyone started making a beeline for the shore, eager to escape the kelpie. I tugged Maisie close, cradling her body in my arms.

Indra helped me bring her out of the water, where she used her sun gifts to dry Maisie's dress and hair. The sapphire on Maisie's chest glinted in the sunlight.

"She's alive," Indra told me. "She might still come back."

"I don't understand." I felt numb. Raw and empty, exhausted from the pull of magic.

"The fact that she's not dead means that she was accepted on the ancestral plane," Josette offered. "In some way, shape, or form, she's communicating with those who dwell there. We can only hope it's truly Gaia and not a malevolent spirit looking for revenge."

Indra shot the pixie a glare, and I resisted the urge to swat at her hovering body like a fly.

"What do we do now?" Hala asked, wringing her tunic of water as she stood behind us.

The druid and nymph had disappeared, likely in the spirit-like form they used to travel faster than we could. The goblin was stalking off into the trees, muttering under his breath, and the leprechaun was sneaking looks back as he slinked away too.

"Damn untrustworthy scum," I muttered.

Josette shook a tiny fist in the air. "They are not worthy! They will be punished by our goddess!"

Indra cleared her throat. "I will take Maisie to the healers and see if anything can be done to keep her strength up while she's, uh … in limbo." She pushed a strand of Maisie's honey-yellow curls out of her face in a very nurturing way. "You need to get to the battle," she added, facing me this time. "We don't know yet if Maisie will be successful, and your army is without a captain."

I nearly rejected her. Ryen was there, as well as Maverick and Diana and Spense and his seemingly unending line of siblings with unrivalled battle experience. I should be here, with Maisie, to make sure she woke up. To give her my magic, if she needed it.

But Indra was right. I had left my queen in a risk that hadn't paid off—at least not at that moment. I needed to be there, to make things right. To ensure that the responsibility no longer fell on anyone else to do my job. My duty.

I turned to Indra, my face hard. "Stay with her."

FIFTY-THREE

DIANA
SHATTERING GLASS

"**G**et out of here," I told Spense urgently. "Warn the armies."

"I'm not leaving you." His eyes were steel, and I knew of all the battles I would fight today, this was not one I'd win.

The human soldier was bedecked in iron, although to his credit, it looked lightweight and well made. His helmet shone brightly, and a peculiar set of white wings, forged from the same metal, bracketed the sides. He took his time coming into the room, armour clanging loudly as he finally stopped a few feet away from the dais.

"What are you?" Vera asked, tilting her head curiously.

"My name is Dane, and I am here to end the war my ancestors started." He pulled up the visor of his helmet, revealing very fae-like features, just as I had seen in Rathe. And just like those humans, his ears were small and rounded, one of the only distinguishable features.

End the war?

"You are here in peace?" I asked, hope surging in my chest.

His gaze snapped to me, and he scowled. "If by that, you mean fighting for the peace that was stolen from us by unnatural abominations, then yes."

Any optimism I had deflated inside me. "We left your realm," I told him, putting an arm out to stop Spense from advancing on the human. "And yet you cannot be happy with that? Instead, you must follow us to *our home* to continue this horrible war?"

Dane bared his teeth. "Our fight was not yet over with you. Just because you fled, it does not mean you escaped punishment."

Icy fear spread through my veins as the prophecy became clear. Words I had barely given any thought to were now ringing true—and my life would be affected by them.

The final battle was about to begin.

"Enough of this," Vera scoffed.

She flung a hand into the air, and with the blast of magic that came from her, Dane should be well and truly incapacitated. But he stood there, wholly unaffected, lip curled in disgust.

Vera froze. "How?" She sent another blast—with the same non-reaction. "You have no magic. You're as dry as a riverbed. How do you defy me?"

Dane spat at her feet. "You are all demons, practicing the devil's work. Our god has granted us with the scientific advancements to be able to strike as his hand would." He tried not to be obvious about it, but for a flicker of a second, his hand twitched at his side, reaching for the metal box on his belt.

I glanced at Spense, who nodded almost imperceptibly. He'd noticed it too.

With Vera distracted, Olys was tending to Sorin, who was sitting up now, thankfully. My gaze flitted around the room, looking for Badras, and Spense bent to whisper in my ear.

"He's gone to warn the others."

It was remarkable how quietly he'd slipped from the room—a good reminder not to let myself get too distracted.

Vera wore no sword, no visible weapons. Her magic was always the deadliest in her arsenal. Without it, she hesitated—something she did not do often.

"We need to close the portal," Spense added.

I chewed on the inside of my cheek. I didn't like that thought—it meant we would end up taking every single human life on Eira's land. And while they had come with the intent to take as many fae lives as possible, this order meant there was no driving them back, no retreat. Without a definitive end to this, there was no way to keep a portal open permanently, like the ancestors wanted.

Kashdan strode into the room, suited up in armour, his grey beard braided. Guards wearing the West's colours flanked him, weapons raised. He stared me down, jaw tight.

"About time," Vera snapped.

"We're in position, My Queen. Awaiting the signal."

Dane laughed humourlessly. "A queen who does not even fight with her army. It is not a surprise really. After all, you cowardly demons are without a high power to fight for—and thus, you fear death. I embrace the day that I am welcomed into the gates of salvation."

Kashdan's face contorted into a mix of confusion and anger. "Who is this?" He peered closer. "Or should I say, *what* is this?"

Without warning, Dane lunged for the older male. Iron glinted, and in the blink of an eye, a silver-handled dagger slashed across Kashdan's throat.

He fell to the ground, hands scrambling in vain to cover the red pumping from his neck. Twitching, eyes wide in alarm, he choked on his own blood. Within seconds, he went still.

The two Western guards launched over their prince's body at Dane, who deftly avoided their attack, moving as quick and lithe as a cat. Only using his dagger, the length smaller than a forearm, he blocked and disarmed them.

When one of the guards went for his sword on the ground, Dane got there first and kicked it away. It skidded across the room with a scraping metallic whine.

"Uh-uh." He tsked. "I can have this dagger embedded in her throat faster than you can get to me. How sad it would be to lose the war before it's begun." He pointed the red-tipped blade in Vera's direction.

The guards looked to the queen, whose face, I noticed for the first time, was shocked. She did not look scared—I didn't think she had that emotion—but surprise was evident in her unusual lack of words. Her eyes flicked to Kashdan's lifeless body, then to Dane.

"I have done you a favour," the human drawled. "Now, your subjects must see how you truly lead." He backed from the room, arms outstretched, cocky grin on his face. "I'll see you on the battlefield, *Queen.*"

I charged after my mother as she whipped through the hallways of the palace. She hadn't waited for Kashdan's body to get cold—in fact, she hadn't even spared her oldest advocate another glance before taking off, his guards flanking her.

Spense and Badras shouted after me to stop, and I knew I should listen to them. Vera was the smaller threat right now, as unforeseen as it had been. I was needed in the making of plans against the humans.

Vera's gown train slipped around a corner, and I leaped forward, landing on it. The jarring halt she had to make was accompanied by her furious strike of magic, which I blocked with my own.

She sneered at me. "Look at what you've done. Your magic was pure and white. Now?" She curled her upper lip in disgust. "Tinged with darkness."

"Can you just listen for a *second*?" I growled. "We need to work together against the humans. We can't fight them divided."

She motioned for the guards to leave us, turning her deadly gaze back to me. "They are still flesh and blood. They are nothing my soldiers cannot strike down."

"Did you not see Dane? The humans can block magic, *and* they're as trained as we are. We're condemning ourselves if we don't unite against them!"

Vera took a step closer to me, and I barely breathed, holding my shoulders back tightly. "If you are so worried, then relinquish your forces to me."

"I can't believe you. I knew you were proud, but stupid?"

My mother's hand shot out, and she caught my chin harshly. Her nails dug in, but I would not let myself wince. "Brave little Diana thinks she knows how to fight a war because there are mentally ill zealots following her. Does it make you feel important when they hang on every word you say?"

I gritted my teeth, refusing to look away from her icy stare.

"Does it fuel your ego that tells you that you have a right to my throne? Hmm?" She used her nails to force my head from side to side, inspecting me.

"I have more of a right to rule Eira than you do," I spat.

Vera laughed darkly. "You don't understand the sacrifices it takes to be successful."

"And you do? What have you ever sacrificed for the good of the realm?"

She watched me for a moment and released me. Pain bit at me, and I smoothed a hand over my chin.

"Well, *you*. Or the original you, I should say."

My heart caught in my throat. "Your first daughter became the queen who brought peace to Eira after your treachery.”

“Unlike you, my first Diana was obedient. So easily moulded. By the time the crown sat on her head, there was not a single move she made that I hadn’t orchestrated. And when it came time to seal the realm so Urdan could never bring his slime back here, I needed something powerful that would bind the magic.” Vera smiled, her teeth bared. “And she was the most powerful thing in my arsenal.”

Frigid cold washed over me, running through my veins like ice from head to toe. “You—you killed her? Your own daughter?”

“I made my sacrifice for the realm, and I would do it again.” She laughed at the horror on my face. “Does that scare you? It should. You might be needed by the time this war is over.”

I swallowed, pushing through my fear. “I don’t believe you. If she died, then how was our line continued?”

“Sacrificial magic has been my pathway to great power—more than you could fathom. You cannot comprehend what I have been able to accomplish. My line—the Lightbringer line—comes from me and me alone.”

My eyes flicked to her left arm, where a faded soulmate tattoo resided under the sleeve of her dress.

She tracked the movement and tilted her head to the side. “This was not my first body, you know. Nor was it the second or third or tenth or twentieth. Each has been an excellent vessel for me to use while giving the appearance of several generations. After ascending, the body is at its weakest point. That is when I take it for myself.”

Bile crept up my throat. I wanted to double over and be sick. “But I saw them—my ancestors. You’re saying they didn’t exist?”

Vera rolled her eyes. “Dumb girl. Of course they existed. I birthed each one myself. They were allowed to have their own life until twenty-two. Then, their body was needed to serve other purposes.”

"You—that's so twisted—I …" My breath came in big gulps as the revelation settled in my head. "You have ruled since the beginning, wearing different faces."

"Is that really so hard to understand?" she mocked. "The best part was that each body was matched with a soulmate—Gaia's attempt to make an offspring that would finally oppose me, I'm sure. So, each body was made more powerful than the last, and I could reap it just as easily."

"My father?" I didn't want to ask; I didn't want to know. But I had to.

Vera smiled, humility slipping off her like water off the rocks. "Ah, yes, Jago Harwell. Handsome, smart. Those nine years before conceiving you were slow, I have to admit. He was not anything special, by any means. Not like the one that nearly helped Iave free herself from me."

A booming crash sounded below, shaking the walls. There was no more fire, but burn marks across the entire hall hinted at structural damage. The palace was becoming more dangerous by the second.

"Why are you telling me this?"

"Your insolent whelp of a soulmate ruined my chance to reap your body after your ascension. You are now *useless* to me." Another rumble shook us. A terrible creak sounded from the walls. "I will have to make a new heir. And you are too much of a liability to the peace of Eira."

She stepped closer, and a haze of magic followed. She was building it, growing it, so she could end me in one move.

The palace shook again. The window beside us cracked, the line running from opposite corners.

"Tell your precious ancestors they'll have to try harder next time."

Before my mother could deliver my fatal blow, I wrapped my arms around her and yanked as hard as I could toward the shiny surface.

The palace began to crumble. Shattering glass was the only thing I could hear as Vera and I went careening through the window.

FIFTY-FOUR

SPENSE
SURVIVE

I flung Bloodletter across the clearing, watching as it sank into the back of the human who had been about to slash his weapon across Badras's torso.

The thud of the body falling caught my brother's attention, and his eyes darted to me. "Bloody cowards, striking when my back is turned," he spat, wrenching my sword free.

I took it up again, my palm sliding into the familiar groove of the hilt.

"They're humans—what did you expect?"

Badras grunted in agreement. "The good news is that they seem to have changed the way their magic-blocking works. They have it on each individual being instead of casting it like a big umbrella. That leaves them vulnerable to wide-range attack."

An idea sparked in my mind, and I hauled the first Unseelie soldier I could find toward me. "Are you a storm user?"

The male blinked in surprise and shook his head. "Fauna. But she is."

He pointed to a female with two long braids that reminded me of my sister. She fought off one of Vera's soldiers and locked eyes with me when I jumped in to help incapacitate him.

"I didn't need your help," she said, her words clipped.

"But I need yours. Storm user?" I barely waited for her to confirm before continuing, "Find a place on the outskirts where you can feel your magic again, away from the humans. Then, fire away—clean shots only."

Understanding flared in her eyes. "I'll need to recruit a few more to help. There's not a cloud in sight—we'll have to summon them from the nearest storm."

"Do what you have to do."

She nodded, scurrying off.

"An interesting idea," Badras mused, easily shoving away his next attacker. "Perhaps we could even use it to drive them to the lake."

"Exactly. As soon as we get them in the open, I'll have the drakes ready."

We continued to support the line, driving back the enemy as much as we could. I positioned myself near the edge of the River Nord, which was dangerously close to spilling over. The water raced furious and fast—the perfect way to conserve strength, especially in my wielding arm. A good shove ensured I was able to move on quickly. Even a kelpie would have a hard time surviving the formidable, churning water.

A problem, we were soon learning, was that Vera's soldiers seemed to be ignoring the humans completely, even when attacked. Sure, they fought back, but it was like they were in a trance, eyes focused wholly on the opposing fae. *Us.* I couldn't imagine Vera would be okay with the humans in the land she was so territorial over, so why had she not given the order to her army?

In a brief moment of pause, I pulled at the magic that Diana and I shared. It was there, strong as ever, but it felt far away. Like an echo. Ignoring the stab of worry at how far she was from my protection, I gave my head a shake and focused back on the problems in front of me. She was capable on her own.

The sky darkened considerably, and I found myself craning my neck to look up, others doing the same. The sun was covered by low-hanging clouds, grey and heavy with rain.

I fought a smile. Lightning shot from the sky, rapid and precise. From the yelling that ensued, it'd hit its target. Rain began to come down sideways, wind pushing it toward the direction of the river.

My Unseelie would not fail. It was I who had taught them after all. I joined back in the fray as, slowly, the battle started to move. The rain didn't stop a war, but it was its own formidable opponent. My storm users pushed the battle to the direction of Silver Lake, and my insides roared with triumph.

The ground was slick, but with the rain and considerable bloodshed, my instinct was to blame the elements.

What I did not think of, however, was the impact more water would have on the already-teeming River Nord.

As I ducked to avoid an incoming knife, my boot slid, and I lost my balance. I flung my arms out, searching for purchase, and stared into the tidal wave coming my way. Angrier than ever, water sloshed up the sides of the riverbed, spilling over onto the cobblestone streets. It was no slow trickle. The force of the wave sent my attacker sliding away, and I struggled against the arm that yanked me backward, hauling me against a huge barrel of a chest.

"It's me! It's me!" Badras stepped away, warily glancing at my sword, which I had begun to swing as soon as he let go of me.

"We need to tell the storm users to stop," I panted.

The river was merciless as it took over the streets, dropping human and fae alike.

"I say keep it coming. It's giving us the advantage to position the battle," Badras argued. "And you're welcome for saving your ass, by the way."

"We're at the lowest point of the city right now! If this keeps going the way it is, we'll be swimming instead of fighting." I eyed the slopes of the house-lined streets. "Any plan we had is out the window. We need to focus on getting to high ground."

More water crashed over the side of the river, and I leaped onto a nearby shipping crate, likely abandoned from a nearby shop, which wobbled concerningly when Badras's weight joined me.

"High ground means retreating," my brother growled. "We lose our power."

"Do you hear yourself?" I shouted. "We have no power left to lose!"

A long-handled axe floated in the water that rushed by. It was knee-height now and steadily growing. Bodies abandoned the fight in a scramble to get high; some climbing the sides of houses or trees. In the distance, I could make out running figures ascending up the hill of the main road, likely fleeing back to the palace. I cursed under my breath. This was where we lost the war.

"On the contrary, brother," Badras yelled. "We'll use the drakes to pull our soldiers from the water. Then, we can use them to drop any remaining humans to the bottom of that river, where they belong."

He grinned madly, and in that moment, I realized that my brother, as strong and unbreakable as he seemed, had also been twisted by our father. Battle was all he knew, and while his strategizing skills were unmatched, he had lost the humanity that was supposed to drive him. He was not unkind or abusive, but he had turned apathetic to the waste of life a long time ago.

My realization was confirmed when he gestured to a floating body in the water. "Let's use that as a raft and get those drakes in the air."

My throat felt dry and tight, and for once, I could not think of what to say to my own brother. Sadness pressed on my chest, mingling with a sort of guilt that made me taste bile.

The body drew closer, and Badras prepared to jump from the crate into the frenzied water.

"There's no other plan," he said, narrowing his eyes at me over his shoulder. "I know what you're thinking, but don't be an idiot. *Survive.*"

He had mistaken my quiet for trepidation of the water, which was probably for the best. When this was all over, I would make sure my brother was all right—not just physically. I would make sure all my siblings were.

"Don't worry about me."

Badras's reply was a loud splash as he hurled himself off the crate and into the treacherous water. He only had to paddle a few strokes before reaching the body, which he flipped so it faced down, and wrapped his arms over the floating piece of chest armour.

I took a deep inhale and launched in after him.

FIFTY-FIVE

AEDAN
HELL IN A HANDBASKET

If we survived this, it would be a damn miracle.

Upon my return, I found Ryen immediately, coming out from the makeshift healer's tent. Some still waited by Silver Lake, but most had been rerouted back here behind the palace after the storm broke up their travelling party.

"There you are," my second breathed. "Thank Gaia."

I looked into the tent and caught the head healer's attention. "There is an unconscious female arriving within the hour. See to it that she gets the same level of care as the high princess would."

Focusing back on Ryen, I led us away. He matched me step for step, guiding me to the battle at a run.

"Don't tell me it's Maisie."

I nodded, mouth going dry at the sight of the cobblestone ground, which was littered with fallen weapons, blood, and the occasional body. As we grew nearer to the fighting, led by the increasing noise of it, the fallen soldiers increased.

"I don't have time to explain it all. I'm sorry I wasn't here when the battle began."

"I figured you had a plan. Is Maisie's state … permanent?"

My throat felt tight. *It can't be.* "Update me."

"Maverick and I have been managing, but since the humans arrived, everything has gone to shit." Ryen veered left sharply, taking me toward the city of Nevelyn proper.

"Humans?"

"Some creature from the realm where Diana was. They've been at war with the Unseelie for centuries—hunted them through the portal to here."

I halted, grabbing my second's arm. "Are you telling me that there are now *three* different parties fighting in this war?"

He nodded. "It's chaos. They have some sort of contraption that blocks magic."

"That's impossible."

Magic had been woven into the fabric of the realm by Gaia herself. It was not something that could be snuffed out like a dull flame.

Ryen shook his head. "I've felt it myself. It's like dead air." We picked back up running. "How do we fight them?"

"They fall by blade, just as we do. We are only limited by our skill without magic's helping hand."

He did not say it, but I knew we were both thinking the same thing. Soldiers were taught not to rely solely on magic, but it was not like a button we could switch off. Whether we tried to use it or not, magic flowed through our veins, acting as a protector of the body. It gave us an extra push of speed or pulled us a hairbreadth farther from our attacker's fist.

We were as good as limbless without it.

"It doesn't sound like we made it to Silver Lake."

Ryen glanced over his shoulder at me. "We haven't been able to attack offensively at all."

Hell in a handbasket—that was what this was.

And as we rounded the corner at the top of Nevelyn's theatre district, the highest point in the city, I knew we were in for a bloody, fatal battle. What had once been a sought-after district for its homes' view of the River Nord spilling from the mountains was now a macabre scene. War, fully fledged, was playing its own symphony, bringing the harsh sounds of clanging metal and shouts all the way up the hill.

Storm clouds had rolled in low, blocking out the harsh sun, rain coming in spatters over the battlefield.

Vera's army wore her colours—emerald and black. They were fluid and unified, easy to spot. Besides the fact that most of Diana's army consisted of the Outcasts, who had no colours or even armour at all, our side looked ill-prepared.

The Nordians and the Unseelie held up their own flags, and the soldiers I'd brought from the queen's army had scrubbed their armour of the North crest, leaving us disjointed and spread out. It was far from ideal, but it was what we had.

"Let's find Maverick and make a plan."

As we began our charge down the hill, movement on the river caught my eye.

"What the—"

Horns started blowing, voices yelling, and the sound of stampeding feet shook the ground. Water was pouring out of the River Nord, flowing like a tide into the streets of Nevelyn. The waves were unnatural in size and speed as they flooded the lowest point of the city.

Ryen had the good sense to drag us both to the side of the road, pressed up against a home, as soldiers of all colours raced up the hill, heading for the safety of the high ground. A large body walked backward through the mess, grabbing at fae as he shouted orders, unmoving when anyone bumped into him.

"Maverick!" I called.

He didn't turn his head, and with the cacophony of noise, I wasn't surprised. There was no safe gap to wait for, so I hurtled myself into the stampede, making my way diagonally through it.

I grabbed at the Nordian's shoulder and ducked as a fist came flying at me.

"Thesand! Thought you knew better than to sneak up on me like that!"

"What's going on?" I yelled, hoping my voice would carry over the shouting.

Maverick turned, and with his tree trunk of a body blocking one side, it was quieter. "River's overflowing. Snow melted too fast, and the rain isn't helping. We've lost any uniformity we pretended to have. Your Outcast leader started giving her own orders," he growled.

I frowned. "Freya was in the Shynin camp."

"I know what I saw."

I knew better than to question the Nordian. "We need to regroup and make a plan before we lose this war." My eyes fixed on a body floating face down in the water below. There were less and less fleers, most having made it up the hill by now or facing a much worse fate. "How many have we lost?"

Maverick twisted his lips. "Too many. I have pegasi units on their way. An aerial attack is looking like our best option."

I remembered Spense's words about the drakes and how their fire burned everything. "It's our last resort. We can't ensure an aerial unit won't take out our own soldiers."

Maverick gripped the front of my chest plate suddenly, and my hand went to the hilt of my throwing knife.

"It's a sacrifice they signed up for. You're going to lose the war if you don't wise up."

His face was red and angry, alpha male coming off him in waves.

I took his wrist and shoved it off my armour none too gently. "Touch me like that again—"

"Help! I need help!"

We both spun. Freya was at the bottom of the hill, dragging a body with a mess of white hair behind her, trying to get it up on the dry road. Ryen was already sprinting down, and we followed.

With Ryen's help, Hollaina was pulled from the water and turned on her side to help get any remaining river from her lungs.

"She just collapsed," Freya panted, placing her hands on her knees.

I traded a look with my second.

She pointed to a large shipping crate bobbing on the water not far from us. "Leo collapsed while he was up there. His legs started to slip off, but I was able to push them back on so he wouldn't drown."

Ryen and Maverick took to the water, barely even having to swim to reach the crate.

While they retrieved the prince of the Southern Isles, I turned to Freya. "What are you doing out here?"

She smirked. "That sounds like concern. I'm touched."

"I'm concerned that you were out here, giving orders like someone in charge."

Her nostrils flared. "I *am* someone in charge. If it wasn't for my Outcasts, you'd be shit out of luck with all those magic blockers, wouldn't you? Did you really expect me to sit around in my camp, letting the war wage while I sat idly by, knitting cross-stitch? I raised you better."

"Actually, you didn't raise me at all."

Hurt shone in Freya's eyes for a moment, but she quickly covered it up. "You have no right to be so condescending. Where were *you* when the battle began?"

This back-and-forth felt better than the strained silence we'd been giving each other lately. Like we were using it to empty out all the feelings that had gone unspoken. But there would be time for that later.

Ryen and Maverick were nearly out, dragging Leo on his back through the water.

Bickering with Freya would have to wait.

"We'll take these two to the healer, and then we'll gather up all the troops behind the palace, on the road that leads to the stables. We need to make a new plan."

Stiffly, she nodded, grabbing ahold of one of Leo's arms as he was hoisted from the overflowing river.

"I'm assuming you know what caused this?" Freya gestured to the limp bodies of the deities.

This was not what Maisie had had in mind when she convened Gaia's Council. But the fact that the deities were all in the same coma-like trance that she was filled me with hope. Something was happening.

"I'll explain on the way. But if they've collapsed, then it's likely that Il—Vera has too. We should try to find her body and get her detained."

Maverick looked over the water that sloshed angrily up the sides of houses. Like a tide coming to shore, it slowly licked closer to us. "With any luck," he grunted, "she's at the bottom of that mess."

"We don't have that kind of luck," Ryen said.

"I want lookout parties searching for survivors. Inform them that Vera is to be brought to me immediately if she's found."

My second nodded.

"That home has a garden," Freya pointed out, looking at the red house to our right, where water had begun trailing close to its front step.

Maverick pursed his lips. "What an astute observation."

Freya glared. "If there's a garden, there's likely a wheelbarrow. Because unless you want to carry these bodies on your own, we'll need something to help get them back to the healers."

I had no doubt that Maverick likely *could* carry both bodies on his own with no issue, but he didn't press the matter.

The Outcast leader went to look, and I found myself turning toward the top of the hill. There it was—that movement out of the corner of my eye. I scanned the horizon, but there was nothing out of place.

I put a hand in front of my face to shield my eyes from the glaring sun and felt all the blood in my body go cold.

Past the top of the hill, on the path behind the houses that led all the way to the palace, there was black. The longer I stared, the more I realized it wasn't just *a* shadow—it was an army of shadows, marching in perfect formation, nearly unnoticeable.

And they were coming right for us.

FIFTY-SIX

DIANA
AND TIME FROZE

There was no worse sound than no sound at all. When you couldn't hear the outside world, your thoughts became a lot louder.

I tried to push through the debilitating ringing in my head as the blackness faded slowly from my eyes, leaving spots in my vision.

My hands, outstretched on the wet grass in front of me, were bleeding. Tiny shards of glass were imbued in them, and if not for my armour, I probably would have been covered in cuts. I reached for any magic that might be available, hoping to heal my hands, but winced when the pull was greater than I could manage.

I used my elbows to prop myself up, sucking in a breath when I saw the remains of the palace.

It was rubble.

What had once stood proud and tall, with turrets and winding staircases and floor-to-ceiling windows, was nothing more than a ruin of rock and ash.

A few feet away, my mother was stirring, groaning softly. I looked around, hoping for anyone who could help me detain her, but there was no one in sight.

Those who had gotten out before the collapse likely put as much distance between the palace and themselves as possible.

My heart kick-started. In an adrenaline-induced frenzy, I tore the armour from my forearm, feeling my lungs fill with air when I saw the tattoo still whole and intact. Spense—he had to have gotten out. Badras and Sorin and the rest—they were okay. They had to be.

Vera was attempting to get to her feet. She was markedly more stable than I was, and I wondered if I had hit the ground first. I couldn't remember anything after deciding to jump.

Or maybe it was whatever darkness she had been dallying in making her strong because she seemed to have no struggle amassing magic around her. The smell of lilacs carried on the breeze, and I caught a variety of florals with it.

It was then I realized where we were. In my favourite part of the garden, once flourishing with lobelia and other flowers of my choosing. The purple buds were sad and wilted, having been suffocated by an inordinate amount of snow, but they were still here. Alive.

They were worse for wear, but they did not give up their fight.

Nor would I.

I pushed to my feet, swaying once my boots were on solid ground. Black dotted my vision before the swirling world stopped spinning. "Don't. Move."

Vera, whose gaze had been on the mess of a palace, turned to me, laughing wickedly. "You do not command me."

She raised a hand, and magic pulled through the air. It swept through my hair, pulling even more from what was left of my braid.

I had known my mother was powerful, but the sheer amount she had readily available was not just frightening—it was terrifying. I still felt sluggish and unsteady, disoriented.

Please, I pleaded to Gaia, to Ouranos, to the deities and anyone else who might be listening. *Help me save Eira.*

"They really put their all into creating you," Vera said, her voice as sharp as razor blades. "Their prophesied child, the one to finally bring back peace."

She stepped closer, and I staggered back.

She grinned, her mouth bloody from her cut lip. "Too bad you'll never do it. You're weak. Small. Even at birth, you were unremarkable. You didn't cry, didn't throw big tantrums of power, as expected from a chosen one. If not for the Unseelie boy, you would have ascended and become mine, without ever questioning what I presented to you. Tell me, does that sound like the leader of a rebellion?"

My ears were still ringing, but the words from my mother could cut through even if I couldn't hear at all. They stung as they made their way to my heart, leaving bleeding wounds in their wake.

"It doesn't matter how I got here," I managed to grind out, my voice shaking at first but finding its fervour. "I will end this."

"Yes," Vera sneered. "One way or another, this will end. Today."

Without another warning, she blasted her magic at me. It hit me square in the chest and knocked me flat on my ass. Coughing, fighting for breath, I rolled to my knees, only to get whipped back again.

My lungs felt like they were in a vise grip, the way they refused to expand to bring in air. Fear clawed at my throat.

"It's too easy," my mother purred.

I looked up to find her standing over me, looking as unhinged and chaotic as I'd ever seen her. Her hair, much like mine, seemed to stand on straight edge, pushing away from her scalp.

"Look how easily you break."

With air finally making its way to my brain, a new pain emerged. Every breath felt like it was tearing knives through my lungs, scraping them away one piece at a time. My ribs had to be broken.

Crackling energy hit the air, palpable and strong. Clouds that had gathered overhead rumbled insidiously, dark and angry. Vera was charging up, and I did not want to be on the receiving end of what she was cooking.

I leaned on my hands and gripped the grass with them, digging my fingers into the squishy grass as deep as they would go. Earth was my greatest strength, and it would be where I found myself now. The echoing beat of my heart resounded in the ground below me.

I reached deep down inside myself, farther than I had ever ventured, and grabbed at whatever I could find. This magic was springy, a little sour, unfamiliar. I pulled at it regardless, using it as a shield as Vera's blast of lightning came right for me.

I could not understand what possessed me in that moment, but I followed my magic's urges and funnelled everything I had into one singular command.

"STOP!"

And time froze.

My mother's face, her outstretched hand, the zap of pure electricity heading my way—it all just … paused. Stuck.

The magic fizzled out, its pull too strong for me to hold on to, but whatever I had done was still reacting.

Vera's blast disintegrated into the air, as if it were a cooked noodle going limp, and she yanked her hand to her chest as if she'd been burned. She stared at me, openly shocked. The world turned brighter, as if the clouds were receding.

An overwhelming sense of Spense settled in my senses, as if he were right beside me. I even looked around for him before realizing it was coming from me. I had used his magic.

Soul magic.

I didn't have time to think about the ramifications of my actions— what I had done to my own, how it would affect Spense—because

Vera grew enraged.

She pulled with everything she had, her face screwed up in focus, and a tremor racked through me. I had put everything I had into stopping the last blow, and I knew innately I could not do that again. Not while I was so dazed, so beaten up physically and mentally.

So, I braced myself, but the blow never came.

My mother lay in a heap on the grassy ground, her body crumpled unceremoniously. There were no outward signs to her that explained why she had collapsed, unconscious. Her face though was telling enough.

I recognized the vacant look in her eyes. I knew I was next.

I knew it would happen right before it did.

FIFTY-SEVEN

SPENSE
NOT GOOD

Panting, soaking wet, I heaved myself to my feet. The body raft had been helpful, if not in a disturbing sort of way. I had killed more than my fair share of bodies, most deserving, some not—which I would forever be atoning for—but being on such a personal level with death had an unexpected effect on me.

Not only did it feel like defilement, but it was also a grim foreshadowing.

Death would come for us all, and we would likely not be expecting it.

We had followed the movement of water down the river, where it was starting to overflow onto the bridge in the Marketplace, and yanked ourselves onto the cobblestone, using the railing.

Badras shook his head like a wet dog, droplets flying into the air. They slid down his armour in rivulets. "What now?"

"We go back to the palace. Find Diana. Regroup." A prickling sensation had begun in my chest, and I rubbed at it. The magic that pulled between Diana and me felt … taut. Like she was farther away than she'd ever been from me since our magic had merged.

I led my brother down the streets I had walked with Diana only hours earlier. When we rounded into the square, he halted me, a big arm flung out to my chest.

"Look who's back," he whispered, nodding his head toward the alley across the way.

The shadows.

They were as ominous and dark as the last time, only now, they held the shape of a body. Dozens of fae, holding shadow swords and marching on silent feet.

"What the hell?"

"Try to control them," Badras urged. "This could turn the tides for us."

I reached out toward the shadows with my magic like I'd done in the West. They enveloped me, and I didn't fight them as they wrapped around my mind.

Kill, they whispered. *Hunt. Kill.*

Halt, I told them.

For a split second, I thought I saw their line waver. But they continued marching as if I had no effect on them at all.

HALT! I tried again, more forceful this time.

To my horror, one shadow soldier cranked his head unnaturally to the side to look straight at me. There was no face, but two sunken holes where eyes might be.

You do not order us.

There was a hard shove, and I faltered back a few steps. The shadows had yanked away from me and continued marching up the street toward the palace.

"These are evolved," I said, my voice shaking as black started to dot my vision. "We have to warn the others."

I took a step, but it was weak. Stumbling. My limbs felt heavy. "Bad?"

I turned to my brother, but he was on the ground, motionless. His eyes were wide open, staring unseeingly at the sky.

Not good, not good, not good.

As hard as I tried to fight the mental fog, it was no use. I couldn't even see my own hands in front of me. Knowing I was about to pass out, I tried to get to the ground so I stood a better chance of not hurting myself.

I heard my knees smack into the cobblestone, and thankfully, I couldn't feel what would have likely hurt immensely. As I braced my hands outward, I swore I heard a voice in my head tell me to stop fighting.

And so I did.

FIFTY-EIGHT

AEDAN
IMPERVIOUS

I was speeding toward the palace, my armour bouncing heavily, when one of my own soldiers flagged me down.

"Go on ahead," I called to Maverick, who didn't hesitate, pushing the wheelbarrow of limp bodies at a startlingly quick pace.

Ryen and Freya followed closely, sometimes helping to tuck in an arm or leg that had bounced off the edge of the bucket.

"We've swept the city for survivors, just as you asked." The soldier was bleeding from his right shoulder, his armour dented and stained.

"And?"

His face showed more than his words could.

Gaia-damn it all.

"We also found two bodies of fae from … the other side. The ones seen in Diana's circle," the soldier went on. "We didn't have the numbers to lift them, but I can show you where we found them."

Two of Spense's siblings—it had to be.

"Take me there."

Cobblestone lined my path through Nevelyn, and my throat tightened when I saw the bodies. Not just Badras, but Spense as well. A quick glance confirmed they, too, had suffered the fate of the other deities we had found.

"You recognize them?"

Numbly, I nodded. Our decision-making party was dwindling. If things continued the way I thought they would, the only one in our original group still able to make conscious thought would be me.

With his help, we were able to pull the limp—and heavy—forms of the brothers to the side of the alley, where they would stay out of sight from the street. Their eyes, like the others, were open and glassy.

Whatever they were seeing, it wasn't the cloudy Nevelyn sky.

This was a disaster.

The only saving grace was the hope that Vera had also succumbed to this vegetative state and her army would struggle without her. She wasn't one to trust someone enough to appoint a deputy. Even Embris could only advise the queen about how to run her army.

Where was my father now? He would have fought at the front with Vera's soldiers if he was on her side—that much I knew. He was many things, but a coward was not one of them.

In an unusual, fleeting ember of worry, I hoped he was far away from all this.

"Stay with them until someone comes with the wheelbarrow to retrieve them," I ordered. "This is very important cargo. See that they're treated as such. Make sure they get to the healer's tent safely."

The soldier nodded, his jaw set. He straightened his chest plate, wincing once when the metal hit his shoulder.

"And get yourself looked at while you're there," I called back.

Dark thoughts swirled as I made my way back through the streets I knew so well. I kept my pace up, unknowing of what I'd encounter at the palace.

What I had not expected was for there to be no palace at all.

It was in absolute shambles. Towers were crumbling, stones slipping and sliding as I watched. The grand foyer was flattened with only cracked pieces of the marble floor poking out. The air was hazy, ash still raining softly.

It made me halt in my tracks. I had become disenchanted with the palace in the recent months, but it was still my home.

Or at least, it had been.

A nearly inaudible hiss of a sword being drawn had me spinning around just in time to dodge a swing of glinting metal. I yanked my knives free, readying them to charge. But as I stared into the smoky, mist-like outline of this shadow soldier, my muscle memory faltered.

I had no idea how to defeat this enemy.

I leaped forward, bringing one of my knives down in a slash across the soldier's neck. The shadow dissipated where my hand had gone through and then rematerialized. Fully intact, it wasted no time attacking me again. Our weapons clanged noisily, even as the soldier was deathly quiet. It might be a nonliving thing, but the blade was very real.

The shadow lunged forward, intending to gut me on the sword, and I jumped sideways. I knocked the hilt from the enemy's grip and slashed through its body again, hoping to find a weak spot.

I had no such luck, and when the shadow was remade, it bent down to retrieve its weapon like nothing had happened.

That was when I made the decision not to die on this hill.

I took off at a full sprint toward the back of the palace, where our army would hopefully be reconvened by now. I focused on my feet as I dodged rubble, bodies, and debris, trying not to roll an ankle. When the first hit came, it shocked me.

The shadow hadn't waited to get closer to me before stabbing, and it was my saving grace. His sword dug into the chain-mail siding of my armour, sending me pitching to my knees. They scraped on the glass and stone of the palace, but I didn't notice, for the pain in my ribs. It was not a life-threatening wound, but the blade had cut me, and blood now trickled from my side down the length of my body.

I put a hand to it, and when I pulled it away, it was drenched.

Shit.

I barely looked up in time to duck under the sword swinging for my neck. I jumped to my feet, ignoring the bolts of pain as I freed my knives.

Only I was no longer fighting off a shadow.

I was fighting off a *horde* of them.

I was surrounded—so much so that their darkness made it hard to see. There were so many that they began to blend into one form, closing in tighter.

Desperate, I gathered my magic and used it to send blasts of power out, like I'd seen Diana and Vera do. It worked to push the shadows away, some even skidding across the ground to the back of the pack. But it had no effect on their mobility or their unwavering resilience to harm.

I tried to shove down the fear that rose like bile in my throat. Escape was my only hope of getting out of this alive.

I pushed through the ranks, using magic to keep them at bay, sometimes having to quickly change directions to avoid a runner. Eventually, I was able to break the circle and drop the tiring magic, making a run for the stables.

Sunlight broke through the clouds, and as I got closer to the stabling, a line became clear. A blindingly light line that separated the cloudy, overcast sky from one of robin's-egg blue. It ran along the grass, not caring how much dirt, cobblestone, or palace rubble was in its way as it went from one tree line to the other.

I had never seen such a weather phenomenon.

Bodies appeared as I got closer to the strange line, waving and shouting—seemingly cheering me on. I was within hearing range now, and cries of, "Don't stop!" and, "Run faster!" reached my ears, spurring me on.

There must be some sort of protection from the shadows behind the line.

I dared not look behind me. It was terrifying to know that there was an army chasing me, one that made no noise as they gained stride after stride.

A sword was thrown when I neared the line, narrowly missing my left side. Another one joined it soon after, cutting it even closer.

I tore through the grass, adding a zigzag to my path now that I had to dodge flying weapons. Ryen waited for me on the bright, sunny side of the line and reached across, his arms outstretched.

Right before I crossed the line, he grabbed me by the shoulder plates and yanked me over. I met a strange resistance—a tightening of sorts—but Ryen's grip was strong. He didn't let go until I hit the ground in the warmth of sunlight.

I scrambled to my feet to watch the shadow army stop dead in their tracks, ominously staring at us as if they could see right through our skin and bone to the souls underneath.

"They won't go near the light," Ryen explained. "Thankfully, we have Unseelie on our side who have quite a proficiency in keeping the sun pointed at us."

"What happens when the sun goes down?" I panted, placing a hand on my side to staunch the bleeding. With my heart rate as high as it was, blood was pumping steadily from the wound.

My second grimaced. "We're not there yet. Let's just enjoy being on the greener side of the grass for now."

"Do you have a healer's tent set up?" I backed away from the line, eager to put as much distance between myself and the shadows as possible.

Ryen nodded, unflinching as he inspected my side. He started toward the soldier barracks, motioning for me to follow. "I'll take you. We pulled a lot of civilians over the line who had been harmed in the palace explosion. Not to mention our own injured soldiers. It's … not looking great, Cap."

I swallowed. "Where's Maverick?"

As if in answer, the sound of flapping wings filled the air. The Nordian general waved his spear in the air, sitting atop one of the famed pegasi. It looked like a normal horse, pure white with a long, untamed mane, but was easily twice the size. The wings were soft and fluffy, like a dove, and spread wide as the beast angled itself toward the ground. It landed with a thud that shook the ground.

"Good to see you're still breathing," Maverick boomed, not moving to unmount. "The human division is on the run. We've spotted them going for cover along the forest line near Silver Lake. Now's the time to strike."

"We cannot spare the arms." I eyed the winged horse, close enough to touch if I were so bold. It looked gentle and harmless, but knowing the Nordians, there was a reason they had chosen these beasts as their war mounts, and it likely wasn't because of their pretty looks.

Maverick scoffed. "I will take a flying unit and get it done. The humans are on the run. They are without arrows to fire at us. We'll pick them off one by one until they regret ever stepping foot in this realm."

Ryen cleared his throat, speaking directly to me. "The drake unit has similar notions. The beasts breathe fire—they want to blast it on the humans from the sky. I'm losing my grip on them without you."

"Well?" Maverick called. "Let's finish this!"

My head swam, and a dull ache throbbed behind my eyes. One

hand still clutching my side, I used the other to rub at my temple. "Everyone needs to calm down. We don't have the numbers for a retaliation right now—nor do we have an answer for what happens to the shadows come nightfall."

"The longer we wait, the more time we give them to hide and plan their next attack," Maverick snapped.

With his war paint, his healthy-sized weapon, his giant steed, he looked every part the terrifying Nordian from the stories. I understood why they'd chosen him as their general.

But I just couldn't bring myself to care.

I started toward the healer's tent again, my fingers slippery in my own blood. It was still flowing, and I did not want to pass out from lack of blood flow; it would confine me to a bed—the last thing this army needed right now.

"Your pegasi are made of magic, right?" I didn't look over my shoulder as I spoke to Maverick. "A piece of the mountain?"

"What of it?" was the general's gruff, annoyed reply.

I leaned into Ryen, grateful for his support. "What happens when they hit the magic blockers of the humans? What if your entire unit ends up falling from the sky, plummeting to their death? Are you willing to risk them?"

There was silence for a moment, save for the jangling rhythm of my armour as I walked.

Then, almost too far away now to hear, "You have an hour to come up with a better plan."

Wind whipped at our backs from the wings of the pegasi as it launched back into the air.

"That goes for the drakes too," I told Ryen. "Unless the flame somehow kills the shadows."

"We tried fire. They are impervious to all harm we've inflicted."

"This is chaos," I muttered.

Ryen helped me to the healer—a stout, old male from Shynin, named Grogio—who led me through a maze of bloodied, battered fae and Folk until we stood in front of the last unoccupied examination table.

After I finally shed all the layers of my armour, the healer surveyed the wound. He poked his fingers around it, not deterred when I hissed in pain.

"This will heal, but you will scar. And it will likely reopen, considering I doubt I can convince you to rest a few days."

He arched an eyebrow, and I shook my head. He tsked under his breath as he got to work, gathering his supplies.

"Where's Maisie?" I asked my second.

"We have a separate tent for the … afflicted ones. I'll take you once you're stitched up."

I nodded, trying to push away the uncertainty that was growing at an alarmingly rapid rate in the pit of my stomach. Thank Gaia the sunshine was protecting the healer's setup.

"Here, drink this." Grogio held a thick, opaque liquid out to me.

I took it, inspecting the sludge as it moved viscously, like syrup. "What is it?"

"Poppyseed and a few other pain blockers. You'll need it when I start stitching."

I gave the drink back. "No, thanks."

Grogio gave me an exasperated look. "You realize I'll be pulling a needle through your skin and pinching it together, don't you?"

"I can't take anything that will alter my mental state." As much as I wanted to, the drowsy-inducing medicine would do me no favours in figuring out how to win this war.

The healer shrugged. "Suit yourself." Wordlessly, he handed me a rolled-up towel.

I collapsed onto the table, lifting my arm over my head so Grogio could access the wound. As he started his work, I placed the towel in my mouth and bit down—hard.

I let the pain take over. It was my reprieve from conscious thought as a host of impatient warmongers counted down the clock, waiting for me to make the decisions that would determine their fates.

FIFTY-NINE

MAISIE
DIVINITY

With Aedan's beautiful blue eyes still imprinted in my mind, I woke up. That might be a generous way to describe it, considering I wasn't quite sure what being awake meant when you weren't in your body.

But it sure felt like I was real, in a physical place.

The grass I sat in was warm and tickled me as a quiet wind made the blades rustle against my skin. Wildflowers popped up here and there, and a big tree reached over my head, shading me from the warmth of the sun.

My subconscious really knew how to pick a paradise.

I was alone, and suddenly, I wasn't. Sitting around me so we made a circle of dents in the grass were faces that were shocking.

Spense was beside me with his brothers and the healer, Meske, fanning out past him, along with a face I had never seen before—female with high cheekbones and beautiful. On my other side was Leo, who, despite our tumultuous history, was perfectly happy and at ease.

But it was the icy-cold eyes of Vera, staring at me from across the circle, that was the most unexpected. The other deities flanked her—Urdan, Kol, and Hollaina. I suspected this was the first time they'd all been together in quite some time.

The four of them did not appear as the rest of us. There was a certain … etherealness to them, to how they materialized. The faces I knew them to wear seemed to flicker in and out, as if they were not their true forms.

It hit me that I was the odd one out. They were all deities or descended from one, and I was just the normal, low-powered rebel who had somehow managed to get to this plane. It was absurd to think I was responsible for bringing them all here. But surely, this could not be a coincidence? And where was Diana?

For a long while, or maybe it was short—time didn't seem to work the same way—we all just sat. Gazes shifted, and looks were exchanged, but the overall energy of the group was calm. In my heart of hearts, I wondered if being on this realm made it impossible to feel such physical emotions as hatred and anger.

The willow tree shook, more than what would come from the gentle breeze. It swayed and shimmied until it was not a tree at all, but a being.

And I knew with an irrefutable certainty that, in this moment, I was sitting before a god.

He appeared male, tall and broad, with long hair that seemed to be made of the ocean. His eyes mimicked the sea green that I'd only seen in paintings of the South. But his face was ever-changing, as if it could not settle on an appearance. It moved through colours and shapes like a mosaic in sunshine.

Ouranos.

It was absurd to ever have doubted his existence. Not only was he real, but his presence also emitted a power so palpable that it rocketed through my limbs. He was more than just the creator. He was the sky and the sea. He was everything in between.

"My creations." His voice boomed with power, but it held a gentleness that was soothing.

He looked at us each in turn, and when his gaze landed on me, I found I could not look away.

"Maisie, you have done a brave thing."

"Am I dead?" I could not stop the words from slipping out.

"That depends on you." Ouranos did not offer any explanation to that less-than-soothing answer and settled his gaze on Vera. "Have you anything to say for yourself?"

To my surprise, her spewing hatred and fervour for violence did not come forward. She was cold though as she shrugged a shoulder. "I was just exercising the free will you tout as your first and most important rule."

"You knew the limits of your gift. The life you were given in exchange for providing magic and protection to the realm. And you spurned us anyway, harming our land and our creations for your own gain." His voice never rose, never scorned, but the admonishment was there all the same.

Vera straightened her shoulders, eyes trained on the grass. "You cannot force me back here."

My eyes shot to the other deities, where Kol and Hollaina were watching with barely contained disgust. Urdan, however, was nearly unrecognizable. He looked younger, softer, as his gaze rotated on each of his children, love and pride for them shining clear.

"Of course I can," Ouranos replied, a note of humour in his tone. "I could chain you to this realm and dissolve you slowly, over eons. Watch as your soul ceased to exist. It would be more than you deserve. Gaia does not share my opinion, however. How fortunate for you."

A tremor worked its way down my spine.

"In fact," the god continued, "she is of the notion that you must all find your own way back here—as mortals."

For the first time, fear shone in Vera's face. "Good thing you're such an obedient lackey then," she spat.

Power pulsed from Ouranos, even as his stature remained deathly calm. "She does not order me, nor I, her. We are equals, one and the same. We are the perfect balance. If I were to decide on a different punishment, then it would be as it should be." He turned to the other deities. "Demekol."

Kol's head snapped up. "Yes."

"Tell me what you think Ilysia deserves."

The male I knew as The Curator swivelled his gaze to Vera, where utter contempt grew in his eyes. "She stole my magic centuries ago and put it in a wolf—my own pet—to mock me. She hid my amethyst and the others' ties and controlled us like puppets. If her soul were to wither away into the ether with no one to remember her, I would not complain."

Vera stared the other deity down with a venomous expression.

The god studied Kol for a moment and turned to Hollaina. "You share this notion, Ilex?"

The princess of the East nodded, her face dark. "She's a plague."

Lastly, Ouranos landed on Urdan. "Lazansus, do you agree?"

The Unseelie king barely spared the god a glance; he was too busy staring at the female I didn't recognize. "I don't care."

"You don't care? Ilysia tied her soul to yours. She cut you off from your realm and the magic there. It is because of her that your mind was twisted and warped beyond recognition. And you don't care?"

I looked to Spense, who seemed to be experiencing the same shock that I was over Urdan's indifference. From the faces of his siblings, they, too, were taken aback.

Finally, the male faced his creator head-on. "I trust in you and in

Gaia. There is no punishment that I could enforce on her greater than your will. I am but your servant."

Ouranos did not change through any of the answers he received, so I had no way of knowing whether or not he was pleased. "What would you do if you returned to Eira?"

"I do not wish to return. If I may plead for anything, it would be not to be trapped in a mortal body again. I had forgotten." Tears pooled in Urdan's eyes, spilling down his cheeks. "This peace, this weightlessness—I have not known divinity for millennia. I am ready to leave that realm behind."

"What of your children? Have you no desire to be a part of their mortal lives?"

Urdan smiled softly, gazing upon the Drakenis line he had created. "They are beautiful, aren't they? I cannot atone for how I treated them as Urdan. They have no need for me, and I do not wish to meddle where I do not belong. I will watch over them, and I will finally be a father."

Emotion swelled in my throat. Vera's atrocities had no bottom. She had turned Lazansus, this gentle and doting deity, into a heinous tyrant.

Slowly, Ouranos nodded. "I have heard all I need to."

He brought his hands together, and I braced myself for an explosion. A burst of unfathomable power. "The deities are no more. Magic has long been imbedded in Eira, and its inhabitants continue to grow and feed it. The land will thrive as long as there is balance. As such, there is no more need for a deity to provide the magic."

One by one, Vera, Kol, and Hollaina lifted into the air, their bodies suspended by an unseen force.

"You will go back to your bodies as mortals. When you die, you will come to this realm as mortals do, and you will face judgment for your sins. Lazansus will remain."

Worry splashed across the faces of those lifted.

"You mean to punish us all?" Kol asked, his voice strained.

"All three of you have lost the divinity that makes you a deity. Gaia and I will shoulder that blame, for allowing you to stay in the mortal realm far too long. It has corrupted you into something we never meant to create. I wish you good luck. Use your *free will* wisely."

With that, they disappeared.

I blinked rapidly, but it was not a trick of the light. They had winked out as if they had never been here at all.

"Now," Ouranos said, rubbing his hands, "Lazansus, are you ready?"

Urdan gave his children one last smile. "Goodbye, my children. I hope you can forgive me." He nodded to the god. "I am ready."

And, just like the first three, he was gone without a trace.

Briefly, I wondered what peace looked like for Urdan. What it might look like for me. If I would be finding out sooner than later.

And then my thoughts stilled because Ouranos fixed his gaze on me.

SIXTY

DIANA
FAMILIAL

I had been here before.

Well, not *here*.

But here.

Did that make sense?

Here was a meadow painted with wildflowers. Birds chirped, and the sun shone warm and bright. There was a circle of fae sitting under a willow tree, but I was too far away to make them out.

I took a step toward them, and grass squished beneath my feet.

Wait. I could feel that.

In all my time in these planes, I'd never once *felt*. I was only a conscious being, floating in the ether.

Did this mean I was truly dead?

The fear I expected to spike never came.

Maybe fear didn't exist here.

I should try to talk to the fae in the circle. See if they knew where we were.

I only made it two more steps before a familiar voice had me turning around.

"Back again already?" Iave teased.

Smiling, I took her outstretched hand, marvelling at how I could touch her, see her in a mortal form. "As nice as it is to see you, this was not my doing."

"I know. It was Maisie's."

I startled. "Maisie?"

Iave nodded, and pointed to the fae under the willow. "She's there now. She was incredibly brave."

Now that I was looking, it was easy to spot the head of honey-yellow curls. She sat with her back to me, next to—*Spense!* I would know those horns anywhere. My heart leaped in my chest. Still no fear, but an altered sort of concern wormed in my gut.

"What did she do? Are those fae—are they—"

"They are not dead," Iave replied. "Maisie's use of Gaia's Council allowed the goddess to channel her and retrieve those souls. They are merely … visiting."

"Can I go to them?"

Iave shook her head, sunlight reflecting off the shiny, bald skin. "You still have a prophecy to fulfil, Diana Lightbringer. You are not ready to meet Ouranos or hear his words."

I swallowed. None of this made sense, and I suspected that it likely never would. "Then, why am I here?"

My ancestor squeezed my hand once. "Will you walk with me?"

Wordlessly, I kept stride with my ancestor, revelling in the softness of the grass beneath my feet, at the peaceful blue sky and the wildflowers that lined our path.

"Are we truly related?" I asked, remembering the truths that my mother had dropped on me.

Iave looked sideways at me. "Of course. Just because Ilysia took control of each ruler, it does not mean the line was not true. In fact, I was the only one before you that resisted her."

"In a history book I found, it called you an Unseelie sympathizer,"

I recalled.

She chuckled. "I was an exploratory adolescent. Once while deep in the woods near the base of Mount Nord, I investigated a cave that I had come across. There was a remnant of magic inside, so I followed it all the way to the gemstone that tied Ilysia to this realm. She had fashioned it into a staff and hidden it away. I'll never forget how I felt when I touched the garnet on the end." Iave smiled wistfully. "That stone had memories—and it shared them with me. It's how I found out about Ilysia—who was parading as my own mother at the time."

"You tried to stop her?"

"I did. I was young, a new mother myself, and I went about it all wrong. I confronted her in front of the region heads. They all died that day."

I swallowed.

"She kept me in the cells under the palace, away from my daughter, Kvista, for weeks, and when she retrieved me, I knew it was going to be my end. But I had taken the garnet from the cave, and I used it against her. I had to kill the body that had been my mother."

"I'm sorry," I said, meaning every word.

"You cannot change the past, Diana." Iave's gaze bored into mine. "Only learn from it. My mother's body died that day, but Ilysia did not. When she recovered and found herself a new body, she killed me. I hadn't seen it coming."

Even in this place of peace, I still felt her words fall heavy on my heart. Vera might have been my mother, but she was gone. Ilysia was what remained.

"Why did the ancestors never pick a different bloodline to rule?"

Iave halted us in front of a magnificent sycamore tree. Its thick, wide trunk reached impossibly high. The leaves sprouting off its branches were the perfect green, full of life and bloom.

"Do you think a different line would have stopped her?" the spirit said finally.

I studied how the wind rustled through the tree, the sound gentle and calming. "No, I suppose not."

We were silent for a few minutes, and when I turned back to Iave, she was watching me already.

"When I met you for the first time, at my ascension, do you remember what you said to me about my name?"

Iave nodded. "I told you that your name was an omen. That you were finally the one we had been waiting for."

"You said that it was almost as if my mother had known—that it was a gift to you. But why would Ilysia have named me for her first daughter?"

"I said your mother, not Ilysia. Vera's soul has always been in there somewhere. The real Vera—the one who existed before Ilysia took over her body. She might not have raised you, but you are still her child, born from a soulmate pairing. Her choosing that name was her way of reaching you."

I sighed, a heavy exhale. "And Ilysia let her do that?"

"I gather she rather thought it was her own idea."

"I don't think I understand."

Iave smiled gently. "Let us pray you never do." She turned to the tree and nodded once. "It's time for us to part. I expect a lot will have changed when we next meet." She began to walk back down the path we had come.

"Wait, how do I get back?" I called after her.

She did not stop. "Do not fret. I leave you in good hands."

The wind picked up significantly, blowing through my hair and bringing with it scents of florals and fruits.

From the tree, as if materializing out of the bark itself, walked the fae I had been eager to see since the day I had repaired the portal. The one that smiled gently, filling me with the kind of comfort only familial love could.

My grandmother, Maeve.

SIXTY-ONE

SPENSE
NEXT ADVENTURE

Urdan's confession and subsequent disappearance left me shell-shocked. Numb. My feelings felt muted, and I wondered if that was part of being in this realm, and I would have to sort through a tidal wave of emotion when I returned to Eira. When I went to reach for the anger I usually kept brimming near the surface, I came up empty.

I didn't know how to feel without it.

Ouranos beckoned Maisie forward, who did so with eyes wide. "You enacted Gaia's Council without the true tools needed and succeeded regardless."

Maisie swallowed.

"You have my thanks," the god said, his voice gentle. "And my respect. You knew the risk involved."

Maisie straightened her shoulders. "I'm prepared to pay the price."

Ouranos cocked his head to one side. "We are not of your world. We do not require payment or sacrifice. Everything we do is of our own volition and freely given."

My heart clenched for Maisie, who had clearly thought she was giving her life when she enacted whatever ritual they spoke of.

She wobbled on unsteady legs. "But the memory in the sapphire—"

"It would be wise of you not to question me." The god did not look angered, but from his tone, it was clear we did not want to see that side of him.

All tension was erased from Maisie, who looked near collapse with relief.

"As for you," Ouranos said, helping the female beside me to her feet, "I think you are ready to rest. Do you agree?"

Her face was unfamiliar to me, but I knew who she was. Our long-lost sister, Jweira, did not look remotely similar to any of Urdan's children, and yet it was obvious. Indisputable. Her magic was as Drakenis as ours.

The voice that only Diana had heard before spoke, melodious and smooth. "I have been ready for some time."

From beside me, Alwyn stood. "You deserve peace, my sister."

One by one, we all got to our feet. Maisie and Leo kept a distance away.

"Thank you for finally saving our father from his misery," Jweira said. "You did not know him as the kind and wise ruler that I did, and you were merciful to him anyway. For that, I am grateful." She turned to Maisie, her eyes softening. "You were incredibly brave and smart. It's because of you that I am free from my cage. In another life, I think we would have been friends."

Lastly, Jweira's gaze landed on me. "Please tell Diana that I will miss her. When my emerald was summoned to her, it was obvious to me she was meant for big things. I could not think of a better last soul to work with." She raised a brow. "Treat her well."

"You have my word." *I will treat her better than myself.*

Satisfied, my sister nodded once. She did not offer hugs or emotional goodbyes, and that felt right. Even though I had never had the chance to get to know her, it was clear that was just who she was.

Ouranos spoke to Leo next, who agreed that he still had goals to accomplish in Eira. His mother might have been ageless, but it seemed Leo was not trapped to her immortality. He simply was the age that he looked. Unlike Sorin, who bowed his head when Ouranos spoke his name.

"As Urdan's children, with the exception of Spense, you have all lived an insurmountably long time—longer than we intended when we made the fae. As you have seen, the mortal realm is for mortals only. When Lazansus's ties to Ilysia, and thus Eira, were cut, it freed you all from his life span."

There was a visible sigh of relief among my siblings. Meske smiled broadly.

"However," the god continued, "your souls have aged. When you return to Eira, your mortal bodies will not be able to account for this. Your remaining days will be vastly accelerated."

My siblings, to their credit, accepted this without much reaction. I could not relate. It wasn't fair—they deserved to finally live a life without war and death, to grow old, as they had been denied.

Sorin took Meske's hand. "How long?"

Ouranos ignored his question. "When I send you back, it is unlikely you will retain full recollection of your time here. I do not know what you will remember and what you will not. You are not meant to have knowledge of what awaits you after your time in the mortal realm is over."

A breeze lifted through the air, blowing gently in my hair and smelling of cloves and cinnamon.

"Yes," murmured Ouranos, seemingly answering the wind. "I agree."

The god began walking, and wildflowers popped up in various colours and varieties on either side of his path. "Come along."

We followed him, and after what could have been mere minutes or a stretch of hours, he stopped us in front of a set of iron gates that stretched high into the blue sky and swung open.

"A word to the wise," Ouranos said. "Those gemstones that tied the deities to the land might not work that way anymore, but it does not mean they do not still have power. If I were you, I would see to it that they are properly taken care of."

"How will we remember to do that?" I asked. "What if we forget what you told us?"

"That is up to you. Now, go."

None of us moved for a beat, until Maisie stepped forward. "We can go home?"

The god gestured to the gates. "Live your life well."

My legs shook as I took a few careful steps toward the way back to the world as I knew it. This realm was lovely, and I had no doubt it would be a peaceful place to rest. But I was not ready. Not *near* ready.

I turned back to thank the god, but Ouranos had vanished. Only us mortals remained.

"What are you all waiting for?" I grinned.

Collectively, running like children, we all gathered at the gates, mouths open as we stared at the impressive size and sheer power coming from them.

Leo was first through, not pausing long enough to look back, and disappeared. Maisie followed closely behind.

I gripped Alwyn's hand. "Come on. Aislinn is dying to see you."

I tugged at her and met resistance. She smiled sadly, and I shook my head.

"*No.* You're coming back with us. You're going to experience the peace we all fought for. You're coming home."

My brothers and Meske gathered around, and Badras wrapped

his arm around our sister.

"Spensey," she said, bringing a warm hand to cup my cheek, "I am home."

"Please," I croaked. "We need you. *I* need you."

Alwyn tsked gently. "None of that now. Where's my headstrong brother? You are incredibly capable of rebuilding Eira without me. You and Diana were meant to. I feel very fortunate to have given my life to help you."

"It's not fair that you don't get to see it come together. What about a great love?"

My sister pulled all of us to her small body, and even though it was not possible on any physical realm, her arms wrapped around us all, drawing us to her warmth. "You all have been my great loves. Diana and my little fox too. We have been through hell together, and look!" She drew back, motioning with her head at our surroundings. "We are not destined to live in endless misery. There is hope for peace. *Finally.*"

Sorin sighed deeply, a content smile on his lips despite the tears in his eyes. "I am so glad you are at peace." He rested his forehead on hers. "I will miss you terribly, but it won't be long until we see each other again."

Olys was next, pressing a kiss to her cheek. "Rest well, sister. You'll need it." He smiled devilishly. "Peace does not mean we will be bored when we join you."

Alwyn laughed, and I tried to soak up every note of the sound. "I have no doubt of that."

Badras swept her into a crushing hug and whispered something in her ear. Her face gave away nothing of what he'd said, and she stepped back to rest her hand on his cheek lovingly.

Last, Meske smoothed her hand through Alwyn's hair, unweaving the braids. When her hair hung in crimped waves down her shoulders,

Meske smiled. "The badass warrior princess's braids can finally rest too."

One by one, my siblings stepped through the gate, each taking one last look as they left, returning Alwyn's grin.

She turned to me and tilted her head to the side. "You will understand one day," she said, and I saw the same look in her eyes as I sometimes saw in my brothers'. Exhaustion, right down to the soul. They had lived far too long already, had seen things no one should have to see. I could not relate to the bone-weariness that my siblings felt after such long lives, but I was not blind. Alwyn was ready to move on to her next adventure.

Finally, I nodded. "I will miss you."

She placed a hand on my chest. "I will be here."

I took her into my arms again, trying to memorize everything about her—from the way she squeezed me to the exact hue of her sandy-brown hair.

When she stepped away, she smiled brightly. "Go. Live your life! Enjoy the peace you've worked so hard for. Tell your children stories of their magnificent aunt Wyn."

A comfortable wind floated in the air, ruffling our hair. I got the innate feeling that it was encouraging me to the gates.

Taking a deep inhale, I nodded. "I love you, Alwyn."

She rolled her eyes good-naturedly. "My brother, the softy. I love you too, Spense."

Even as everything in my body begged for one last hug, one last glance, I turned away. I did not look back, and I would not, even when she spoke again.

"And remember," she said, humour in her voice, "I'm going to bring up every stupid thing you did when we meet again."

Laughing, head clear and heart full, I stepped through the gates.

SIXTY-TWO

DIANA
NOT READY

I launched myself into my grandmother's arms, savouring the feel of her, squeezing tight.

"Diana"—she chuckled—"I hoped we would not meet again this soon."

"Iave told me that Maisie brought me here."

Maeve nodded as I pulled away. "She did not intend to."

"So, why am I here?"

I followed Maeve to the grass, where we sat cross-legged together. In all the years I had known my grandmother, I had never seen her so relaxed.

"Plenty of reasons. But they are not for you to know. I will tell you that you are not going to win your fight against Ilysia."

I sighed deeply, my shoulders sagging. "I don't know how I am expected to beat her. She's got more power than the entire army combined! She's always a step ahead. What can I even do?"

"Do you really think so low of yourself and the allies you have surmised?"

"Well, no—it's not that. I just don't see a way where we win."

Maeve tsked. "There is always a way. There are countless ways. Countless variations of each and every occurrence. You need only pick the right one."

That … helps nothing.

"What happens to my destiny if I don't choose correctly?"

"My child, you *are* your destiny. Every choice you make is the correct one. That is what free will truly means."

I rubbed at the back of my neck, surprised to find my hair long and unbound, clean from tangles and grime. "It's confusing here."

My grandmother chuckled. "It is because you are not truly of this realm. Not yet."

I looked over my shoulder, hoping to get a glimpse of my friends around the willow tree. But there was nothing, only a field of wildflowers. "I don't want to fail them."

"Failure is not inherently bad. There is much to be learned from failing."

"What is there to learn if I'm not able to kill her? Everyone who has been counting on me to reclaim Eira's freedom is going to suffer because of my shortcomings."

Maeve's eyebrows drew close. "The inability to kill without remorse, without questioning yourself and your intentions, is a strength. Kindness and mercy have and will always be the rarest of qualities."

"I won't hesitate to kill her if I get the chance. She's evil. There is no peace with her still breathing." The words were hateful in my head, but they came out more defeated than I had thought they would.

"Are you sure? She raised you. Surely, there is a part of you that still loves her."

Tears pricked at the back of my eyes. I willed the emotions away— it was far too painful to examine them. "How can you defend her after all the atrocities she's committed?"

"Do you think it was easy for me to watch as Ilysia left my body to inhabit my daughter's? Or deal with the repercussions of the irreparable damage she had done to my mind and body? I wasn't able to save Vera from my fate—that is why I did my best to keep you from Ilysia's indoctrinations. I had very little time left to live when she moved into Vera's body, but I hope I helped change *you*."

Emotions I had been trying to keep down welled in my chest as I took my grandmother's hand. "You did."

She squeezed once, staring ahead. "Ilysia has made choices that affect the lives of everyone in Eira—some from other realms as well. As have you. As has your soulmate. But Gaia will not forsake us. It is in our nature to get lost sometimes. But there is always a choice to heal, should we choose that path."

"What if she doesn't want to heal?"

Maeve shook her head gently. "That is not for you to be concerned with."

I bit on my bottom lip. As much as I wanted justice, the fight was leaving my veins. It felt liberating to leave this in someone else's hands.

"Was Ilysia one of the fae under the willow tree?"

"Would that change anything if she was?"

If she was here, speaking with Ouranos, surely, that meant something. Something important. Maybe she would change her ways after being here; maybe she would see the evil in her actions.

Grief suddenly clouded my thoughts, a hauntingly sad melody in my head. I would never have a mother again. Ilysia had raised me to know love, as strange as it was to admit. She had taught me how to wield magic, how to conduct myself with grace and poise, how to be diplomatic. Maybe it had all been an act, but it had been real to me.

And it was painful to watch that dissipate in front of my eyes.

I looked back up at the goddess. "Will I ever meet her—my true mother, Vera?"

"That is not up to me."

A comfortable silence stretched out between us.

"I'm tired," I admitted.

"You have done a most wonderful job," Maeve said, nurturing. "You do not have to go back."

Surprise lanced through my chest. "I can choose that?"

My grandmother nodded. "If you are ready to rest, you will find your peace here." She tilted her head to the side, studying me. "But I do not think you are done."

I considered her words. This realm was alluring, made of pure love and light. But when I thought of staying here, something in my chest twinged.

Staying meant peace, certainly, and to be with my grandmother and all my lost friends, like Anten. It meant waiting contentedly for the rest of my family.

But it also meant that I would not see Eira rebuilt to its glory. That I would not see Spense for a very long time, or kiss him, or feel his arms wrapped around me. It meant I would never have children of my own. I would miss out on watching Maisie and Aedan's inevitable love story unfold and all of life's little twists as we aged.

I was not done.

I was not ready to die.

I turned to Maeve, and she smiled.

"I thought so."

SIXTY-THREE

ÆDAN
UNSOLICITED

"If you pull much harder, you won't have any hair left," a healer warned, eyeing me. She smoothed a salve over Maisie's forehead, rubbing it in circles gently.

"You let me know how *your* hair is faring when you become solely responsible for an entire realm," I snapped back.

The healer harrumphed under her breath and continued her way through the tent, applying the salve—which she had claimed would focus magics and inner consciousness—on the heads of the others who were affected.

Maisie. Spense. Badras. Sorin. Olys. Meske. Hollaina. Leo. No sign yet of Diana or Vera—or Urdan for that matter.

The thought that I could not help them—did not know what was going on—drove me crazy. It brought worry and nausea to my stomach and sent my thoughts spiralling.

"The hour is nearly up," Ryen said softly from his spot near the entrance.

My hand returned to the back of my head, where tugging on the long strands of hair seemed to be the only thing I could convince my body to do.

I needed to get myself together. I had never been so out of touch with reality before. I had gotten myself through every problem I'd ever encountered—without help. I could get through this now.

Except every time I repeated that, it sounded less believable.

Raised voices from outside the tent carried inside, and Ryen opened the flap to investigate. When he turned back to me, he was shell-shocked—an expression I could not recall ever seeing on my second's face.

"Aedan," he started, and my heart leaped at the tone of his voice. "It's—"

Without warning, a body pushed through and entered the tent, immediately making it smaller in here, sucking up all the air. His presence was a force, one I knew all too well.

"Father." My voice came out softer, smaller than I had planned.

Embris stalked to me, face unreadable, and in my shock, I could not even tell myself to pull my weapon free before he yanked me to his chest, arms enveloping me.

My father was … hugging me.

Stiffly, I returned it. What had started as awkward quickly turned into a comfort I hadn't known I needed, and soon, we were squeezing one another tightly.

When Embris pulled away, he placed a hand on my shoulder. Maybe I was seeing things in this dim tent, but his eyes looked watery.

"I'm so relieved to see you're alive."

"You could've seen to that yourself had you freed me from the cell."

He had the decency to look ashamed, removing his hand from me.

"You don't know how hard it was to leave the palace, knowing what was happening to you. I did what I thought was best, as I have always done. There was something I had to do."

His words filled me with bitterness, eating up any residual affection that had been drummed up from the hug.

"Something more important than making sure your only son saw the light of day again?"

Quietly, Ryen slipped from the tent, his shadow lurking right at the entrance.

"Do you want to have it out, or shall we save that for after the war is won?" Embris growled.

My arms opened wide. "Win the war? We're screwed. We stand no chance against these shadows—not even if our army was at its best."

"This is war, boy. Where did you get the notion this would be easy? It's not. It'll take everything you have from you, and when you somehow find the strength to keep going, it'll take that too. But you can't give up the fight. The moment you believe you're toast, you are." Embris took a glance around the tent, at the sleeping bodies, and shook his head.

He grabbed me none too gently by the arm and dragged me outside.

"You see that?" He pointed toward the sun, which had dipped lower since I'd arrived. "When it slips down and leaves us in darkness, those shadows will have the advantage—and they'll use it. We can't let it get that far. Once night falls, we're in their domain."

I glanced across the line in the grass. They weren't visible from this far, but it did nothing to reassure me. I knew what was out there. "We don't even know how to kill them. Marching on them now is a death wish."

"Have you tried using the fae that are currently controlling the sun? Surely, they can channel it into blasts that could take one out."

"That could work!" Ryen exclaimed from behind me. He glanced between us when we jumped at the sound of his voice. "Sorry, I figured now's not the time to worry about social restraints."

Embris nodded. "We should talk to them immediately."

This version of my father I knew well. He was the captain of the queen's army, taking charge and putting confidence into plans. But what surprised me was how normal he acted around the Unseelie. Not only was he accepting the Folks' presence, but he was also actively involving them in an important part of this war.

"It would take a lot of energy from them," I said, thinking out loud. "And I would bet they've used up a lot already with this." I gestured to the line. "But if they could imbue it on our weapons, give us direct sunlight to fight with …"

The three of us did not need to say another word. We fell into line as we headed straight for the sun-wielders.

"So, what was it?"

Embris, sitting on a stool in the tent crudely being used as an armoury, paused in the middle of sharpening his sword. "I'm going to need more information than that."

I slid my knife down the whetstone angrily, sending a spark flying into the air. "What was the highly important, all-encompassing 'something' you had to do? The one that kept you away from fighting this war?"

He set his weapon down, leaned against his knees, and levelled me with a look. "What do you know of Vera's true identity?"

I did not flinch away from the stare that used to make me look down. "Everything."

Embris nodded, and a strange emotion played over his face. It was almost sympathy. "I'm sorry you had to learn that on your own. I had hunches over the years, but I dared not speak them to anyone. It was dangerous information."

"A heads-up would have been nice. If not to me, then at least to Diana. She deserved to know the monster her mother truly was."

Instead of answering with his usual aggression, my father sighed heavily. "Perhaps you will understand one day, when you have children of your own. Every choice I made was to protect you—and Diana. I would do it all again." He resumed sharpening his blade.

"When I learned of the items that ground the deities to this realm, I knew Vera's would have to be destroyed if we wanted to truly kill her. So, I waited.

"There was only one time when she did not take me with her as a guard. She did not even take Delios. In my twenty years in her immediate service, she had never left the palace grounds without me. So, when she left that night to what she had said was an unexciting trip to the Academy, I followed her. We trekked all the way to the base of Mount Nord, to the caves underneath. Vera went into one for all of five minutes and was on her way again."

I ran a thumb along the edge of my knife, satisfied with its wicked sharpness. "Did you go in?"

"I couldn't."

"What do you mean?"

"It was warded." Embris stood, sheathing his sword. "But I knew then that was where she was keeping it. When things started to go south in the palace, I went straight for it. And that's where I was this whole time."

I frowned. "But you've been gone for weeks."

"You try getting through a deity's wards," my father growled. "I'd chip away at it for hours until I passed out from exhaustion every day. Then, I'd wake up and repeat the process. It wasn't pleasant."

I got to my feet, double-checking my armour and weapons. We would be expected outside momentarily. "If the wards are that tight, we will need Diana to try to get through them. As Ilysia's daughter, she should be able to do it."

Embris scanned the room once more and headed for the exit. "No need. I was successful."

"What?" I scrambled to catch up with him.

He gave me a glowering look over his shoulder. "When I set my sights on a goal, I accomplish it. That is the Thesand way."

Gods, that's annoying.

I lengthened my stride until we were pace for pace. "And? Was her tie to the realm in the cave?"

"Not only hers, but another's as well."

I didn't let my surprise slow me down. "Demekol," I wagered. "He said Ilysia had stripped his magic away."

"You have met another deity?" my father asked, his baritone voice as close to surprise as I'd ever heard.

I nodded. "And you have too. Hollaina is Ilex."

Embris's jaw tightened, but he was a practiced soldier. He was prepared for the unexpected. "I take it then that Urdan is the last one?" When I confirmed it, he swore. "We have a bigger job ahead of us than I predicted. Finding Vera has never been of more importance. She's already incapacitated, and we cannot find her? It's unacceptable."

This time, I did halt, wrenching my father with me, a hand on his arm. "Let's get something straight. I will not take this from you. You were *gone*. I stepped up. I have been leading this army—*my* army. You have no idea what I have done to protect the realm in your absence. I have made every decision with the greater good in mind. We are low on fresh, rested soldiers. I have a scout looking for Vera and Diana, and that is all I can sacrifice right now."

I did not relinquish my hold or my eye contact, surging ahead when Embris opened his mouth.

"I know you're used to running the show, and I value your knowledge and expertise. But you *will* answer to me, or I will have you detained. Our army is made of Seelie, Unseelie, fae without magic, Nordians, and all types of Folk—all of whom have sworn fealty to me. They need one leader if they are to stay united, one voice. And I am that voice. So, if you cannot get on board with that, then you need to tell me now."

My father studied me for a few moments. I let go of his arm when he finally nodded.

Gruffly, he said, "I'm proud of you and the work you've done here. I don't want you to think I disapprove. It is muscle memory for me to step into the captain's role, but I apologize. I can see that role no longer belongs to me."

Internally, I took a deep sigh of relief, one that shuddered through my very soul.

"Thank you," I replied curtly.

We continued walking, and for the first time in my life, I was innately comfortable with my father at my side. It felt right.

As we approached Ryen and Maverick, menacing with his feet on the ground and his steed flying overhead, formations and plans began to rearrange in my head. This would take some fine-tuning if we were going to make it work.

"Can I offer my advice?" Embris asked.

I wondered if he had ever spoken those words out loud before. It was certainly the first time I had witnessed my father not give his opinion unsolicited. If we weren't in the middle of a war, I could have smiled.

"Tell me."

SIXTY-FOUR

MAISIE
FOREVER

On the other side of the gates, I found more meadow. Confused, I wandered in a circle, waiting for something—*anything*—to happen. Had the god decided to keep me here after all?

"My child, a moment, and then you might return to your friends."

I spun and instantly knew who I was standing before. Gaia's face was somehow every race of Folk at once, every colour, shape, size of the beings she had created. It was beautiful, ethereal, and the glow that radiated from her was warm. I looked into her eyes, feeling an incredible pull of safety, of love.

"I have heard your pleas, Maisie," she started, her voice soft, like sunshine. "I know you ache for the kind of love you see in your friends Diana and Spense. That you feel as if you cannot accept your current partner out of fear."

She was my creator, but still, it surprised me that she knew me so well. That she had *listened* every time I spoke to her. Although I wasn't sure yet about calling Spense my *friend*.

"I do not have a soulmate for you, Maisie."

Even here in this peaceful realm, I swore my heart caved in. "Oh, I see."

Her gentle hand tipped my chin up. "But not because you do not deserve the very best love. Soulmates were originally my creation to strengthen those in times of great need. Every bond served a very precise purpose, and it was never my intent for my beings to look to them as the only way they could be truly happy in relationships. I only ever want free choice for my creations."

Something very humble crossed Gaia's glowing face. "In truth, there will not be another pair of branded soulmates in your lifetime. The realm will see peace for many years to come, thanks to the efforts displayed by you and your friends. Do you see now how powerful love is, even without the physical display of a bond?"

Slowly, I nodded. "Yes, I understand."

Gaia studied me for a moment. Under her scrutiny, I knew I could not hide anything.

"Are you unhappy in your love for Aedan?"

"No! No, he's amazing. Sometimes, I can't believe that he actually wants to be with me. His love is something I never thought I would have."

"But you worry."

"I know it's not the way you designed us to be, with free will and all, but there's an undeniable … *safety* in knowing that you're meant to be with that soul. That he was hand-picked by my creator specifically for me."

Gaia gave me a knowing look. "All my beings are made with the opportunity to do what they may with their time in this realm. Though soulmates are no longer prominent, that does not mean I do not have a hand in who is made for whom."

She placed a hand over my eyes, closing them softly. "Go back to your friends, Maisie, and enjoy the life you have been given. Enjoy the choices you are free to make, and when you and I meet again, I hope to look back together on a life filled to the brim with everything your heart desires. It is what you deserve."

That pure, unfiltered love filled my heart, my soul, until I felt like I could burst. Her strong, unwavering power took hold of me, and when I opened my eyes next, I was looking up at burlap, my sight blurry.

The sensations began to fade, my mortal body unable to hold what my soul could, but the unwavering *fullness* stayed. I hoped it always would.

Burlap was replaced with the most beautiful blue eyes.

"Maisie," Aedan breathed, leaning over me. "I was so worried. Everyone woke up before you." His face was dirty, streaked with blood, his hair sticking out in every direction, but he had never looked handsomer.

I reached up and clasped my hands behind his neck, pulling him down to me. I kissed him with every bit of love I could wring from my heart, marvelling in the sensation of his lips on mine. He was sweet and salty and so *Aedan*. It was a blessing, I realized now, that I had the freedom to pick who my heart belonged to. And I was so lucky to be able to choose him as mine.

When he finally pulled away, emotion shone in his eyes, his smile the most unguarded I had ever seen on him. "What was that for?"

With his help, I sat up, keeping him close to me. "To show you how much I love you. And that I choose you. Every day, always."

Aedan's eyes widened slightly, and he grinned, leaning in to kiss me again. And again and again. "I love you, Maisie, so much. I choose you for all the rest of my days. Be mine forever."

I laughed because there was no other way to let out the emotion inside of me, and I soaked up all his love. His forehead rested on mine, and I looked down at our joined hands in my lap.

So quick that I almost thought I had imagined it, a swirling bracelet of black ink wrapped around my left wrist, a matching one on Aedan's. They glinted at me, the lines moving like waves, and disappeared.

I gasped, and Aedan tilted my head up.

"Everything okay?"

Thank you, Gaia.

My smile was so wide that my cheeks hurt. "It's perfect."

SIXTY-FIVE

SPENSE
WAKE

As soon as I opened my eyes, I flung the sleeve of my tunic up. The tattoo on my left arm swirled with inky-black colour, winding its way around my skin. I breathed a sigh of relief.

I sat up in the cot I had been lying on, glancing around the room. All my siblings were stirring, squinting in the dim light of the tent. The still body I presumed to be Maisie's was blocked by Aedan's large frame. But there was no sign of Diana.

"Spense." Sorin was the first to get to his feet, testing his weight gingerly. "We need to talk."

"Where is she?" My voice felt raw and raspy as it clawed its way from my throat.

Aedan's head swung around. "Diana wasn't with you—wherever you were?"

"No." This I was sure of, even as my recollection of *where* I had been began to rapidly fade.

Alarm passed over the captain's face before he smoothed it away. "She must have not been affected. We found all the unconscious bodies, except for her, Vera, and Urdan."

Urdan was no longer a threat, but there was no time to explain that now.

"Vera—Ilysia—was with us. That means she's woken up. Diana is in danger."

Badras's low voice rumbled from behind me. "The stones."

At his words, something pulled at my memory. It was hazy, reminding me of the days when I had first arrived in Eira and could not remember anything beyond my own name.

"We have to find them before Ilysia does," Olys agreed.

All I could recall were bits and pieces of conversation. An unfamiliar voice, Urdan's uncharacteristic goodbye, and something about … *gemstones.*

"Does anyone remember if we were told where they are?" I asked.

Everyone shook their heads.

Leo stood over Hollaina—his mother—with his brows drawn. "Maisie had Ilex's sapphire. I do not know where the others are, but Ilysia's will be well hidden. She had Demekol's and Lazansus's, too, at one point. The hunt to find them could take years—decades. We need to find Ilysia and let her lead us to them."

Aedan stood suddenly, his hand still grasping Maisie's. She did not look awake yet.

"I have them—the garnet and the amethyst. They belong to Ilysia and Kol, right?"

Leo looked to him sharply. "How?"

"Embris. He has been hunting for years. We have them here, at this camp, under guard. Unfortunately, I don't know about the last stone."

A hopeful sensation surged in my chest.

"Urdan had it," Sorin reminded me. He stood next to Meske, who had sat up, her legs dangling off the side. "When we found him in that cave, he was clinging on to it for dear life." He traded a look with Olys. "Guess it really was his dear life."

"Great." I leaped from the cot. "You guys head to the Unclaimed Land. Get the last stone. I'm going to find Diana."

Sorin's hands met my chest, blocking me before I could cross the room. "Listen, brother. I know you're worried about Diana. But she's strong and capable. The best way to help her now is to destroy the stones. If Ilysia gets her hands on them, we're done. You heard Ouranos."

My brow wrinkled. *Ouranos? Is his the unplaceable voice I remember?*

"You can handle finding the stones without me," I argued, pushing Sorin's hands away.

"You alone shared the same magic as Urdan. You're our best shot to destroy it," Sorin implored.

"I need Spense here," Aedan cut in. "He can control the shadows, and we have an entire army just waiting for the sun to go down."

I ran my hands through my hair, exhaling deeply. "I tried to influence the shadow soldiers, but I couldn't. Your best hope to get rid of them is to kill Ilysia, and that's what I'm going to go do."

"Think about this," Olys said. "What if you find Diana, but Ilysia isn't with her? What if she's already gone to retrieve the stones?"

A small gasp from Maisie had Aedan turning away from us, speaking to her in a hushed tone.

I kept focused on my brothers. "We don't know that."

"We don't know anything, except for the fact that the stones are what will turn the tide for us and win this war," Sorin said. "Please, brother. We need you."

"And stop insulting Diana by rushing to defend her. She's proven that she doesn't need protecting," Badras said.

I let the thought of leaving Diana to her own devices wash over me until the fear subsided to a manageable pang. Without that clouding my judgment, I could think clearer. As much as I hated it, the smarter choice really would be listening to my brothers.

With a glare shot in Badras's direction, I said, "Let's go get that gods-forsaken stone and finish this."

"I will help you destroy the stones. They once tied me to this realm, and I would like to see them destroyed."

We all spun to face Hollaina. Leo was helping her stand, holding firmly to her arms. Kol, already standing quietly near the tent flap with his hands folded in front of him, agreed.

Sorin nodded. "Thank you. We will need you both."

"You should stay with Aedan." Leo, finally satisfied with his mother's ability to hold her own weight, looked at us. "Spense, Kol, Hollaina, and I will be enough to destroy the stones. Your years of battle knowledge, including your brothers'," he added, nodding to Badras and Olys, "will be better served with the army."

"He's right." Aedan had detached himself from Maisie, now awake and watching intently, and joined us near the centre of the tent. "Our plan involves heavy use of Unseelie magic—any insight you could provide would be invaluable."

My brothers looked at me, and I agreed. "I can take care of it. Stay; make sure we win this."

"Take a few minutes to fully wake up from whatever that deep sleep was," Aedan said, his voice taking on that of a captain making orders.

A while ago, earlier this week even, falling under his captaincy would have pissed the hell out of me. I wasn't sure when it had changed, but I was pleased to see him seamlessly fit into the role.

"We join the army in ten."

I followed my siblings to the only body who hadn't yet moved. The small one in the corner with long hair spilling over the sides of the cot and a mouth that curved up like it was holding a secret.

"She's already cold," Meske murmured, brushing stray hair from Alwyn's temple.

A heavy sadness landed in me like a weight.

"Does anyone—do any of you remember seeing her?" Olys asked, a tremor in his words. "I remember talking to her, but it's fuzzy … I can't think of what we said."

"Neither can I," admitted Sorin. "But I know that whatever she said, it was probably something to do with us not spending our days mourning her."

Badras nodded. "She would want us to go kick some shadow ass."

Like my brothers, I couldn't recall speaking with Alwyn on that plane—wherever we were. Any memories at all were fading quickly, like water slipping through my fingers. I remembered *her* though. And her arms around me. Crushing me to her in that enthusiastic way of hers.

When I thought of that, I felt peace.

"I'll get her cleaned up and ready for a proper burial when this is all over," Meske said. "She would hate having this balm on her forehead forever."

"Balm?" Badras rubbed his temples and made a face of disgust when his fingers came away coated in the medicinal-smelling clear paste. "Ugh, *that's* what that reek is."

I cleared my throat. "What are your thoughts on our father? If I'm remembering right, he did not return to his body. Should I bring it back to be buried?"

We all exchanged looks.

"Whatever you feel is right, Spense," Sorin finally said. "Urdan certainly does not deserve it, but Lazansus … I don't know. I am glad I got to meet him though."

Badras clapped me on the back. "He's dead—he won't care what we do with his body. If you feel like lugging that giant pair of wings back here, then go for it. Burn him, leave him there, throw him in the river—it hardly matters."

"Real sensitive, Bad," Olys muttered.

Badras opened his arms. "We've got more important issues than how to deal with the dead body of our psychotic and abusive father." Then, he added, "For a male whose favourite words were *that Seelie bitch*, he really went soft, huh?"

"I definitely was not expecting that," I agreed.

It hadn't sunk in yet that he was gone. That the male responsible for making our lives miserable would never torment us again. That he had been as much of a victim as we were.

"It doesn't change the way he treated us," Olys said darkly. "Or the deaths he was responsible for."

"We have death on our hands too," Sorin reminded him. "All we can do is move forward and attempt to do better with the time we have left."

Something nagged at the back of my mind at his words—something that pertained to time and not having much of it. Ominous as it was, I couldn't link it to anything.

I pulled the chain on Alwyn's neck until the chunky emerald appeared from under her breastplate. Gently, I unclasped it, smoothing my sister's hair again as I pulled Jweira's former prison away. The gemstone felt empty now, the life it contained no longer trapped within its green walls.

"Let's go do better then."

SIXTY-SIX

MAISIE
TRUE POTENTIAL

Aedan was entirely too distracting as captain with his take-charge voice and hard-set features. There was a beauty in it, the way his mind didn't slow even for a second as he charged forward with plans and orders.

When he finally landed on me again, his eyes softened. He came to stand in front of me, where I was still sitting on the cot with my legs off the side.

"Now, you," he started. "I don't have to worry about you sneaking off to do something noble again, do I?"

If only he knew how good that guess was.

I smiled demurely, hoping that would placate him so I wouldn't have to lie. "How are you managing with Embris being back?"

Aedan took my hands in his. "He's the reason we have the gemstones for Ilysia and Kol. Apparently, he's been suspicious of Vera for years. When Hollaina showed up after Diana's disappearance, he went straight for the cave where he knew they were hiding."

"Wow. I would not have thought that he would be the saviour in the darkest hours. I mean, no offense, of course," I added quickly.

Aedan shook his head in disbelief. "Neither did I."

I squeezed his hands. "But you didn't answer my question. He's okay with you leading instead of him?"

A smile ghosted across Aedan's face, one that I couldn't wait to spend more time coaxing out of him once this was over. "He is. I'm actually enjoying working with him."

The tent flap opened, and Embris himself strode in. He eyed our joined hands, gaze flicking to me once, but if he had anything to say, he kept it to himself. "Are you ready?"

Aedan nodded. "Let me grab the others."

With him striding to the other side of the tent, I was left alone with Embris. "Maisie," he acknowledged, tilting his chin.

The servant in me would have bowed her head and mumbled a greeting steeped in respect. But the warrior in me—the one who had met her creator and come back, the one who had sacrificed her life for the realm—she knew her worth. She was an equal to Embris.

I straightened my shoulders. "I hear you're the one to thank for finding the gems. You've turned the tides in our favour."

"Just doing my duty," the former captain replied gruffly.

Silence stretched between us, and a sort of awkward tension poured from Embris. I didn't let it affect me though. For once in my life, I was comfortable in my own skin. And I wasn't about to let anyone or anything take that from me.

"Thank you," Embris blurted suddenly.

"For what?"

"For being with him, for being what Aedan needs." Embris watched his son, a soft look on his face. "I can see the change in him. He needed you to grow into his true potential."

"I needed him too," I answered honestly.

Aedan crossed back to us, joined by Sorin, Badras, and Olys. Embris motioned for them to follow him, and they filed out of the tent.

"I have to go." Aedan pulled me to his chest.

I wrapped my arms around his neck, breathing in that earthy smell of pine. "Be safe."

"I'll come back to you," he vowed. He kissed me gently—a sweet promise. "You'll stay here?"

"I'll see how Meske is doing." It wasn't a lie. Even if I had no plans to stay after checking in on her.

"Good idea." Aedan kissed me again and stepped back. "I'll see you soon."

"I'm holding you to that, Thesand."

With a final grin over his shoulder, he was gone.

The second the tent flap fell back down, I jumped from the cot.

Spense was the only one left, shoving a few items into a small pack.

"Where's Meske?" I asked him.

He looked up, surprised. He blinked a few times, and I got the feeling he had been lost in thought. "She went to join the other healers."

I'm going to count that as checking in on her.

"Okay, well, good luck with the stones." I marched toward the back tent flap behind him, where I could slip out unnoticed, only to pause next to him. "She's going to be fine on her own."

His face was hard. "I know."

"Good. Can you—can you feel her?"

Spense nodded.

"Can you feel *where* she is?"

"You're not staying, are you?" he asked knowingly, scrutinizing me.

I shrugged. "I'm not much of a healer."

He held my gaze for a few beats and finally nodded slowly. "It's not like a map with a pinpointed location. But I can tell you that I feel … *drawn* to her. To the gardens behind the palace."

I could have laughed. It was so fitting.

"I'm going to find her," I promised. "I'll kill the familiar Ilysia uses to harness Kol's magic, and then I'll let Diana channel me to finish her off."

He studied me for a moment. "I underestimated you."

"Don't worry." I dared to pat him on the shoulder as I brushed past. "I did once too."

SIXTY-SEVEN

DIANA
WARRIOR

My head pounded with the force of a hundred anvils.

Shifting on the grass, I opened my eyes. A pair of icy-blue ones stared right back at me.

I jolted, sitting upright. My head throbbed painfully. Ignoring it, I tried to make sense of the face before me. She wore my mother's clothes, along with her signature disdainful expression, but she was no longer Vera.

With high cheekbones, plush lips, and white-blonde hair that ran down to her knees, she stood, shaking off the bits of glass that clung to her, still covering the ground from the explosion. It would be impossible not to know her though. The eyes gave her away.

This was the true face of Ilysia.

"Ah," she crooned, her voice cooler, lighter than before. "There you are."

She stared past me, beckoning with an outstretched hand. A low growl had me scrambling to my feet, spinning around.

Delios stalked out of the gardens, his grey fur matted with debris and blood. His lips lifted in a snarl as he passed me, keeping me in his sights as he sat dutifully at Ilysia's feet.

I had no weapons. My magic was no match for hers. And I was

entirely alone.

Faintly, I wondered how far I would get if I ran. Would she set the wolf on me? Or chase me herself?

Somewhere in the distance, the unmistakable roar of battle crashed. My fae were dying to protect this land from *her*. They raised their swords and banners in my name. I would not—*could not*—fail them now.

My brain felt fuzzy, and I couldn't remember why I had passed out. Splashing images of dreams played through my mind, ones filled with warmth and willow trees and a cool breeze. My only advantage was that Ilysia had also lost consciousness; otherwise, I wouldn't have woken back up.

It proved she was fallible too. I just needed time.

"So, this is your real face."

The deity smiled, lips turning up into a haunting look of a predator. "Do you like it? I must say, it feels good to be back in my own body. It's been a while." She made a show of stretching out her arms. "There's so many more things this one can do."

To accentuate her point, a bush to her right went up in flames, the fire hungrily engulfing it until nothing but charred branches remained.

To my own credit, I held back my flinch as heat warmed my side. "That body will fail," I promised. "And you will not be able to jump into another." My words were a threat, but the reaction they received was more than I had expected.

"The punishment given by the gods is no consequence to me," she sneered. "I can work around it. They seem to forget I have been forging myself into this land for millennia."

My brows furrowed, and I worked on a swallow. Clearly, the time we had been unconscious held pertinent information—and perhaps a weak spot I could use to finally best the deity.

Ilysia picked up on my confusion though. Her grin widened gleefully. "Oh, how wonderful. You don't remember."

I clenched my jaw. There was nothing I could say to prove otherwise, but staying silent felt incriminating too. "Perhaps we are recalling different things. In your memory, did the gods also tell me how to kill you?"

The bluff was bold, but a sliver of uncertainty flickered over Ilysia's face before she masked it. At least it would buy me time.

Come on, think, I urged my brain. *She always talks about how she is Eira. Her power source must be rooted in something from the land. What am I missing?*

"If you had what it takes to take my throne, you would have done it already." Ilysia knelt next to her wolf, smoothing her hands down his thick mane of scruff.

As she began to whisper to Delios, a glow radiated from him. Light at first, playing tricks on my eyes, until it illuminated him like a silhouette.

Ilysia stood, keeping one hand on the wolf. The other she held up, its glow retained in her palm. Then, she closed her fingers, and a snap of energy burst from them.

I didn't even see it fly through the air until it connected with my chest, sending me flying backward. I hit the ground with a thud that pulled the air from my lungs. Wheezing, I forced myself back to my knees, even as panic set in at how little I could breathe.

Ilysia's laugh was as grating as knives in my ears. "See what I mean?"

Delios had been at her side since my earliest memories and well outlived the usual life span for a wolf. He listened only to her and obeyed without hesitation, sometimes without spoken command.

It had been so obvious that he was a familiar. A conduit. She hadn't even tried to hide it.

And no one had ever realized.

I would have to be smarter than this. This queen had not raised me to think outside of the world I knew, to question reality or true motives. Why would she have when it suited her better that I be in her complete control?

I was still learning how to trust myself at the same time I was dismantling my blind trust in everyone else. It was a tightrope I kept losing my footing on, but every step gave me more balance.

Nothing that came out of Ilysia's mouth would be beneficial to me in any way. She only spoke to further her gain—lies came naturally to her. Cursed lies, darkened truths, and broken oaths.

So, I would have to believe in myself instead of her words. I would believe in my ability to best her; I would believe that she spoke no truths about escaping the gods' punishment.

It gave me focus, clarity.

Separate them. Kill the wolf.

With air working its way back into my lungs, I gathered my own magic, stalking forward. Hesitation would only hinder me, so I sent blasts of magic right to the arm that connected the deity to the wolf.

Ilysia snapped her hand back, hissing. Almost immediately, the glow winked out.

"Wrong choice." She seethed, rubbing her reddened fingers. "But that's the thing, isn't it? You are *still* too soft, even after all you have gone through. You are delusional to think you have the strength needed to control this realm. You don't have the killing blow in you."

"The inability to kill without mercy *is* a strength," I said, surprising myself with the words.

Ilysia shrugged. "If you say so." Almost lazily, her gaze landed on her wolf. "Delios," she said, her tone bordering disinterest, "kill."

The wolf swung his giant head toward me, amber eyes locked on mine. His muscles bunched, and that was the only warning I got before he sprang into the air. His plate-sized paws landed on my shoulders and drove us both down.

Pain radiated from the areas his claws gripped on to me. I shoved at his massive body, and he evaded my knees easily. He had to be twice my weight, and it was getting harder to push his head away from my neck while keeping an eye on the razor-sharp teeth as he bit at me.

I reached into my magic and sent it his way, but the blasts bounced off him like he was being shielded. Desperate, I focused my energy on finding a way into his mind so I could bend it to me, like I had done with Ilysia before. The last time had been on accident, so I had no idea whether I wasn't doing it properly or if it just wasn't working on him.

He was not even a true wolf. Did he even have a mind I could control?

Delios's hot breath made me ill to my stomach. My arms trembled to keep him away, even as a fang skated over my cheek.

Gaia, help me!

A scream tore through the air. At first, I thought it was mine, but it was not one of fear or pain. It was a battle cry.

A blade appeared through the wolf's throat, its steel clean as the metal winked at me. If I thought Delios would whine or yelp, I was wrong. His body stiffened, cracks forming all over his fur, as if he were made from glass. And then he shattered.

The pieces disintegrated immediately, floating into the sky like ash. The blade withdrew from its outstretched position, and the wielder swung it through the air. I drew in a breath as I realized who stood there.

The warrior was nearly unrecognizable with a hard face and

narrowed eyes. They wore no armour, bore no weapon other than the sword that was missing half of its handle. But there was no doubt about it, shocking as it might be.

The warrior was Maisie.

SIXTY-EIGHT

SPENSE
SHATTER

I had thought I would feel differently, standing over the body of my dead father.

To be fair, the male didn't deserve tears and a black mourning veil. But I struggled to drum up more than a pitiful kind of sadness when I looked at him.

Mostly, I felt free.

Urdan's body looked ready for a funeral. It was almost comical to think of him arranging himself in that way, waiting for death to come.

He lay on his back, clutching a staff over the centre of his chest. The gemstone in the claws of it was pitch-black, opaque, with jagged edges. It reminded me of obsidian, like the throne he had built in Ivywall. But this was different—obsidian was shinier, like glass. I wasn't an expert on precious stones, but I believed this to be hematite.

"For someone who lived such a tortured life, he had a dignified end." Hollaina's voice was soft beside me. I hadn't even heard her come to my side. "You know, before the war, he was a good companion. I much enjoyed the time I spent with him."

Kol grunted from my other side. "He was a show-off."

That's more believable.

"Let's get this over with." I grabbed the staff and slid it from my father's grip.

His fingers stayed curled around the air, even after it was free.

Leo, still lingering near the entrance of the cave, as if afraid it would swallow him whole, reached for the pack hanging across his shoulder. From it, he pulled Hollaina's sapphire and Kol's crown of amethyst, passing them to their respective deities. Ilysia's staff of garnet he kept for himself.

"How do we do this?" I asked.

Kol and Hollaina exchanged a glance. "Well," the former began, "Hollaina and I will start the process. We should be able to destroy at least two on our own. You'll both have to be readily available in case we need to channel from you."

"Sounds like you didn't need me here." I crossed my arms.

Hollaina shook her head. "We are powerful, but we know our limits. If we fail, you and Leo will need to finish the job."

My eyes flicked to the prince of the South. His jaw was clenched as he mirrored my stance.

"How hard are these stones to destroy, truthfully?"

"They are as tied to the land as they were to us. I would imagine severing the link will need some … persuasion." Kol ran his hand along the cluster of purple gems imbued in the crown he held. "They are an extension of the gods, are they not? Things like this are meant to last. They are timeless."

"Are you quite certain you're up to the task?" Leo tested the grip strength of the claws holding the garnet on the staff, his usual indifference lining his tone. "You have not practiced magic for some few odd centuries."

Kol's face soured. "The time I was without magic is far outweighed by the eons I spent using it to shape this land. Don't insult me."

"Did that make you feel better?" I muttered to Leo.

"Nothing that comes out of his mouth does," he replied.

Kol had been insufferable after the return of his magic on the way here. A cloud of ash, apparently containing his long-lost magic, had flown through the air at top speed, making a hair-raising hissing noise, and circled around Kol until it all went up his nose. Hollaina had pulled us to the ground just in time for the once deity to explode with power, blasting through several trees, where our bodies had been moments ago.

The last half hour of the trip had included Kol *giggling* to himself and exclaiming every few minutes how good he felt with his magic back.

Knowing that Maisie had succeeded in at least part of her ambitious plan calmed the piece of me that wouldn't quit its worrying about Diana. If I went looking through our shared magic, I found hers active and warm, but other than that, it was quiet. I wasn't sure whether or not that was a good thing.

Hollaina lowered herself to the smooth rock floor, crossing her legs. "Let's get started. The sooner we finish this, the quicker we can put it all behind us."

With all of us seated in a circle and the gemstones in the middle, a charge stretched through the air. There was a lot of power gathered in one place.

Kol and Hollaina joined one hand, the others resting on the garnet first. Their eyes were closed, and they were breathing deeply, but it was questionable whether something was actually happening.

Until I felt it. A vibrating hum echoed off the walls of the cave, reverberating through my bones. A shiver worked its way down my spine.

Leo's gaze was intense as he shifted between watching his mother and Kol. I focused on the garnet between them. It began to wiggle and writhe, as if trying to escape them. Its red hue flared brighter and brighter. A high-pitched squeal, similar to a boiling kettle, was the only warning we got before the gem shattered into tiny pieces. A crack ran along the staff, the wood turning brittle.

Breathing hard, the two fae did not waste any time before moving on to the hematite. The magic in the air was heady. Strong. The darker pieces of my own magic were starting to wake, eager to partake in the power.

"Shouldn't you wait a minute?" Leo asked, alarmed. "Give yourselves a chance to catch your breath?"

If Kol or Hollaina heard him, neither responded. They did not move as they worked.

"Maybe it's better that they keep focused," I offered.

Leo's jaw clenched. "They're in mortal bodies now. They're going to get themselves killed."

I didn't say it, but deep down, I wondered if that was the intention. As we watched, hair began to stand up on the back of my neck. A different magic had joined the fray, and I recognized the oily unpleasantness.

Dashing to the entrance, I cursed when my suspicion was confirmed. I motioned to Leo. "We've got company."

The prince joined me, a colourful string of cuss words leaving his mouth—admittedly much more impressive than mine. "She must have sent them for the stones."

Six shadow soldiers marched steadily toward the cave, their eyes unseeing and their blades drawn. Roots and branches did not deter their path, their ... *bodies*—if you could call them that—pushing right through anything in their way.

"Did anyone ever figure out how to kill them?" Leo asked.

My brows pulled together. "I don't think they can be killed.

They're not really alive, are they?"

"Aedan said something about using Unseelie magic against them. What do you know of that?" Leo looked ready to grab me by my shoulders and shake the information out of me.

What kind of Unseelie magic would affect shadows? Soul? No. Storm? Unlikely. Fauna? Nothing plants and animals can do that I can't. Which means …

"Sun magic. It makes sense—shadows are the lack of sunlight. That must be what's affecting them."

Leo looked to the approaching soldiers, then to the cave, where the hematite was glowing brightly. "Take care of it. They're going to need me."

"I can't fight them and wield the magic at the same time," I hissed, grabbing his elbow as he turned away. "Help me."

Leo's gaze was sharp as he yanked out of my grip. "Once the stones are destroyed, I'll join you. Surely, a male of your skills can hold off a siege for a few minutes," he sniped.

I bit my tongue as a less-than-polite response came to mind.

The shadows continued their methodical pace, like Death moving on silent winds toward his next mark. The magic I pulled forward was slow and a little unsteady at first as I channelled the sun. I thought of Sorin and his lessons, growing up—how he likened the sun to a giant, unyielding force. It could not be strong-armed; it had to be directed without interrupting the natural flow.

I placed a shield of sunshine in front of the cave entrance, relieved when the soldiers stopped before it, unable to move through the warmth.

It wasn't my strongest suit, but it would have to do.

"This isn't going to hold them forever." I expected to see Leo channelling with the others when I turned around, but found him hovered over Hollaina, speaking in her ear with a worried expression.

The magic held as I took a few steps back, so I felt safe enough to approach the others.

The hematite exploded, its pieces shattering across the cave floor loudly.

Again, without hesitation, Kol and Hollaina reached for the crown of amethyst and kept going.

Leo's hand, outstretched, shook as he tried to get either of the once deities' attention. "Let me help you," he urged.

"Can't you join them without having them touch you?"

The Southern prince shook his head. "It would do nothing. They have to accept me."

And so we watched—with me stealing glances at the entryway—as they shattered the amethyst. After the gem broke, there was an obvious exertion to the both of them. Kol's hair was stuck to his sweat-plastered forehead, and Hollaina panted rapidly.

When they reached for the final stone—the sapphire—it was slower, sluggish.

"Take mine, damn it!" Leo kept pushing his hand closer to his mother, who spoke through gritted teeth, "I told you, we know our limits."

"You're beyond them!" he shouted. "Your limits are nonexistent anymore!"

"Fine," Kol grunted. He took a hand off Hollaina's shoulder, beckoning for Leo to take it. He locked eyes with me. "Consider this me calling in on my side of our deal. Don't let him stop, no matter what happens. *I mean it.*"

Leo placed his other hand on the sapphire, and the magic around them flared brighter with the addition.

As the sapphire began to glow, a surefire sign that it was nearly destroyed, Kol started retching. His pallor was ashen and grey, and his eyelids fluttered. In one jerky motion, he fell backward, releasing his hold on the power.

He shattered like the gems before him, the pieces wispily floating like ash through the cave and out the entrance.

Demekol was no more.

The strain on Leo was prominent as he took over Kol's place. If I were confident that I could hold the sun magic over the door subconsciously, I would have stepped in. But it was taking most of my concentration as it was.

Hollaina's skin began to flush in that grey colour, her pants turning into gasps.

"No!" Leo gripped his mother tighter.

"Don't. Stop." Hollaina gave the magic her all, right to the very end.

When she collapsed, joining Kol in the wind, it was graceful.

The power was solely in Leo's hands now—literally and figuratively. His face twisted into an emotion so full of anguish and rage that I nearly felt it myself.

With a roar that would have sent even Badras running, he released a blast of power so massive into the stone that it broke instantly. The light of it filled the cave, and I brought an arm over my eyes.

When the brightness finally dimmed, Leo stood, his face vacant. Wordlessly, he pushed past me to the cave opening, where I realized my magic had failed. Sunlight no longer flooded the entrance.

"Leo, wait!"

I ran toward him, but faltered when the prince walked right through and into the trees without raising a hand. The shadows were nowhere in sight, the air completely devoid of their oily energy as well.

Had Leo banished them with his power surge? Or had they been called off?

The prince didn't look back as his form disappeared into the wooded land. I considered following him, maybe even convincing him to return to the fight. But as I took a step in his direction, something stirred in my magic.

Diana. I felt her presence like a branding iron in my brain.

She was featherlight and gentle at first. And then, without any warning, she *yanked.*

SIXTY-NINE

DIANA
I'M NOT SORRY

The scream that wrenched itself from Ilysia's throat was ear-piercing. Her horror quickly morphed into rage, her mouth twisting into a wretched snarl as she fixed her gaze on Maisie.

It all happened in a matter of seconds. I scrambled to my feet, lunging for my friend. Maisie took my hand, and her warm, honey-sweet magic seeped up my arm. Ilysia's attack came barrelling toward us, and with my other palm outstretched, I watched as a buttery-yellow barrier kept her magic from touching us.

All was silent in that moment. Where I thought a large boom would sound from the meeting of our magics, it was the opposite. Even the whoosh of the air that blew my hair around my face, covering my eyes and getting stuck in my mouth, was soundless.

"You think one lowly servant can give you enough power to defeat me? You're wrong!" Ilysia spat, hysterical.

I gritted my teeth as more force pushed back at me. Maisie's loaned magic was keeping me from a swift defeat, but I had not channelled before. Nor was I familiar with Maisie's magic. How long could she go before I took too much?

But there didn't seem to be another way to get the upper hand.

Even if I managed to redirect this hurricane's worth of magic, I needed an offensive plan.

"Don't hold back," Maisie grunted, her unused hand balled into a fist at her side. "End this."

She was standing and balanced, her feet firmly planted. She would be okay for a few more minutes.

I knelt, Maisie following me, and placed my free hand on the ground. Using our combined magic, I tunnelled deeper, sending quakes and quivers through the wet earth. When it reached the soggy grass beneath Ilysia's feet, it was a rumbling shake.

The force of it knocked her off-balance, stemming the outpouring of her magic. While she struggled to find solid ground, I gathered as much force as I could risk taking from Maisie and struck.

The blast hit her square in the chest, knocking her down. I did not relent, and when she put up a shield around her, I continued to push at it—at her.

Ilysia's defensive magic would last considerably longer than I could attack. She was old, experienced, and undoubtedly had tricks up her sleeve. I needed something aggressive to turn the tide in my favour.

I needed *more*.

It was almost too easy to reach out and find Spense. He was connected to me in more ways than a mortal brain could fathom, as much a part of me as my own magic was. His essence was tipped in that dark purple hue that coloured every one of my dreams, and it came to me easily—almost eagerly.

As heat spread through my left arm, I understood it. I understood the importance behind soulmates, the reasoning. We were powerful on our own, but this—*this*—was what soulmates were meant for.

The words of the prophecy were clear in my head. *Two become one.*

"Hope you don't need this," I muttered, ignoring the painful thought that even though the magic was coming willingly, it didn't mean he had no need for it. Knowing Spense, he would send it all to me even if it was his last resort.

With his power fuelling mine and Maisie's magic supporting me, I channelled every bit of it toward her.

The queen on a stolen throne. The imposter. The female who had raised me.

Memories of my life within the now-ruined palace walls flooded my head as I pushed on. Recollections of magic lessons and picking out dresses and shared laughter—all with someone I, along with the whole realm, had considered my mother.

I mourned the memories, letting them fly away with any hurt I still held for her. I was free—free of her, free of the betrayal, and free of my obsessive thoughts.

I was the rightful queen. I had been tasked with keeping this realm and all its fae safe. The female before me was no longer a blood relative with a complicated history. She was an enemy and a risk to my peace.

As she blocked me, the earth around her began to fall away, sinking with her. Now a few feet lower, she had to increase her shield to protect her newly exposed areas.

Ilysia fought against me with all her might, resisting and pushing me away until her strength started to fail. It happened slowly at first, dings and nicks in her shield. But when she crumbled, it was fast. The shield around her exploded in a puff of smoke, magic flying like shards of glass into the air.

Without it, she was exposed.

The final blast hit all of us. I flew back, wincing as I slammed against the muddy grass.

The hole I had made was now a small crater—and it was quiet.

Slowly getting to my feet, I crept to the edge and peered down.

Where I expected to find a body, there was none. I scanned the edges and up the sides and then—

A hand gripped the soil, inches from my feet. Withered and clawed, it flexed morbidly as the bony arm it was attached to started to haul itself over the lip of the crater.

Swallowing, I backed away, gathering what was left of my drained magic. Maisie came to my side, chest heaving. Her eyes were hollow, cheeks gaunt. She held her arm out.

"No," I told her. "You're too weak."

She shook her head, mouth firmly closed, as if she was worried that speaking might be the final act to use up the last of her energy. Her palm opened, drawing my eye to the knife that she balanced there—crudely made with a jagged edge. She must have picked it up from the battlefield when she found the sword.

I knew what she wanted me to do with the blade. My throat dried at the thought.

My magic was near useless right now, but it was still my first choice. I took the blade anyway, tucking it into the empty hilt I still wore, my sword Soulweaver long since lost.

Ilysia hauled herself over the edge, her wilting body crumpling into a heap. She gasped loudly, the sound rattling in her lungs.

She looked moments from death. Selfishly, I hoped that I wouldn't have to finish it myself.

Hesitantly, I crept forward until I was standing over her. Ilysia's gaze flickered to me as I knelt down beside her, keeping a healthy distance between us.

"Didn't think … you had it … in you," she wheezed. Her long white hair was wispy and thin, clinging to her dry and cracking scalp. Wrinkles surrounded her face, so deep and grooved that her eyes could barely open.

"I hope that wherever you go from here, you can be healed," I said softly, gaze wandering over her sunken form.

It was as if all the years she had stolen were taking revenge on her. Even before my own eyes, her muscles visibly atrophied.

Ilysia coughed once, using that to propel herself to roll on her side, facing me. "I can make this right again … I can be your mother the way I should have from the beginning. Let me borrow from you …"

I frowned, unsure of what she was talking about as she grasped my left hand and sandwiched it between hers, which had turned bony and frail.

"Just give me a bit," she rasped. "Just a taste."

Her eyes glazed over, and she closed them, shuddering. When they opened again, gone was the icy-blue colour, black in its place. Wholly, unnervingly obsidian *black*—from top to bottom eyelid.

I gasped, realizing what she meant to do, and tried to pull myself from her grip. But for as small and weak as she looked, she held on to me with surprising strength, squeezing my fingers until they felt like they might burst.

Her smooth lilac magic scented the air, and our joined hands warmed. I could feel as she pulled at me, could feel as my magic was yanked toward her—

And then it stopped.

She gurgled, a wet, slapping noise, and I looked down to her throat.

Where a knife disappeared into it.

I hadn't even felt my arm move, yet there it was, outstretched in front of me. Holding the handle of the blade. I let go, my hand falling to my lap with a slap that didn't register.

Ilysia's hands slipped from mine, and her eyes slowly shifted from black back to blue. She coughed and retched, only accelerating the blood that seeped from the wound. She leaned back onto the grass, dropping ungracefully.

Blood pulsed from her neck, and then she was still.

My mother was dead.

I willed myself to move, to get up and stop staring directly at the wound that steadily bled her life force, even without a heartbeat to pump it. Her blood was my blood and all the queens that had come before me. It was like watching an entire kingdom's worth of blood sink down into the bodice of her dress.

"I'm sorry," Spense said quietly.

I looked up, surprised. I wasn't sure when he had gotten here, but the way he watched me made me think he had witnessed what I did. He offered me his hand.

Slowly, I blinked as I turned away from Ilysia's body. My neck felt stiff, my eyes watery from staring too long. "Sorry for what?"

"That it had to end like that. And that you had to do it." His face hardened. "But I'm not sorry that she's dead."

The world felt fuzzy and swirling, and Spense's words only half made it into my brain. Groggily, I accepted his hand, and he pulled me into his arms.

There, in his safe embrace, I felt brave enough to admit the words I had been afraid to even think.

"I'm not sorry either."

SEVENTY

AEDAN
FERAL

Sunlight made swords heavier.

They still swung smoothly with a sharp arc, but there was that extra … *something*. Even if you discounted the warm glow that came off it like waves, there was just a feeling that the weapon in hand was no ordinary chunk of metal.

The magic imbued within the swords was our saving grace. When they made contact, the shadows lost their vapor and became solid where they were hit.

They didn't stay down forever though. Without the weapon in the body, they became shadows again, and it was only a matter of time before they were back on their feet.

It wasn't ideal, but at least it gave us a fighting chance. We couldn't afford to leave our valuable altered swords in the bodies.

We fought for what seemed like hours when, in reality, it was likely not even one. The fact that we were not making any progress, only holding them off, was something I tried to keep from entering my mind.

"Ryen!"

My second spun around from where he had just beheaded a shadow.

"How many have we lost?"

His face was grim. "We're already being pushed back. We need a miracle."

A curse left my mouth, followed by one from Ryen as he pointed to the sky.

What in Gaia's name?

Along the horizon, where the sun had slowly been setting, a blast of light bounded across the skyline. Blinding and greenish, I barely had time to blink before it disappeared in a winking blip.

Ryen and I exchanged glances. I waited for the explosion to follow—or whatever disaster was being thrown at us this time.

All was quiet. In fact, it was nearly calm.

And then the battle erupted again, sending Ryen and me into opposite directions.

The moment I had time to take a breath and look for my next mark was when I realized that we were winning. There were far more shadow soldiers littering the ground, their half-physical bodies bleeding in the places they were wounded.

They did not heal. They did not stand up again.

I didn't question it or how the green light was involved. Looking a gift horse in the mouth wouldn't burn me today.

I raised my sword in the air. *"We finish this!"*

A chorus of echoing roars answered back. I caught sight of Embris yelling his own battle cry.

Searing pain erupted in my left shoulder, spreading through the limb like wildfire. I dropped my hold on the sword I was yanking from a fallen shadow.

Gasping, I lurched forward, landing on my knees as the world tilted.

"The mighty Aedan Thesand, felled by an untrained courtesan," a voice cooed. The owner stepped in front of me, her stained skirts swishing. Jamey smiled cruelly. "A shame."

With my other arm, I reached behind me and felt for the source of the pain. A handle protruded from my back, small and grooved. The bitch had stabbed me.

"You know what your mistake was?" she continued, clasping her hands in front of her as if she were at a royal party instead of a bloody battlefield. "You got too cocky. Stopped looking behind you."

My fingers curled around the hilt of the weapon. I gritted my teeth and yanked as hard as I could. I couldn't stop the grunt of pain that accompanied it, but when I pulled it around, it was a relief to see how small and dainty it was. Petite and easily concealable, popularly made for self-defence, it had the ability to do damage when used correctly. Had this one been a few inches to the right, it would've hit my heart.

But it wasn't, and it didn't.

"And your mistake," I growled, getting to my feet, "was that you missed."

Smugness bled into fear as Jamey's eyes widened. She backed up a step and faltered when she tripped over a body. She went down on her ass hard, her hands slipping through the muddy grass.

I flipped her blade over in my palm. It was finely made with a row of diamonds along the hilt and a padded handle. She had probably never used it—or any weapon—in her life.

I would enjoy using it on her.

With each step I advanced, she scrambled backward, her head whipping back and forth from me to the terrain.

It was pitiful. Pathetic really. It almost made me consider sparing her.

Almost.

I let the chase continue until she unearthed a blade from a fallen soldier. She got to her feet, holding it with both hands out in front of her.

If I had my own sword, it would have been an easy parry. Jamey's weight was entirely forward, the weapon dragging her down. But I only had a knife, slick with my own blood.

"It didn't have to end this way." I took a step.

Jamey reset her grip, shifting her weight from foot to foot.

"Had you chosen the right side, you could be safe and guarded right now." My eyes flicked up and down over the ruined gown she wore. "But you offered your services to someone who would have seen this realm torn apart by hate and discrimination. For an empty promise of a throne that had already been claimed. For *greed*."

"Everyone thinks they stand on the right side," she sneered. "I would rather die out here in the mud than bow to Diana. I give it a month before Eira turns on itself. She doesn't have what it takes."

"You won't be around to find out."

I moved too quickly for her to react. In a heartbeat, I had my leg wedged between hers, sword dropped, with one arm around her neck and the other holding the knife to her ribs.

"I'm surprised." Jamey did not fight me, her limbs locked into place, but the rapid thump of her heart told me her nonchalance was feigned. "Murder doesn't seem like Diana's style. Are you going rogue, Deputy?"

My teeth gritted together. "You're right. Diana believes in mercy. In second chances—even if I don't." I moved the knife from her ribs to her throat. "So, I'll give you a choice. Admit your wrongdoings and pledge your life to the new and rightful queen or lose it."

Jamey's throat moved against my blade as she worked on a swallow.

Her pulse was quick, untamed, as she silently considered.

Predictably, she burst into action, landing a well-aimed kick to my kneecap and loosening my grip. She wiggled and flailed against my hold as she continued her escape. My knee flared hot with pain, but I kept my weight on my other one.

I had her dress sleeve clenched around my fingers, and she started ripping the fabric to get away. She scraped at me, her nails digging deep into my hand.

She was scrappy—I'd give her that. But at the end of the day, she was small and untrained. I dived forward, letting my weight carry us both to the ground. Jamey's kick had done some damage, and when my knee drove into the hard surface, I felt a sickening snap, followed by the telltale crunch of bone breaking.

There, with her limbs trapped, she stared up at me with such a hateful expression that I wondered how she had ever pretended to enjoy my company.

"Say it." I drove the knife closer to the skin on her neck, blood welling up on the blade. "Say you regret your actions. That you have remorse."

She breathed heavily, her throat's movements sending more red trickling down my knife. Her upper lip curled in a nasty smile, and when mixed with her dirtied appearance and ragged hair, she looked downright feral.

"I hope these Folk you so lovingly protect slit your throat in your sleep."

Jamey was a stranger. She held no more humanity, no empathy. She was gone.

And good riddance.

It only took a slight flex in my wrist to finish it.

Afterward, I got back to my feet, waiting for the guilt to seep in. But nothing came. And so I left her there, lost in the bodies of the battlefield, and limped away to rejoin my army.

SEVENTY-ONE

DIANA
MALE OF ACTION

I found Finnvarra at the edge of the forest surrounding the stables, trotting around with her tail high in the air, trumpeting loud breaths through her nose.

Someone had let all the horses loose, and while that would be a pain in the near future when it was time to retrieve them, it was probably a safer bet for the animals.

It had taken all of my resolve to catch the flighty mare and wrestle her into a bridle. The only saddles remaining in the stables were the beginner's training ones, and considering they were half my weight, there was no way I had the strength to lift one over my head.

Bareback would have to do. Finnvarra barely stood long enough for me to use a fallen tree as a step, and when I landed ungracefully on her back, she took off running.

Reseated and balanced, I let her less-than-weary legs follow the sound of the waning battle, where shadows were dissolving around swords left and right.

Aedan noticed me right away, running to sweep me in a hug as I slipped from the side of my horse. I held tight even though my side screamed in pain, his familiar scent the only thing keeping me grounded. When he pulled away, he brushed a tear from my cheek that I hadn't known had escaped.

"My mother is dead." It was the first time I had said those words aloud.

My longtime friend nodded. "I heard. Word of Queen Vera's death is spreading like wildfire."

"I suppose that's for the best."

Maisie had broadcasted it to anyone who would listen on our way to the healer's tent behind the remains of the palace, where I made her promise to stay put. All the maladies and fatalities surrounding the area clotted thick in my throat, reminding me that it was my orders responsible. It had chased me all the way to the stables.

Aedan motioned for someone to come take Finnvarra for me, but I shook my head, gripping on to her reins. She was a tether keeping my feet on the ground.

"When you're ready to tell me how it happened, I'll be here."

I tried to muster up a smile for his sake. "I really couldn't have done it without Maisie."

Aedan froze, his face falling into one of horror. "I should have known she wouldn't stay put. Just … tell me she's all right."

Sorry for blowing your cover, Maisie.

"She is. I left her with the healers, and she said she would stay there."

"I've heard that before," Aedan grumbled. "Where's Spense? I'm surprised he hasn't found you yet."

"Badras and Sorin needed help with the other half of our army— the ones who couldn't get across the water. They gathered on the other side of Nevelyn. I sent Spense there."

"I still find it hard to believe he would leave you to come alone."

I shrugged. "It was easier to convince him now that the ancient, all-powerful deity hell-bent on my death is no longer a threat."

Aedan looked at me like he wanted to question me on the flippancy of which I'd spoken about my dead mother, but to my relief, he left it alone. "She might not be a threat anymore, but this war is far from over."

I pulled my shoulders back. "I know. That's why I'm here."

"Then, let me update you on everything I know." Aedan snapped into captain mode, almost unrecognizable as he slipped into that role.

As he filled me in, we moved into the heart of the camp, where exhausted soldiers were collapsed on the ground, covered in cuts and scrapes—some even worse off with mangled limbs and missing appendages. Their swords remained clean—supporting a strange and undeniable fact that the enemy they had been fighting was not made of flesh and bone.

I shook my head. "Ilysia's power was terrifyingly unchecked. I know we thought Urdan was behind the shadows, but he was so far gone … I think she was able to use the link between them to control the shadows." I stopped abruptly, a hand landing on Aedan's arm. "That means she was behind the shadow attacks on the citizens from the last few months."

"If the afflicted wake now that Ilysia's dead, I suppose we'll have our answer."

Checking up on the poor souls that were in an unconscious stasis had sadly moved to the bottom of my recent endeavours.

I will see every fae in this realm thrive, I promised myself. *That starts with winning this war.*

Aedan led me into a tent that had clearly been put up hastily, the back drooping and the flap assembled wrong so a corner piece was not covered by it. Inside, I was met by a group of fae I was shocked to see working cohesively.

Embris—looking as sharp as ever, even with blood seeping from a cut on his temple—was in deep conversation with Maverick, the Nordian responsible for my first heartbreak and who had vowed vehemently he would never descend the mountain.

Ryen unfurled a map of the North over a table, placing paperweights in the corners.

All looked up at my arrival.

"Diana. You're okay." Relieved, Embris rushed to me with arms open, hesitating when he was a few steps away.

Once upon a time, he had been like a father figure to me. He taught me how to ride a horse, how to use a sword, how to knock an assailant on their ass. But he knew what terrors Ilysia was capable of. He knew for *years*. And he had not told a soul.

Aedan had told me of his father's role in retrieving the gemstones that were in the process of being destroyed and how he had never been on Ilysia's side.

And so I could not condemn Embris. Or even hate him.

But I had not forgiven him for allowing me to live under the thumb of such evil without so much as a warning. Not yet.

The obvious rejection of my not moving into his embrace splashed cool hurt over his features, but after a terse nod of his head, Embris returned to the table, where I joined him.

The giant Nordian stared me down as I approached.

"Maverick," I greeted coolly, breathing an internal sigh of relief when he dropped the eye contact first, dipping his head.

"Nice to see you again, Princess. You have grown even more beautiful in our time apart." He flashed that wide grin, the one that used to make me giddy.

"You might be the new general, but you will still address me by my title," I said. "Which is Queen."

Maverick smirked. "I was hoping you'd say that."

Having shed the armour that was mostly ruined from my tumble out of a window, I rolled the sleeves of my tunic up and propped my hands on either side of the table, leaning over the map. "Well, shall we?"

The males jumped into action, any awkward tension or hesitation disintegrating.

"From what Maverick's flying units have told us," Ryen stated, "the human party has retreated into the tree line surrounding Silver Lake. They'll likely camp out there until they decide their next attack."

"Any chance they could be retreating?" I asked.

Aedan pointed at the map, dragging his finger along the distance between the lake and the palace, which now stood in ruins. "We have been separated for long enough that they could have all gone through the portal by now if that were their plan. Considering the portal lies somewhere in the lake's immediate area, it's pretty clear that they are biding their time to attack again."

I bit my bottom lip, feeling the broken skin wince in pain. I hated that I didn't have the confident answer a queen should have. I hated the fact that I couldn't be self-sufficient, that I had to risk dragging others down by relying on them.

But that was what a counsel was for. These fae had years of experience on me and keen eyes for strategy that I had not been gifted with.

I could hate it, but I would still push my pride aside. It was not a weakness to lean on them. It was a strength.

I took a steadying breath and turned to Aedan. "Do you think we should wait them out or attack first?"

He considered this, taking a moment to lock eyes with Embris. "We're not at full capacity, and there's still the trouble with not knowing the extent of their magic-blocking devices. But the longer we wait, the bigger the list of unknowns grows. We should strike while they are unprepared."

Embris cleared his throat. "I agree. Given that they are taking refuge near the portal, it's not a far jump to assume they could be awaiting reinforcements."

Maverick nodded his agreement.

"All right then." I pointed to the map. "How do we move our army to Silver Lake without being noticed?"

Aedan shared a look with his second. "The biggest problem lies with crossing through Nevelyn's inner city. The river flood took out most of the theatre district and down the lower section. It's still underwater."

"That's where I come in."

The new voice had us all spinning, the males reaching for their respective weapons.

Leo held his hands up in a sarcastic submission. "If you stab me, you might not win this war."

"What are you doing here?" I peered around him, wondering if Hollaina and Kol were far behind. We could use the extra hands—especially ones that could wield powerful magic.

"The stones were destroyed. You're welcome, by the way." Leo strutted into the tent, his shoulder brushing mine as he came up to the map. The Southern prince was full of his usual breezy confidence, but there was something off about it. The attitude was forced. His eyes were hollow.

I opened my mouth to ask for more details, but he charged on ahead.

"I will create portals here, here, and here." He pointed out three spots on the palace grounds, making a triangle around the area we stood in now. "With several working at once, the army should be able to get through fairly quickly. Whoever goes first through each one will have to be prepped on where to come out. I'll leave the specifics of the locations to the army leaders," Leo continued, the sneer in his voice unmistakable. "But in my opinion, the best option would be to position them to surround the human army, wherever they might currently be."

There was a moment where nobody spoke, the prince's words still registering.

"Wait, what are you talking about?" I grabbed Leo by the upper arm when he barely stifled an eye roll. "Your plan is not only to make one portal—which we don't even know can be done individually—but *three*? This will kill you, Leo. No ifs about it."

For the first time, I saw the real Leo. One whose jaw clenched as he tried to rein in the deep pain he was drowning in. He was defeated.

"I know my limits."

"Why are we entertaining this?" Embris scoffed. "He cannot do it. Three? He will collapse before getting through the second. That's if he can make *one* on his own."

"I wouldn't be so high on yourself, Ex-Captain," Leo snarled. "I seem to recall you kissing Vera's ass until it no longer suited you."

Aedan placed a hand on Embris's chest as the male took a determined step toward the prince.

"Stop," I warned them both. "These petty quarrels waste time."

"Let the deities work, won't you? We'll let you know when your input is needed."

That activated not only Embris, but all the males in the tent as well, including Ryen. They bristled, their bodies locking up.

I turned on Leo, levelling him with a glare that he returned. "That's uncalled for."

"With the seal around Eira broken, portals are no different than any other magic. They just take discipline, focus, and skill. Are we finishing this or not?" He crossed his arms over his chest, clearly fine with having four extremely skilled warriors in the same tent who hated his guts.

Sighing, I looked to Aedan. "Is there any other way we can get across the water?"

"No," he bit out. "Not as fast or efficiently as what Leo suggests."

"Wipe that smirk off your face," I told the prince, who did not wipe anything. "Give me a few minutes, and I'll find fae to help you with the portals. You can channel them or work together. As long as they work, I don't care."

Leo didn't spare any of us another glance as he left the tent. "I don't need anyone. I'll do it now. Be ready to go through them."

My molars ground together.

"What a piece of work," Embris growled.

Maverick shrugged. "I can respect a male of action."

"Let's get in position." Aedan motioned for them to get moving. "But know we go on Diana's orders, *not* his."

"I take it, the deities are gone." I stood next to Leo in one of the three circles he'd made in the dirt by dragging his foot through it.

"Far from it." He stared ahead, expression tight. "Here you stand, as do I. Your soulmate and his litter-sized group of siblings. We're almost overpopulated, don't you think?"

His snark and attitude had always been off-putting, but now, it cracked open a piece of me that had broken with Ilysia's death. "I'm sorry that you lost her. I lost my mother too."

Still, he didn't look at me. "Don't pity me, Diana. I won't be insulted when I'm doing this for you."

"You can put out your cold and uncaring exterior all you like, but I understand your pain. I don't pity you. I *relate* to you. And lately, I have found it easier not to battle that hurt alone."

Leo pulled a deep sigh in through his nose. "Is your army ready yet? The longer the buffoons take to shuffle into a line, the more ammunition the humans build."

Slowly, I nodded. "All right, Leo. We'll do this your way then."

Behind me, Aedan spoke to the soldier who had volunteered to go through the portal first—the one who had the responsibility of directing the landing point. He looked to me and nodded.

The two other circles had their own lines assembled with Embris and Maverick each guiding one. They both gave their affirming signals.

"May Gaia give you the strength for this," I told Leo.

He had refused to entertain the idea of having a backup supply of magic in the form of a willing fae to channel. Even when I had warned him that my own magic was still dangerously low and I would not be able to step in if he faltered, Leo was adamant.

"She already has." Then, with a forceful clap of his hands that sent sparks flying into the air, Leo began to work.

SEVENTY-TWO

MAISIE
CONQUERED

"Body incoming!" The shout from the flap of the healer's tent had me jumping to my feet, wariness be damned.

Meske tried to push me back to the cot I had been resting on. "Don't push yourself."

Two Outcasts carried a body into the tent, hurriedly following the instructions of the head healer, Grogio, while picking their way around the overcrowded floor.

"I want to help." I joined Meske at the cot where the body had been placed and slapped a hand over my mouth to stifle my gasp when I saw who it was.

Leo struggled for breath, his chest rising and falling in uneven bursts. Meske got to work right away, checking his pulse and propping him up to breathe easier.

"What happened?" She didn't look away from her job as the fae who had brought him in explained that he had collapsed on the field.

"That seems to be happening a lot," Grogio muttered.

Meske shot him a look.

The skin of the Southern prince was tinged in blue, his lips nearly drained of all colour at all. Black lined the underside of his eyes and the tips of his ears.

"I've never seen such a thing," Meske admitted. Considering her age and experience, that was saying a lot. "Can you hear me?" she asked Leo, who struggled to open his eyes.

"A complicated magic attack." Grogio was brusque as he started adding ingredients from his wall of herbs. "Without knowing the specifics, we'll have to give a blanket remedy and hope he can regain the energy he needs to heal."

Slowly, Leo shook his head. "Not … magic," he croaked. It was so quiet that Grogio didn't hear him, continuing his mixing.

"What is it then?"

The male had always filled me with a strange mixture of dread and fear, accompanied by a begrudging interest. There were times I had dared to imagine a situation like this, where I held the power over him—where he begged me for my respect. I had not dreamed of a time his life would be in my hands.

He began to shiver, his teeth audibly chattering. "Used too much."

Meske retrieved a blanket from an empty cot and placed it over him. She took one of his blue hands in hers and rubbed gently to generate heat. "Too much magic?"

Leo nodded again. The effort seemed a lot for him.

"There is not much we can do for you." Meske was soft and kind with her words. "I learned of this in my training. Your body drained itself too quickly to replenish your magic—essentially removing it entirely from your system." She clucked gently. "You should not have pushed yourself that far."

"Could he channel someone else's magic to help replenish his own?"

I looked down at the prince. He was a shell of the once-mighty, proud presence in any room he deigned to enter.

Meske shook her head. "Unfortunately, no. In order for him to channel, he would need his magic. I'm afraid with how he looks, he has very little left."

"Could it regrow with time and rest?"

"I wish I could give you a confident answer." The healer sighed. "I assume that it is possible—magic is resilient—but he is very far gone already."

"It's okay," Leo rasped. "I don't regret it."

Grogio took that moment to come bustling back, attempting to get a thick, foul-smelling liquid down the prince's throat, and Meske pulled him away.

"You can't die," I told him, emboldened by the privacy we fell into. "You never got to beg for my forgiveness."

Confusion crossed his face, the first emotion I had seen on him since his arrival. "And what am I sorry for?"

"You can't really think that the hours I spent with you were consensual."

His brows drew together slightly as he tilted his face to meet my eyes. "You never said no."

I did not drop his gaze. "You never asked."

He coughed, the sound weak. "Then, I suppose we have both learned from this."

The girl who felt as if she could not refuse the Southern prince was long gone, a distant memory. Although I couldn't say that I wanted to be in his company, it was still a slight shock to find that I had forgiven Leo.

More importantly, I had forgiven *myself* for the way I'd treated and thought about myself. For believing that my worth was tied to how I served others.

I had spent my whole life thinking I was less than those I worked for, and it had made me weak, cowardly, and jaded. Now, even as I began the process of shedding the layers of distaste and hatred I had built up around myself—a process that could take years—I would not look back on my life with regret.

Everything I had done led me to where I was now. Someone who could hold her head up high, who understood that her path of life looked different from others and that was okay; it didn't make her any less worthy.

Aedan might have kick-started that journey for me, but he could not take the credit for my change, as much as I loved him for it. I'd conquered this all on my own. I had loved ones around me, a family, but at the end of the day, I didn't *need* them. All I needed was right inside of me.

I placed a hand on Leo's shoulder, fighting not to jerk away when sharp cold bit at my fingers. "Some good that lesson will do you now."

He laughed once, a short, abrupt sound. "Don't let the South go to an idiot's hands."

"Wouldn't be the first time."

Leo smiled faintly, struggling on a swallow. "It is nice to meet the real Maisie. Even if I only get a few minutes with her."

He didn't speak again. I stayed with him until his last breath after he slipped into a quiet sleep. After, I pulled the blanket higher over him and left Leo in my past.

SEVENTY-THREE

SPENSE
BAD

With the magic-stifling still in effect, the Outcasts took the brave and dangerous position of being on the front line. Wholly unaffected, they fought with fervour while magic users worked from farther back, sending blasts of wind or bolts of lightning. Overhead, the drakes and pegasi worked seamlessly together, dipping in and around each other, their shadows nearly blocking out all light from the sun. Drakes aimed blasts of fire at the back of the human brigade, and the ones who survived the flames were taken down by Nordian arrow from the air.

Folk of all types whipped past me, weapon of choice raised. Pixies, who disoriented their foe by flitting around the head, worked in tandem with the small goblins, who then cut the distracted enemy down at the knee.

If someone was in need of help, there was an answer to their call.

Elf, brownie, Seelie, Unseelie—it did not matter.

Even though the humans were far from retreating, we were getting closer and closer to Silver Lake by the minute, and that meant our plan was slowly working.

It was poetry.

I fought next to Olys for some time, until we were separated by a large swarm of Night Pixies, grouped into a hive, dropping all sorts of their poisonous inventions on attackers.

There came a point in every battle where it shifted from one side to the other. Eventually, no matter how long it took, someone began to win. After what felt like hours of fighting, I had yet to see it. We were still evenly matched; the humans' swordsmanship was remarkably good, and without our magic on the front lines, we were vulnerable.

Too many fae bodies lined the ground.

Fae that were fighting for their freedom—some who had never known it before and still offered their lives for the cause. Fae that I had promised to take care of.

This ends now.

"Hey, give me a leg up." The soldier nearest to me, one of Aedan's, nodded, interlocking his fingers and getting to one knee.

I placed my foot in his grip and used my higher vantage point to see what waited on the other side of the battle field. I scanned the humans, who were still coming in droves from the forest, until I found what I was looking for.

The helmet with the white wings fought a Nordian a mere three lines from me.

There you are.

I hopped down from the soldier's hold, racing in Dane's direction.

I was slowed significantly by wayward swords and oncoming attacks, but nothing could redirect my focus. The human leader was in my sights, and he was causing a ruckus around him.

He yelled words that didn't reach my ears. The soldiers he fought fell easily; his comrades backed off to give him the space he was clearly trying to make.

I pushed my next attacker away without much effort, kicking them in the ribs once for good measure before closing the distance to the prey I was tracking.

"Bring me the queen!" Dane roared. "Let me best her myself!" He waved his sword in the air, slick with blood.

The fae who were near dared not approach, choosing opponents of more equal skill.

"The queen is dead!" I yelled back at him. The fighting between us jumped away, eager to avoid what was gearing up to be nasty, until there was only open battlefield separating the human from me. "And soon, you will be too."

Wings flapped overhead, drawing my attention to the sky. Badras leaped from the side of a pegasi mid-flight, landing in a roll and springing to his feet.

"Don't touch him," my brother growled. "That one's mine."

Dane laughed loudly. "I will be sure to bring your severed head to your little queen pretender when I go for her next."

Badras charged, a battle cry ripping from his throat.

He and Dane met in a clash of swords. Dane was large and muscular for a human, but Badras still towered over him. The brutality of their fight drew the attention of those surrounding us.

As eager as I had been mere moments ago to take Dane myself, there was no resistance in me as I watched my brother spar. He was ancient and impeccably skilled, and I wondered what twisted way he would devise to punish the human.

Both males grunted and swung heavily, neither going for the agile tactic. They put the entirety of their considerable strength into their drives. The force of their swords meeting echoed through across the lake.

This had been going on too long without change, and Badras knew it. He risked his chest as he feigned a stumble and placed himself behind Dane, getting one of his tree-trunk arms around the human's neck. Dane was much too skilled to be trapped in a headlock, however, and hooked a leg around Bad's knee, sending them both to the ground and breaking the hold.

Both used the moment to recompose themselves, and they were back at it again with their swords.

The soldiers of both sides closest to the ring were getting antsy. Some took steps forward, some jeered, and some watched with an empty hunger in their eyes. I wondered who would break first.

As if conjuring it myself, one of the humans ran at Badras's exposed back with a rapier. It was all too easy for me to take control of his mind. The magic pulled at me greedily, released from the clamp I had been holding it down with.

Stop, I commanded.

His legs planted themselves on the ground, the momentum of his run sending him catapulting over himself.

The next order was on the tip of my tongue, dancing around in my head. *Turn that rapier around and walk through it*, the soul magic begged me to say.

Trying to shake its influence was like washing tree sap from your hands; the more you scrubbed, the stickier it got.

Commotion snapped me away. Badras's sword had dinged Dane's helmet, and he grabbed the human by one of the wings, yanking him down. They grappled on the grass, swords abandoned.

The wings were proving to be Dane's downfall, as Badras used them as grip holds, smacking Dane's head into the ground over and over.

I started forward. *Is it over?*

The human brought his knee up, trying to dislodge the giant fae, but Badras held on. He took one of the wings and snapped it clean off his helmet. In a fast, calculated movement, he slashed the jagged edge of the wing across Dane's throat.

Vindication that the human died as he had arrived, killing Kashdan, petered out when Badras slumped to the ground beside him.

I barely registered how the battlefield reacted to the human leader's death or which way the stampeding was going. I raced to my brother's side.

He was trying to sit up, but slumped back when he saw me. A knife stuck out from Badras's ribs, finding the slit between his two pieces of torso armour.

"The bastard got me." He laughed, dark and humourless.

I knelt beside him, leaning as much of his weight onto me as I could without him snapping at me. "Bad."

"Yeah. Yeah, it is bad," he joked weakly, joined by a wheezy laugh.

I covered the gaping hole with my hands, pressing as hard as I could. "Just stay still," I told him.

Diana had attempted to teach me a long time ago how to use magic for healing. The lesson never really sank in, but I thought back to the day in the meadow and what it'd felt like when she healed my cuts.

"Don't." Badras coughed. Blood trickled down his chin. "I can feel you messing around down there. Just"—more coughing—"leave it. I don't trust you as far as I can throw you to fix this."

My hands were hot. Whether it was from the heat of Badras's blood or the magic I was attempting to direct there, I didn't know.

"You're so stubborn," I gritted out, pleading with my magic to do something instead of sit in my hands.

I pictured a sewing needle pinching his skin back together, and the magic was clunky in response, clumping and zigzagging through the wound.

Screw this.

"You!" Soul magic clamped down on a pixie that had been flying past, sending her zooming down to me. *"Get a healer—now!"*

She raced away, and I ignored the guilt. The only blessing was that I was entirely too focused on the mess in front of me to be affected by the dark magic's pull.

My brother coughed again, and my hands became slimier.

"Stop coughing. Someone's coming to help."

"Is that—is that an … order?" His voice was barely audible now, scratchy and thin.

I swallowed my fear, willing my voice to stay steady. "Yes. Don't make me get Sorin."

Badras laughed—or what sounded like an attempt to laugh. "Make sure they write s-songs about me."

"You'll be around to hear them."

He met my eyes then, growing serious. "Don't … you dare make this … emotional, Spense."

Each breath he took sounded more and more laborious, until I could almost hear it rattling in his lungs.

"Let me have … a hero's death."

I clamped my jaw to keep the tears that pricked at my eyes from surfacing. That was likely the emotion Badras didn't want to see.

"You're a hero," I told him.

He nodded faintly. "Damn … straight."

He breathed heavily a few more times, and then his chest was still. My heart could have burst. Anger, sadness, disbelief all warred for my attention, but I couldn't focus on one. I couldn't focus on anything.

I was as numb as I had been when I saw my father's body.

What emotion could *possibly* be enough for the severity of this? My life had been built around my siblings. Three brothers and a sister. I had already lost one, and now, cruelty had struck again.

My brother, the protector. My brother, the provider. My brother, who I would no longer get to see every day. He was gone.

Badras was dead.

SEVENTY-FOUR

DIANA
LIFE GOES ON

Somewhere on this battlefield, Spense was suffering. A thick, choking sort of anguish filled me through our shared magic, making it difficult to decipher which emotions were actually my own.

It was hauntingly similar to his reaction upon Alwyn's death, and I wondered which of his siblings he had just lost.

I was no stranger to the hurt of loss by now, and it certainly was not going to get any easier. The battle was waning, with fewer and fewer humans left—most retreating back to the portal. But I could barely focus on the fact that we were winning—that we had won.

The price of it was so high.

Would I ever be able to justify this? Their lives?

From my spot on the highest point overlooking Silver Lake, I could see most everything. Aedan was easy to spy with his shouts echoing over the hills and the water. The Nordians showed no mercy, always choosing to fatally wound instead of disarm. The Folk worked in tandem, their various skills proving unique and irreplaceable.

And then there were the Outcasts, led by their fearless leader at the very front of the line. Despite her age and seeming lack of muscle and nourishment, Freya forged ahead tirelessly.

The humans were turning tail one by one. The portal near the edge of the woods shimmered and swayed as they retreated through it.

It was absurd—almost. To try and wrap my head around the fact that it was *over*. That ever since the moment Spense had come barrelling into my life, we had been moving toward this moment. Destiny, fate, prophecy—all words that did not hold as much meaning to me as they used to—had played out.

What happened next?

I watched from atop Finnvarra's back, still without a saddle. She tossed her head impatiently, sending her orange mane flying in waves. I could tell she itched to gallop down the grassy hill, to make her own mark on this war. But her job was to keep me upright. My limbs shook from exhaustion, and as I lost balance here and there, my mare corrected us.

When the last human disappeared through the portal, raucous cheers erupted. And they did not stop. I was certain the celebration could be heard on Eira's southernmost beach.

I could not bring myself to join them. This was their win. They were the ones who had risked their lives, who had lost friends and family. They did not need me to swoop in and collect their glory.

Hoofbeats, dulled by the grass, alerted me to Sorin. He steered his horse—who I recognized as one of the palace-bred mounts—to my side. "Your fae have been looking for their queen."

"She's dead."

"She looks pretty alive to me."

Sorin's gaze didn't falter. He never did. Everything he said, every move he made, he stood wholly behind. I hoped to come close to that level of confidence in my lifetime.

"I don't know how to do this." The words came out shaky, and I looked to Sorin, pleading. "How do I rebuild this realm from the horror it's seen? How do I ensure peace?"

Sorin nodded to the fae by the lake, still celebrating. "You take it one day at a time. There will be ups and downs, but life goes on whether we want it to or not. They will heal from this. As will you. All you can do is what feels right, Diana. And from what I have seen, you have a good grasp on that already."

"I don't want to rule all of Eira." The admission took me by surprise, and once it was out in the world, for only Sorin's ears to hear, my shoulders dropped with the loss of a weight I hadn't realized they had been holding. "It doesn't seem fair to me that three regions are ruled by someone who doesn't reside there—who doesn't know what they truly need."

"That's wise. And what a great opportunity you have to create worthwhile, lasting change. There's no better time."

I met Sorin's gaze, his features firm and encouraging without being condescending.

"You are not alone, Diana," he continued. "We will help you." Warmth heated in my chest, calming the anxiety that had been flaring bright. Soothing the painful burn of trepidation and fear of failure.

I gathered Finnvarra's reins. "Shall we?"

Sorin smiled. "You go. I have a healer to hug."

He rode back the way he had come, and I urged my mare to descend the hill. She was careful at first, picking her steps with concern to my weak body, but soon, she was flying across the grass. Her orange mane moved like flame as her hooves pounded the ground. Above us, pegasi soared. They flew on real wings, but they could not catch Finnvarra.

The wind filled my lungs, and for the first time in a long, long while, I felt free.

I dropped the reins, opening my arms wide, revelling in the feel of it. When we reached the army—my army—we were met with cheers and weapons pumping the air. Finnvarra slowed, and as we made our way through, the crowd offered her pats. Some patted my legs too. We had not seen the bloody battle that these warriors had, but they still celebrated me.

They rejoiced in the fact that I had killed my own mother.

That was something that would always be hard for me to accept. And maybe one day, I could be at peace with it. Like Sorin had said, life went on. Choosing to move forward each new day didn't mean I was forgetting the past, but rather learning from it. Making every decision with the hope of never returning to the darkness.

And it was such a blessing to see all the Folk represented. Not one body here cared what race their fellow soldier was. It was harmonic. Beautiful.

Aedan caught my eye from a few feet back, smiling. Even Olys offered a rare grin, the sight downright shocking.

Finnvarra halted in front of Spense, bloodied and wearing the same exhaustion I felt. There was sadness in him, but also joy. Relief. The look we shared communicated more than words ever could.

We endure.

We always would.

SEVENTY-FIVE

MAISIE
NATURAL HABITAT
ONE WEEK LATER

The death count was high.

Eira would be mourning for some time. It was a strange thing to grieve while also celebrating the freedom we had gained. A bittersweet blend of joyous melancholy.

"What will happen to them?" I watched as bodies of various sizes wrapped in canvas or blankets were carried from the healers' area.

What had started as one tent led to multiple and spilled into the outsides as well, creating a ward as big as a street. The palace was still a disastrous mess, but it had worked in our favour to use brick from the rubble to build up structures and walls where we needed them.

Meske washed her hands in the pail of water at the foot of the tent entrance. "Various rituals. Some Folk will be buried; others burned. The nymphs and pixies have their own ways of returning their fallen to Mother Earth that are private." She stood, shaking her hands to dry them. "Sorin dropped by with the news that Diana is hosting a mass memorial to honour all the dead tonight. The bonfire is being built as we speak."

When word of the war's end had spread, fae from the outer cities in the North had started to appear, coming in droves. The arrival of the Folk was a shock, to be sure, but most handled it gracefully, offering their help to rebuild what was left of Nevelyn and the palace. There were some who could not accept the newest members of Eira and made their opinions quite clear to Diana, who calmly held fast to her new decree, abolishing the verbiage of Light and Dark fae and included every race of Folk as citizens.

There would always be those who feared change and could not understand those different from them. What might end up being a radical group was a problem for another time. It was amazing to me that there had been absolutely no pushback on Diana as their queen. She had not sat upon a throne or claimed the title, but her Northern citizens had bestowed it on her anyway.

And with Cretis reinstated as High Mother of the Gaians, a better age was beginning to emerge in their strict religion—one where they led with love first and prejudice second. I wasn't sure why, but I was absolutely certain that Gaia would approve.

"I heard that massive groups from each region were spotted on their way here. That they should all be here by tonight. It will be the largest gathering of fae Eira has ever seen." I reached down to retrieve the rolls of gauze that had fallen to the ground, wiping the dust from them.

"It's about time they do," Grogio muttered, having eavesdropped on our conversation from the corner, where he inspected the half-healed stomach wound of a soldier. "They would not fight for their queen when she asked for their aid. I hope she demands their fealty."

Meske shook her head softly as she attended to her own patient.

"Diana won't condemn those who were under the control of Vera. They could not see the truth. As long as they come in peace, they will see for themselves the peace that she has brought *them*. They will fall in line." I was sure of that.

In the days following the last human's departure, Diana had worked tirelessly to organize and plan Nevelyn's rebirth.

Everyone had. We all pitched in where we could, whether it was repairing the homes damaged by the flood or making a big meal to feed whoever was hungry.

It was chaos, most certainly. But it was a cohesive chaos.

"A queen must have a strong hand," Grogio replied. "She'll lose that throne if she's complacent."

Grogio had been born in the Unclaimed Land, an Outcast through and through. He had followed Freya for years, who had been hardened by the world and jaded against those who used magic. It did not surprise me that he held this opinion. He would learn in time that Diana's biggest strength was her mercy. Her ability to be kind even though the recipient didn't always deserve it. She had already proven that leading with loyalty was multitudes stronger than leading with fear.

I tried to picture this response toward Vera and couldn't. The public had not truly loved her. Not like they were learning to love and trust Diana.

We worked for a few more hours, falling into an easy rhythm. I had found a soothing sort of meaning in this work. Meske had shown me more complex things, like mixing balms and tinctures. Grogio had begrudgingly allowed me to observe his technique as he stitched up large wounds. It was exciting to feel useful like this. It wasn't the kind of servitude I was used to; it was better. There was a power in healing.

Aedan's arms snaking around my middle startled me from the powder I had been crushing. "I called your name twice," he said, his breath tickling my neck. "You were so focused."

I twisted in his arms, wrapping mine around his neck and

delighting in the wave of butterflies that took flight when he smiled and those damn dimples appeared. "It's easy to get lost in this work."

He dipped down to plant a kiss on my lips. "I'm glad you enjoy it. Do you think you'll pursue this further when everything settles down?"

"I think so." I nodded slowly. "I can see myself doing this for a while. Helping others in a meaningful way. My mother came by yesterday actually and said I looked like I was in my natural habitat. So, I guess healing agrees with me."

Aedan twirled a finger around a piece of hair that had come loose from its hold. "As long as you're happy, you can do whatever job you'd like. How is Ada?"

He had met my mother on accident a few days ago, when he and I were in a line for stew and my mother was serving it. Ada was fairly unflappable, so the scream she let out when she saw our joined hands had given me such a fright that I dropped my bowl of stew.

"She's cooking for hours on end and gets to order fae around, so it can't get much better for her." I laughed. "She asked about you. I swear she only came to visit me in hopes of seeing you."

And who could blame her? Aedan had won over my mother instantly with his good looks and charm.

"We'll spend an evening with her once we can all breathe again," Aedan promised, making my heart flutter. "Your father, too, if you'd like."

I nodded, kissing him again. I was still so wildly grateful for this male.

"The memorial is starting soon," Aedan murmured, pulling away. "Are you coming?"

"I have a bit left to do, and then I'll probably come by for the bonfire," I told him. "I'll see you later?"

He nodded, dropping a kiss on my head. "Don't work too hard."

I smiled as he walked away, the warm feeling not leaving me, even after he left.

Don't work too hard. Never once in my life had I been told that.

If only he knew that for the first time ever, I didn't feel as if I was working.

SEVENTY-SIX

AEDAN
BOND SO UNBREAKABLE

"I want to thank you all for being here," Diana started, standing on a large slab of marble that used to be the foyer floor of the palace.

She hadn't wanted to make her first official address from the ruins, but we had convinced her that it was an important piece in showing the fae from all factions that we were rebuilding Eira from the ground up.

Spense and I working together was new, but it *was* working.

"Each and every life that was lost for our new freedom will be honoured for years to come. This very spot will be made into the largest garden the realm has ever seen. Every flower, tree, and shrub will have a place, just as every name we lost will be immortalized within."

Cheers sounded, families hugging each other.

"While I am grateful for your trust and belief in me, I know I cannot rule without help. In the weeks to come, expect big changes in the way we used to run our courts. If you know of a leader in your community, someone you would trust to speak for the voiceless, bring them forward to me. As well, a fae from every faction of Folk will be chosen by their peers to join Gaia's Council, which will preside over any official meetings to provide a nonpartisan vote." Diana was perched high over the crowd, but she was not above them. She spoke earnestly, unflinching from eye contact.

"With the Folk reunited, we predict that the land—and our magic—will change exponentially. While that might be scary or troublesome at first, we have to keep our minds and hearts open to the change. The fae who are new to this realm belong here just as much as those who were born in Eira. You are all welcome to stay in the North as long as you would like. Gods know, we can use the help rebuilding."

That earned a laugh from the crowd.

"I am hosting a bonfire tonight as a memorial to the lives we lost. With respect to the differing funeral rituals that have been observed, this is more of a celebration than a mourning. We thank those who are not here to see the dawn they helped to usher in."

Diana could not even finish her speech or the closing remarks she'd agonized over, switching out words until the wee hours of the morning. The fae closed around her, yelling their approval and pushing others out of the way to get close enough to hug her.

Spense and I watched closely for the signs that she was getting overwhelmed, but she handled it well, her smile never wavering. She spoke to every single fae that waited for a turn to see her and didn't rush any of them.

Endlessly humble, Diana would never say she was the driver of the revolution. In fact, she probably would shake her head and say that this was no revolution—this was fate.

Whatever you wanted to call it, there was no going back now.

I couldn't wait to see where it took us.

"You seem awfully happy." I joined Freya around the bonfire, which was easily bigger than an average home.

It had been built up with driftwood from the flood, as well as any flammable debris that could be found. I had it on good authority that the gnomes had placed bodies in there as well, but I chose to pretend I had never heard that.

The Outcasts' leader turned her head, the orange glow of the fire casting shadows across her face. "Aren't you? The war is over."

"Generally, the idea is to be respectfully reserved at memorials."

Freya drank deeply from her cup. "Those who lost their lives did so willingly—to serve a higher cause. We should honour them by making the most of the freedom they fought for."

Her words made sense. Not that I would ever tell her that.

She motioned to the cane I had taken to using as my knee recovered from Jamey's blow. "Will that heal?"

"Yes. I'll probably have a permanent limp, though."

Freya nodded stoicly, as if it were her own soundness she was giving up. "All for the cause."

"Will you be sticking around long?""Depends."

"On?"

My mother looked at me. "How our lovely Diana decides to rebuild the political landscape. I deserve a voice in how it shapes up."

"A voice, yes. But she will not tolerate a bully in her court."

Freya tipped back the remaining contents of her drink. "Good thing I'm not planning to be in her court. Besides, I'm not a bully. I'm just not afraid to bring up the controversial subjects."

"Would faking one's death and disappearing into the woods to lead a rebel organization count as controversial?" Embris's dry tone split the air between us, and Freya's eyes widened.

I had the innate urge to flee as my parents stared each other down.

Finally, Freya smiled. I did not know her well enough to see through her acts, but it seemed sincere enough.

"Embris. It's been a long time."

"Well, that was your doing." His voice was gruff, his gaze locking on to the fire.

Now, my father I knew well—and this was one rare tell that he was uncomfortable.

"I would like to explain everything to you—when we have a more opportune time. I owe you an apology for how it went down."

To her credit, Freya had offered me the same. To sit down and really talk—and listen—to each other. I wasn't sure if our relationship could be healed, but in the spirit of new beginnings, I agreed to try.

Embris looked to me, brow raised.

I shrugged. *Not getting in the middle of that.*

"That ... could be arranged."

A nod passed between Embris and Freya, one that held a tinge of softness. It was a shock to my system to see them together, like one of my boyhood dreams come to life. I still couldn't see how they had worked in the first place—they were both stubborn as hell and preferred to be the leader. But maybe that was the point—they never *did* work.

We stood in a civil sort of quiet for a few moments, watching the bonfire attract more fae to its wavy red flames. As much as it was a funeral, Freya was right in the fact that the survivors were in generally good spirits. It was not a party by any means—thank Gaia the Nordians had gone back up the mountain a few days ago, or that might have looked different—but it was not a sad, wallowing event.

It was largely thanks to Diana's speech before the bonfire was lit.

She honoured the Folk while inspiring the fae that were native to Eira.

She was already a beloved leader.

Pawl approached, eyeing up Embris like he was ready to brawl, and I decided that was my cue to leave. There was someone standing alone who I wanted to see anyway.

Diana kept her gaze on the flames as I came up beside her. "That looks complicated," she remarked, motioning with her head toward my parents.

"After what we've gone through, that'll be a walk in the park," I replied.

She bumped my shoulder with hers. "We have gone through a lot, haven't we? Would you have ever predicted we would end up here?"

A huff of laughter escaped me. Of all the ways I had pictured my life going, this did not come close. A year ago, I would have said the biggest hurdle in my life was living with a hard-ass of a father and loving a girl who didn't love me back. "Not in the slightest."

She turned to me, her hazel eyes glowing from the fire. "Somehow though, it feels right."

Her gaze travelled to the other side of the camp, where Maisie was speaking with a goblin. He gestured to the bandage on his neck, and she listened intently, a hand on her chin.

"I'm happy for you both," Diana said. "You deserve to be loved like that."

I nodded to Spense, who was standing with his brothers across the fire, but kept looking at Diana every few minutes, as if he was worried she would disappear. "As do you."

She took my hand, leaning her head on my shoulder. A gesture that would have had me weak in the knees not too long ago now filled me with deep comfort. What had started as a childhood friendship strengthened into a bond so unbreakable that it bested war and death.

"What do we do now?"

A smile pulled at my lips. "What we have always done. Except now, instead of Princess and Deputy, we get to play Queen and Captain."

"You think we'll do well in those roles?"

"Only one way to find out."

She laughed. "Whatever happens, I'm glad it's you taking this walk with me."

"Always," I promised, kissing the top of her head. "One day at a time."

SEVENTY-SEVEN

SPENSE
HAPPY

"Thank you for being here," Diana said, shaking the hand of Lord Nimshar.

He nodded, face grave as the hood of his green mourning robe swayed over his head. "Hollaina sent word in her final days that you were worth following. So, on behalf of the Eastern Plateau, I offer my sincerest gratitude for saving this realm and pledge our allegiance to you, as long as you may reign."

"Your words are so kind." Diana beckoned Nimshar closer, dropping her voice. "I have always thought you were admirable in your undying loyalty to the East and the welfare of the fae there. I have a plan that involves more conservatorship for the citizens and more power for the head of the region. Can I keep you in mind for something like that?"

Nimshar blinked in surprise, mouth opening slightly. "I would very much like to be considered, My Queen."

"Good. You are my first choice anyway. Expect to hear about a meeting in the next few days, once I get a bit more organized." She smiled. "In the meantime, I would like to introduce you to someone."

Diana waved at someone who had just filled up their mug of tea— supplied by the Brownies in their traditional style of mushroom and fig—and gestured for them to join us.

"Benton," she greeted. "I would like you to meet Nimshar. He rules in the Eastern Plateau, the region I was telling you about back in Rathe."

"Pleased to meet you." Hesitantly, Benton shook the male's hand, smiling nervously.

I had met the male on a few occasions, whenever Alwyn could drag him to the palace for a break from the human-infested city of dirt and dust, as she called it, but seeing him now was such a change from his usual grumpy, unflappable self.

I had to remind myself that as the Folk settled into Eira, not everyone would feel at home right away.

"Benton has a proficiency with air magic," Diana explained to Nimshar. "He was one of the only Seelie left in Rathe after the fae were split. Might you find a place for him in your court?"

Nimshar cleared his throat. "Well, no one in the East gets a position without earning it, of course." His face softened. "But you are most welcome with us airheads—that's what we call ourselves within our borders. To survive in what I'm told was a hunting ground for fae, you must be made of the right stuff. I am certain you'll fit right in."

"That was kind of you," I said to Diana once we left a relieved Benton talking with the Eastern official.

She leaned into me, slipping her hand into mine. "It was what felt right."

I placed a kiss on her temple. "You have done a remarkable job this past week. In case you don't hear it enough."

She looked up at me, light from the fire dancing in her eyes and lighting up her smile. "You tell me every day."

"Doesn't mean it's enough. I'll tell you every hour if that's what you need. Every minute—"

"Okay, okay." Diana laughed, pulling me in for a kiss. "You're the best."

A small, frenzied form with a halo of bright red hair came barrelling toward us.

I managed to call out, "Incoming!" right as Shela collided into Diana, squeezing her tight against her chest.

"Thank the goddess you're alive." The resident Academy scholar pulled away, examining Diana for injuries. "If you had died, I would've killed you."

Diana laughed. "Thank you for your help with the prophecy—and for working with Pik. It set a great example for the fae and Folk working together."

Shela wagged a finger. "Don't think you can butter me up so I'll forget how many books you currently owe back to the Academy."

"Yeah, about that …"

"You'd better not be about to tell me that they're under that giant pile of rubble."

Diana lifted her shoulders sheepishly. "Maybe they survived the explosion?"

"I'm sure we can forgive the books, considering your queen just saved the entire realm from a vicious deity," I cut in.

Shela surveyed me, sighing finally. "Can't argue with you there. I am an academic after all, and one thing we love is irrefutable logic."

Diana took her friend's hand. "We will need your help now that the victims of the shadow attacks have woken up. They—"

"Are missing their own shadows, I know," Shela answered eagerly, her eyes lighting up. "How positively *puzzling*. I can't wait to run some tests."

Diana and I shared a look. Shela looked way too maniacal when she spoke like that.

"Besides," she continued, "I've been looking for a change of scenery. The dusty, old Academy is getting boring. No one will let me redecorate either."

"I can have a horse for you on the first trip back south."

"See, this is why it pays to have friends in the palace. I knew it was a good idea to befriend you all those years ago. Hey, I've never been to the Southern Isles. What's the hottie situation like down there?"

"All right, all right." I steered Diana's shoulders away. "The queen is busy. Lots of subjects to speak to, decrees to make. Nice seeing you, Shela."

Forever getting the last word in, Shela called out as we walked away, "Don't be jealous of the Southern hotties, Spense. You'll always be number one in my heart!"

Diana giggled all the way to the fire, where I found us a spot she was less likely to be recognized. She was happy to speak to whomever and solve whatever problems she had to, but I had to make sure she was taking breaks too.

"Shela was raised in an orphanage, you know," she said after her laughter subsided. "It's why I chose to work with unhomed youth when I had the opportunity."

"If you name the home here after her, she'll never fit through the door. Her head will be too huge."

Diana, among her many endeavours, had been working with the fae who ran the orphanage in Rathe to build new homes not only in the North, but also in every region for the displaced youth. She was not leaving anyone behind in the new Eira she was creating.

"Don't worry," she assured me softly. "I was planning on naming it after Alwyn anyway."

I brought our joined hands up, planting a kiss on the back of hers. "I've been thinking," I started, leading us to rest on a newly vacated wood log, "since accessing soul magic again and with the shadows, I'd like to take a break from the soul fight for a while."

Diana's brows pulled together. "What do you mean?"

Letting go of her hand, I placed both mine on the soft earth below us, which was slightly warmed from the proximity to the fire. I closed my eyes, searching for magic below the surface. There. Grasping on, I pulled the magic back. A fist-sized lump of obsidian broke through the earth, reflecting the flames on its shiny exterior.

I held the gem out to her. "A little better than all that tourmaline, right?"

She laughed. "If only we knew back then how powerful you truly were." She turned the stone over in her palm, admiring it.

"I want to put the soul magic into that."

Diana looked up sharply. "That's—"

"Don't say it's not possible. I've seen gemstones used for all types of magic. If it can tie a deity to the land or keep a soul imprisoned, surely, it can contain a malevolent magic."

She softened. "Your magic is a part of you. And anything that's part of you is not malevolent. I don't understand. I thought you had a handle on it?"

I nodded. "For the most part, I do. And I'm giving you all the credit for that. But I don't want to fight it anymore. Sometimes, I don't want to use magic at all because I'm scared I'll awaken it. It's like a bomb, and I never know when it will go off."

Diana studied the obsidian a bit more, nodding slowly. "Well, let's see what we can do with this. Maybe one of the Folk will have a better idea. Or Shela can find us something at the Academy. I don't want you to live like that, Spense, but it might not be possible to separate the soul distinction from your magic." She looked up at me, jaw set. "But we'll try everything we can."

Gently, I took the stone back from her. "We'll table it for a later date. Once the queen has her land in order and has a moment to breathe again."

"It feels weird, to call myself queen," she admitted. "But I suppose I won't be the only one. If my citizens like my new structure, we'll have four more kings or queens. Chosen by their subjects."

"It's perfect." I pulled her in close to my side. "*You're* perfect. The fae have been controlled for so long, told who was going to rule them and for how long. By choosing their own leaders, it will cement the freedom you promised them."

She wrapped an arm around my middle, resting her head on my chest. "I hope they see it that way."

"They will," I promised. "Although are you sure about the Unclaimed Land getting a seat? Freya will end up the biggest thorn in your side in the coming years—I can see it now."

Her laugh shook us gently. "I just hope they pick a different name now that the land *has* been claimed."

"Knowing her, she'll probably keep it just to be difficult."

A council made of five rulers, each selected by their own regions, working together to keep Eira in balance and harmony, was the best idea Diana had ever come up with. Hell, the best idea that *anyone* had ever come up with.

It would take a lot of work and probably some friction as everyone settled into this new system, but with my soulmate leading the charge, I had no doubt its success was guaranteed.

"Are you happy?" I asked her sometime later, when the bonfire had dulled to a flickering flame and the crowd dwindled to a few dozen.

Diana's magic spoke for her, surrounding me in that beautiful lavender light. "I am happy." She pulled back just enough to meet my gaze, those hazel eyes forever my undoing. "Or I will be."

"Oh? What does this queen need to make her happy?"

"Only one thing." She smiled. "A king."

427

EPILOGUE
TEN YEARS LATER

The soothing call of the mourning dove hooted softly through the misty air. Dew collected on my boots, the sun's first rays touching my skin.

Both my hands were full, but that was the way I liked it these days. One holding Spense's and one wrapped around the chubby, small fingers of our daughter, Ellery.

As we ventured deeper into the gardens, morning shadows created light shows on the foliage unique to this particular place. The flowers were hybrid crosses of the region's native plants, the trees and shrubs the same. My favourite was the dynamic mixture of the Northern willow and the Eastern dogwood, its branches long and weepy, the white blossoms reaching toward the ground.

It grew right above the headstone of Jweira, covering the ground with its snowy flowers.

We stopped there first, and I showed Ellery how to brush her magic across the broken pieces of emerald encased in the marble. She giggled, delighting in the breeze that lifted her curly, dark hair in response.

Spense knelt beside us and helped Ellery's twin brother do the same. Dorian was stoic, gazing seriously at the gem's jagged pieces, his hazel eyes laser-focused. They were not yet three years old, but already, their personalities were clear as day.

"Shall we continue?" I took Ellery's hand again, and she led me deeper into the garden, occasionally getting sidetracked by a butterfly or a bright flower.

I didn't mind taking the extra time to see the world through my daughter's eyes. We had no plans, no worries, nothing urgent in the back of my mind. All the time in the world.

Eventually, we made it to the clearing in the quietest, farthest point of the memorial gardens. The sun shone brightly, pleasantly enveloping me in a warm hug. We let go of the children's hands, and they raced each other through the archway, grown into a wall of ivy.

Aislinn was already there, sitting cross-legged in front of Sorin's grave. He had passed peacefully in his sleep just over a year after the war ended, his hair grey and his bed surrounded by his dearest family and friends. Meske had gone three days later. Since the last anniversary of their passing, Aislinn spent nearly every morning here alone.

When the children got to her, she grinned and jumped up, lifting them into the air one by one and spinning them around. Aislinn, now sixteen, was positively idolized by Ellery and Dorian.

Spense took off his backpack and unfurled a rolled-up blanket, smoothing the corners down. Taking a seat on it, he proceeded to unpack a multitude of food containers, lovingly sent by Ada.

The four of us joined him, and I paused while unclasping the lid of a delicious-looking hummus. "Should we wait for them?"

Spense laughed, nodding to Ellery, who had gotten into a bag of candied pecans all on her own. "Try telling her that."

I drank it in. The smiles of my family. The way the lines around Spense's eyes crinkled now and how he had taken to wearing a bit of scruff on his cheeks. The glint in Ellery's eyes that was entirely Alwyn and how she looked like her father's clone. The gentle quiet of Dorian as he processed the world around him, unflappable in his curiosity. The gratitude I felt that Aislinn, our little fox, had blended into our family seamlessly and how she treated the twins like her own siblings.

My heart was full to bursting.

In my head, I spoke to Gaia like an old friend. *Please, let me live in this moment forever.*

The squeals and laughter of children pierced the air, followed by thundering footsteps.

"Gods, they're like an alarm system," Aislinn muttered, shaking her head.

"It's a fair warning to run while you can," Spense said under his breath.

I elbowed him, even as a smile tugged at my mouth.

Four children of varying sizes came barrelling around the corner, locking on to us. They all had the lightest-blond hair imaginable with the same set of blue eyes and dimples. But the best part about the horde of them was the giant grins that never seemed to leave their faces.

This was the future I'd envisioned all those years ago. Pure, unfiltered happiness. These children had never known—and would never know—the pain and suffering of war.

Remi immediately hurtled himself into my lap, his tiny fingers getting tangled in my hair. Kara, the eldest, sat next to Aislinn, complimenting the way she had braided her hair today. At nine, she was desperate to distance herself from the younger kids.

Norden leaped onto Spense's back, using his horns as handholds, and his partner in crime, Coren, followed suit. Ellery held her bag of pecans close to her chest, which was valid, considering how often one of the Thesand herd "shared" her food. Dorian continued to eat his raisins, unbothered.

Aedan came running after them, his limp visible at this speed, calling out, "Sorry!"

Behind him, a very pregnant Maisie waddled into view. Her face was flushed, a hand on her belly.

"It's okay." Spense managed to untangle himself from the boys, plopping them onto the blanket. "We stopped expecting you to be on time years ago."

"You'd think that with the baby due in less than a week, she would be resting," Aedan chided as his wife got closer. "But where did I find her this morning? In the infirmary, stitching up a patient."

"What are you saying about me?" Maisie narrowed her eyes, within earshot now.

"Just how beautiful you are," Aedan replied without missing a beat.

I pressed my lips together, stifling a laugh. He was right though. Maisie was glowing, her skin soft and hair shiny. Pregnancy agreed with her, which was good, considering it seemed to be her permanent status lately.

"Come sit." I patted the ground next to me. "Get some food before the children devour it."

Aedan helped Maisie to the blanket, not letting go of her elbow until she swatted him away good-naturedly. The captain of the Northern army was terrifying in battle, impossible to outwit, but when the armour came off, he was the biggest softy I'd ever seen. He doted on Maisie and made a huge effort to spend quality time with each of his kids. He had grown his hair longer, grey threading into the blond, and didn't let his knee keep him from chasing after his goals.

I was so proud of him. My oldest friend.

"How are you feeling?" I asked Maisie as our husbands divvied out food.

She blew out a breath. "Like I can't wait to walk normally again. I swear, this is my last one."

I offered her a cup of Ada's sweet citrus juice, and we touched our glasses together with a clink. "That's what you said last time."

Maisie's face softened, and I followed her gaze to where Aedan had their youngest, Coren, in his lap, helping him remove the pit from a fig. "Well, can you blame me?"

I placed my head on her shoulder. "No, I can't."

Eventually, the children finished eating and started a game of tag, darting around the various bushes and shrubs. Aislinn humoured them, moving slow enough for little legs to catch her. Even Dorian, who had slid into my lap when Remi got up, joined them after a few minutes. He stood out in the open, yelling out warnings when someone got too close to a gravestone. He got tagged a few times, but he ignored it, much preferring his job as bossy rule keeper.

Without a child in my lap, I stretched my legs out, propped on my hands behind me. It had gotten much warmer, but the breeze in the air kept the temperature perfect.

A perfect day.

"Ten years," Aedan remarked. "That was a blur."

I couldn't help but agree. Here we sat, in a garden I had promised to build at the end of the war, where our most precious family was buried.

Where I had come after the frustrating council meetings when Freya made me so mad that I would have preferred sleeping on a bed of thorns than go back the next time.

Where I had found Spense after Olys died two years ago, on his knees in the courtyard, head bowed in grief.

Where we had watched the rarest flower in Eira bloom under the blue moon sky, its black petals unfurling to reveal a rainbow of colour inside, and I had told Spense he was going to be a father.

The past decade had been filled with joyous highs and strength-testing lows, but we'd managed to keep our heads above water as we forged our new world. I knew I could not have done it without these three fae sitting beside me.

"Embris sends his regards, by the way," Aedan started. "He finally got the portal in the capital to stop spitting out squirrels from that forest realm. He needed Shela for it, but if Freya asks, he fixed it on his own."

I laughed. "Glad to hear it. Shela doesn't need the ego-fluffing anyway."

"He should be here in a few days," Maisie said. "He wants to be here for the birth."

"What a lucky baby," I reply. "They get the king of the Western Shores at their christening."

"Don't be too excited," Aedan muttered. "The queen of the Unclaimed Land will never be outdone by Embris. Which means we get both of them at the same time."

Freya and Embris had buried the hatchet when Kara was born, but separation was better for them. Once they started bickering, you might as well just leave the room; there was no getting in between that.

The queen of the Southern Isles—now, she was another story altogether.

"What do you predict in our next ten years?" Spense asked. "I hope to retire, personally."

I shook my head, chuckling. "As long as the North wants us, we'll lead them."

Spense tucked me into his side, planting a kiss on my head. "You lead them, and I'll be your arm candy. Compromise."

"Isn't that what you do already?" Aedan asked jokingly.

"As long as we continue to have days like this, I don't mind what the future holds," Maisie said softly, a hand on her belly as she watched her children play. "I hope none of them ever have to pick up a sword."

I pulled Maisie closer, looping my arm in hers. Aedan pressed against her other side, linking the four of us. Magic tingled in the air of its own accord, reacting to the deep bond we had all cemented. Even Spense's—muted from placing most of it into the obsidian he kept buried with his father—could be felt.

This moment right here was worth everything we had all endured since Spense had come crashing into Eira and set our lives on a trajectory no one had seen coming.

And I would do it all again for this.

For this peaceful forever.

THE END

ACKNOWLEDGEMENTS

Another book in the rearview mirror, and the thank-yous haven't gotten any smaller. It takes a village! This book was difficult to write in many ways; not only because I was wrapping up the series that'd been sitting in my heart for years, but also because I wrote the majority of it while in the midst of some indescribably *crazy* life changes.

First and foremost, I have to thank God for the ability to pursue my passion every day and for blessing me with stories inside to share.

Thank you to my team behind the scenes, starting, of course, with my amazing editor, Jovana Shirley of Unforeseen Editing. You are truly a master, and I get so much better sleep at night, knowing my books have been through your fine-tooth comb!

Thank you to Julie and the rest of the talented people at Books & Moods. Once again, you've designed a stunning cover that I am proud to share with the world. I am continuously grateful for your formatting skills that make the inside of my books just as beautiful as the outside.

Thank you to my little team of early readers and online friends who have been with me since *A Kingdom of Dark Truths* and continue to spread the word about my books. I wouldn't be where I am without you.

To my little family: Evan, Milo, Lucie, Finn, and Eli—You guys are what keep me going. I'm so lucky to have such a good place to come home to when I leave the fantasy worlds behind.

Mom, Dad, and Hayley—You guys are the best supporters and cheerleaders I could ever ask for. I miss you all terribly and cannot wait for our next reunion. (P.S. Dad, you're still winning.)

To my friends and family who have continued to support me and my goals by reading, sharing, reviewing, and gifting my books—You all have my deepest gratitude.

For the readers who have stuck with me, with my characters, with the world of Eira—Thank you from the bottom of my heart. It's because of you that I can continue to do what I love. I'm so excited to have you along for the ride—and there's so much more to come!

To Diana, to Spense, to Maisie, and to Aedan—I'm sorry for the troubles you had to endure from my typing. Thank you for letting me write your stories. May we meet again.

If you enjoyed *A Kingdom of Broken Oaths*, please consider leaving a review on Goodreads, Instagram, Amazon, or another platform of your choice. They go a long way toward helping indie authors like me!

ABOUT THE AUTHOR

Lauren Lowther is the author of the Dark Truths Trilogy. She has been reading and writing since she learned the alphabet, writing her first book about a lobster and his crustacean friends at six years old. She is rooted in a love for stories with adventurous storylines, unique plots, and sweeping romance—all of which you can find in her books. She lives in the Pacific Northwest with her husband, two rescue pups, and two sassy horses, who are constantly trying to outdo each other's giant personalities.

To stay updated on book announcements and more, follow Lauren on Instagram *@authorlaurenlowther* or visit her website *laurenlowther.com*.

www.ingramcontent.com/pod-product-compliance
Lightning Source LLC
Chambersburg PA
CBHW061052210726
48294CB00001B/111